Nemesis

Blake Detective Series, Volume 3

Jon Mason

Published by Jon Mason, 2023.

This is a work of fiction. Similarities to real people, places, or events are entirely coincidental.

NEMESIS

First edition. November 2, 2023.

Copyright © 2023 Jon Mason.

ISBN: 978-1916757066

Written by Jon Mason.

To my mother, from whom I inherited my love of literature

# Nemesis

One

The trials, tribulations and success of my training were behind me. On the horizon and getting closer day-by-day were the ensuing criminal proceedings. In the meantime, armed with my limited knowledge and experience I had to learn my trade as a police officer.

I took formal occupation of my Mirfield abode seven miles from Westleigh. A ground floor one-bedroomed flat. Rented and furnished by Joe. I had no rent to pay. All I was waiting for was Lucy. The all-clear from the doctor and the insurance money from the accident she was now the proud owner of a new Benly.

I heard it well before it came into sight. With the throttle wound open it could produce an ear-splitting 10,500rpm and 15hp. It was a great bike.

After overnight rain the roads were drying. A weak sun attempting to make itself known. I was standing on the footpath helmet in hand when she stopped beside me. Her grin visible through the visor. Engine off. Bike on stand. She dismounted, removed her helmet and threw her arms round my neck kissing me as hard as she could. The smell of her perfume, the patchouli on her leathers, and her skin were a heady mix. It was almost as if she were trying to leave an indelible impression – *This one is taken, hands off.* The moment accompanied by a fanfare from a couple of passing vans.

An elderly lady contributed to the scenario. 'Young people these days. Such wanton behaviour. No self-control. I don't know what parents are coming to.'

To which Lucy responded in true Lucy style, 'You're only jealous.'

'Good morning,' I smiled. 'It's nice to see you too.'

'I've had to wait almost a week for that,' she said. 'I called your Mum and said we would be late. I want to see the flat. And, I've brought you a flat-warming present.'

'Come on then,' I said as she fished a ribbon-wrapped parcel from the pannier and followed.

She had an appraising eye. 'This is nice,' she said in all seriousness. 'Is it carved in stone or am I allowed to make changes?'

I had to laugh. 'You mean you wouldn't anyway?'

She grinned and nodded.

'Change what you like but go easy on the girly stuff.'

There was an answering look of exasperation. 'Give me a bit of credit,' she said and wandered across to look in the bathroom, kitchen, and bedroom.

'Here's your prezzie,' she grinned and handed me the parcel.

I slid the ribbons off, unwrapped it and smiled. 'Flat warming present? You meant bed-warming.'

There was an answering smile as she unzipped her jacket and slipped it from her shoulders. She was naked. 'Better pull the curtains.'

Two

1730 Monday. I presented myself at the police station for my first shift as a police officer: Half nights: 6 – 2. Exhilarated and ready for the off. After the briefing I left the station in company with PC 'Jim' Tyndall. 'Just treat it like a training exercise, like those you did at Pannal, Brian,' he said. 'Keep it simple. Don't worry about comments of finding something useful to do instead of persecuting motorists. Most of the silly bastards never check their bloody cars anyway.' Two minutes later a 'cyclops' as Jim called them appeared. Just as Jim said. Keep it simple.

That was my first offence. If the driver had checked his car it wouldn't have happened.

'It's as simple as that, kid,' he said. 'Think of it as a road safety lesson, teach 'em to think.'

There were a couple more minor offences before mealtime, or snap, as Jim called it. Return to the nick for sandwiches and a cuppa, accompanied by numerous questions. Oh boy. We took our meal at 10pm. With the 2-10 crew and Sergeants Meadowcroft and McGill there were ten grinning coppers in the office. On the rest room table was an open copy of the latest issue of the Police Review. I had my own copy at the flat. I knew what was coming.

Sergeant Meadowcroft, a sixteen year veteran, five ten, thinning dark hair and stocky, pointed to a column on the right-hand page: Those who had come top on the latest courses. 'I take it there was only one 547 Blake on that course?'

'Yes, sergeant,' I said.

'Well done,' there was a series of echoes.

The sergeant turned the page back and laughed. 'And this?' He pointed to an article about Sergeant Palmer. 'Well?'

'Somebody put the kettle on and get Brian a cuppa, he'll be dying of thirst,' said Jim.

'Guilty, Sergeant,' my grin matched his. I almost disappeared under a welter of back-slaps.

'Locking a Sergeant up? That's a wet dream,' offered a north-eastern accent. Followed by howls of laughter.

'All right, Stan ... Now then young man,' said Sergeant Meadowcroft. 'The unexpurgated account, if you please.'

It didn't take long and I managed to start eating my sandwiches and swallow some tea. There were plenty of questions. A high percentage regarding whether I'd caught Sergeant Palmer and the Matron at it. And, had I clocked Matron's tits or anything else. Eventually, with a warning from both sergeants not to spill the beans to the Westleigh Chronicle the late turn crew departed. With me now working on their patch they were sure to try it on.

There were raised eyebrows when I asked if I should type the files before returning to patrol. Even more when I started typing. I'd finished in less than twenty minutes, all three files.

'Bloody Hell. You'll be handy typing like that, Brian,' offered Stan, the man with dreams of arresting a sergeant: big, raw-boned and happy-go-lucky from Sunderland. The detached beat officer from Midstones.

The voice of Sergeant Meadowcroft cut across the conversation, 'No he won't, you'll do your own files, Stan. If you start submitting files as neat as that I'll know, all right?' Stan grinned and nodded.

'Blake,' Sergeant Meadowcroft said. 'Don't let this load of idlers put on you, let them do their own files. Now, it's time you were out.'

Nothing had been mentioned about the incident at the Spartan's race track.

A steady walk into the town centre, Jim asking questions about where I'd learnt to type and why. I told him about university which he followed by an almost startled, 'And you've joined the bloody police?'

Without mentioning Dad, that would keep, I told him it was something that I'd wanted to do since childhood. Jim still thought I was mad.

The memories of that night drove me. Not just because I wanted to be a detective sergeant but I was fifty percent him. The more I achieved the more I was taking him with me.

'Every night we check vulnerable property, especially the rear,' Jim emphasised. 'You never know what you might find.' Across from the Post Office, in Lowside, there is a narrow covered passageway that Jim told me led to a cobbled delivery yard for the local shops. Vehicular access was direct from Bradford Road. The sound of voices and someone walking on broken glass met us half way. My heart rate picked up. Jim grabbed my tunic sleeve, put his finger to his lips and eased himself to the front. The yard was small, about twenty yards by thirty and illuminated, for want of a better word, by an ancient guttering gas lamp. There was enough light to see one lad struggling to get through a broken window without injuring himself on the glass still in the frame. Another youth walking backwards and forwards a yard or so away. 'Come on, bloody hurry up before the coppers find us,' he hissed at the other.

I'd slipped my handcuffs out of my pocket as we entered the yard. The one who was walking about looked up. 'Bloody Hell, run.' he shouted. Before he had chance to move more than a couple of yards I'd grabbed him and handcuffed him round the gas lamp. He was too shocked to react. I set off after the other. Jim was built more for comfort than speed. A trail of sweets spilling from the thief's coat pocket showed the way. I caught him by the bus station about a hundred yards down the road and marched him back through cheering pedestrians. Jim was sitting on a dustbin in tears of laughter. 'Welcome to Westleigh, Brian,' he said, wiping his eyes. My first prisoner protested volubly and glared at him, 'We've done nowt lerrus out.'

'Let me introduce the brothers Smith. That really is their name. The one keeping the lamp post company is Damian, and the one you've got hold of is Christopher.' I cautioned both of them and told them they were under arrest for shop breaking.

At the station Jim was still laughing, 'You've never seen owt like it Sarge,' he said, and shook his head. 'Brian was like a whippet. He 'ad Damian cuffed before I 'ad chance to breathe. Scared these two witless.'

Carl Beatty, the office PC, called the keyholder for *The Little Sweet Shop*. I presented my evidence to Sergeant McGill. 'And you handcuffed him round that gas lamp?' he queried, a broad smile across his face.

'Yes Sergeant,' I replied. 'Was that wrong?'

The Sergeant nodded. 'Different, Blake,' he said. 'Just different, but not wrong. Well done, it's a good arrest, these two are a nuisance.'

I searched them both. Damian Smith had his pockets full of sweets. Twenty packets of cigarettes stuffed inside his shirt. Christopher Smith, the elder of the two, had a dozen packets of rolling tobacco, a box of bars of Cadbury's milk chocolate, £5.9/- in loose change inside his coat and, a screwdriver and a few loose sweets in his coat pocket. The remainder were scattered down Bradford Road.

Detention sheets completed. Prisoners in the cells. C.I.D. would interview them in the morning. A message was passed to Stan to inform the parents.

Whilst I was typing Jim was spreading the news amongst the night shift. Sergeant McGill left a short report for the information of

Inspector Jeavons. Not exactly a break in at the Bank of England, but it had been a great first shift, just as I'd hoped.

Three

Thursday afternoon I called the Secretary to the Westleigh Rugby Club receiving an invite for the following Tuesday training session. So far so good. I missed the game. It would be good to get back on the field. According to the local rag I found in the office they were a good team. I might or might not get a game but it would be good to get back in action.

The evening similar to Wednesday, three minor traffic offences and a warning to a group of rowdy youths in the market place. After meal it was dead - it poured down. The only people enjoying the weather were us.

It might have been Friday Night is Music Night on the radio, but in Westleigh it was pay day and we were short staffed.

After meal I patrolled with Sergeant Meadowcroft. There were a few noisy groups who quietened down when we appeared. We were in Albion Street walking towards the Town Hall when we heard the shouting.

'Come on little chickens. Come to daddy. Come and be sliced.' It might have been funny had it not been for the broken bottle the man was waving about. 'Come on little ... Oh look, two big black turkeys just waiting to be sliced. Come on little turkeys. Come to daddy.'

'Put the bottle down, Fred. Before someone gets hurt.'

'Get back in your hutch Meadowcroft,' Fred replied waving the bottle in our direction. 'It's carving time.'

'Can I Sarge?'

'Don't get hurt, Blake.'

'I won't.' I began to walk towards the bottle waver.

'Look, the little turkey wants to be sliced.' He thrust the bottle towards me. I knocked his hand to one side and applied a chokehold. Took the bottle and cuffed him.

The sergeant gasped. 'Where on earth did you learn that? It wasn't at Pannal.'

'No Sarge,' I grinned. 'I'm a martial arts instructor.'

Malcolm Swinderby, the office PC on night duty, insisted he was placed in the cell furthest from the office so the sound of him banging on the door wasn't too loud. I typed my statement of arrest. He would be charged and bailed to court in the morning.

Saturday was different. I was on half-nights and back in company with Jim Tyndall. We were turned out early from the office, even before the briefing, to deal with a shoplifter at the local Buy Smart supermarket, recently opened in Broadway. Attracting the wrong type of customer.

Mike Preston the deputy manager greeted us. In his office, overwatched by a member of staff was a woman wearing a beige gaberdine raincoat and black shoes. She was holding onto a pushchair containing a baby that looked and smelled as if it needed a bath and a change.

'I was in my office looking through the window,' said Mr Preston. 'I observed this lady take these.' He indicated seven tins of baked beans on his desk. 'She looked around and slid them into the pushchair behind the baby. At the till she paid for these,' he indicated two further tins of baked beans. 'Tendering a £1 note. She made no attempt to pay for the seven tins of beans and left the store where I stopped her, told her what I had seen. She denied it and I called you.'

Jim nodded at me. 'Is what the manager said, true?' I said.

The woman nodded. 'Yes,' she said.

'I can add that she was given enough change from the purchase of the two tins of beans to pay for those she stole.'

I have to admit that I had felt sorry for her but she did have enough money to pay for them.

I checked with the divisional collator. Wendy Green, aged 27, had three previous convictions for shoplifting.

Stan did an address check. It was correct. However, her children were at home. The baby was her neighbour's. She was trying it on thinking that with a small baby she could get away with it.

We made our 8pm point at the telephone kiosk close to the fire station. We were told to come in and take an early meal, there'd been intelligence there was going to be some trouble between a couple of local gangs.

The first report was from a road traffic car. A known member of one of the gangs and three others in an old Comer van registered number PCX 74 had just driven past Oakenshaw church. They would be with us in less than five minutes. Leaving a couple of Special Constables to keep an eye on the town centre, Inspector Jeavons split what was left into two groups, one under his command and the other Sergeant Meadowcroft's.

The plan was simple. Most gang members have a sheep mentality and follow where others lead. Their views were that the best place to hide a tree was in a wood. The best place to be in a ruckus was in a middle of a large crowd.

'Blake,' said Sergeant Meadowcroft. 'Your job is to obtain full details of the drivers and issue a ticket to produce his documents. Check the registered number against the excise licence and report for any offences. If the excise licence has any alterations or is displayed on the wrong vehicle the driver will be arrested.'

'Yes Sergeant.'

We stopped every car as they approached Westleigh. I had two prisoners for theft of excise licences and three reports for no excise licence, plus forms issued to produce driving documents. Four passengers had to walk home.

Of the eight cars where there were no apparent offences the occupants were advised that if they entered the town and exited their vehicles they would be arrested and charged with the offence of 'conspiracy to cause affray'. There were one or two who complained that it was a free country and that they had the right to drive into Westleigh.

They were given the choice. Take the advice or appear before the Magistrates on Monday morning. In the end no-one drove into town. There were only the two Specials plus the six of us, and that included the Inspector and the Sergeant. That would have been an interesting evening.

I spent the remainder of the shift with Jim interviewing my prisoners. Sorting out the offences. Entering the details in the Offence Book and typing. I got off duty at 3.30am.

Four

2-10 Sunday was generally a quiet shift. At three o'clock Sergeant Meadowcroft picked me up from my point. There had been a report that Mrs Rose Baxter, aged 86, living on the Turnton Estate hadn't been seen since Friday. Her house curtains were still drawn. The chances were that she had died. Her son couldn't get in. The door was bolted. A small group of neighbours were discussing how the old lady would be missed. What sort of funeral she would have? Would it be a decent ham tea? They could have waited until we knew whether or not the old lady had died or not. Using the Sergeant's penknife, we managed to slide the window catch and open the living room window. Being the youngest and the most agile I was volunteered to climb through and unlock the door. Son Eric was reticent about investigating and finding her dead.

I didn't have the time to stare but the house was like a new pin. Just about to unbolt the door when I spotted a prone bare leg through the kitchen door. An elderly lady in nightdress and dressing gown, right slipper missing. An injury to the left temple. She was still warm to the touch No reaction to light when I raised her eyelid. No carotid pulse. Mine was increasing.

The sound of someone walking in the first floor bedroom.

I motioned to Sergeant Meadowcroft and whispered what I found.

'Are you all right?'
'I'm fine, Sarge.'
'Upstairs. I'll follow.'

Half way up the staircase I stepped on a loose board. Sergeant Meadowcroft was close behind.

The footsteps stopped. I launched myself upstairs shouting. 'This is the police stay exactly where you are.'

I headed for the rear bedroom. The window was open. A young male was climbing out. 'Stand still,' I shouted and managed to grab the right sleeve of his anorak. He wriggled like hell to try and slide out of it and was succeeding. 'Sarge, I've got the sleeve of his anorak. Can you get round the back.'

'Will do.' Sergeant Meadowcroft turned and ran down stairs. Seconds later I heard the back door open.

I managed to grasp his shirt collar with my other hand as he tried to jump. He was in danger of hanging himself. Sergeant Meadowcroft appeared. 'Well done, Blake. You can let Taylor go now. I've got him.'

Andrew Taylor, 25 years, five six, had been out of prison for two weeks having served eighteen months of a two year sentence for factory breaking. I cautioned him. I'm arresting you for ...' and looked at Sergeant Meadowcroft.

'Suspicion of causing GBH.'

'I'm arresting you on suspicion of causing grievous bodily harm to Rose Baxter.'

'I didn't do it.' he protested. 'She were dead when I got in. I could see her through the kitchen window. Honest.'

'Blake, you will accompany the body to the mortuary. Some forces, like Leeds City, have dedicated coroner's officers. We don't. We are all coroner's officers. In view of the circumstances, until we know the result of the PM, this is a murder enquiry.' He went to the phone box fifty yards away. Within minutes a road traffic car arrived to act as a communications vehicle. Stan turned up to take over when I left.

Eric Baxter was standing with a group of neighbours. 'I've very sorry, Mr Baxter,' I said.

'My mother's dead?'

'I'm afraid so.' I looked at the neighbours. 'Could someone get him a cup of tea, please.'

A Mrs Raistrick, the next door neighbour took him by the arm. 'Come on, love. Let the police do what they have to do.'

Taylor was carted off to the station by a second traffic car.

Detective Constable Fred Smith arrived. I put him in the picture as to what I had observed and what Taylor had said. 'I had a quick look in her eyes there are no petechiae.'

He frowned. 'How do you know about petechiae?'

'I tagged a module of anatomy onto my exercise physiology degree. The professor was only too pleased to pass on interesting bits when he knew I was intending to join the police.'

'Dark horse,' he said grinning. You kept that quiet.'

'I've only been out of Pannal a few days. Didn't want anyone to think I was bragging.'

'Fair enough. Show me.'

He had a quick look at the body. There was no obvious bruising. 'Come on,' he said as he stood and motioned with his head. 'Let's have a look.'

The yard was paved. Standing on tip toe I could barely see Rose Baxter's left shoulder.

'Could Taylor see her as he claimed?' said Fred.

'He's a climber but even so it would be difficult, she's lying between the kitchen table and the sink. He's only about five six.'

'But not impossible?'

'No, but he would have to have had some way of getting the extra height. I could hardly see her at all.'

'So what could he stand on?'

'If he was alone the only thing would be the dustbin and that's over by the gate; at least ten yards away. He's not going to carry it to the window take a look inside and put it back.'

'Conclusions?' he said with a grin.

'He's lying.'

'I agree. At least about being able to see her as he claimed. Any signs of an attack on the door?'

A quick examination of the door and frame. 'There are some marks here that look weathered.'

'They're old marks. Rose has been a regular target over the years, ever since her husband died.'

'Taylor?'

Fred nodded and smiled. 'Great question. Yes. He made the marks with a screwdriver when he broke in. What's next.'

'I take it Taylor was arrested.'

'He was.'

'Who was the arresting officer?'

Fred smiled and nodded. 'Stan Turnbull. He had been a friend of Rose's husband. They both played in the darts team at the Flying Horse. He kept an eye on Rose after her husband died.'

'I'll have to have a chat with Stan.'

'Yes, he'll fill you in. In fact he'll be here soon. You're doing well so far.'

Any further discussion kicked into touch by the arrival of Doctor O'Keefe, the Divisional Police Surgeon. He felt for the carotid pulse and looked up from his crouch. 'Death certified at,' he checked his watch. '3.45pm. The head wound looks to have been caused when she fell against the table here,' he said pointing. There was congealing blood and hair adhering to the wood. 'The post mortem will answer the question as to why she fell. I'm afraid that is up to you gentlemen. She is flaccid and warm. Rigor mortis has not yet begun. I estimate that death occurred ...'

'Less than two hours ago,' I said under my breath.

Doctor O'Keefe stopped and looked at me . 'What did you say?'

'I was just musing, Doctor,' I said.

'You said less than two hours ago, Pc?'

'Blake, Doctor.'

'How did you know that? Have you a medical qualification?'

I had to smile. And, as I explained the Doctor did as well. 'I have a degree in exercise physiology, Doctor, with an added module of anatomy. The one covering post mortems.'

'Excellent. And, yes, I estimate within the last two hours.'

'Judging by the blood on her face and the table that injury is recent.'

'I agree, is that relevant?'

I glanced at Fred. He nodded. 'Yes Dr. I arrested someone. He was trying to climb out of the window.'

'Excellent. If there is nothing else gentlemen, the pathologist will answer your questions.' He turned to leave. 'I shall follow your career with interest Pc Blake. Good day.'

As he left Stan Turnbull arrived. 'It's that little bastard, Taylor, you've arrested?'

'Yep. He was trying to climb out of the back bedroom window.'

'Good. Should have had a rope round his neck,' he said with some vehemence. 'Save the country a load of expense. Rose was a harmless old dear. I've lost a tea-spot and a good informant ... Oh, there's somebody enroute from Forensic. I'll hang on here if you want to get hold of the neighbours.'

Bearing in mind I'd arrested Taylor climbing out of the window there was nothing new from the neighbours. He only lived a hundred yards away. Talk about crapping on your own doorstep.

The photographer was leaving. 'Will you hang on,' I said. 'Before he goes, Fred, there's something I'd like to establish.'

'Ok. What did you have in mind?'

'Taylor's sightline.'

I explained to Stan what I had in mind. 'If it'll help to get Taylor convicted I'll bare my arse in the Flying Horse. Where do you want me?'

Stan was a good three inches taller than me. So, with the casement window open and him standing outside against the wall with his arm extended, I took the wooden clothes prop from the kitchen corner placing it close to Rose Baxter's head and rested it against the sink.

'Stan, just put your thumb where the prop is.'

Photographs taken. Prop back in its rightful place I measured Stan. To within half an inch it was seven feet. Taylors story that he could see Rose Baxter whilst standing on tiptoe was a non-starter.

The undertaker arrived waiting patiently in his hearse.

Twenty minutes later a Dr Jenkins arrived from the Forensic Science Lab., took swabs and hair samples and left.

Leading the hearse Fred stopped at the police station. 'Nip inside Brian, ask Sergeant Meadowcroft for the mortuary keys.'

I thought that a bit strange. However they were in the key safe in the sergeant's office. It was a two minute drive to the Council Yard. The mortuary was in the corner behind the gate backed against the outer wall.

The mortuary could only be described as functional. A couple of dissection slabs. A sink, water heater a small cupboard and not much else.

A tag tied round her right hallux bearing: the date, her name and my details We undressed her. They were faint but signs of bruising were appearing on both upper arms, as if someone had had a firm hold. 'Interesting,' said Fred. 'Tomorrow we'll see what they really are. In the meantime.' She was covered with a sheet. The clothes placed in evidence bags for forensic examination, just in case, although there was no sign that her underwear had been interfered with.

There were bobbies everywhere including Inspector Jeavons and Detective Inspector Greening. Five eight. Receding greying hair. Weather beaten lined face and well jowled.

'This is your first murder, is it lad?' Detective Inspector Greening smiled.

'Not exactly, sir,' said Sergeant Meadowcroft. 'Blake is the one who arrested an instructor at Pannal.'

DI Greening's eyes lit up. 'Are you indeed. So, locking up the likes of Taylor are just run of the mill?'

'I wouldn't put it like that, sir,' I said.

'Can we have a word, sir,' said Fred.

Inspectors Greening, Jeavons, Sergeant Meadowcroft, Fred Smith and me were in the inspector's office Fred outlined the circumstances.

'A clothes prop?' said the DI.

'Yes, sir. A straight edge.'

'I get the idea. It's a hypotenuse. And Turnbull with his arm fully extended.'

Yes, sir. He's three inches taller than me and against the outer wall, the tip of the prop was level with his fingers. To within a half an inch, seven feet.'

'That screws Taylor's comment about seeing Mrs Baxter as he claimed. Well done. That was good thinking. We'll have to wait and see what the PM turns up. However, Taylor has some serious questions to answer. Next, Smith get Taylor a change of clothing, shirt , pants and footwear. We'll keep him in overnight and put him before court in the morning. Get a remand to police cells pending further enquiries. We'll hold his interview until we have the pathologist's report. And you young man, your father was, I understand, Douglas Blake.'

'Yes, sir.'

'A little late but my condolences.'

'Thank you.'

Now, it would be unseemly to allow you to be involved in Taylor's interview, but, I want you to sit in as an observer. You may take notes but not speak and, you will ignore anything that Taylor may say to you, understood?'

'Yes, sir. Thank you.'

'Sergeant, you'll oversee Blake's pocket book and statement?'

'Next on the agenda, sir. Blake will be attending the PM.'

'Yes. Have you witnessed a PM before, Blake.'

'Yes, I have, sir.'

The DI nodded. '10.00am tomorrow. You know where?'

'Yes, sir.'

'Good,' he turned to leave.

'Before you go, sir,' I said. 'Eric Baxter, Rose Baxter's son, was the one who notified us that his mother hadn't been seen. He only knows that she's dead. He hasn't seen her since ...'

The DI looked thoughtful. 'No. A couple of reasons. One, the PM takes precedence. Two. The Westleigh mortuary is not the most salubrious of places. We will have to see what the Coroner decides re disposal. Then we can make a decision,

Circumstances alter cases. I was now working Monday and with a bit of luck taking Wednesday off instead.

Five

1030 am Monday. The mortuary was full: Professor Snodgrass the Home Office Pathologist and his assistant. DI Greening. DC Smith. Me. And the photographer.

'Good morning, gentlemen. A busy day today,' The Professor looked round. 'A new face,' he said looking at me over his glasses.

'Pc Blake, sir.'

'Well Pc Blake, if you feel dizzy at any time please sit down. I've a busy day and haven't the time to carry out two PMs this morning.' The comment raising a laugh.

'That's all right, sir. I saw several at university.'

'Really? Mr Greening have you any problems with me giving Pc Blake a little test enroute?'

'None whatsoever, Professor.'

Why did I feel nervous when the professor smiled at me?

Sheet removed the professor said. 'Mrs Rose Baxter. Eighty years of age, approximately five feet three inches tall and well nourished. Signs of bruising to both upper arms,' He nodded to the photographer. Both arms photographed the professor continued. 'You can see Mr Greening that the thumb impression is on the inside of her upper arms and the finger impression on the out.'

'She was held from behind.'

''She was. And tightly as well. The bruising is well developed.'

He transferred his emanation to her groin. 'No bruising to the genital area. Right, let's turn Mrs Baxter over.'

It made me feel angry. In the middle of her back was a large bruise. 'It looks as though the assailant was annoyed, that's the impression of a sports shoe or something similar,' said the professor. The photographer placed a right-angled ruler around the bruise and took two photos. 'You have the suspect's shoes, Mr Greening.'

'We certainly do, Professor,'

There was silence as professor opened her back. 'This lady had osteoporosis. You can see here the vertebrae are crushed.' We moved back so that the photographer could get his shots.

'Would that be enough to kill her?'

'In my considered opinion it would. It would have been incredibly painful. That in itself could have triggered a heart attack. But I will be able to tell you more when I have examined the heart.'

Back sewn up Mrs Baxter was turned over. The professor nodded to his assistant. With his circular saw he split the sternum and opened the chest. It didn't smell too bad, although Fred smith looked a bit queasy. 'Pc Blake, what is that?' With his scalpel he pointed to something descended from the upper left chest, looped beneath the aorta and ascended on the right side before disappearing into the throat.

'Thanks, Professor.'

'Any ideas?'

Time to take a stab. 'The recurrent laryngeal nerve?'

'Excellent. Why is it odd?'

'Because it innervates the larynx but instead of the direct route from the spinal cord, a distance of two inches, it takes the circuitous route, like driving from Leeds to Bradford via Gateshead.'

'And?'

'It's one of the proofs that Darwin was correct and Genesis was wrong.'

'If you ever get tired of being a policeman come and see me. Now, we have work to do.' A few seconds later. 'This lady was on borrowed time. That,' he pointed to a bulging descending aorta, 'Is an aortic aneurism. If that had ruptured she would have been dead in seconds.

But she didn't. She had had a heart attack but not one that would have killed her. Do you know what medication she was taking?'

'Sorry Professor, no.' said Fred.

'No matter. You can see here, the marginal branch of the right coronary artery and the dead tissue. This is relatively uncommon but is associated with atherosclerosis, the build up of plaques in the arteries.

Examination concluded. 'Mr Greening I will let you have my report within the next two or three days. The injury to the head was superficial. In my opinion, although she was an elderly lady and had a worsening picture of health the cause of death was the injury to her spine.

Taylor had been remanded to police cells. I was now joined at the hip to Fred Smith. Shown as the arresting officer and DI Greening the officer in the case. The paperwork was unending. I did the typing, which help to reinforce what I was doing and, I had a hard copy.

By the time I finished my shift I felt knackered. Bought myself some fish and chips and had an lonely early night. Much to Lucy's annoyance.

Six

Following a morning visit to Salendine Nook I invited myself to Lucy's. There was a face I'd seen before fitting an alarm system. 'Don't I know you?' I said.

'Where you from?'

'Huddersfield, Salendine Nook.'

He shook his head. 'Sorry. Don't know it.' He said and carried on. I wasn't so sure.

I gave Liz a pillion to the track. The police had given her the ok to clear the remains of the shed.

Seeing the empty space was as if a weight had been lifted. Liz said that she and Lucy felt the same. I asked her to call Anne and let her know.

The Spartan's walking wounded from the accident in Rotterdam where Lucy's father and Lester Roberts – one of the mechanics - had lost their lives, were servicing their bikes. None of them had been seriously injured and all of them back in the saddle. Neil made himself known. He had called Anne a couple of times. He looked concerned. 'Would they mind if I went across?'

'Neil, you don't have to ask. Make Anne's day.'

They told me later that he arrived in time for tea. Jennifer smiled when she answered the door. 'Anne,' she called over her shoulder. 'You have a visitor. He looks hungry.'

Liz had a perpetual smile. 'Everything all right?' I said.

'Lucy told me about her flat-warming present.'

I think I blushed. It felt like it. 'Oh. quite a surprise.'

'Please be careful, Brian. It's easy to get carried away at your age and Lucy can be headstrong. You've only known each other a few weeks,' she paused and smiled. 'But a gross?'

'She seems to like me.'

Her eyebrows raised a few notches. 'You think?'

Lucy arrived thirty minutes later and draped herself round my neck. 'Will you stay tonight? Mum won't mind, honest.'

'Yes, but what about?'

She had a vicious grin. 'I ordered two boxes, just in case. Besides,' she whispered. 'I want you to fuck me.' The shadow of her father seemed to have dissipated.

Lucy worked at the Vernon's office in Leeds. I shadowed her in Wednesday morning. Then took the time to visit the New College and speak with the Head and one or two of the Masters. It was good to see the old place again. They were delighted when former pupils took the trouble to pay them a visit. They weren't too sure about me being a police officer. Something about me being over qualified? Nobody had linked me to the Palmer case in the newspapers. I didn't enlighten them.

1600 I met with Giles Cameron, the journalist from the Headquarters' Press Conference, at the flat.

I handed him his coffee and waved him to the settee. 'You wanted to tell me something about my father?'

He took a sip and a deep breath. 'Let me set the scene. In the early 1930s my father was an accountant and we had a nice life. We lived in a detached house in north Leeds close to Roundhay Park with no apparent worries. My parents had survived the depression because my father had investments in the United States as well as in the UK and Europe. Then the Wall Street Crash occurred. The firm went bust. We lost the house, everything.

My father, much older than my mother, suffered a heart attack and died. We had to move out and rent a one bedroomed vermin-infested flat in the city centre. It was a shock to the system. There was no money for school fees and I attended a school in the city centre. I was bullied at school and joined a local street gang more for protection than anything else.

I got to enjoy what my father would have described as being very naughty. And because they thought I had a posh voice it fell to me, if we were caught, to apologise and promise not to do whatever it was, again.

We used to sneak into the goods yards and play on the wagons. Even wait until they were hooked up to a shunter and go for a ride. If we were spotted, run like hell.

It would be Whitsuntide 1936. It got to, *I dare you*. Causing damage, sneaking into the backs of shops and stealing. It was getting ramped up. Then your father appeared. I got caught and taken to the police station.

He was intrigued. I spoke correctly and didn't swear like the others. My clothes still looked of better quality. Some of the other kids were dressed in no better than rags. He asked where I lived. I told him. Then he asked me where I'd lived before that. He took me home and I got a caution. Mother was horrified at what my father would have thought.

He came back the next day and said he knew of a vacancy in the Co-op as an office clerk. If she wanted it she had to be at Beeston Co-op for 8am the following day. He even gave her £2 out of his own pocket because there were some flats close to the Co-op. That must have been a lot of money for a police constable in those days. Also there was a school not far away.'

'You're not going to tell me I have half-brothers and sisters running round, are you?'

He laughed. 'No, nothing like that. She got the job and repaid your father a month later. She did well and later she got a job in the finance department at head office.

To cut a long story short, during the war she became a supervisor. One day, in 1940, the son of one of the Directors visited. He was a Captain in an artillery regiment. They were married in 1941,' he smiled at me. 'I do have a half-brother born in 1942. He's at Sandhurst.

I went to university. My one regret from this was that I never got to thank your father for what he had done.'

'That's quite a story,' I said. 'Thank you for telling me. Would you like to see my mother. I think she'd like to hear.'

His step-father was killed on the road to Arnhem during Operation Market Garden. His mother died two years ago of pneumonia.

I rang Mum and told her. They arranged to meet the following week.

Seven

That evening I had my runout with Westleigh. They were a well-appointed club supported by a local engineering company; they even had a floodlit pitch. They were a friendly lot, except some of the backs and their outside half who appeared to see me as a threat to their established order when they found out how much experience I had. As the song went, *There may be trouble ahead.*

Back to work on Thursday, Taylor would be interviewed at 2pm. Jim Tyndall had called in sick. So I would either sit in the office counting paper clips or patrol on my own.

I'd only been out for twenty minutes when I spotted someone acting suspiciously in the car park at the rear of the Town Hall.

He caught my attention by strolling up and down the rows pausing to peer inside random cars. He hadn't seen me. I made sure that he did. He ran. But not far. A search produced a thin piece of flexible plastic. A couple of pieces of bent welding rod for opening quarter-lights. A screwdriver and a dozen recently issued vehicle excise licences. He was quite embarrassed walking through the town centre handcuffed to me. It was good public relations.

Fred Smith was in the office when I arrived. 'You don't half make work for yourself, Brian.' He said and laughed.

I carried out the interview with Stan. My prisoner, Brian Jacks admitted everything; he couldn't really do anything else. He was charged and bailed to magistrates court in four weeks. It was 1.30pm before we finished the paperwork. Just time to snatch a sandwich and cuppa before interviewing Taylor.

Fred smith brought an apprehensive Andrew Taylor up from the cells and sat him in a chair across the table from DI Greening and himself; I sat behind the DI.

'You know why you were arrested Andrew?'

'I didn't kill her?'

'But you know why you're here?'

'Something about GBH.'

'That's right. Now, I'll tell you that you're not obliged to say anything unless you wish to do so but anything you say may be put into writing and given in evidence.'

'Yeah, Yeah, heard it all before.'

The DI smiled. 'I'm sure you have, Andrew. But this is the first time since you got out of prison.'

'Too bloody true.'

'Right, tell me in your own words what happened that Sunday afternoon.'

'I already told that copper behind you.'

'I know, but he's brand new and I want to hear it from you to make sure I got the right tale. So, in your own time, what happened?'

'It were Sunday. Nobody about. I just had a look.'

'Through the kitchen window?'

'Yeah.'

'And?'

'She were lyin' on her face.'

'Where exactly?'

'On the floor.'

'Between the kitchen table and the sink?'

'Yeah, She weren't moving. So I thought.'
'You'd take a wander round and see what you could lift?'
'I've already admitted that.'
'You said she was lying there. You're only five six. How did you look in and what did you see, exactly.'
'On tiptoe. Plain as day.'
'And just how much could you see?'
'What's all this about?'
'I just want to establish what you saw. Exactly what could you see?'
'She were face down on the floor, like I said.'
'Could you see both shoulders.'
'No, just one shoulder and her head.'
'Thank you. Then you decided to go in?'
'Door were unlocked so I did.'
Did you check to see if she was still breathing.'
'I could see she wasn't.'
'How do you mean; you could see she wasn't.'
'Well, when you're breathing your chest goes up and down, dun't it?' She weren't movin."
'So you didn't kneel down and physically check.'
'No. Are you happy now?'
DI Greening paused for a few seconds. 'Andrew, you're lying.'
A worried look passed Taylor's face. 'Naw. I've been straight. Honest.'
'Andrew, you're five six. Do you know what a sightline is?'
'Sure, it's what you can see.'
'Look at these photographs.'
Fred Smith handed the photographs to the DI. 'This shows the kitchen table on the left. Mrs Baxter's body in the centre. The sink unit below the window you claim you looked through on the right. See how little room there is?'

'What of it?'

'Now this,' He pushed a second photo across the table. 'You can see Pc Blake holding a clothes prop by the side of Mrs Baxter's head. The clothes prop leaning against the sink and protruding through the window.'

'Well?'

The DI pushed the third photo across the table. 'This photo is taken outside. You can see PC Turnbull with the clothes prop against his outstretched hand. That point is seven feet in the air. Yet, you claim that you could see Mrs Baxter's head standing on tiptoe. I don't think so.'

A look of fear fixed itself on Taylor's face.

'Have you any explanation? Or were you hoping we wouldn't check?'

Again no response from Taylor.

'Shall we accept that you weren't telling the truth. When you looked through the window Mrs Baxter was nowhere to be seen but she confronted you when you went through the back door.'

'Aye, all right,' he said at last.

'Now we're getting somewhere. So much easier when you tell the truth. Is that what happened?'

Taylor nodded. 'Near enough.'

'Then what?'

'She walked into the kitchen. When she saw me she said she was going to tell bobby Turnbull and have me sent back to prison. She turned and walked away, tripped and fell banging her head against the table. That were it.'

'How did she get the bruises?'

Taylor scowled. 'What bruises?'

'Fresh bruises that showed someone had grabbed her hard from behind and left imprints of their hands on her upper arms.'

'Nowt to do with me.'

'And can you explain this?' The DI pushed another photo across the table.

Taylor looked and began to shake. 'What is it?'

'Don't be naïve, Andrew. You know what it is. It's a photograph of the impression left by your trainer when you stamped on Mrs Baxter.'

'No, I never. I didn't stamp on her back.'

'Really. I didn't say where the bruise was. You are right though the bruise is on Mrs Baxter's back and according to the forensic science people the impression matches your trainer. Size six with a chunk missing from the lefthand side of the heel. Look at this.' DI Greening took Taylor's trainers from a paper bag. 'These are yours. You can see this here,' he pointed to the heel on the left trainer. 'See, this missing piece. It matches exactly the photograph. You stamped on Mrs Baxter's back. She suffered from a medical condition called osteoporosis which makes the bones very brittle. Your stamp broke her spine and that is what killed her. That, Andrew, is murder.'

Taylor was almost in tears. 'I didn't mean to. When she said she was going to turn me in I grabbed her and asked her not to. I didn't want to go back inside. I pushed her and she fell and banged her head.'

'And you stamped on her back because you were angry?'

'I just wanted her to keep her mouth shut.'

'You succeeded. Stand up.' DI Greening took the form passed by Fred Smith and signed it. .Taylor gripped the edges of the table and stood. 'Andrew Taylor, You are not obliged to say anything unless you wish to do so but anything you say will be written down and may be used in evidence. You are charged that on Sunday 15th September 1963 you did murder Rose Baxter contrary to Common Law. Have you anything to say?'

There were tears in Taylors eyes. 'I didn't mean it.'

DI Greening wrote Taylor's reply turned the form and said. 'Andrew, sign the form there,' he pointed. Taylor signed. 'Before we take you to court do you wish to talk to your solicitor?'

'No, useless twat he was.'

The DI turned to me. 'Got your cuffs, Blake?'

Eight

It was a classic. An immaculate 1940 Rover16 sports saloon in black, belonging to Mr Wainwright, a local stationer at the corner of High Street and Lowside. A man of bad habits: ignoring the parking restrictions and leaving his car unoccupied outside of his shop with the engine running. Often so close to the junction that vehicles attempting to enter or leave Lowside were impeded. I could never catch him. It was either driven away before I could reach him or he had wandered off.

Only three days ago I'd spoken with Mrs Frazer, the manageress. She said that it wasn't the first time this had happened but Mr Wainwright waved her comments away.

It was beginning to bug me. My time would come.

I slipped across to Huddersfield that evening. Mum told me about her meeting with Giles. It had gone well and brought back some happy memories.

Thursday of the following week. I'd been at Westleigh for four weeks. I was walking along Bradford Road towards the bus station, my next point was a half mile down the road towards Hecton. The Coach and Horses pub across the road. A middle-aged man hurried out. He called across to me before hurrying off. 'You'd better get in there lad, there's going to be some bother.' There was an Ariel Square 4 parked outside

I'd been told that under no circumstances should I enter licensed premises unaccompanied. This was to prevent allegations that I had consumed alcohol on duty, or become involved in some other nefarious activity. However, it sounded as if I had to do something other than just wait outside. The Coach and Horses was an old pub, low ceilings, plenty of beams, old battered tables and an uneven floor. It was very quiet. The licensee, Alec Jones, was standing behind his bar. Five of his six customers clustered at the far end. One of them, a young lad in blue jeans and a grey shirt was rubbing his left cheek.

'Are you all right?' I said.

He pointed to the sixth customer sitting next to the door. 'Bought a pint then slapped me hard across the face.'

'That's right, officer,' volunteered Alex Jones. 'I've barred him and told him to leave.'

Between forty and fifty, unshaven, long greasy dark-brown hair tied in a pony tail, his hands and finger nails were filthy. Worn leathers and boots. At his side a full-face motor cycle helmet.

Sitting quietly smiling to himself as he drank his beer. I made a quick trawl through my knowledge of the licensing laws.

I turned to Alex Jones. 'Tell him again.'

Jones looked at the motorcyclist. 'I've told you you're barred. Now leave.'

He lifted the glass, 'Cheers,' he took another drink.

'The licensee has told you you're barred. It's an offence to refuse.'

'Cheers,' he said and raised his glass. 'I'm waitin''

'Did you hit the lad at the bar?'

He was confrontational. 'It was just a love tap. Why don't you fuck off home Sonny Jim? Play with yer toys. I'm all right just waitin' fer Meadowcroft.'

'You're talking about Sergeant Meadowcroft?'

'Yeah, the fuzz.'

'I am the police.'

He looked me up and down. 'Ha. I've told you, fuck off home Sonny Jim. Play with yer toys.'

I cautioned him and told him that I was arresting him for assault. He threw his head back and laughed.

One or two at the bar warned me that he was a nasty bastard and the police had been called. I put my helmet on the table. Before he could react, I stepped forward, grabbed him by the front of his leathers, pulled him forwards my elbows tight against his ribs and hauled him to his feet manoeuvring him towards the door, 'You're nicked, Sonny Jim', I said.

I hadn't got hold properly. He was a strong man. Face like thunder he swung his left arm breaking my grip. 'You're fuckin' dead,' he said, put his right hand in his jacket pocket. A second later he was wearing a spiked knuckleduster. I blocked the punch aimed at my head with my forearm. Slid my hand down to the wrist taking a firm hold. Stepped forwards rotating beneath his arm and wrenched his arm up his back throwing him off balance. He tripped against the edge of a floorboard and caught a chair full in the face. There was a lot of blood. Within ten seconds I had him cuffed and the knuckleduster in my pocket. Sergeant Meadowcroft burst through the doors. The sight of a traffic car pulling up outside was equally welcome. Alec Jones slid the pint of beer indicated for me seconds earlier beneath the bar counter. Not that I would have drunk it, but it was thirsty work.

I don't know whether the Sergeant was pleased that I was still alive or because I had arrested the self-styled *El Diablo*, or, to give him his proper name, Vivian Smedley. Sergeant Meadowcroft stayed to take the witness statements whilst I went with the prisoner to the cells at Hecton courtesy of the traffic car.

The duty Inspector took one look at Smedley and dispatched him to hospital for a check-up. It wasn't a long job. Clean him up then transport him back to Hecton. He didn't cause any further trouble. After a short interview which consisted of a series of 'no comments' from Smedley, he was charged with offences of common assault. Violently resisting arrest. Being in possession of an offensive weapon. And, failing to quit licensed premises. He was detained pending his appearance at Hecton Magistrates Court the next morning. When I returned to Westleigh Sergeant Meadowcroft had already departed. I didn't have the opportunity to ask why Smedley was waiting for him, but I deduced that it wasn't to wish him a Happy Birthday.

Nine

0945 the following day I introduced myself to Inspector Felton, the Prosecutions Inspector, in No.1 Court at Heckton Magistrates Court. It was busy, police officers and civilians milling around, and plenty of chatter.

'Interesting start you've had to your career, Blake. A murderer so soon,' he paused and smiled. 'Back to today. With Smedley you've two cases this morning. You've picked a good one to cut your teeth on,' he said. 'When Smedley is produced, he'll come up from the cells directly into the dock. I'm going to tell the Magistrates that the assault charge has been dropped.' He anticipated my question. 'The complainant made a secondary and withdrew the original. It's not a problem.' I nodded. 'Then I'll ask if I can put an alternative charge to Smedley.' I was puzzled. He smiled. 'Because Smedley broke your grip and put the knuckleduster on after you had taken him into custody I'm putting an additional charge of unlawfully attempting to escape. Cover all the angles. Mind you, if Smedley is as talkative as he has been in the past he won't answer. If he won't, a not guilty plea will be entered and a solicitor appointed, probably Mr Reeve, the man sitting over there with the briefcase on his lap.' He pointed to a man aged about forty-five with receding sandy hair, wearing a brown suit. They exchanged greetings. 'Be careful, he's as crafty as a box of monkeys. He'll do anything to get under your skin. Just think before you answer and don't let him rile you.'

'I'll be careful.'

'If Smedley does plead guilty, and there's a first time for everything, you can stay in court. But as it's your first time you will give evidence. I will inform the bench as such and lead you through it. Mr Reeve will probably ask you a few questions. Watch for the low ballers. You understand what I mean?'

'Yes sir.'

'If he pleads not guilty, or refuses to speak at all then you will leave the court and wait outside to be called. You're happy with that?'

'Yes sir.'

'There will be three magistrates today,' he continued. 'The Chairman will be a Mrs Brocklesby. She's a stickler. When she's sitting, she owns this court. She will probably cut you some slack because it's your first time. The other two are a Mr Baxter and a Mrs Frith, address them as Your Worships. Just one last quick point, they'll be here in a few seconds, Mrs Brocklesby is never late. Why did you tackle him on your own? Smedley's an animal. Why didn't you wait for some back-up?'

I frowned. 'He was on his own, sir.' He gave me a funny look. But the Inspector's question made me understand Smedley's attitude when I told him that he was under arrest.

Ten

The door to the magistrates retiring room opened. The court usher entered. 'All stand.' Mrs Brocklesby was about fifty and plump, brown shoulder-length permed hair. She was dressed in a no-nonsense brown worsted two-piece, a white blouse and no doubt sensible shoes. She had a determined jaw. I wondered as she took her seat whether instead of declaring defendants guilty or not guilty, she gave the 'thumbs up', or, 'thumbs down'. Mrs Frith, about ten years older, wearing a slimmer version of Mrs Brocklesby's two-piece with a yellow blouse. Mr Baxter, a charcoal grey single-breasted suit, white shirt and blue tie. All were wearing spectacles and Mr Baxter a hearing aid.

Smedley was produced. I was shocked to see the amount of bruising to his face. It looked as if I had given him a good going over with a club. Inspector Felton got permission to withdraw the assault and add the unlawful attempt charge. Smedley refused to speak. A not guilty plea was entered. He was returned to the cells and Mr Reeve given time to interview his client. In five minutes he was back. His client was a man of as few words with him as he had been to the magistrates.

Alec Jones was in court for less than ten minutes, then it was my turn.

Inspector Felton explained that it was my first case and sought permission to lead me through the evidence. They agreed, as did Mr Reeve. It was when I said that I wanted to affirm instead of swearing on the bible that there were one or two askance looks.

My initial evidence must have mirrored Alec Jones. The Inspector asked me what Smedley had said and I replied simply that he had sworn at me, forgetting what I had learned at Pannal. Mrs Brocklesby interrupted and smiled in my direction. 'Officer, you must tell us the exact words you say the defendant used. We've heard it all before. We won't be shocked.'

'Very well, your Worship,' I replied. 'He said, "Fuck off home Sonny Jim. Play with yer toys."' That got a laugh in court.

Mrs Brocklesby's boom of, 'Silence in Court,' ended that.

Inspector Felton was still smiling when he asked me what happened next.

I told the court that I cautioned Smedley and told him that I was arresting him and why. That Smedley laughed again so I picked him up out of his seat. I realised then that Mr Reeve was taking copious notes. When I got to the bit about disarming Smedley Mrs Brocklesby interrupted again. 'Pc Blake? How far from the defendant were you at this point?'

'Slightly more than arm's length, your Worships.'

'And at this point he was wearing the knuckleduster?'

'He was, your Worships.'

'And you say that you blocked his punch. Could you explain please?'

I demonstrated the block and explained the move.

'And you weren't injured during this exchange?'

'No, your Worships, just a little out of breath.'

Mrs Brocklesby smiled and had a bit of a confab with the others, 'Thank you,' she said and looked at Mr Felton. 'Inspector?'

There were no more questions. Then it was my first time to be cross-examined.

'Your first time in Court, Pc Blake?' Mr Reeve opened with a smile. I confirmed that it was.

'And how long have you been a police officer?'

'This is my fourth week out of training school, your Worships.'

'What was your paid employment prior to joining the police?' I told him that I wasn't in paid employment prior to joining the police. After what Inspector Felton had said I was volunteering nothing. His eyes narrowed slightly as he picked up that I wasn't going to step onto one of his landmines. He looked as wary as I was. 'Might I enquire just what you were doing?'

'I was reading exercise physiology at East Midlands University, your Worships,' I replied.

He smiled. 'Excellent,' he replied. 'You got your degree?'

'Yes, your Worships a 2:1.'

'Very good, but not a first?' he countered.

I wasn't having that. 'Not quite, sir. Did you?'

He flashed me a glance, cleared his throat and shuffled through his notes. Out of the corner of my eye I saw Mrs Brocklesby smile, then she leaned over and said something to Mr Baxter. Then my ego collapsed. 'Pc Blake, please remember that you are here to give your evidence and answer questions, not to ask them.' I felt so stupid. A simple yes would have sufficed without tripping over my ego. I apologised and glanced at Inspector Felton who was shaking his head. Mr Reeve looked up, a faint smile on his lips. Mrs Brocklesby turned her gaze on the Solicitor, inclined her head and looked at him over the top of her spectacles, 'Mr Reeve,' she said, in a tone that suggested enough.

'Your worship,' he acknowledged with a faint smile.

After that it was straight forward. His questions were to the point. After a brief confab the Magistrates found Smedley guilty. I was shocked when the Inspector read out Smedley's previous convictions. He had over a dozen, mostly for violence. The last some ten years earlier for murder. He had been released on life licence just one week ago. Smedley was remanded in custody until a recall to prison could be arranged. Mrs Brocklesby said that my actions had been exemplary. I had probably prevented a serious incident. She would be writing to the Chief Constable.

Inspector Felton shook his head as I approached. 'I did try to warn you,' he said, then smiled. 'Well done, not many probationer's first appearance in court is because they have single-handedly arrested a violent criminal.' I didn't mention Sergeant Palmer or anything else.

I had the next case as well. Fred Manning, 45 years, a welder. The would-be turkey slicer. He pleaded guilty to being drunk and disorderly and fined £10.

Eleven

Walking down the steps of the Courthouse I got a surprise. Mr Reeve caught me up, 'No hard feelings?' I accepted his hand. 'You did well without taking the arrest into consideration. A lot of probationers struggle at first.' Then he changed tack. 'Was that karate you used to subdue Smedley?'

'Not really. But I am a martial arts instructor in Huddersfield.'

'My daughter's twenty. She's interested in learning. Would that be too old?'

'Not at all. If you like I'll find you a good club.'

He handed me a business card. 'Thanks. I appreciate it.' We shook hands and parted company.

It started to rain.

Back at the station Sergeant McGill called me into his office. He told me about Smedley and Sergeant Meadowcroft. There had been a fight between rival gangs of bikers. Smedley had beaten another gang member to death using a knuckleduster. It had been Sergeant Meadowcroft who had managed to get the handcuffs on Smedley. He promised to return the compliment. On release Smedley had found out when Sergeant Meadowcroft was working, only I had been in the way.

After a cuppa and a sandwich, I grabbed my helmet and set off to patrol Town Beat 1.

Northgate. A certain black Rover16 Sports Saloon passed me going in the same direction. It stopped outside Wainwrights. The driver left the car and entered the shop. Even from this distance I could see the exhaust fumes. I made a note of the time. Like a moth drawn to a flame I began to walk faster.

I'd turned the engine off and removed the ignition key before writing as much as I required in my pocket book. I had a bit of an audience comprised of pedestrians and a couple of local shopkeepers: 'You're wastin' your time lad'. 'Yon bloke pisses int' same pot as your boss'. My pocket book back in my pocket I heard the shop door open. It was the driver. Swarthy complexion. Aged about fifty-five. Five feet seven. Dark greying hair curling over his collar. Clean shaven. Wearing a dark grey suit beneath a dark Crombie overcoat. I thought the loose-fitting bracelet around his right wrist looked effeminate. It looked as if it had been fashioned from an old Albert chain; you know the sort, flattened links. A small engraved oval plaque in the centre. He wore highly polished black shoes, and a scowl.

'Is there a problem, officer?'

'Yes, sir,' I cautioned him. 'You're parked under a no parking sign and too close to the junction. It should be a minimum of fifteen yards. I've had several complaints that you do this habitually. In fact, I spoke with Mrs Frazer about this only the other day and I have previously left notes on the steering wheel asking that you desist. In addition, you quit the vehicle without switching the engine off and removing the ignition key.' I reported him for the offences.

He forced a smile and put his hand on my arm. I told him to remove it, which he did, answering with a scowl.

'Well officer, you know what it's like in business, always trying to be in two places at once.'

'You still have to have consideration for other people using the road. They have to comply with the law as well.'

His mood changed. 'Don't you know who I am? Can't you give me the benefit of the doubt?'

I pointed out how close he was to the junction and that he was parked underneath the sign prohibiting parking. 'Mr Wainwright, there is no doubt.' That didn't help although the few assembled locals were enjoying it.

'There is an order in Westleigh, officer. I am an Alderman.'

'That makes no difference, Mr Wainwright. I would have thought that a man in your position would set a good example.' I gave him a ticket to produce his documents and handed him his keys. 'Good day, Mr Wainwright. You have five clear days from midnight to produce your documents.' I left him spitting feathers.

'Your superiors will hear of this.'

I just had enough time.

I was about a hundred yards from my point when Sergeant Meadowcroft pulled up alongside and motioned for me to get in. He looked grim. 'Have you been speaking to Alderman Wainwright?'

'I reported him for traffic offences, Sergeant.'

'Is your book up to date?'

'Yes, Sergeant,' I said and handed it over.

He read the last few pages. 'Good,' he said and initialled the entry and endorsed his own pocket book.

'Is there a problem?' I said, although the question was, with hindsight, superfluous.

'Yes, he's made a formal complaint to the Inspector about your attitude. You dealt with him in full public view causing him severe embarrassment.'

'If you check my pocket book index, Sergeant, there are several other entries regarding Alderman Wainwright's flagrant disregard for the law. Also, complaints from drivers and other shopkeepers about him. I spoke with his staff the other day asking them to remind him. And I've left notes in his car which he chose to ignore.'

He nodded. 'I don't know what the Alderman said to Mr Jeavons but, to put it mildly, whatever you've done has touched a very raw nerve. He wants to see you.

Twelve

'Pc Blake, sir,' Sergeant Meadowcroft announced. I marched in and stood to attention in front of Inspector Jeavons' desk. He looked angry.

'What the deuce do you think you're playing at, Blake?' he demanded.

'Sorry sir. I don't understand.'

If looks could speak. 'I'll spell it out for you, Blake. Alderman Wainwright. What do you think you were playing at?' He sat there glaring at me.

'Sir, he's in the habit of ignoring the parking restrictions outside of his shop. I've had numerous complaints. I have left notes with his staff and on his steering wheel. Three days ago I spoke with one of his staff about his ignoring the restrictions, but to no avail. He drove passed me and parked his car beneath the no parking sign. When I reached the shop the car was unoccupied and with the engine running, so close to the junction with Lowside traffic was having difficulty in gaining access or leaving.

'Pah. Why not just issue a caution?'

'Sir, he should be parked fifteen yards from the junction. Your instructions were that I couldn't issue a caution for the first three months.'

'Blake is correct sir,' said Sergeant Meadowcroft. 'Those were your instructions.'

The Inspector glared at us both. 'Don't you know who he is? He's a man of substance in this town. Holds a position in this society. He's a God-fearing man. We go to the same church for God's sake.'

This conversation was turning bizarre. 'But our oath says without fear or favour, sir. The fact that ...'

The inspector stood and slammed his fist onto his desk. 'I do not need you to tell me what our oath is, Blake,' he spat the words out. 'And, I've heard reports that in court this morning you chose to affirm. You did not swear on the Holy Bible.'

'I'm an atheist, sir. I don't accept the existence of the supernatural' I said, trying to maintain my equilibrium. 'Affirming has been legal for almost two hundred years.'

I thought he was going to have a fit. Sergeant Meadowcroft didn't look too happy either. Inspector Jeavons leaned forwards across his desk taking his weight on his clenched fists. I could see the tension in his jaw and the tiny muscles round his eyes dancing. 'Without faith, Blake, you have no moral compass. Without a belief in God and the redeeming power of the love of Christ you are nothing.' Then he seemed to relax a little. 'Look, you've had an excellent start to your police career. I'll arrange for you to have some religious instruction, set you on the right track.'

This was way over the mark. 'Sir, under no circumstances will I agree to that.'

He stiffened. 'If you want a career in the police, Blake, you have no choice. You will comply.'

I thought I was going to explode. The commandant at Pannal had made me aware when my atheism came to his notice that many senior and other officers were religious. What the Inspector had just said was unacceptable. There was no way I would comply. Was this the end of my dream to follow in my father's footsteps? As for what Lucy might say?

'Sir, I did not join the police to have religion rammed down my throat. If that is what you intend I tender my resignation with immediate effect.'

'That, Blake,' he said, 'will be my pleasure to recommend under Regulation 10 as not likely to make a good and efficient officer.' He held his hand out. 'Pocket book.' I handed it over. He scribbled something and threw it across the desk. 'Now, get out!'

I was blazing. I don't recall feeling like this since my father's murder and screaming at the vicar, accusing him of being a liar – I had prayed for Dad to come home. The vicar had said in Sunday School if we were good, God would answer our prayers. He didn't.

Sergeant Meadowcroft opened the door. 'Do not do anything precipitous. Go and make yourself a cup of tea. I'll see you shortly.'

My head was spinning. What had just happened? Jack Kneeshaw, the Pc on desk duty, heard every word. Asked if I was all right. I didn't answer. I went into the Mess Room to the sound of raised voices from upstairs.

Thirteen

The sound of Chief Superintendent Williams' voice yanked me back to the present. To my surprise there was now a plain clothes officer sitting alongside him. Dark suit. Light brown receding hair. Brown eyes. An open face displaying a few laughter lines.

'Blake,' the Chief Superintendent picked a report up from his desk and looked me straight in the eye. 'I'm going to read to you the two-week report submitted by Sergeant Meadowcroft last week:

'Pc Blake is a mature officer who in the last two weeks has shown exceptional talent. His punctuality, dress and demeanour are excellent. He is fitting in well and has been readily accepted by his colleagues.

He is quick to learn and not afraid to seek clarification, if necessary. Neither is he afraid to make operational decisions as the need arises. A very promising start.

Inspector Jeavons agreed: *I concur with Sergeant Meadowcroft's comments, a sound start.*'

He put the report back on the desk. 'I also have a report here from Inspector Felton with regard to your attendance at Court yesterday, including a reference to the comments made by the Chairman, Mrs Brocklesby. Also, a report from Detective Inspector Greening re your arrest of Andrew Taylor, and the prosecution files prepared by you concerning Jacks and Smedley.

After the discussion that you had yesterday with Inspector Jeavons I received a telephone call from Sergeant Meadowcroft, so I am fully aware of the circumstances, but I would like to hear it from you.'

The Chief Superintendent removed his reading glasses and looked at the young officer. Silent. Immobile. Stony-faced. Standing to attention in front of him. Pausing for a moment he picked up Pc Blake's personal file and handed it to the officer at his side. As the Chief Superintendent turned back to look at Blake. Detective Chief Inspector Graeme Valentine opened the file.

'Blake,' the Chief Superintendent began, 'There appears to be a disconnect between the various reports that I have read, and what I have in front of me. Two reports both dated yesterday. One submitted by yourself tendering your resignation. The second by Inspector Jeavons recommending your dismissal under the provisions of the Police Act: *that you are not likely to make a good and efficient officer.* Would you care to explain?'

I glanced at my commanding officer, 'Personal reasons, sir,' I replied. Then fixed my gaze back on the clock across the Market Square.

'That, Blake, is patently obvious. Would you care to expand?' He gestured with his right hand inviting a reply.

I maintained my stance, looking directly to my front. 'Incompatibility with Inspector Jeavons, sir.'

'That is also patently obvious,' he continued. 'One of the most, if not the most important jobs that I, as divisional commander, have to do is to ensure that all probationary constables under my care, and I use the term advisably, gives of his best. That the regime that operates at his sub-divisional or section station provides the training, support and guidance to make that possible. One of the ways in which I monitor this is to ensure that every piece of paper submitted by probationers crosses my desk. That includes those submitted by you. With regard to the report submitted by Sergeant Meadowcroft I would disagree in one regard. Having read everything that concerns you, I would describe your progress as exemplary, not merely promising. Somewhere along the line there has been a catastrophic breakdown.

I am also acutely aware of your arrest of Andrew Taylor and, Vivian Smedley two days ago. Not to mention your arrests whilst at Pannal.'

Pc Blake was the third probationary constable to resign from Westleigh in as many months. The Chief Constable wanted to know why. So did he.

The Chief Superintendent held his hand out, 'Your pocket book, Blake,' he said. He read the last twenty pages without comment, closed the book and placed it on his desk.

Fourteen

There was no reaction from the young officer until he spoke again. 'Blake, I know that you have wanted to join the police since before you were eight years of age. And, I know why. DCI Valentine and I both knew your father well ...' he paused and turned to look at the detective.

The DCI looked up from the file he was reading and studied my face, I was confused. 'You're Douglas Blake's son?' he said.

'Yes sir,' I replied. I had no idea who this DCI was. Why was he here?

The DCI smiled. 'I wondered why I'd been summoned here today,' he said looking at the Chief Superintendent, who simply returned the smile, 'May I, sir?'

'Please.'

'Are you familiar with the circumstances surrounding your father's death?'

'A little, sir,' I replied. The others noticing the tightening of his jaw and the muscles round his eyes.

'Before you begin, Mr Valentine,' interjected the Chief Superintendent. 'Blake, there's a seat behind you, sit down.'

'I'll be fine, sir,' I remained standing.

'That wasn't a suggestion.'

I sat.

The DCI began. 'Your father, Mr Williams and myself were all probationers at the same time. Your father and I at the same station. We all eventually joined C.I.D. It was your father who arrested Magnus Yarney for the original murder, that of a young woman, an eighteen-year-old working prostitute called Christine Jones. Yarney had been diagnosed as a paranoid-schizophrenic with religious delusions. He claimed that he had heard God's voice telling him to cleanse the world of sin. However, those who knew best thought him to be safe as long as he took his medication. He hid his tablets. One evening he met Jones, a very pretty girl. He took her up to Littletown where he violently assaulted and raped her. Then cut her throat. It was later established that he hadn't taken his medication for two days.

About an hour after the event he walked into Hecton police station, put the murder weapon, a craft knife, on the counter and asked to speak to someone in C.I.D. During subsequent interviews carried out by your father, and in the presence of a solicitor, Yarney made a full confession maintaining that he was carrying out God's will. Your father was a Detective Sergeant with less than eight years in service, a rapid promotion in those days.

During the post mortem, semen was found not only in Jones's vagina but also in her trachea and oesophagus.

At Leeds Assize Yarney was found unfit to plead and detained at Her Majesty's pleasure. He was suspected of other offences but refused to answer further questions. He died in custody nine years ago.

However, some twelve months following the date of his initial arrest Yarney claimed to have fallen and injured his shoulder. He was transported to the local hospital to be assessed and allowed to visit the toilet unsupervised. The warder was out of sight having a cig when Yarney made good his escape through the toilet window. He had a five minute start before the dumb bastard who was escorting him raised the alarm.

The area was searched without trace. An hour later we received a 999 call to the effect that a woman's screams could be heard coming from a detached property in Garden Lane, Littletown. I was a DC and attended with four uniforms. It was Yarney. He had followed a Mrs Collins and her seven year old daughter to her home. Yarney put a vegetable preparation knife to the young girl's throat and ordered the mother to scream or he would kill the girl. She screamed. Then ordered her to call Hecton and speak to your father. By pure chance he was on duty. Mrs Collins spoke to your father, then Yarney followed suit. He would surrender to your father leaving the mother and daughter unharmed. We had the house surrounded when DI Spencer arrived followed by your father. Shortly afterwards by a dog handler and ambulance. Yarney, satisfied that it was him allowed the woman and her daughter to leave. Unbeknown to anyone outside, Yarney had tucked a chef's knife underneath the belt at the back of his trousers. As Mrs Collins and her daughter walked passed your father Yarney pulled the knife out and lunged, stabbing your father through the heart. The ambulance crew couldn't help. I arrested Yarney and was looking into your father's eyes and talking to him when he died.

During a subsequent interview I asked Yarney, why? He said that it was punishment for interfering in God's plan. Bearing in mind that he initially surrendered himself that is simply bizarre. So please don't ask me for an explanation.'

They weren't to know it but my mind was back when I was eight. I had just found out that my father had been killed. I wouldn't say that I was in turmoil but it was hurling some unpleasant memories around..

Fifteen

There was a full thirty seconds of silence before the Chief Superintendent spoke. 'Are you all right, Blake?' he said. The pain on my face must have been obvious. 'That can't have been easy.'

That was an understatement if there ever was one. 'Yes, thank you, sir,' I replied. 'It was fourteen years ago. My mother would never talk about it or allow anything in the house that referred to it. I never heard her discuss it with Joe, although there were certain things I picked up later on suggesting he knew far more, but they ensured that me and my sisters were protected. Having listened to Mr Valentine it seems somehow more real now. It's brought a lot of unpleasant memories back.'

'Would I be correct in thinking that it was Inspector Jeavons' remarks about religion that triggered this unfortunate train of events?'

I nodded. 'Yes sir. I found his comments concerning religion and his insistence that I must take religious instruction or else totally unacceptable. Also, his defence of Alderman Wainwright simply because of who he was.'

'I understand,' the Chief Superintendent smiled. 'But I will advise you now, shouting at a senior officer no matter how severely you feel you were provoked will not be tolerated in future. Do you understand?'

This is novel, I thought. Am I going to get a chance to retract? I felt suitably admonished for my outburst. 'Yes sir. I understand.'

'Good,' he said, 'Now Blake, what do you want to do about this report of yours? In view of the circumstances, along with my comments and recommendations, I shall have to submit all the relevant paperwork to the Chief Constable. It is a serious matter. One that I discussed at some length with Mr Barton yesterday evening, and which must be dealt with as soon as possible. If you still wish to resign from the force that is your prerogative. I will accept your decision without further comment. However, you have shown that you have a good future within the police service. Should you decide to stay then I guarantee, certainly for the next month whilst this mess is sorted out, you will be working under the direct supervision of Mr Valentine. It is your choice.'

I felt the stress drain from my body in seconds. For the first time in over fifteen hours the feelings of nausea and despondency lifted. 'Yes, sir. Thank you, I'd like to stay.'

Chief Superintendent Williams breathed a sigh of relief. 'Good,' he said. 'Once we have finished here, what I shall require from you is a report stating that having had time to reconsider you wish to retract your decision to resign. Secondly, an offence file in relation to Alderman Wainwright. Submit them through Mr Valentine. Can you manage that?'

I was forced to smile. 'Yes sir, I can. But can I ask a question about Yarney?'

'What would you like to know?' DCI Valentine said.

'Did Yarney act alone? I definitely remember reading that Yarney couldn't drive. Littletown is some distance from Hecton.'

The two senior officers looked at each other. This was better. 'That's a good question,' responded the DCI. 'One that was asked many times and never answered. Yarney refused to say how he got the girl to Littletown or himself to Hecton. Covered in blood as he was, we know that he did not travel by public transport. Also, that the rape and murder occurred where he said. That was where we found the body. There was no evidence of any vehicle in the vicinity. No sightings. Tyre tracks. Nothing. We have to assume that the answer to your question is yes. Yarney took his secret to the grave. Any other person or persons involved kept their mouths well and truly shut.'

'Would that suggest sir, that any of the people involved or any vehicles used might have been local. Had every reason to be there and any sightings ignored because of that?'

'You're like your father, Blake,' the DCI laughed. 'That's a damn good point, and the answer is yes.'

'Sir, with regard to his absconding from the hospital toilet ...'

'You were going to ask if he had somehow arranged transport, or perhaps the whole thing was planned from the outside and the information passed to him?'

'Yes sir.'

'Again, that answer has a high probability. We thought so at the time. I still do. Someone chose Littletown as a destination. A link to the murder of Christine Jones.'

For the second time that day I smiled. 'if I might, sir, just a couple more questions.' Why didn't Yarney kill the woman he took hostage, and why didn't he just pick up the phone and dial 999, did he say?'

DCI Valentine smiled to himself. It could have been his father speaking. 'Yarney's philosophy was that the woman was married and therefore had committed no sin by having a child. She need not be *cleansed,* as he put it. The daughter was, in his mind, pure. However, that did not mean in his twisted version of reality she was innocent. She was female. It was Eve in the Garden of Eden who tempted Adam bringing about the fall from Grace. He terrified the girl and her mother because he could. Because of the Genesis myth hated all females. Terrifying the mother and the girl, making the mother scream was part of God's punishment that he, Yarney, inflicted. According to the staff at Broadmoor where he was originally assessed, it gave him some kind of sexual gratification. In simple terms Yarney was an outright bloody nutter.'

Sixteen

The atmosphere had relaxed considerably. That did not mean there was nothing left to ask. There was plenty rolling round inside my head. DCI Valentine picked up the Smedley file. 'Did Inspector Jeavons mention Smedley's arrest at all?'

'No sir. He only talked about my choosing to affirm instead of swearing on the Bible, and Alderman Wainwright.'

The DCI looked at the Chief Superintendent. 'That's worrying in itself, don't you think?'

'Yes, I do, and it's in my notes.'

'Blake,' the DCI said. 'I hear you're an exponent of Karate and this is what you used to subdue Smedley?'

'In part, sir,' I replied

'For how long?'

'Since I was nine sir,' I smiled, remembering the first time I saw Joe. 'That's how we met Joe. He was the Karate teacher.'

'Joe as in your stepfather?' He smiled as he dropped that one on my toes.

'Yes sir,' I replied, my brow well and truly furrowed. 'The same; but you know about Joe?'

This time they both smiled. 'Yes,' replied the DCI. 'Both my and Mr Williams' wives have kept in contact since your father's death. Still exchange cards at Christmas. Your mother has kept us fairly well informed. In fact, we were all at the wedding when your mother and Joe married.'

'He's been a fantastic stepfather to me. Initially I used to think that was being disloyal to my real father. Of course, it wasn't. Now they have Clive we've got a great family.'

'I'm sure you have,' the DCI paused. 'Your Pannal exploits apart, I know your experience is limited but tell me, which in your considered opinion is the more important, the crime or the criminal?'

That caught me by surprise, but both the DCI and the Chief Superintendent were watching me like hawks. I got the impression that after the issue with my resignation this was the main event. I couldn't help smiling. 'Thank you sir.'

The DCI looked me in the eye. 'It's not a test, take your time.'

I raised my eyebrows and exhaled. 'Well, from what little I've seen,' I began, then paused and frowned. 'It would have to be the criminal, sir.' It seemed to be the right answer.

'That's a very definite answer, Blake,' he said. 'Why?'

I thought for a few seconds. 'Because society always plays catch-up. Much of our law was taken from biblical sources. Thou shalt not kill. Bear false witness etc. Although in more enlightened times we no longer execute adulterers or homosexuals. But unless this activity was already occurring within society the laws wouldn't have been seen as necessary. From my experience,' I paused and concentrated. 'Cinemas aren't listed buildings. It's not an offence to be found inside when they are closed unless damage has been caused or there are thefts from the kiosk, office etc. However, it's quite commonplace these days. Hopefully that will be amended in the not too distant future.'

'In the new Theft Act,' replied the DCI and paused. 'That will do. You're not married, are you?'

'No, sir.'

'Anyone in your sights?'

'Very much so, sir,' I said with a broad smile. 'Her name is Lucy Vernon.'

'As in daughter of Bill Vernon?' said DCI Valentine.

I started. 'Yes sir.'

His brow furrowed. 'You were at the Spartan's track at Tadcaster?'

'Yes sir.'

The deafening silence broken by the DCI. 'Getting information out of DI Thewlis is like trying to get a straight answer from a politician.' 'What can you tell us without breaching The Act.'

'The trial will be at the Old Bailey within the next three months, sir. I am the only one required to attend.'

'I don't suppose you know who the trial judge will be?'

'Lord Justice Nevison, sir.'

'Nevison?' said the DCI. 'He's a hanging judge, or would be.'

'Who else was there?'

There seemed no point in hiding those who were at the press conference so, here goes. 'Lucy, my sister Anne and Elizabeth Vernon, Lucy's mother.'

Both the DCI and the chief superintendent looked puzzled. 'They were present and yet not required to give evidence?' the DCI said.

'They didn't witness the murders, sir.'

There was an askance look between the two senior officers. 'I think that's enough, Mr Valentine. We'll have to wait for the trial report for the details.'

'The trial is *in camera*, sir,' I said and smiled. 'and with respect could I ask a favour?'

'*In camera?* Including the Press?'

'I don't know, sir. Just that it's *in camera*.'

He nodded. 'Now, what would you like to ask?'

'With the death of Bill Vernon the pressure on Lucy and her mother will be high enough ...'

'Without adding to it,' Interrupted the chief superintendent. 'I think we can manage to keep quiet Mr Valentine.'

'I think we can, sir.'

'Back to the point I was raising,' said the DCI. 'Under normal circumstances we all chat. You being a probationer it's only natural that you would discuss what you do as a police officer with your family and friends. Providing you don't go blabbing to the press that isn't generally a problem. However, what I am about to disclose will not be divulged to anyone. Not your family, girl or other friends, or Uncle Tom Cobbly. Do you understand?'

This sounded interesting. 'Yes sir,' I tried not to appear too enthusiastic.

'You can tell them you are on secondment. I run a department of twelve detectives. You'll meet them all later. As you might surmise we target known criminals or those not in the system and brought to our notice.'

I hunched myself higher on the chair. 'However, this is not the instant gratification from a quick collar. A shop lifter or a thief climbing out of the back window of a shop and landing in your arms.' He paused and looked me in the eye. That was in my file. 'We wait until we have the evidence. For the simple reason that the people we target are intelligent and resourceful. We obtain as big a picture as possible before we move in unless something forces our hand. Our aim is to put them away for a long time. It can be cold, wet and at times seemingly fruitless. Sometimes we're wrong, but we keep going until we know. One of our target groups we believe are transporting small items of high value; what that is we have no idea. We need information. Tell me, does the name Michael Grant mean anything to you?'

'I do know a Mick Grant, sir,' I said. The Mick Grant I knew seemed ok, but I suppose Doctor Crippen did as well. 'He plays rugby for Gomersal. I played against him last week.'

'He's the one,' confirmed the DCI. 'How well do you know him?'

'To be honest, sir, I've only met him a couple of times and that was to play rugby. Last week's was a good close match. Afterwards we all got together in their clubhouse for a drink, a few sandwiches and just chatted. We're more acquaintances that share a love of rugby than friends, but yes, we got on all right.'

'Good. One of my team was following him. He overheard you talking to someone about your course at Pannal and made a note of your bike. We were making arrangements to borrow you when I received a call from Mr Williams last night. Grant's been a petty criminal for several years. When he developed interesting friends and far more cash than a machine operator at Burnley's Mill should have we took notice.

The task I have in mind for you is to develop a friendly relationship with Grant. Friends talk. He may divulge something useful. We also have to consider that he may, bearing in mind you are going to tell him the story of why you are no longer a police officer, report back to whoever pays him. That may lead to him attempting to recruit you. Should he do that we will have to tread with the utmost care. We have his routine plotted. He uses one particular watering hole. Are you still interested?'

I would have been mad not to. 'Yes, sir.'

He smiled. 'Very well, are you on your motorbike?'

'Yes, sir.'

'Until further notice no uniform. Go home. With the exception of your staff cuffs and warrant card, you can leave those at the office, bundle everything up and leave it in a conspicuous place in your living room should anyone look through the window.' He handed me a card. 'Be at this address in ninety minutes.'

'I'll be there, sir.'

'Does Grant know about your father?'

I'd always made a point of not telling anyone. 'Not from me he doesn't, sir.'

'One last thing before you go,' the Chief Superintendent smiled. 'Tell us about Sergeant Palmer.'

I heard the conversation start as I closed the door, just not what was being said. My head was almost spinning. My heart was thumping. What a turn round from yesterday. There really was a light at the end of this tunnel and it was getting brighter by the minute. Pleased that it wasn't a train heading my way.

'You're happy with him, Graeme?' The Chief Superintendent asked as the door closed.

'Promising, sir,' replied the DCI. 'He's certainly not the sad and angry little boy we saw after Douglas was murdered. He's got the right credentials. We've just got to dampen his enthusiasm a shade. I was going to say we're not looking for Bulldog Drummond but he already is. I won't demean what he's just told us by comparing it to James Bond.'

'Well, excepting the last eighteen hours, his enthusiasm has delivered spectacular results. He's mature and intelligent. The rest is down to you and your team.'

Seventeen

An hour later I arrived at a faded green door in James Street, parked the bike and pressed the buzzer. It might have been faded on the outside. Inside it was freshly decorated. A dozen desks each with its own mini-switchboard. Seven of them occupied. Two of the occupants recognised me and raised their hands. I smiled in return although I hadn't a clue who they were. A separate room for communications: telex, teleprinter and radio console. What caught my eye were the large boards containing numerous photographs and notations. On an adjacent wall a similar board covered by a large sheet.

DCI Valentine sat me down in his office. 'Blake, ignoring what you told Mr Williams and myself, which was unbelievable, you have to develop a thicker skin. You can't allow yourself to rise to the bait like you did with Inspector Jeavons. You won't last two minutes. You've a great deal to learn about being a policeman. Keeping calm is one of them, irrespective of how severely you're provoked.'

I wasn't aware that we had any female detectives in the force. There were two updating the board. The chatter ceased as I followed the DCI, standing at his left shoulder. We were joined seconds later by the two remaining members of his team.

He introduced his supervisors. 'This is my two i/c, DI Mark Henderson.' Mid-forties, six feet and built like a tank, clean-shaven, plenty of laughter lines, salt-and-pepper hair. 'DS Peter Cartwright.' Five ten, early thirties, stocky, dark hair and an open face. The two who had just entered. 'DS John Nicholson is sitting to your left.' He was mid-thirties with dark hair and a winning smile. I acknowledged them all. 'You'll find out who the others are in due course.'

There wasn't a sound as they looked at me, expectation writ large on their faces. 'This,' he indicated me, 'is our rugby playing probationer, Pc Brian Blake. He'll be with us for the next four weeks. And just in case you're wondering, he is not here looking for a sergeant to arrest.' Like the Co-op's Gold Seal Margarine my fame was spreading. The explosion of laughter subsided. 'He will try to slake your curiosity later. Now is not the time.'

One of the female officers spoke, 'Sir?'

'This is WDC Elizabeth Farthing, for some strange reason generally known as Penny.'

I smiled. She was a slim brunette, I thought in her mid-thirties, around five seven, attractive and wearing a wedding ring. 'Hello,' she said. I acknowledged. 'Penny or Liz,' she answered pleasantly. 'It doesn't matter which. Sir, I was in the DHQ canteen less than thirty minutes ago. It's now obviously false, but there's a rumour that Pc Blake is suspended pending dismissal for having threatened to strike Inspector Jeavons.'

DCI Valentine turned to me. 'The power of the rumour mill,' he said. 'All right, settle down.' Order restored he continued. 'Yes, the rumour is false but do not comment or say anything to contradict it. It suits our purpose. That is with the blessing of the chief constable. Yesterday evening,' he continued. 'I received a call from Mr Williams to the effect that he thought he had found the officer we were looking for to participate in Operation Gateway. As a result of that conversation I attended his office just over an hour ago. The officer in question was Pc Blake, whom I had last seen, fourteen years ago?' he looked at me for confirmation.

That made me smile. 'Correct sir,' I replied.

'Makes me feel old,' he laughed. 'That occasion was the re-marriage of his mother. Pc Blake's father, Douglas Blake, a DS, had been murdered whilst affecting the release of two hostages and the re-arrest of one Magnus Yarney two years earlier. Pc Blake was just turned eight. I was present when Douglas was stabbed. He died in my arms.'

Now every eye was on me. I wasn't used to being the goldfish in the bowl.

'However, Pc Blake's grown up since then. He's even started shaving.' He paused, waiting for the laughter to subside. I grimaced and rubbed my chin. The atmosphere was certainly relaxed. 'The meeting that I had with Mr Williams concerned the matter for which Pc Blake has allegedly been suspended. It is true that Pc Blake and Inspector Jeavons had a full and frank philosophical disagreement, as a result of which Pc Blake stated that he would resign rather than comply with Inspector Jeavons demands.'

'I'll bet, sir, that it was over the fact that Pc Blake affirmed in court yesterday, instead of taking the oath.'

'Yes, DC Jackson, it was.' The DCI turned to me. 'DC Jackson was the one who spotted you at the rugby match. And that information like everything else stays in this room. It was whilst I was perusing Pc Blake's file that I realised who he was. The facts confirmed Mr Williams' suggestion that Pc Blake would be suitable for our purpose. Although in the job for only four weeks, during that time however, he's shown me just what he is capable of. He's a motor cyclist and he knows Michael Grant through playing rugby.' There was a sudden flurry amongst the others. 'He can also look after himself. As referred to earlier he appeared in court yesterday for his single-handed arrest of Vivian Smedley. According to eye witnesses in ten seconds flat. And if you're too young to know who Smedley is, the last time he was arrested, and that was for murder, it took half a dozen just to hold him down.

'Last but by no means least he knows how to think. Not only has he a degree, but the incident at Pannal shows a maturity that many seasoned police officers do not have. If you'd like to ask him any questions before we put him to work, fire away now.'

Before anyone could speak the DCI continued. 'One last thing. Arrangements are in progress to make Pc Blake disappear from our Admin. Although I'm sure he will be pleased to know that he will still get paid. And, with the exception of this office I want him kept away from all police premises for the next month. If we haven't got anything useful by then we can return him to active duty, and,' he turned to me, 'I want you divorced from your present life at Westleigh as much as possible for the next four weeks; that includes rugby.'

DI Henderson joined in. 'Blake, I've spoken with Inspector Felton in Prosecutions and any pending cases that you have will be arranged for at least five weeks hence. All Prosecutions correspondence to be directed to you here.' I nodded in acknowledgement.

The questions didn't come thick and fast, mainly about why I joined the police after my father's death and attending university.

My answer was simple, 'Why are you detectives? I think it's the best job in the world.' I don't think they were convinced.

PC Jackson asked about karate kicks. I invited him to participate in a short demonstration, promising that providing he stood stock-still he wouldn't get hurt.

'Why me?' was the plaintive protest.

'Because you opened your big mouth,' was the general answer. Although several others had been going to ask the same question, or so they claimed.

DC Jackson was about the same height as me except more comfortable around the waist. I asked him to stand in the doorway to the telex room, put his sandwich box on his left shoulder. I took my shoes and socks off to comments about sweaty feet and that I was going to take a running jump. I turned sideways on and flicked the sandwich box from his shoulder. I picked it up returning it to its owner.

'How in bloody heaven's name did you get your foot so bloody high? I'd tear my nuts trying to do that.'

'You haven't got any nuts,' came a female reply. That was Jenny Sendrove the other female detective

'Ha bloody ha'.

'I started to learn when I was nine,' I said, joining in the laughter.

The meeting broke up shortly afterwards with several officers leaving. Inspector Henderson and DS Nicholson told me what they thought I should know about Operation Gateway. Nothing. My task was to befriend Mick Grant and, without pressurising him find out as much as I could. The more I knew about Operation Gateway beforehand, the greater the risk that I could let something slip and, as they put it, screw the entire effing show. I understood their logic, although it wasn't exactly what I'd expected.

The DCI had told me that I had a lot to learn as soon as possible. This was certainly no quick collar. No instant gratification. I was beginning to feel like the proverbial black cat wandering into a pitch-black cellar hunting for a black mouse that might not be there.

I went across to Huddersfield. Frankie was there on her own. 'I can't stop. I'm on secondment for the next month. If anyone wants me you can reach me here.' I handed her a note of the number and left.

Eighteen

All the curtains were pulled. Lucy was wearing an incredibly sheer bra and pants and an expectant smile. She had a great figure. 'Seeing you've forgotten where I live, I'm here.' She gave a great impression of the Vitruvian Man. 'Like what you see?' She reached behind, unhooked her bra letting it slide down her arms. The things I have to do. 'Bloody stupid question.' I stripped off. Scooped her up and ran into the bedroom, tripped over the bedside mat and dumped her on the bed.

'Well if that's what you think of me,' she sat up trying not to laugh. 'I'm going home.'

My arm round her waist I dragged her into bed. 'You're going nowhere.'

'She reached up and stroked my cheek. 'I do like it when you're masterful. Make love to me.'

Straddling her I slid down the bed, hooked my arms under her thighs and buried my face.

I was lying on my side supporting my head in the palm of my right hand. 'Now, have you got that?'

She could be plaintive when she wanted. 'Of course,' she said lifting her head from the pillow. 'I'm not stupid.'

'I know you're not, but sometimes ...'

She grinned at me. 'You've been seconded for a month but only the family can know and they're to tell no-one. Everybody who asks, especially strangers, have to be told that you've resigned over a bust-up with your inspector and you're looking for another job, or, going back to university.

How's that?'

'Perfect.'

'Good,' she reached up and stroked my left cheek then down my belly and took hold of me. She smiled. 'What you did before with your tongue. Do that again than we can go out for a meal. My treat. I don't fancy sex on a full stomach.'

She called home. She was staying.

Nineteen

1145 the following Tuesday. It was bright and sunny with a gentle easterly breeze. I'd parked my bike down by the river in Low Street and joined the multitude of late morning shoppers in Bridgefield. I took five minutes to look at the bikes in Vernon's; their Head Office where Lucy worked. There was a brilliant Yamaha I would have loved to own, if I'd £500 to spare. What was I thinking? *Come on. Get your head straight. You've resigned from the police. You have no job and no money.* I was apprehensive. *Would he turn up? What if I let something slip?*

A hand on my shoulder. 'Brian? Brian Blake?' Mick Grant's voice. Right on time. Relief. 'I didn't know you frequented this area,' he said. I turned and we shook hands. He was a couple of years older than me. A couple of inches taller. He played at outside centre for Gomersal. Just like the photographs at the unit. He was a smart dresser. Sports coat. Cavalry Twills. Brown brogues. Brown check shirt. A lovat green raincoat. It must have cost him a pretty penny.

'Hello Mick, I didn't know you did either,' I replied. 'Just casting envious eyes over this beauty. It's too much for me and likely to remain so for some considerable time.'

He looked over my shoulder and scowled. 'You won't get me on one of those things for love nor money,' he said and shuddered. 'Death traps they are.'

'Only if you fall off,' I laughed.

'You still won't get me on one,' he frowned. 'A grotty four wheels is always better than a shiny two. Anyway, I thought you were a copper. Plenty of brass these days. Won't take that long to put the readies together.'

'Long story,' I said. 'Yes, I joined. Now, I'm on my way out.'

He looked genuinely shocked. 'But it's only what, three, four weeks?'

I nodded. 'Since I left training school? That's about right,' I said. 'But it's not what I thought it would be. I had a blazing row with the Inspector. I told him I was resigning. He said he was going to recommend my dismissal. Here I am in no-man's land just waiting to get my cards.'

'Bloody Hell,' He retorted as we approached the Bridgewater Hotel. 'I often call in here if I've got time,' he said. 'Come on, I'll buy you a pint. You look as though you need one.'

The Bridgewater was one of those hotels built before the First World War when Britain ruled the waves and most other things. Now exhibiting a fading grandeur. It was still four star, just had the corners rounded off. Nevertheless, it had an excellent head chef and a comfortable lounge bar.

There were only half a dozen in the bar when we arrived, including Liz Farthing and Derek Myers, another of the team. Both enjoying a cup of tea and what looked like toasted currant teacakes. No doubt on expenses. I chose a table about five yards away whilst Mick bought the drinks.

'Go on, Brian, get your laughing gear round that.' He put the drinks on the table and sat.

'Cheers Mick,' I took a good swig.

'What you gonna do now? Don't you feel you've been cheated? All that bloody hard work?'

'That's one way of putting it,' I paused and took another mouthful. 'Totally pissed off. What comes next? Not sure. I've got to do something. My stepfather's been great in the past, but another two years university? He's not happy at putting his hand in his pocket too often. I've got to find some way of earning some cash.'

'I know a few people,' said Mick, after a few seconds of exercising his grey matter. 'Don't hold your breath. I can always put a few feelers out if you like. See what might be on offer. You never know.'

'Cheers,' I replied. 'That's good of you. I'd appreciate that.'

'No problem,' he said. 'How do I get hold of you?'

I chuckled. 'Now I've no other commitments?' I said. 'I should have been playing at Tandem on Saturday and Wyke the following week, but for obvious reasons I'm keeping my distance from Westleigh. I can always meet you here, if that's ok.'

'Fine by me,' he replied. 'Saturday's a bit on the sharp side. How about a week today?'

'You're on,' I replied. 'And thanks. I'll get the beer in next time.'

He grinned and nodded. 'Fine,' he replied.

'Anyway, that's enough about me. What about you? That's some good gear you're wearing. Have you won the Leger or something?'

'As it happens, I did,' he laughed. 'That was in '62. Stuck a pin in the racing page of the Daily Mail and picked Hethersett. I put a fiver on the nose and the bloody thing won at 100/8, that was £62.10/- in my pocket.'

'You put a fiver on a horse,' I gasped. 'Streuth. As for £62.10/- that's a month's wages for me, before stoppages. But I thought you worked at Burnley's Mill?'

This time he laughed. 'Not for a while, Brian. Thanks to Mr Littlewood.'

'Littlewood?' I queried. I must have looked puzzled because I was.

'Yep, Littlewood's pools,' he grinned, and whispered. 'The jackpot.'

'Bloody hell.' I blurted out; I couldn't help myself.

He was on a roll. 'Any eight from ten. Forty-five lines at a penny a line. That's three shillings and nine pence.' He grinned. 'Just shy of half a million quid.'

My face must have been a picture. 'There are a lot of people know that I won. But not how much.' He gave me a knowing look. 'I'd be grateful if that stayed between us.'

I winked. 'Of course.'

He leant back on his chair. A self-satisfied look on his face. 'Betty and me, we bought a nice house between the park and the ring road, for cash. 'Nice big gardens for the kids. We have a boy and a girl. I bought a bright red MGA, my pride and joy. That lives in the garage these days and I had to buy an A55 Cambridge. I'm not complaining. I even invested in my aunt's business. She owns Yorkshire Air Holidays and opened another branch last month. Things are looking good at the moment.'

What else could I do but congratulate him. I would see him next week at the same time. As I left the hotel the penny dropped. I could have kicked myself. If he won half a million quid he could have bought himself a couple of helicopters and a dozen Rollers, so why did he buy an Austin Cambridge? There's nothing wrong with the A55. Not exactly what you would expect from somebody with that amount of money, even if he was being careful with it.

Twenty

Liz Farthing replaced the handset, turned to Inspector Henderson. 'It's true sir,' she said. 'A Michael Grant with the address we have in our files did win a substantial amount in November 1962. But it was £15,000 and not the £500,000 he claimed. Nowhere near enough to buy the house where he lives and to finance his current lifestyle. Bearing in mind that we now know he left Burnley's nine months after the win, the little toerag's lying through his back teeth.'

Following the debrief and a few phone calls we had a good picture of Michael Grant. Personable. Good rugby player. A gentleman of leisure with insufficient means of support. I have to admit that although I couldn't claim to know him well I liked what I saw. Initially the deceit made me feel uneasy. It was looking as if he was up to his eyes in something he shouldn't be. That was when it began to dawn on me what being in C.I.D. was all about; even if Dad had ever done anything like this. What a job. Great.'

Over the next two days I worked with Sergeant Cartwright and Liz Farthing checking out Mick Grant's home and his aunt's travel agencies, making enquiries to find out just what, or who, Mick Grant was.

The day prior to my next meeting with Mick we had information from numerous sources including the Post Office who supplied copies of his telephone bills. He made a lot of telephone calls, including overseas. Also details of his tax affairs from the Inland Revenue. However, the big surprise came around three o'clock when the DCI took a call from Chief Superintendent Williams.

A well-dressed man answering Mick Grant's description had presented himself at Westleigh a day earlier. He asked to see me with some cock-and-bull story about me helping his mother when she had broken down. Wanting to give me a bottle of Black Label as a thank you.

Sergeant McGill had explained that I was no longer a police officer. They couldn't help with the address; all relevant records having been sent to HQ. The sergeant was aware that I lived in Mirfield, but didn't remember the address. Grant left the nick and drove off in a red MGA sports car leaving the scotch on the sergeant's desk, as he said, *For the police Christmas raffle*, probably expecting the sergeant to drink it himself. Fingerprints lifted from the bottle, which was placed in the Connected Property store, were confirmed as Mick Gran's.

It appeared that Mick Grant had progressed from juvenile stupidity to something in a different league altogether.

Right on time. 'Take a pew, Mick. I'll get the beer.'

'Cheers.'

'Right,' I said when I placed two pint glasses on the table. 'You look happy enough. Good news?'

'Yup. My Aunt Marjorie, Marjorie Simmonds, I told you about her last week, is looking for somebody. Not sure what the job is and she wants to see you tomorrow morning in her Yorkshire Air Holidays office in Town Street, Horsforth.'

That was it.

The only issue I had was his claim that he didn't know what the job entailed. Why didn't I believe him?

Twenty One

You could smell the paint. Everywhere clean, crisp and tidy. There were two young couples talking with members of staff and a young man leafing through the myriad brochures in the wall-mounted racks. The door marked 'Office – Staff Only' opened and a woman, who I took to be Marjorie Simmonds appeared, she smiled. 'Brian?'

I nodded.

She invited me through. About the same age as Mum, taller, slim and attractive. A brunette with permed shoulder-length hair. She wore a white blouse with 'Yorkshire Air Holidays' embroidered across the left breast pocket, the same as the girls downstairs. A dark grey slim-line skirt and black high heels.

Her office was light and airy, aided in no small measure by the full-width full-height window that overlooked Town Street. An aroma of fresh coffee.

Two photographs on her desk with a couple of facing dining chairs. Adjacent to the window a small coffee table surrounded by four comfortable-looking easy chairs. To the side, a coffee-making machine and cups. Unusually, or at least I thought so, a telex machine in the corner to her right of the desk. She knew what Mick had told her about me from rugby and our conversation at the Bridgewater. Plus, whatever he gleaned from his visit to Westleigh and anything from any other enquiries that he might have made, which couldn't have been much. Bearing in mind what we knew about Mick Grant I think I had a slight advantage. I still felt a twinge of apprehension.

After initial introductions we shook hands.

'Take a seat,' she pointed towards the window. In the café opposite Liz Farthing and Derek Myers. Seconds later. Whirring. The aroma of ground coffee pervading. 'How do you take your coffee, Brian?'

'Black, no sugar, please,' I said, looking at the grinder. 'That's a neat device,' I said.

'Italian. De'Longhi. They're the best. I can't abide instant. No body.'

I took a sip. 'It's very good,' I said.

She sat opposite pulling the hem of her skirt down and turning her knees away from the window smiling as she did so. 'You'll have to buy your mother one.'

'I'll put it on the list.'

She had a pleasant and easy-going manner. Over the next fifteen minutes covered what had been my life without intruding too much into the family. I didn't have to lie.

'Now, this breach that you've had with the police. Is it permanent or is there any chance that you might re-apply?'

I cast my mind back picturing the row with Inspector Jeavons. 'No, Mrs Simmonds. That is unlikely. I'd like to go back to university. But, that's maybe for the future.'

'Fair enough. A little bit about me. I have several business enterprises on going. There's Yorkshire Air Holidays and several hair and beauty salons across the West Riding. I also provide a courier service. That's where you come in. The fact that Michael tells me you ride a motor bike is of interest. I'm looking for someone I can trust. Someone who can get the job done with a minimum of fuss. Your job will be to deliver to the addresses on the envelopes that I give to you. There will always be a return envelope which must be in your hand before you release yours. The position is self-employed and I will pay you £30 a day. No bike no money. No sick or holiday pay and, no expenses. You pay your own tax and stamp.'

I did a quick mental calculation. £30 per day was £150 per week. £7500 per fifty weeks. I'd read somewhere that the chief constable was paid £5000 per annum. Two days a week would equal my monthly salary. What was the catch?

She smiled and took a drink of coffee. 'Well. What do you think? A two-week trial?'

I nodded. 'Thanks. I can't think of any reason why not.' I was still getting paid and probably wouldn't be allowed to keep the extra, but at least someone else would be paying for the petrol. 'I have no idea about self-employment though.'

She reached across her desk and passed me a business card. 'Go and see these, they're a stationers in the High Street. They'll put you right. It's quite simple. A record of income and outgoings in relation to the business. The difference is yours, less tax etc.'

She cleared the cups. I picked my helmet up from the floor. 'Brian, how do you fancy earning some money today?'

That took me by surprise. 'Er, well, yes,' I replied, smiling.

'You were at East Midlands University.'

'Yes, I was.'

'Do you know Rutland Water?'

'Yes, I've been there a few times?'

She unlocked the right-hand desk drawer. Handed over a brown envelope. Addressee: Nigel Ridley, Mead Cottage, Oakham Road, Hambleton – three doors from Pamela's parent's weekend cottage. I hoped to hell that she wasn't there. 'I know the road. If there's no-one at home?'

'Bring it back. If there are any problems just give him your apology and return it to me.'

'I understand.' A bit of a strange procedure but she was the boss.

'Good. How long will it take you?'

I glanced at the clock on the wall.' Depending on traffic?' I mused. 'About two hours each way, give or take. Time for a break. I should be back here between 4pm and half past.'

The smile returned. 'Excellent,' she declared. 'And you'll need this.' She opened a small black cash box. Removed several bank notes. Handed them over and relocked the drawer. 'Just check to make sure that it's all there.'

Six crisp £5 notes. I thanked her and put the money in my left breast pocket. The envelope my inside pocket. So far so good. The only thing that I could call dodgy was that there was no signature for the money. £30 was a lot of money. I'd learnt from Joe that everything above board went through the books. That entailed a signature or some other form of documentary evidence to substantiate the transaction. Mrs Simmonds had just handed me thirty quid and no signature.

I collected my helmet and had a thought. 'Mrs Simmonds, what happens if there's a problem and I can't get back in time? Do I hang onto the envelope until tomorrow, or what?'

She paused for a moment then turned and opened a small box on her desk handing me two business cards. The first was for her Horsforth office. The second was her personal contact details: home telephone number and address. 'Depending on the time call the office. If that isn't successful, home.'

Liz Farthing and Derek Myers left the café heading for the car park a hundred yards further up Town Street. I noticed one of the photographs on her desk. I was no horseman but it was a photograph of a racehorse. 9 on the saddlecloth. 'Yours?' I said with genuine interest.

'Yes, it is,' she smiled picked up the photograph and handed it to me. 'One of my little indulgences from running a successful business.'

I nodded, took hold of the frame and looked at the horse's name on a small plaque at the bottom. 'Hairanair,' I read out aloud. I noticed she was smiling, 'Hair-an-air?' I repeated, and then laughed. 'You named your horse after your businesses, that's very clever.'

'Thank you,' she sounded pleased.

Might as well follow up on a successful trend. 'Do you race?'

She frowned and shook her head. 'Oh no,' she said. 'I like to ride but I'm not a race jockey. In any case she's a chaser and way out of my league. Cost me a pretty penny. Had a couple of runs. Sixth out of eight in her first. Fourth out of ten last time out. Missed out on a place by a short head. I won £40 prize money. Her trainer thinks that if she continues to improve she may be good enough to enter in the Cheltenham Festival next March. So, who knows?'

I handed the photograph back. Time to leave. 'Well, good luck with the horse.' I opened the door following Mrs Simmonds down stairs and out of the shop.

'Between four and half past then,' she said.

'I'll be here,' I felt exhilarated as I fastened my helmet. Kicked some life into the bike. Checked the road. U-turned and headed for the ring-road.

Out of sight of Mrs Simmonds I spotted Liz and Derek in my mirror and pulled in. They drew alongside. I shouted the address I was heading for and why. The time I expected to be back. Derek gave me the thumbs up. Liz reminded me to go straight to the office. Both wished me 'good luck.'

Twenty-Two

The open road. A long run ahead with someone else paying for the petrol. The A1 was calling. The only hindrance about five miles north of Newark. Two lorries had embraced. That was where a bike came in handy. Cars crawled. In first gear I paddled down the centre of the road. The copper on point duty north of the accident glad to wave me through and out of the way.

Memories of the cottage in Oakham Road filled my mind, the vast majority very pleasant. All involving Pamela. The clouds had dispersed. The early afternoon sun was warm. I reached Mead Cottage at the same time as Nigel Ridley was parking a very nice dark red 3.8 Jaguar. Thankfully, no trace of any vehicle outside the cottage three doors away. Like all the others in Oakham Road the front gardens were tidy, hybrid-T roses in full flower and hedges trimmed.

I dismounted. 'Mr Ridley?' I called, removing my helmet.

He looked at me as if he had a nasty taste in his mouth. 'Who are you?' he demanded.

'Are you Nigel Ridley?' I asked again.

He looked at me for three or four seconds. 'Yes,' he replied with some reluctance. 'Who wants to know?'

'I've a letter for you from Mrs Simmonds.'

He looked aggressive and thrust his hand out. 'Hand it over.' It wouldn't take much effort to dislike him. I took a deep breath. Now I understood Mrs Simmonds' attitude when I asked if there would be any reply. 'I understand there's a return. I have to have possession of your return before I hand it over.'

He thrust his hand out again and stepped towards me. 'I've told you. Hand it over. Then I'll decide.'

'Mr Ridley,' he really was an annoying man. 'I'm not here to debate the matter. If you want the letter I'm carrying then get me your return envelope. I won't ask again. If you don't I shall just go back. It's entirely up to you.'

He narrowed his eyes and looked me up and down a couple of times then turned on his heels. 'Wait there,' he ordered over his shoulder, unlocked the front door and disappeared inside emerging a minute later. The envelope that I was carrying contained one or two sheets of paper. The one he thrust in my direction was quarto, folded over something about an inch thick, and flexible. 'Marjorie Simmonds,' he pointed to the envelope. There was a piece of transparent sticky tape over the name. He turned the envelope over. 'This is my signature across the seal. I've put tape over it so that you can't look inside or help yourself to the contents. Tell the bitch from me that one of these days she'll get what's coming to her. I hope she burns in Hell.'

It was pointless saying anything else. Without another word we exchanged envelopes. I couldn't tell by feel what it might be.

The only incident on the return journey was Pamela's car heading towards me as I approached the outskirts of Oakham. I accelerated past. She slowed down, but I'm fairly sure that she recognised me. *Can't be helped*, I told myself. The last thing I needed was Pamela, in spite of the memories. I stopped for a sandwich north of Newark and got back to Horsforth at 4.10pm.

Mrs Simmonds thanked me. Locked the envelope in the desk drawer and said with a half-smile. 'Did he say anything? Cause any trouble?'

'You were expecting trouble?' I said. Had I been set up?

She put her tongue in her cheek and ran it across her teeth. 'He goes through a little routine. Although we have a good working relationship. What did he say?'

'Nothing much. He asked after you. Nothing more.'

'Then you haven't been to the right address.' A broad smile creased her face. 'Now, what did he say?'

'Ok,' I said frowning, which made her smile all the more. She didn't explain. It was nothing to do with me. 'He said that he'd taped over your name and the flap so that I couldn't tamper with it or interfere with the contents. Then he said to, "Tell the bitch from me that one of these days she'll get what's coming to her. I hope she burns in Hell."

'That's better,' she said laughing. 'That's Nigel ... 9am tomorrow, Brian. This time there are several drops, all local.'

Twenty-Three

The city centre traffic was a pain. The debriefing intensive. A second-by-second account of my interview with Marjorie Simmonds. Contact details of both home and business. Apart from being astounded at how much she was paying me just for riding a motor bike they were interested in the horse racing aspect of our conversation. Liz Farthing was detailed to contact Weatherbys a.m. tomorrow. The place to go for bloodstock enquiries. You learn something every day.

Enquiries were made at the Criminal Record Offices at Wakefield and New Scotland Yard regarding both Simmonds and Ridley. Neither were recorded or wanted. Follow-up enquiries were pencilled in for the following day. There was some discussion about the package I brought back. I described it as accurately as I could. There were a few suggestions. One that appeared more likely than the others: they were bundles of tightly wrapped Bank of England notes. If that were the case what was she selling? Drugs? And what was I delivering? The meeting broke up.

The DCI waved me into his office and pointed at the chair opposite. 'You've already told her you need to put some money in your pocket. They will expect you to be seen spending, but not over the top. Make time to visit the stationers Simmonds mentioned just in case she checks. Keep full records and receipts. Now, pocket book and a full report.'

The next morning I left Horsforth with four envelopes to be delivered and four to collect.

- Scagglethorpe, just off the A64 Leeds to Scarborough

Road.
- Reighton, south of Filey.
- Market Weighton.
- Monk Fryston.

It's a good job they were *all* local. However, it was easy money. The weather was on my side. Four envelopes delivered. Four collected. All approximately the same size as yesterdays. None problematical. I collected my £30 at 3.30pm and reported back to the office. I was debriefed and brought up to speed with the enquiry. There wasn't much new stuff. Dismissed. I went back to my flat, had a shower then rode across to Huddersfield.

Twenty-Four

I waved at Frankie through the window. Dismounted. Opened the door and walked into a wall of four very angry looking women and a puzzled sub-teenager. All talking at once.

Confused wasn't the word. I put my hands up. 'Whoa. What's the matter? And one at a time, please. Mum, what's up?' I was beginning to get the picture.

'After all Joe's done for you and you treat him like this.' Mum was angry. If what they were thinking had been correct she would have been justified. 'If you've got problems we're all here to help. Why not talk it through?'

The girls joined in. 'Yes, why not,' was the gist. They were all talking over each other, again.

I put my hands up. They quietened. 'Who've you been talking to?' I was smiling now. I knew exactly what had happened.

Frankie took the lead. 'You should have been working 2-10 yesterday. I called Westleigh to leave you a message to come over. Sergeant McGill told me you'd resigned. He was surprised we didn't know. Stop laughing, Brian. It's not funny. I'll bet it was Pamela. She never wanted you to join the police.'

That was getting beyond a joke. Pamela?

'Frankie, Have you forgotten Lucy so soon? I haven't seen or heard from Pamela in months,' which was true – I couldn't see the driver's face. 'I haven't come over for a row. If you want answers, kitchen and tea. And how did you know I should have been 2-10?' I was drawn by the smell of one of Mum's meat and potato pies.

It was Clive who answered. 'They've got your duty roster on the fridge. They check it every day. I think they're daft.'

We reached the kitchen. 'We are not daft, shorty,' protested Jennifer. 'We're interested.'

'I still think you're daft,' Clive was nothing if not stubborn.

Sitting round the kitchen table the painful silence ended when they all had their cups in front of them. 'What did Sergeant McGill say?'

They all began to talk at once. 'One at a time, please, Frankie?'

'He didn't go into details just that you'd resigned about a week ago. Is that true?' It was almost an accusation.

'About ten days ago, yes,' I said and took a drink of tea as the cross-examination began again. I reached for my warrant card sliding it to Anne.

She picked it up and frowned. 'This is your warrant card.' She was more confused than ever. I smiled and took another drink of tea.

There was confusion around the table. One of my sisters began to look acutely embarrassed. 'You haven't resigned then?' Anne said.

'I did. But I remember that about ten days ago I came over and left a note with someone. A different number to ring instead of Westleigh if anyone wanted to contact me. To prevent this from happening.'

'It wasn't me,' declared Anne, looking round the table.

'Or me,' echoed Jennifer.

'Or me,' added Clive, not wanting to be left out.

'And it wasn't Mum, Dad or Clive,' I concluded, as everyone looked at Frankie. Her face buried in her hands.

She looked up at four pairs of accusing eyes and one broad grin.

'Sorree,' she wailed, 'I forgot.'

'Frankie,' admonished Mum. 'All this fuss and palaver.'

Sorry? she didn't need to flash an SOS with her eyes; the look on her face was quite adequate.

The others weren't so kind.

'You idiot!' was Jennifer's contribution, followed by Anne's.

'Sorry? That's rubbish. What were you thinking of?'

'Girls are rubbish!' from an admiring little brother.

'All right, she didn't do it on purpose,' Mum said putting her arm round Frankie's shoulders. 'There's no harm done, is there?' she looked at me.

'No,' I replied. 'At least not that I'm aware of ... next question?'

'*Are* you still a policeman?' asked Jennifer looking as puzzled as everyone else.

I pointed to my warrant card in Anne's hand. 'Outside of this room most people that I know think I've resigned. Less than twenty know otherwise. That includes all of you. Please, for goodness sake keep it to yourselves. No discussing it with your friends or at the club. That includes you Clive. I want your promise that you will say nothing to anyone.'

'Not even Dad?'

'It's all right, Clive, I'll talk to Dad. You can talk to him or Mum at home but not outside, all right?'

Everyone agreed, although the girls seemed reluctant. Mum said she would remind them if necessary. I promised to explain later. Mum promised to keep the note safe once Frankie had retrieved it from her room. Half an hour later Joe arrived home. Frankie was left to explain her foul-up. Joe suggested in future it might be a good idea to cross-check before jumping to conclusions. 'Did anyone think to ring Brian's flat?

No-one had.

Joe and I had a quick confab in the library after dinner. He was more concerned about what he had heard from a friend in Dewsbury about Smedley than anything else. He knew Smedley by reputation and wanted to make sure I was all right. I told him I was working with the C.I.D. for the next few weeks. That was all I could say. He, like Mum, promised to keep an eye on things.

Half past eight. I had my leathers on when the phone rang. Joe answered. 'Yes, he's here,' he handed me the phone. 'It's a Mr Valentine.'

'Thanks, Joe,' I wondered what the boss wanted.

'Come on, give him some privacy, it's work,' he shepherded everyone into the library.

'Yes sir?'

'It sounds busy.'

'There were seven for dinner, just like old times.'

'Good,' he replied. 'Families can take your mind off things.' I wouldn't have put it like that. He continued. 'I want you in the office for 0800 tomorrow.'

'0800,' I confirmed. 'Yes, sir, I'll be there.'

Twenty-Five

0745 I was the last to arrive. Everyone seated and facing the Michael Grant wall, now displaying a reasonable likeness of Marjorie Simmonds.

'Things have moved rapidly over the past forty-eight hours,' said the DCI. Using a long pointer he indicated Marjorie Simmonds's photograph. 'Marjorie Simmonds, reputed aunt of Michael Grant. Not yet established. Born Marjorie Brooks, May 21st 1918 in Halifax. An only child. Her parents worked in the tailoring industry. Secondary modern education. Joined the army in 1938 until 1941 when she was discharged with ignominy after receiving six months for misappropriating army property. Fancied herself as a bit of an entrepreneur.' The laughter faded. 'Probably because this offence was purely of a military nature there is no record at CRO. That will be rectified as soon as possible.

She opened a hair salon in 1945. In 1946 met and married one Nigel Ridley,' he paused and looked at me. 'Yes, the same. They were divorced in 1953 after she cited him for adultery. There were no children. She's kept herself clean since then. Well, hasn't been caught. She now owns seven hair and beauty salons in Leeds, Brighouse and Halifax. Four years ago she opened a travel agency. Two months ago her fifth, her Head Office in Horsforth. She told Blake she provides a private courier service. Although, all that seems to happen is that Blake hands over one envelope that contains one or two folded sheets of paper in exchange for something more substantial, something about the size of a five or ten pound note. An inch thick and flexible.

This expansion of hers is rapid, although the tax people have no issues with her. Neither have the local authorities. She employs almost seventy people and has no debts. Everything appears to be above board. Yet, when Grant suggested that Marjorie Simmonds might be looking for somebody, he turned up at Westleigh trying to prize information out of the duty sergeant as to whether Blake's claim to have resigned was in fact true. That in itself is fishy. Grant also lives in a very nice house just off the Harrogate Road at Moortown, bought twelve months ago for cash.' A comment which brought a few whistles. 'On the positive side, she provided Blake with her personal contact details. Grant and Simmonds live within four hundred yards of each other.

That brings us on to Nigel Ridley, unfortunately we have no photograph as yet, but Blake describes him as 5'11", proportionate build, dark brown wavy hair, dark eyes, smart dresser, three-piece suits etc and drives a dark red 3.8 Jaguar. Lives in Hambleton, Rutland. His manner is brusque, aggressive and obnoxious. Sounds like a nice man.'

'Very easy to dislike, sir,' I volunteered from my seat at the rear, to a few laughs from the team.

'Quite,' he replied. 'According to the military, Ridley was born in Halifax in 1915, attended Halifax Grammar School and joined the Royal Marines in 1935. He is reported to have served with distinction. Full details of his war exploits are not available. However, he received a field commission and took part in the D-Day landings, awarded the MC. Resigned his commission in 1947. He got into a few scrapes over Mess Bills and gambling. That is as much as we know. Enquiries are continuing. Blake,' he continued. 'You're the only one who has met any of the group of individuals including the four recipients you visited yesterday. Give us a brief run down. From the front,' he said as I stood up. 'We don't want cricks in our necks.'

Inspector Henderson produced two large board-mounted maps on easels. My job, identify the exact location of the drops with black pins. The hair salons were already marked with blue pins and the travel agencies green. A red pin stood out in Holywell Beck, a few miles from Halifax, where her mother still lived. A further red pin in Park View Mews, Moortown for Grant and a third for Simmonds. Small notes were placed adjacent to the black pins noting the details of the various recipients together with time and date when I made the drop.

My knowledge of the Yorkshire region had been pretty good before I started but it was being stretched. I knew my way to the various towns but every single house was imposing, most within large grounds. Mrs Simmonds told me that over the next four days I would make a further twenty drops.

Twenty-Six

There were no days off. If I wanted the job, I worked.

- Day one. Monday. all in South Yorkshire: Darton and Wombwell, both just outside Barnsley. Chapeltown and the Rivelin Valley, Sheffield, lastly, Penistone.
- Day two: Tuesday. Newmillerdam, Wakefield. Emley. Almondbury, Huddersfield. Sowerby Bridge and Hebden Bridge.
- Day three: Wednesday. It was a long day: Wetherby, York, Darlington, Whitby and Pickering.
- Day four: Thursday. The third call was directly opposite Pannal Ash. A beautiful half-timbered 16th century manor house. Manicured lawns and specimen trees.

I rode passed a line of executive cars. The front three limousines. I began to feel very uneasy. Voices through the half-open door. I gave the bellpull a hefty yank. The conversation stopped. A male voice. 'I'll see who it is.

An impeccably dressed young man about my age and height came to the door. Apart from the white shirt he was dressed in black. Highly polished shoes. That answered that question. He looked at me as if he knew me. I didn't know him from Adam. 'Can I help you?' he said.

I held up the envelope, 'I have a letter for Mr Hugo Carver,' I said.

'*Sir Hugo*.' he replied with emphasis, 'is not available, but I will take it and see that he gets it.' He held his hand out.

That, I hadn't expected. 'I apologise. I wasn't aware,' I said. 'I'm supposed to hand it directly to Sir Hugo and no-one else. I understand he is expecting it and there will be a reply.'

'Just wait there, please,' he said, turned to go then paused. 'Could I enquire who sent the letter?' he asked as an afterthought.

'Marjorie Simmonds,' I said. His eyes narrowed. Without another word he retreated into the house.

I picked up the name '*Marjorie Simmonds*' and '*reply*', but it was the voice that answered that gave me a shock. I smiled to myself. At least I would be prepared. 'Hermione, leave this to me.'

I only had to wait for a couple of seconds as the figure of 'the old man', the now retired former Chief Superintendent and Commandant of the No.3 District Police Training Centre, Mr 'Archie' Andrews, appeared. 'Now listen you ....' He began, then paused when he realised who I was. 'Blake? What the deuce?' Had it not been for the circumstances it would have been funny. 'Is this what you do since your resignation?'

'Good afternoon, sir,' I said. 'You're well informed.' I handed him my warrant card. 'If I can't trust you, I can't trust anyone.'

He glanced at the card and handed it straight back. His eyes narrowed and I could almost hear the cogs spinning inside his head. 'Thank you,' he said. I put the card back in my pocket. 'Who are you working for?'

'DCI Valentine, sir,' I replied. 'I apologise for the timing of my visit. Had I known ...'

He waved his hand. 'It's no matter, but we can't talk here. Come with me.'

Curiouser and curiouser. A knight of the realm and a retired senior police officer who held sway with the occupants. I followed him into the hall. It was one of those houses where the hall literally was a 'hall', probably the largest space in the house. Everything was dark oak: beams, walls, floor, doors, stairs, handrail and gallery. Without the obvious circumstances for the gathering it must have had a brooding atmosphere. Whether they were all aware of the reason for my visit I didn't know. However, the conversation of the two dozen or so people present died as we appeared, their eyes fixed on this unwelcome intruder.

'Hermione,' Mr Andrews said as an aside to a plump woman about fifteen years his junior. Hermionies weren't too common on the ground even in Pannal. 'There's nothing to worry about. We're just going to use Hugo's office. Give us five minutes.' She made no reply, just nodded.

I was ushered into a small office and the door closed behind us. The chatter commencing straight away. The solitary window gave views across the lawns towards the training school. Blocked owing to the presence of a huge Cedar of Lebanon. The office was well lit by fluorescent lights; definitely out of time. A large oak desk, three chairs, three filing cabinets and shelving along two walls. The office of a busy man.

He turned and we shook hands. 'C.I.D. sooner than expected, Blake?' he said with a smile.

'Very much so, sir.' I returned the smile.

He paused as if considering what to say next. I suppose it was as awkward in its way for him as it was for me. This was the first conversation that we had had outside the confines of the establishment across the valley. He was a retired chief superintendent with forty-four years' service. A former detective superintendent. Now I was the police officer. Part of a team investigating what appeared to be a serious crime involving his friends or family, one of whom, the recently deceased owner of the name on the envelope. Now he was just plain mister. I still called him, sir.

'Just to salve my curiosity,' he smiled. 'If you have no objection. These rumours surrounding your resignation?'

'There are several, sir,' I held back the smile. 'Is there any in particular you had in mind?'

'Really?' His eyebrows lifted a notch. 'The one I heard concerned your Inspector ordering you to take religious instruction?'

'Inspector Jeavons. Yes, he did. It was either comply or resign. So, I submitted my resignation.'

'I see,' he nodded. He probably remembered the talk that we had had whilst I was a student. 'Does that fit in with this subterfuge?'

'It does, sir.'

'Well, don't tell me anymore. You know the rules. But is there anything further with regard to that other matter.'

'Not a lot, sir. The trial will be held at the Old Bailey in the next two months.'

'Old Bailey? Somewhere I've never been. That will be an experience. Have you any idea why the Press Conference was not broadcast.'

'I think the easy answer to that, sir, is that I don't earn enough.'

He laughed. 'I'll bet there aren't many people who do.'

'I have my ideas but who am I? However, if I were to hazard a guess it was because of a name that was mentioned by one of the journalists. The service of a D-Notice. But I don't know.'

'Hmm. Do you have any idea what is in the envelopes you deliver, or the responses you collect?'

'We have ideas. However, Mr Valentine thinks that we should hold back on interception until we know the full extent of the network we're dealing with.'

'Quite,' he acknowledged, pausing before continuing. 'I have no intention of interfering but have you considered what course you are going to take when my cousin arrives?'

So, it was family. I hadn't thought about it but considered that this might be the perfect opportunity to find out exactly what was in the envelope. With his permission I called the DCI, appraised him of the situation and sought permission to open the envelope should one be forthcoming. He agreed and said to call him back just as soon as I had the information.

Twenty-Seven

No sooner had I put the phone down than there was a sharp knock at the door. The woman Mr Andrews had spoken to earlier entered, followed by a very pretty girl, about my sisters' age. Dressed in the ubiquitous black and carrying a large tea tray. Last but by no means least the young man whom I met on my arrival. A quick glance was all that was necessary to know they were siblings.

'They've all gone,' said the plump lady to the old man.

The old man turned to the visitors. 'Introductions ... this,' he said indicating the plump lady, 'is my cousin, Hermione, Lady Carver.'

'Lady Carver,' I acknowledged. 'Please accept my condolences. I apologise for intruding at this time.'

She scowled as she scanned me up and down. 'Thank you,' there was ice in her voice. 'Anything from that woman is an intrusion. However, from the manner in which Richard is speaking with you, you are not what you appear to be.'

Before I could continue, the young woman who had been studying my face interrupted. 'I thought that I recognised you when you arrived. I do now,' she sounded excited. Her accent was certainly not Westleigh secondary modern. 'You're Brian Blake,' she said. Her brother grinned. Her mother looked at her in surprise. 'You *are* a policeman.'

I couldn't help smiling. 'I am?' I looked at the old man who simply shrugged.

'You know you are,' she continued in her excitement. 'You used to do martial arts on the playing fields every morning. You gave a fabulous demonstration at your passing-out parade.'

'I did?' I said. *But how?*

She sighed in exasperation. 'You should know that the only people that Richard speaks to under the age of fifty are either Byron or myself.' She nodded at her grinning brother, 'or policemen at the training school. And, you are neither myself nor Byron, *ergo*, you are a policeman.' she finished with a flourish.

I had to laugh, so did everyone else. 'If your facts are correct,' I said, although I was certain that they were not, 'then I suppose that your logic is as well. Do you speak to anyone else under fifty?' I asked the old man.

'Isabel, I speak to many people under the age of fifty who are not police officers,' he said with a smile.

'Oh, bother.' she declared looking annoyed with herself.

'You should also know,' added Byron, 'that we used father's field glasses.'

'And,' continued Isabel, 'you haven't denied that you are a policeman. You're acting under cover. How exciting.'

The old man smiled and looked at me over his glasses, as if to say, *'get out of that'*.

I had to laugh. 'That is true,' I conceded. 'The investigation involves Marjorie Simmonds.' I'd already mentioned the name. It was pointless trying to hide it. 'I need an undertaking from you two.' I looked at Isabel and Byron, 'Whatever you hear stays within this room, no chattering ... The only people who know anything about this are in this room ...'

Isabel and Byron looked at each other and then at their mother, who made no comment. 'You're trying to tell us,' said Byron, 'that if anything is heard that could be traced back to this conversation it is because we have broken a confidence?'

I nodded. 'Or, you could just wait outside.' I wondered how they would react being told that they might have to vacate a room in their own home. I felt easier when I saw their mother toying with a smile.

Inquisitiveness won the day. There were a couple of hurried glances between them. 'All right,' said Isabel. 'We both agree.'

'I agree,' confirmed Byron.

'Very well,' I said and looked at their mother. 'Lady Carver, I'm sorry to have to ask this but when I leave I have to make a telephone call to explain why this visit did not go as planned. Could you tell me how your husband died?'

She sighed and looked out of the window. 'He suffered from rheumatic fever as a child,' she answered, her voice flat. 'Eventually it caused heart problems and he required an operation. He never recovered from the anaesthetic.'

'I'm very sorry,' I replied. It wasn't necessary to say anything else. Of the things I studied at university, the effects of exercise on the body in relation to a series of medical conditions, including several severe ones.

One of the effects of rheumatic fever is to cause calcification of the coronary valves interfering with the flow of blood through the heart and lungs. A necessity of using portable oxygen to deal with increasing breathlessness etc. It was not a good way to die. The operation was one of the largest that could be performed without opening the skull. A huge operation in terms of risk with no guarantee of success. Had that been me I too would have taken the risk. I would rather die under the anaesthetic than suffer the long term alternative.

'Lady Carver, earlier you alluded to the fact that your husband had been receiving correspondence from Marjorie Simmonds for some time. Do you know for how long?'

'Most certainly,' she replied, removed a key from her pocket, walked behind the desk and crouched. There was a slight squeal as the safe door was opened, followed by the rustling of paper. When she stood, she was holding four quarto envelopes. 'Hugo kept impeccable financial records,' she said. 'In here is a record of every transaction he made with that woman.'

The small red hard-backed book was a revelation. Inside the front cover were Marjorie Simmonds' full contact details. The first page was blank. Overleaf it listed by date eighteen horse races, the latest entry five weeks ago. Different dates, courses, distances and horses. It listed the trainers. The stakes and returns. But the thing that stood out above everything else was that every horse had won its race. The stakes were enormous - £1000 per race. The returns indicated that the odds varied between 4/1 and 17/1. Sir Hugo had kept a running total of the profit and the amount he paid Marjorie Simmonds. The amount I was due to take back to Horsforth this afternoon was staggering.

'This is impossible,' I gasped and did a quick mental calculation. Assuming there were only the twenty-five pick-ups there was £900,000 floating about somewhere.

'I agree,' said the old man, looking over my shoulder.

'What is?' demanded Isabel, her curiosity boiling over.

'It's all right,' said Lady Carver. I looked across at her. 'Hugo told us what it was all about shortly before he died. They know the same as I, but we don't know the details and I am intrigued to know what you mean.'

'I'm no expert,' I said. 'I've never placed a bet on a horse in my life. But a friend at university did, his father owns a couple of high-street bookmaker's. He told me that 98% of those who bet on horses lose,' that brought a gasp. 'There are numerous factors that determine which horse wins, from breeding, the state of the ground, weather, jockey, type of race and even luck. If a gambler can win, say four out of ten bets they are doing very well. The bets your husband placed? Eighteen bets. Eighteen winners. That's why I said it was impossible. However,' I continued as something sprang to mind. 'There is perhaps a possibility ...'

There was a pause of several seconds before Byron spoke. 'You mean that someone interfered with, i.e. drugged one or more horses?'

'Yes,' I replied. 'Not for one moment would I suggest that your father had anything to do with that. If indeed it happened. I have no doubt that we can find out. In any case the circumstances don't support that scenario.'

'Could someone do that,' asked Isabel. 'Drug all the horses?'

'They wouldn't have to,' said Byron, 'just one.'

Her brow furrowed briefly. 'Oh. Of course,' she replied. 'That makes sense.'

'Hugo used to own an investment house,' said Lady Carver. 'He was very astute. He made people a lot of money on the stock market, including us. He told me that he had realised there was something amiss and wrote the Simmonds woman a letter. A copy of that letter is in here,' she said, handing me another envelope. 'Her reply is also there. Neither make good reading.'

She was quite correct. In her husband's letter he pointed out the statistical impossibility of, at the time, ten consecutive winners. That as far as he was concerned there were some dishonest practises taking place and wanted no further part in her scheme. He also mentioned the seriousness of his medical condition.

In her reply Simmonds dismissed his argument telling him that it was not illegal. He had made substantial profits at very little cost. If he took further action she would leak his involvement to the press. The family would pay the cost of the adverse publicity that would flow his way. She would expect his continued participation.

The old man was visibly shocked. 'This is appalling, quite appalling,' he said. 'Why on earth didn't Hugo come and see me, Hermione? I would have made sure something was done sooner. We could have stopped this.'

'I know, Richard,' there was a note of anger in her voice. 'At the start it was the shame. Towards the end as you know he became confused. I only discovered the truth during the last two weeks. For that woman to threaten disgrace on the family to keep this ongoing is nothing more than blackmail.'

I wasn't so sure. 'With respect Lady Carver,' I said, 'I don't think she would have contemplated taking that course of action. She's astute and would realise the release of that information would point the finger straight back at her. At that time your husband was vulnerable. She relied on the fear factor to keep him under her thumb.'

'And,' the old man chipped in. 'If the figures in Hugo's notebook are representative, those participating are making a very good profit,'

There were no dissenters.

Of the other two envelopes, one contained letters giving details of which horse to bet on in which race etc. On each one Sir Hugo had written the stake and the return, plus a figure of £2000 written in red ink.

Lady Carver opened the letter that I brought; it was the same. It was for a horse named Sally Simpleton running in the 3.30pm race at Catterick, just two days away. Like all the others it had instructions that the bet should be placed in the last few minutes before the race started.

'Unless I'm mistaken,' I said picking up the last envelope. The name Simmonds written on it. It was the same dimensions as all the others I'd collected. 'This contains the £2000 referred to in the previous letter. I spoke with DCI Valentine just before you brought the tea. He is of the opinion that if this letter was forthcoming we should open it and count the contents.'

Lady Carver wanted nothing to do with it. I opened the envelope. Byron counted the money: Forty £50 notes - £2000.

I made a quick phone call to DCI Valentine to bring him up to date. He agreed that I should call Mrs Simmonds with my story to see how she responded. One of the team would rendezvous at the junction of the A61 and the Leeds Ring Road and take possession of the evidence from Lower Grange before I made the last call at Boston Spa. The Vernons. I would call him again should there be any change.

Everything wrapped and stowed in the nearside pannier. The earlier collections in the offside. I shook hands all round. Lady Carver seeking reassurances that Marjorie Simmonds would go to prison. Something I couldn't promise.

The light was fading. It began to rain. I rocked my bike onto its stand next to the phone box in Star Beck. Gathered my thoughts and called Marjorie Simmonds.

This was no time for finesse. 'Marjorie.' I almost shouted down the phone. 'What the hell have I gotten into?'

There was a nervous edge to her voice. 'Brian, calm down. What on earth is the matter?'

'Several things,' I began to hyperventilate as if I had been running. 'Firstly, the address, Lower Grange, Pannal, is opposite the Police Training School that I've just left. Anyone could have seen me.'

'You're just a courier,' she said in a calming voice. 'Just delivering letters and collecting replies. Is that all?'

'Not exactly,' I kept my tone terse. 'They were upset when I asked for *Mr Hugo Carver*. He's a Knight and he's recently died. They had just returned from the cemetery after the burial.' Time to lay it on a little bit. 'They knew about you.'

Now she was definitely nervous. 'What do you mean they knew about me?'

'As usual I had the letter in my hand. I asked for *Mr Hugo Carver*, which put their collective backs up. I told them I had a letter to be hand-delivered. They asked who had sent it. I told them it was you.' There was a nervous intake of breath on the other end of the line. 'I was invited in and grabbed. They took the letter. Bundled me into some sort of office and locked the door. It's taken me ten minutes to get a window open and escape. This is the first phone I've found.' It was a bit on the melodramatic side and having the desired effect.

There was an extended silence. 'Marjorie, are you still there?'

'Be quiet, Brian,' she snapped. The tone of her voice making me smile. 'I'm thinking ... Did they open the letter?'

'Haven't a clue,' I replied. 'Not as far as I could tell when they locked me in the room.'

'Is that the last one?'

'No, there's one more at Boston Spa.'

'How long will it take you to get to my home?'

'Fifteen minutes, give or take.'

'Ok, skip the last one until tomorrow. Bring the others to me now. I'm at home. See you in ... just a minute ... Did they say anything?'

'As they were closing the door I heard someone say something about calling the police. That's all I need. I've left the police and wasn't intending to get involved in some criminal enterprise.'

'Pull yourself together for God's sake, Brian,' she snapped. 'If it happened ten minutes ago and the police hadn't arrived before you got away it's not going to happen now.'

'You think?'

'Of course,' she paused. 'Have you got a passport?'

That caught me off balance. 'A passport? Erm, yes, it's at my flat.'

'Good, do you know Lockley Aero Club?'

'Yes.'

'Right. Get off home and I'll see you at Lockley tomorrow morning at 5am. Bring your passport and a change of clothing.'

'I'll be there.'

'Don't be late.' She put the phone down.

Twenty-Eight

0455 Friday. The moon was full. A biting northeast wind. I rocked my bike onto its stand in the lee of the Lockley Aero Club clubhouse. The only shelter apart from the two hangers some hundred yards away to the left. Somewhere in the darkness a reception party. Last night I'd contacted the DCI and met Derek Myers at the pre-arranged point. Everything from Lower Grange handed over. The first two collections of the yesterday still in my pannier.

0530. The wind now driving hard from the west. More to the point it was chucking it down. I got what shelter I could in the clubhouse's recessed doorway. A few seconds later the DCI appeared out of the shadows.

'Good morning, sir,' I said. In spite of my kit I was cold, even if I was dry, which is more than could be said for Mr Valentine.

He nodded. 'You're certain it was here at 5am?'

'Positive sir.'

'Well, it looks like she's played us. We'll give it another 30 minutes just to make sure.'

DC Kevin Riley had been parked forty yards from the drive of her home; a large detached house in its own grounds surrounded by high hedges. The house had been in darkness on his arrival. At 0500 still no sign of life.

0700. the DCI put his hand in his pocket. Jacko came back soon after with a stack of bacon sandwiches. At least that brightened the atmosphere.

0900. Horsforth. Told by Christine, the manageress, Marjorie Simmonds had not arrived. Neither was there an answer from her home. Said I'd call back at noon.

1100. Kevin Riley and Colin Anderson informed by Christine there was still no news and messages had been left on Simmonds' answering machine. There were no other contact numbers.

For the umpteenth time Nigel Ridley slammed the phone down. 'Bitch.'

Simmonds' house was checked and secure. The phone unanswered. No answer to repeated use of the doorbell. Her car secured in the garage. The neighbours questioned. She lived alone. No-one had heard of a husband or any other male in the five years she had lived there. There were few visitors.

House to house enquiries were carried out. Farrells, the next door neighbours provided the number for her mother in Halifax. She hadn't heard from her daughter for the last four days. Was Simmonds in hiding or was there some other reason?

DCI Valentine frowned as he put the phone back on its cradle. He pushed his chair back. All eyes on him as he wandered through the doorway.

'£900,000, Blake?' He asked, traces of a smile playing round his mouth. 'Every punter paid her two grand for each race and a minimum of twenty-five.'

'Yes sir,' I replied. 'A minimum £50,000 per race. Eighteen races.'

He raised an eyebrow and smiled. 'No offences committed,' he said. 'It's hers to keep. Almost.'

The protestations began. He raised his hand. 'There are several factors to take into account, and Blake, this does not detract in any way from the work that you or anyone else has done and will continue to do. Nor must you take it personally. I agree with your assessment of the letters you have from Lady Carver. Technically it could be construed as a borderline blackmail. It's mean-spirited and it's petty. However, Sir Hugo is dead. He can neither make a statement of complaint nor give evidence. In any case, the County Prosecuting Solicitor would run a mile if that file dropped onto his desk. No further action will be taken. You don't have to like it. That's just the way it is. Do you understand?'

'Yes sir,' I replied. To be honest that thought had also crossed my mind. But he was right, I didn't like it.

'Next,' he continued. 'Horse doping has been in the press once or twice over the past year or so. However, it's one thing that I've never been involved with, so just to clarify matters I called the experts at the British Horseracing Federation. They called me back half an hour ago. What they said was very interesting. Almost exactly the same as you told me the day that you joined us.' He paused and looked at me. 'Do you remember your answer when I asked you the question: which is the more important, the crime or the criminal, and why?'

'Yes,' I said. 'The criminal is most important. It's the action of the criminal that results in the law being changed. The law plays catch-up.'

He nodded. 'And the relevance in this case?'

I thought for a moment. 'There's no further action re Sir Hugo Carver because of his demise,' I mused, continuing in the same vein. 'And we thought that eighteen straight winners in this case meant that horse doping was involved. However, the British Horseracing

Federation have knocked that idea on the head ... The law is in place with regard to fraud. So, it *has* to be the evidence. I can't see anyone admitting to doping horses unless there was a lever of some sort. That must mean ... the science? The ability to detect whatever substance is used.'

'So far, so good,' he replied. 'But what if the substance that gives the horse a significant edge also happens to be medication prescribed by a vet?'

There was a stunned silence.

'You get the picture?'

'I take it, sir,' said DS Nicholson, 'That it happens? With the vets?'

'According to the British Horseracing Federation, yes,' he replied. 'I suppose you could say it was one of the laws of unintended consequences. To put this into context. No matter how much the statistics may point to this being a case of doping, which in itself is nowhere near enough, there is no suggestion never mind evidence that any drug was used lawfully or otherwise. I've sent them a telex with all the details. That includes Marjorie Simmonds' horse and trainer.

Sooner or later she will turn up. There are four different trainers involved, excluding Marjorie Simmonds'. Their only link with her that we can ascertain is that she sold information about horses which proved to be very beneficial to those who purchased it. That, is not an offence.'

'So why did she run, sir?' I asked before anyone else grasped the opportunity.

'Good question. We may never get an answer. Could have been fear brought on by the conversation that you had about the police becoming involved, but my guess is tax, or, a combination of the two.'

There were several blank looks, including mine.

'I get it,' DI Henderson volunteered. I'll be blowed if I did. 'Marjory Simmonds ran three successful businesses and we know that the tax people were happy with her accounts for two of them because we checked. However, the vast amount of potential income she was receiving through this scheme of hers, had she kept proper books, would have meant that she would have been paying 90% tax on *everything*. If the figure that Blake provided was correct she would have been liable to pay £810,000 in tax on the gambling alone, leaving her with an almost pitiable £90,000. Now, that would have been a crying shame,' he said shaking his head as we joined in the joke. 'It was however off the books. We knew from the start something was dodgy when she paid Blake cash-in-hand and no signature.

'Punters, on the other hand would have had to pay the betting tax of 9%. Either on their stake or the winnings. That is their choice. Whether Marjorie Simmonds ever placed any bets we do not know. We do know that the tax people had no knowledge. I agree with Mr Valentine. In all probability it was to avoid paying tax. She couldn't take the risk of the police getting involved and the tax inspectors taking an interest. She just cut and ran.'

'Any questions? No? Good,' the DCI declared before anyone had a chance to speak. 'This enquiry is almost at an end. The last thing I want is random property clogging up the office. Blake, take the last envelope that you have from yesterday and deliver it. Afterwards, take whatever you have, the envelope or the money plus yesterday's packages and drop the lot off at Horsforth, and get a receipt. Not your personal police receipt book, please,' he said to broad grins all round. My personal receipt book had West Riding Police printed across the top of each receipt. 'I've got one in my desk you can use. Full report when you get back along with the receipt.

'Jenny, take everything that Blake brought back from Lower Grange and return it to Lady Carver. Explain the current state of affairs and that the money is legally held. They can do with it as they wish. And, in your usual tactful manner why no action is possible with regard to the letters.'

'Sir,' she acknowledged.

'Come on everybody,' the DCI clapped his hands. 'DS Nicholson, let's get moving on Michael Grant.'

'Could I have a quick word, sir,' I collared the DCI as he was returning to his office.

'Come on,' I followed. 'What is it?' He said as he sat.

'Sorry, I forgot to mention this earlier.' I handed him the final envelope. 'This is addressed to William Vernon, sir. Lucy's father.'

He had a grim smile. ' A bit late for him now he's dead.'

'Yes sir. If I can't deliver it in person I'm supposed to return it, albeit Simmonds is playing hard to get.'

'Well, after yesterday we know what the contents are. So why not just return it.'

'Bill Vernon was an undischarged bankrupt. The house and all the business assets were transferred into his wife's name some time ago. She's the brains behind the business. He, according to what I've been told, was a liability; hence the bankruptcy. I'm wondering if Liz knew.'

'It's not police business,' he said adopting a humourous expression. 'But you're wondering, as a dutiful future son-in-law there might be a spare £2000 lying round waiting for you, or someone like you, to collect.'

I returned the smile. 'That, and if he's a long time investor just how much more they may be.'

'Very well. Are you all right doing this on your own?'

'Yes sir, I'm fine.'

'Be mindful. And don't spend too much time. I want you back here as soon as possible. In your own time do what you like but, if anything crops up which is not straight forward you call me on this number or at the office.' He handed me his card.

Twenty-Nine

There must have been 40 bikes; all immaculate. The bikers for the most part tidy but a large contingent who could be clones of *el diablo* wearing leathers with Hell's Angels across the back. Amongst the badges red and black wings. Menstrual oral sex with either white or black women. For them there were no boundaries. This was not good. Then I saw continental number plates. They must have accompanied the coffin. Assuming I was just another biker I was treated accordingly. 'Has anyone seen Liz or Lucy,' I said to no-one in particular. Numerous fingers pointed at the house.

Neil appeared out of the throng. 'Hi Brian. Surprised to see you here. Thought you'd be working.'

'I am, Neil. Where's Liz or Lucy?'

'In the kitchen making coffee. What do you make of this lot?'

I looked round. 'Questionable?'

'Too right. Liz isn't happy. There are some pitching tents in the back garden.'

'When's the cremation?'

'This afternoon. This lot have been drinking all morning.'

'I'll have a quick word with Liz. Keep an eye on them.'

Lucy draped herself round my neck to jeers from some of the bikers.

'You said you had man,' laughed one biker with a huge matted beard and a strong German accent to the amusement of half a dozen others.

'She's got one,' I said to ribald laughter.

A few raised their beer bottles. 'Cheers,' to more laughter

'If you say,' replied the original.

Lucy and I turned our backs. 'Can't you get rid of them?'

'Not on my own. Have you another phone?'

'Dad's office.'

Several pairs of eyes followed us through the door at the rear of the larder. 'Lucy, lock the door.'

It didn't take long to explain it to the DCI. 'Do they know you're a police officer?'

'Not unless one of the Spartans has told them, and from what I've seen they're keeping out of the way.'

'Ok, leave it with me. Try not to inflame matters.'

As he spoke someone rattled the door and banged on it with his fist. 'Lucy, your father has something that belongs to us. We're not leaving without it,' the accent English. 'Be sensible.'

'What is it?'

'That doesn't concern you.'

'If you don't tell me I won't recognise it.'

'Stop wasting time. Your mother is out here. Hurry before something unpleasant happens. You don't want that, do you?'

Time to get worried.

'If anything happens to my mother I'll kill you.'

'Of course you will,' he said and laughed. 'Be a good girl or I might lose control of my friends. You have five minutes.'

'Sir?'

'I heard. Does Lucy know what they're after?'

'Not a clue.'

'Leave it with me.' The phone went dead.

'Any idea what they meant?'

'No,' she was getting angry. 'I'll tell you this, Brian. After what happened at the track I'm not putting up with any of their crap.'

I'd never heard her like this before. 'What did you have in mind?'

She opened the bottom left-hand drawer in Bill's desk and put a box of shotgun cartridges on top. 'We keep these to get rid of vermin in the garden and on the track. Time to get rid of some more ... now where is it?' I hadn't seen the shotgun on the rack behind the door. Within seconds it was loaded.

'Are you serious?'

'They're not fucking coming into this home and threaten anybody never mind my mother.' Then she turned and smiled. 'Look after me won't you?'

'To the end of time, darling,' it was time to get very worried.

'Good. Put some cartridges in your pocket. When we leave lock the door and pocket the keys. We walk side-by-side. Ok? We'll see how they like a taste of their own medicine.'

'I don't argue with anyone carrying a loaded shotgun,' I said, wondering what the hell she had in mind.

She took a deep breath and exhaled. 'Let's go.'

If this went wrong we were all in the shit. Was I nervous? You can bet your life I was.

The conversation died as we left the pantry. Liz was standing in the far left corner a Hells Angel either side.

One of the bikers separated from a knot of half a dozen, smiled and walked towards us. 'Common sense prevails,' it was the same voice. 'That was a good decision, Lucy. Have you got it?'

'Fuck you.' Now she was blazing. Before anyone could react she swung the shotgun out from behind my back fired one shot into the ceiling and rammed the barrel under his chin pushing him backwards into the corner. There was total shock. 'Mum, come over here.'

No-one tried to stop her as plaster dust began to settle on the kitchen table. There had been little opportunity for the pellets to spread and daylight could be seen through the hole. I'm certain that was in Lucy's bedroom.

'I'm very good at shooting vermin. I can't miss from here. You come over here with my father's coffin pretending that you cared about him. You're just thieves. Now get your tents and any other crap and leave. Keep away from the crematorium. Don't come back here or to the Spartan's track. I was already talking to the police when this piece of shit rattled the door.' She pushed the shotgun further under his chin. 'They heard everything. Now go, before I spread your friend's brains over the wall.'

The one with the matted beard stepped towards her. 'You have only one shot, Lucy. Then what you gonna do? Eh? Where is it? Hand it over or else.'

'Have you got this one, Brian?'

'I have.'

I applied a choke hold as Lucy turned and rammed the shotgun into the bearded one's gut. 'True, I have just one and you're the nearest. It's your choice. Get out or face the consequences. Well?'

Before anyone could move four bearded men burst into the kitchen.

'Karl, wir haben einen Schuss gehört,' His eyes popped when he saw the shotgun. ' Was zum Teufel!'

Lucy never flinched. 'Back off. Try and take the shotgun and it might go off accidentally.'

With a bad grace Karl raised his hands and backed off. 'The police are coming. We go,' he glared at Lucy. 'For now.'

Within two minutes they were gone, leaving their friend behind. Whether they would take heed was anyone's guess.

Lucy began to shake.

'Are you ok?'

She shook her head. 'You said you couldn't manage it on your own.'

Managing to stifle a smile I teased her fingers from the trigger guard and made it safe then tapped Lucy's prisoner on the chest. He was shaking more than Lucy.

'Right. Keep your mouth shut. On the floor. Face down. Hands behind your back.

I got one cuff on when our new friend protested. 'I'm a police officer.'

'Of course you are,' I said. 'So am I.' and snapped the other cuff.

'Fuck.'

I cautioned him. 'I'm arresting you for conspiracy to steal.'

There was no reply.

I turned to look at Liz. 'Are you all right?'

'I am now. But Lucy what on earth got into you? Look at the ceiling. That's your bedroom.'

'Oh, I didn't think. I just wanted to get rid of them.'

'I wish I had a film of that,' I said. 'It was masterful.'

'I had to do something, Mum. But I'm glad it's over. I'm still shaking.'

I put my arms round her and squeezed. 'We can see that. Better?'

She nodded. 'A bit.'

Neil was standing in the doorway and pointed at my prisoner. 'Did I hear him say he was a police officer?'

'Yes, you did.'

'When they were leaving the one with the beard like a haystack said to the one next to him. "The prick said it would be a piece of piss."'

'Interesting. Have they all gone.'

'Every single one. A couple of the lads have followed to watch where they go.'

Thirty

First to arrive was a Traffic car. He took one look at the prisoner. Looked around and smiled. 'Why's he cuffed?'

'Conspiracy to steal.'

'He's a DS on the drug squad. Aren't you Sarge?'

'I told him. But I had a shotgun under my chin.'

'You told me after the shotgun was taken away. You didn't mention rank. Not that it would have made any difference. You were the leader.'

Details were circulated and observations requested.

Several officers, including an Inspector Merton arrived. I identified myself and talked him through the sequence of events.

'Your shotgun, your ceiling Mrs Vernon, no problem. However my superiors may instruct that the shotgun be seized.'

'They'd been drinking for three hours Inspector and it wasn't coffee. They'd been making salacious comments about Lucy and me. God knows what might have happened. It was self-defence,' Liz protested.

'I've seen the bottles outside but we shall have to see.'

Detective Sergeant Round was relieved of his cuffs and transported to Wetherby Police station.

DCI Valentine, DS Nicholson and Kevin Riley arrived thirty minutes later. 'Blake, before I forget your court warning has arrived. Don't forget.'

How could I forget a trip to the Old Bailey?

'I take it you haven't had the opportunity to mention the reason you came here in the first place?'

'No sir.'

'I wondered why you were here,' said Lucy. 'What was it?'

'First things first. Brian, you write your statement. I'll take Lucy's. John, you take Mrs Vernon's. Kevin, see how many members of the Spartans' were present and get cracking on their statements. Get them out of the way. I know it's not our job but we're here.'

Thirty minutes later we were all seated round the table with fresh cups of coffee.

The DCI nodded to me.

'Liz, did you know that Bill was engaged in gambling, horse racing?'

Liz was shocked. 'You're joking. Even he thought it was a mug's game? Are you trying to tell me he was.'

'Does the name Marjorie Simmonds mean anything to either of you?'

Liz and Lucy looked at each other. 'His bit on the side?' said Liz.

'Not as far as we can ascertain,' I said. 'She ran a very successful gambling syndicate and Bill was a member. That's what I've been doing. Working for Mr Valentine trying to find out what it was about. I discovered yesterday what it was. I've got the next horse to back here.' I pulled the envelope from my inner pocket. 'It runs in the 3.30 at Catterick tomorrow. I would hand this over in exchange for the commission to be paid for the previous race.'

'Why didn't you tell me?'

'Lucy, I couldn't. I would have been skinned alive.'

She smiled. 'Like I'm going to do to you later.'

'Correct.' I returned the smile and handed her the keys. 'Have a look in your Dad's safe and see if there is an envelope or a small package about eight by four and an inch thick. It might be addressed to Marjorie Simmonds.'

She was back in thirty seconds with the package. 'Is this it? How much is there?'

'Count it.'

'But doesn't it have to go to this Simmonds woman.'

'I will just return the envelope marked Deceased. Tell them he died in an accident in Holland last month. His widow checked the safe there was nothing there for her and isn't interested in taking over.'

'And that's legal?' Said Liz.

'It is Mrs Vernon,' said the DCI. 'It's your money. But speak with your solicitor.'

Lucy skipped past her mother. Took a knife from the block, slit the package and looked inside and ran her thumb across the notes. 'But there's a fortune,' she gasped and handed it to her mother. 'And this is commission?'

'Yes, there's £2000.'

'But how much did he gamble?'

'Each race he had to place £1000 with a bookmaker.'

'How can people afford to gamble so much?'

'With the greatest respect to this house, Lucy, the addresses I delivered to were more like country mansions with their fair share of Rollers. They weren't short of a bob or two.'

Liz was shocked. 'But where did Bill get that kind of money. It certainly wasn't from the business. I would have known.'

'We don't know. But after the first race he would have been in profit and that would have financed his other bets. If he had been in the syndicate as long as some members he would have made a profit in excess of £100,000, tax free.'

Liz was having trouble in grasping the numbers. 'What?'

'Do you think that's what that biker meant when we left Dad's office. When he asked if we had it?'

'I don't think so. £2000 isn't much to split between what? Thirty or forty bikers.'

'£100,000 might be.' Commented DS Nicholson.

'If it's true, you could buy a lot of drugs with that,' added the DCI.

'True sir, but it would take up fifty times the space and weigh a lot more.'

'What do you think he meant, sir?' I said.

'I've no idea. They should find out when he's interviewed. Something small, maybe a key or something similar.'

'Where are you going?' I said when Lucy headed for the pantry.

'To empty the safe.'

Five minutes later we had our answer. There was nothing in the safe that would answer the question.

Liz put the £2000 in the cutlery drawer and filled the kettle.

'There is something else, sir.'

'And that is?'

'It might not be £100,000,' I said and paused.

The DCI looked puzzled for a moment. 'You mean the nine hundred?'

'Yes, sir. We know about Marjorie Simmonds business empire and for the most part it was all in order. She had no apparent contacts with the continent but, we know someone close to her who did.'

'Of course. Mick Grant. I must be getting slow.'

'If you're right, Brian,' said DS Nicholson. 'That would make sense. But it would also mean that Marjorie Simmonds and Lucy's father were business partners.'

'As Marjorie's courier do you think that I might get more information out of her mother, sir?'

'On your own?'

'Yes, sir. You trusted me to do the courier bit. I've got the two packages from those other drops and, I haven't been paid. I could hand them over and return the envelope I was supposed to deliver to Bill.'

'Before you go any further,' An aghast Liz's voice broke through. 'Nine hundred? Is that £900,000 you're talking about?'

'It is Mrs Vernon. I'm sorry, we shouldn't be discussing this in front of you or Lucy. And this is a possible scenario. It is what we believe to be the amount of money floating round in this betting syndicate that Bill was involved with. We just don't know at the moment. I am asking that you both keep this information to yourselves until we know, one way or the other. But I will tell you as soon as we know.' The DCI turned to look at me and smiled. 'Very well. When you leave here get yourself across to Halifax and speak with Gertrude Brooks. You have the address?'

'Yes, sir. 13 Pissybeds Lane, Holywell Beck. I'll find it.'

Lucy burst out laughing. 'Pissybeds Lane? There is such a place?'

'There is Lucy,' said the DCI. 'Pissybed is the old name for the Primrose. It a diuretic. Hence the name.'

'Oh. I used to eat them when I was little.'

'Better not eat any more,' said Liz.

'And Brian?'

'Yes, sir, an unmarked receipt.'

'Indeed. That's £4000 you're handing over.'

Thirty-One

DC Driver arrived to take statements.
'We've saved you some time, Driver,' said the DCI handing them over. 'Has Sergeant Round said anything?'
'Not to us, sir. But a DI Thompson, Drug Squad, was ranting on the phone. I was out of the office. The Sergeant and the Inspector are at a fatal on the A1, near the racecourse.'
'You're not saying the gaoler let them talk?'
'Afraid so.'
'Did the gaoler hear what was said?'
'No, sir. Sergeant Round ordered him to leave.'
'Damn. John go back with Driver just in case.'
'Yes sir,' he said as he and DC Driver left.
Valentine thought for a few seconds and snapped his fingers. 'The stock. Did you check the stock? Brian, pass me the shotgun.'
The front door bounced off the wall. The sound of running footsteps along the hallway. An irate man burst into the kitchen. 'Which one of you is Blake?'
'I am,' I stood. 'Who wants to know?'
'What the fuck do you think you were playing at? That's two years up the spout.'
'Who are you,' I said. I guessed this was DI Thompson.
'I'm asking the questions. What the fuck were you playing at?'
'Then I'll ask the questions,' the DCI stood. 'I'm Detective Chief Inspector Valentine. Who are you?'
'DI Thompson,' he snapped. 'Regional drug squad.'
'Regional drug squad, what?'

DI Thompson glared at Mr Valentine. 'Sir,' he said at last.

'Detective Inspector, you will immediately ameliorate your language and apologise to Mrs Vernon and her daughter for your outburst ... I'm waiting.'

The DI sighed. 'Yes, sir,' he turned to Liz and Lucy. 'I apologise, ladies. It was uncalled for.'

They both nodded.

'Now perhaps you would explain.'

'Sir, it's taken two years of damned hard work to get Sergeant Round accepted into that Chapter to the extent whereby they trusted him.'

'As long as he delivered.'

'Maybe. But it's all gone to waste since Blake stuck a shotgun under his chin.'

'I didn't.'

He glared at me. 'Don't' lie. It doesn't suit you.'

'He's right, Inspector,' said Lucy. 'He didn't. I did.'

He gave her a scathing look. 'You? Don't be silly, Miss.'

'It was me, Inspector, so don't look at me like that. I'm not going to be pushed round by scum. Brian was on the phone to Mr Valentine when your Sergeant rattled the door and told me I had five minutes to deliver what they wanted. What they thought I knew they wanted, or else. I hadn't a clue. We couldn't wait for the police.' She pointed to the hole in the ceiling. 'That was the first barrel. Then I rammed the shotgun under your sergeant's chin and backed him into the corner. Then some big guy with a haystack for a beard threatened me, saying I'd only one shot left. Brian looked after your sergeant and I transferred my shotgun to this other's gut. Explained very politely that they weren't welcome and they left. They were threatening my mother and me. If you would like me to demonstrate I'm more than ready.'

'I don't think that would be necessary, Lucy,' I said and turned to the Inspector. 'Sir, when I arrived they were about forty bikes here. You'll have noticed the beer cans outside. The bikers well on their way to getting pissed. Planning for an overnight stay. Pitching tents. The comments about Lucy, my fiancée, and her mother sent less than subtle signals about what was likely to happen. Are you suggesting for one moment that they were acceptable collateral damage?'

'Of course not,' were the words. His eyes said otherwise.

'It's not for me to say ...'

'All right, Brian,' interrupted the DCI. 'I think you've made your point. Now Inspector what is this object? If you think it's here perhaps Mrs Vernon and her daughter can help.'

DI Thompson looked agitated and shuffled his feet. 'Not here, sir. Outside.'

The outer door closed. I handed the shotgun to Lucy. 'Mr Valentine said something about the stock. What did he mean?'

Her eyes lit up. 'Oh, I'd forgotten.' She said and unclipped the end of the stock. There was a metallic tinkling as a key bounced on the floor tiles.

'What the.' I snatched it up and handed it to Liz.

The Door opened. Mr Valentine and DI Thompson entered. DI Thompson's eyes fixed on Lucy and the shotgun.

'I'd forgotten about this,' said Lucy offering the shotgun.

DI Thompson almost snatched it from her and tipped the contents out. Cleaning rods and a brush. 'This is all there is?'

'There's only what you see, sorry.'

I didn't care whether he believed us or not.

'And there's nowhere else it could be?'

'Not here,' said Liz. 'Although I have a key to the safe this was Bill's province. We kept out. If he was going to hide something it would be here.'

'What about the track?'

'There is an office down there but Bill did not have a key to that safe.'

DI Thompson gave Liz a puzzled look.

'Bill was too fond of high risk which is why, well before he was declared bankrupt, every asset from the house to the entire Vernon's business was transferred to my name. I run the business. Bill concentrated on the Spartans and racing.'

A shocked detective inspector gasped. 'He was bankrupt?'

'He was. And now ...?'

A chastened DI Thompson left to break the news to *them upstairs*.

A question remained in my mind. Of all the points he could have raised why did he only mention Bill's bankruptcy?

'Was there anything? I take it you looked?'

Liz handed the key to the DCI.

Mr Valentine turned it over in his hand. 'Midshires Bank safety deposit,' he said. 'Mrs Vernon, it would be best to contact your solicitor as soon as possible, he will advise you. Certainly a court order will be required to gain access.'

'Thanks, I'll do that.'

'Also we would like to be there when the box is opened. And I am expecting someone else who has a valid interest to arrive shortly.'

That someone was DI Thewlis.

Hello Roger.'

'Good morning to you, Graeme. You made it sound urgent.' First name terms? 'Good morning ladies. Pc Blake. I never expected to be back here so soon.'

'Inspector Thewlis, was my husband engaged in espionage?'

'In simple terms, Mrs Vernon, yes he was. Whether he knew what he was doing we may never know. It was possible that he thought he was doing a favour for the man he knew as Peter Pederson but he spoke with some very interesting people. None of it points any fingers at you or your children or, any member of the Spartans other than Lester Roberts.'

'And it was an accident?'

'To the best of our knowledge Mrs Vernon. Now then, why am I here?'

It didn't take long to run through the sequence of events.

'I can understand why, after what you endured, you took that course of action,' said Inspector Thewlis. 'But if you will pardon the pun it could have backfired. However the '£100,000 or even the £900,000 are huge amounts of money. If that is the reason for the invasion I can see why. And bearing in mind we were interested in your husband why Mr Valentine called me.' He turned to the DCI. 'What do you propose?'

'First, Brian is going across to Halifax to speak with Gertrude Brooks, Marjorie Simmonds mother to hand some cash over and try to ascertain where her daughter is. Then back to the office.

'By the way, Mrs Vernon, what time is the cremation?'

Liz checked her watch. 'In forty five minutes, the limo should be here in twenty.'

I left the DCI and DI Thewlis talking with Liz. Lucy came to see me off. The door closed she threw her arms round my neck. 'I'm pleased you turned up. I don't think I would have had the courage otherwise,' she said and grinned. 'Can I come over tonight? After Dad's cremation I'll need some proper comforting.'

'What about your Mum?'

Lucy adopted a faux hurt look. 'You leave her alone.'

I kissed her on the nose. 'You know what I meant, Dopey. You've got a key.'

She smiled oh so sweetly, dropped her right hand and grabbed me by the front of my leathers. 'This is the only key I need.'

I was on the point of leaving when Charlie and Jack, the two Spartans who had been following the Hells Angels, returned.

'Hull,' said Charlie. 'Waiting for the next ferry. Around three.'

'I'm off,' I said. 'But my boss, Chief Inspector Valentine and a Detective Inspector Thewlis are in the kitchen. Have a word with them.'

Thirty-Two

1400 13 Pissybeds Lane, Holywell Beck, Halifax. A small but tidy mid-terrace house in a row of about twenty. A freshly painted dark green front door and small front garden. Allotments over the wall opposite. In fact all the houses just as tidy.

Bike on its stand I noticed the curtains twitch as I opened the garden gate. Before I could knock the door opened. 'Yes?' The tone was curt and the lady about five feet two wearing a smock over her dress.

'Mrs Brooks, Mrs Gertrude Brooks?'

'Who wants to know?'

'My name's Brian Blake. I was your daughter's courier. She seems to have disappeared and I have some property for her. I went to the office at Horsforth but no one has any idea where she is.'

'Better come in,' she turned and walked away. 'Shut the door, lad.'

A man aged about forty, greying hair swept back, ruddy complexion and wearing a pinstriped three piece business suit seated in an arm chair adjacent to the fireplace. 'This is Mr Wright, Marjorie's solicitor. We were just talking about her. You're the policeman.'

I smiled. 'Ex-policeman.'

'I heard,' she said. 'Fell out with your inspector over religion.'

'You're well informed. I did. Ordered me to take religious instruction, or else. I resigned.'

'A man of principle.'

'I like to think so, Mr Wright.'

'Now Mr Blake,' he said. 'What is it that you carried for my client?'

I fished Bill's envelope from my leathers and handed it over. 'I handed these to the people named on the envelopes in exchange for one of these.' I showed him the packages.

He held the letter up. 'Why have you still got this particular envelope?'

'Mr Vernon died in a road accident a few weeks ago in Rotterdam. Mrs Vernon didn't want to know. She did check the safe but there was nothing addressed to Marjorie Simmonds. My instructions were, if there were any problems to return the envelope.'

'I see. And how many drops did you make on that date?'

I got the impression that the goodly Mr Wright was one of Marjorie's clients. 'On this date there were four. And from the look on your face two things spring to mind. Where is the fourth? And, you are one of Marjorie's clients.'

A faint smile crossed his face. 'You are very perceptive, Mr Blake. And?'

'I suspect that these packages contain cash. I could have kept them and disappeared. I could have lied. Said there were only three. But I didn't … The third drop that day was addressed to a Mr Hugo Carver …

' … And my client arranged to meet with you at the Loxley Aero club?'

'Yes. At 5am. It was cold and I got soaked. I wasn't amused. I don't mind the time or the getting wet. But it's the distrust and the fact that I haven't been paid.'

'And how much did my daughter pay you?'

'£30 a day, Mrs Brookes.'

'That's very cheap for what you were carrying,' said the solicitor.

'Why, what was I carrying?'

'Each of these packages contains £2000, or should do.'

'£2000!?' I said, trying to sound surprised. 'It would take me almost three years to earn that and before tax. One day I carried five. Is that why the police are trying to find her?'

'I don't know. They wouldn't tell me. Have you been to the office?'

'Yes, Mrs Brookes,' I said. 'I used to hand them to your daughter. I didn't want to just leave these packages with the staff. They told me about the police.'

'It's not just them either. Ridley's looking for her.'

'Nigel Ridley? He was my first drop. Down at Hambleton in Rutland. Nasty piece of work. He's been here?'

'He has, and *he is* a nasty piece. Charming to your face but don't turn your back. We tried to warn Marjorie but she wouldn't listen.'

'And you don't have any idea where she is?'

'I have no idea at all.'

'What do I do with these packages? I don't want to keep that amount of money in the house, Mr Wright.'

'I'll take them if you wish, Mrs Brookes.'

'That would be a weight off my mind.'

I handed the packages to the solicitor. 'I don't want any comebacks, Mr Wright. Could I have a receipt, please?'

'Of course.'

The next ten minutes we spent watching Mr Wright count the bank notes. '£4000,' he said. 'Mrs Brookes would you be averse to paying this young man for what he's done?'

'No, Mr Wright. As he said he could have kept the money and disappeared. We might never have known. Pay him for four days. I'll want a receipt though.' She said and laughed.

I handed the receipt and the £120 to the DCI. 'She paid you for all four day and he offered you a job?'

'Yes, sir. I wasn't sure whether Mr Wright wanted me to study law or take a different route. He wants me to think it over then go for a chat.'

'Well, your name is sure to be on the front page of the papers after the trial. So I think a visit to return the £120, with you in uniform, together with Mr Henderson. Can't be seen to profit from our charade.

Thirty-Three

Monday a.m. I felt my butterflies stirring.
My court date at the Old Bailey was next Monday.

The enquiring minds of my colleagues filled, eliciting comments such as – 'how is it you get all the fun?'

Now it was back to Mick Grant.

1030 The back of DS Cartwright's car, Jacko in the front passenger seat. 200 yards short of Mick Grant's house. Fifty yards ahead a dark blue two-ton van - Bolton's Hauliers on the side in white. The van indicated left and stopped two yards beyond Grant's driveway. The van driver applied full left lock and began to reverse. With a loud cracking the rear-nearside suspension collapsed preventing the wheels rotating blocking the driveway and half the road. A cloud of rust settled on the footpath.

Reminiscent of the Keystone Cops the driver floored the accelerator, let the clutch in and stalled the engine. They were going nowhere. Both driver and passenger panicked and made a dash for the rear where Mick Grant and another tearaway had one door open and were trying to offload the contents

DS Cartwright coasted up behind them and radioed for back-up. Jacko and I decamped.

It was like dropping a fox into a rabbit warren. I heard Jacko say to the driver's mate, 'Hello Benny, need a hand? You spend more time in Armley than the Governor.'

I grabbed Mick Grant. 'Hello Mick, fancy meeting you here.'

He took one look at me, 'Oh fuck. This is the thanks I get for getting you that job is it, you bastard.'

'We can talk about your Aunt Marjorie later.'

Benny cuffed to the steering wheel and Mick to Benny, Jacko pocketed the ignition keys.

Two minutes later Derek and Penny arrived in convoy with a dog handler, the local sergeant and a couple of Pc's.

The dog ferreted the others out of the rhododendrons in sixty seconds. That was that.

That partially answered the question of how Mick Grant managed to live the life. He'd become a modern-day Fagin. In the past he might have been a machine minder at Burnley's Mill, but over time he'd built up quite a list of contacts across the West Riding.

Their most recent haul, twelve rolls of the finest Huddersfield worsted lifted from the storeroom of Austin Brothers, Elland, the night before. How the hell they got all twelve into the back of that rust bucket I couldn't begin to hazard a guess. All I can say is that the chassis twisted when the suspension collapsed and they couldn't get them out.

What Mick Grant would have to say about his continental telephone calls was anyone's guess.

Marjorie Simmonds was not Mick Grant's aunt. A close friend of his mother's, it was an honorary title. She supplied him with the winning bets, free gratis. Even advanced him his initial stake of £250. Neither did he pay commission. He was a wealthy man so why did he get involved in this criminal venture? I suppose the answer has to be that stupidity knows no bounds. His answer? He got bored.

Apart from the four arrested at Mick Grant's home there was a separate arrest that day. Neville Pearman, the storeman at Austin Brothers who'd tipped him off. Over the next two days we netted eleven prisoners and recovered over £27,000 worth of stolen property. Jenny was the appointed Exhibits Officer. I was her assistant. The officer in the case was DS Cartwright.

I was taking advantage of a few minutes slack when Inspector Henderson poked his head round the door. 'Blake, leave that and grab your coat.'

Terry McCloud, one of Mick Grant's rhododendron loving associates had identified the premises where Grant stored his property. Search warrant in hand we were now en route to the premises.

There were four lock-ups in a block at the end of an unmade road in the shadow of the railway arches. It was an interesting afternoon.

In the left-hand unit there were a dozen phosphor bronze castings. In the next about a half ton of lead sheeting which appeared to have been removed from some church roof. The third was empty. The fourth contained twenty-three boxed television sets, later identified as having come from a burglary four nights earlier. Grant had been a busy boy.

Thirty-Four

I would be returned to operational duty at Westleigh in two weeks. This time on rota three, keep the rotas in balance. Christmas Day and Boxing Day would now be my rota days off. In the circumstances that was fortuitous. The DCI would submit a report as to my future suitability for service in C.I.D. at the end of my probation in twenty-two months. Passing my sergeant's promotion examination at the first attempt would not be a hindrance.

1030 Tuesday. Liz, Lucy, Mr Cadogan the family solicitor, accompanied by Messrs Valentine, Thewlis and yours truly were escorted to Midshires Safe Deposit. Giles Greenwood, the assistant bank manager unlocked the first of the two locks and left.

Liz took a deep breath, unlocked the second and opened the top. 'It's very small,' said Liz. 'I thought it would be bigger.'

There were just five items. Three passports, all current and none in Bill's name. An even bigger surprise were the two additional safety deposit keys.

'Chief Inspector, what on earth was I married to?'

There was no answer.

Nobody knew or admitted to knowing the three men. I logged details and placed the passports in an evidence bag.

Giles Greenwood was summoned and unlocked both remaining boxes. The DCI confirmed they kept a record of the times and dates the boxes were accessed. Greenwood said if a court order was produced they would compile the details. The police would not have access to make their own record.

That was questionable.

The second box, much larger, elicited whistles. Bank notes in denominations of £10, £20 and £50. The value? Very high.

'Is all this ours, Mum?'

'I don't know, Love. I doubt it. Did you check your Dad's diary?'

'Yes. He backed eighteen horses. The details of the races and the result. His stakes are written at the end followed by a letter and ringed. I don't know what that means.'

Mr Cadogan looked as shocked as everyone else.

'I'll have a look if you like,' I said.

'Yes, do that,' said the DCI. 'But after today you will be helping DC Sendrove. This case is not ours. Now, let's get this money out and see what there is.'

There was a lot of money. Beneath the bank notes were ten packages wrapped in white paper. The DCI picked one up weighing it in his hand. 'Roughly two pounds,' he said and made a small slit with his pocket knife. White powder. 'If this is what I think it is I wouldn't like to guess the value. Forensic can do the necessary. Not ignoring the money, I would imagine this is what your unwelcome visitors had in mind.'

'Sir, is this what DI Thompson told you about?'

'It is. Said he didn't know the quantity. But ....'

Liz was in tears. 'What happens now, Chief Inspector?'

'I wouldn't worry too much Mrs Vernon. You had a very enterprising husband. At what level he was involved is yet to be determined. No doubt both you and your daughter will be questioned. Mr Cadogan will be able to help you.'

'I don't specialise in criminal matters, Chief Inspector. I will liaise with one of our younger partners, Jeffrey Garden, if Mrs Vernon has no objections.'

'Not at all Mr Cadogan.'

The third box contained £1000 in denominations of £10 and £20 notes.

Thirty-Five

The DCI beckoned me into his office and pointed to the vacant chair. 'How serious is this relationship with Lucy.'

'Very, sir. We're planning to get married on her twenty first. That's New Year's Eve.'

'I'm a pretty good judge of character and the reactions of both Lucy and her mother tell me that they are not involved. However, you have to submit an application to get married. If there is anything that rubs off on her or her mother it could be seen as a barrier to having her married to a police officer. With so little service you are in a cleft stick. What would you do if permission were to be refused?'

That was a no brainer. 'Resign, sir.'

'Throw away your career?'

'Not as I see it, sir. I've been a police officer for weeks. Everything that has been said about my future are just words. Nothing is carved in stone. Look what happened to my father. And had the Captain not dropped his pistol when I tackled him I could well have been shot with who knows what results. What Lucy and I went through was real. If your situation arose and I chose my career over Lucy I would be damaging two lives. Yes, I want to be a police officer but there are limits.'

'I thought that would be your answer. In that case I want an application from you now. I will carry out and submit the interview. Remember, there is still the possibility should the worst happen that your appointment would be terminated. There is nothing I could do about that. What do you want?'

'I'll submit the report, sir. And if the worst comes to the worst I can always have my chat with Mr Wright.'

At least he laughed. 'So you could. But do that report, then go and see Lucy and put her and her mother in the picture. I'll sign you off duty ... But before you go. You've never said anything about a Captain and almost being shot?'

'It slipped out, sir, sorry. I'm not supposed to say anything about it. Maybe after the trial. It was mentioned at the press conference but wasn't aired. The Chief was there.'

'I don't need to know any more.'

An hour later we were drinking tea at the Vernon's. 'The question is, Lucy, would you like to get married on your birthday?'

'If you want to, Lucy, say yes.'

'Well, yes. But couldn't you still be dispensed with?'

'I could. But it's not about what might happen to me. It's about us. Mr Valentine will be in touch to carry out an interview to see if you're suitable to be a policeman's wife.'

There was an answering grin. 'Thanks. When?'

'He'll call.'

The phone began to ring.

'Tomorrow at 7p.m., Mr Valentine,' Liz turned and gave a thumbs-up.

'Good. Next we have to tell my family. Do you want to come with me. If you do, bring a change of clothing. We can stay there – in separate rooms. I'll get you home early tomorrow.'

Three pairs of questioning eyes focussed on Lucy.

'No, I'm not,' she laughed. 'Yet.'

'You're not yet, what?'

'Mind your own business, Clive,' said Anne. 'You're too young.'

Lucy smiled at the others. 'Pregnant.'

'Oh, is that all.'

'Clive?'

'What, Mum? They all talk about it at school.'

Now all eyes were on Clive. 'What? Oh I'm off. I've got my homework to do.'

'So why the rush?' said Frankie as the door closed.

Lucy glanced at me and nodded. 'You'd better tell them. Everything.'

The girls sat there fingers interlocked elbows on the table resting their chins. 'We're waiting,' said Jennifer. Something that Lucy found amusing.

'I've told you all about the limitations placed on police officers.'

'Yes,' said Anne. 'You can't get married without permission in case Lucy is a mass-murderer, gun runner, drug dealer or distils illicit liquor.'

'And,' said Jennifer. 'You can be turfed out on your ear at any time within the first two years. Unless you keep your nose clean.'

'But it's not his nose we're talking about is it?' said Frankie as all three collapsed in hysterics. Lucy blushed.

'Frankie, really.'

'Relax. Mum,' she replied and kissed her on her cheek. 'It's just a joke.'

Joe disagreed. 'Enough,' he snapped. 'Cut out the inuendo. Clive is eleven. To him they are just words. Hopefully they are to you as well.'

'But,' interjected Frankie.

'Never mind but. Brian and Lucy haven't come across here to be baited by you three. Brian, like all police officers signed the Official Secrets Act. What he's going to try and explain is, in all probability, covered by it. So listen. If you want to be treated like adults start to act like them. What has Anne told you about what she heard and saw at hospital when Brian took her to visit Lucy?'

'Nothing,' said Jennifer.

'Right, take a leaf.'

I'd never heard Joe speak to the girls like that. They looked chastened. How long would it last?

'The first bit isn't covered. But it is relevant. They could withhold that permission which would mean I would have to resign if we wanted to get married.'

'But if you had permission,' said Anne. 'You could get married but they could still turf you out.'

'Yup, or suggest that I resign. Hopefully it won't come to that. It's not just that. As my wife Lucy could not be involved in control of a business that involved the selling of alcohol, anything to do with firearms or, for example, a post office.'

'That makes sense,' said Joe.

'Those don't apply and you're good at your job so, what's the problem,' said Frankie.

I looked at Lucy. She nodded. 'Tell them.'

'The problem is Lucy's Dad.'

'But he's dead,' said Jennifer.

'What did Shakespeare write? The evil that men do lives after them ...'

'The good is oft interréd with their bones,' Lucy finished the quote.

'Enquiries following Lucy's father's death turned up some pretty dangerous contacts. People that you wouldn't want to be within a thousand miles of. And activities which, had they been discovered before his death, could have sent him to prison for a long time.'

'And so far there is nothing to link either Lucy or Liz to this?'

'So far, Anne, no there isn't,' said Lucy. 'And I haven't a clue what it might be. Mum and I were completely in the dark.'

'That's as much as I'm going to say,' I said. 'What you've heard stays in this room.'

'We can't set a date until Brian gets notification. In any case neither of us are religious so the ceremony will be at Leeds Registry Office.' She paused and beamed a smile at the girls. 'I'm looking for three bridesmaids. Do you know anyone suitable?'

Lucy was chatting to Mum and the girls. I caught Joe in the garden. 'Bad?'

'German or Dutch-biker-gangs.'

'Nuf said.'

'Have you spoken to Liz recently?'

'No, In the circumstances I held off.'

'Give her a call. I think she'd be glad of a positive distraction.'

Wednesday to Friday was dealing with the property from the Mick Grant case including a visit to see his wife. She claimed she hadn't seen or had any contact with Marjorie Simmonds either. A further check was made with her mother in Holywell Beck, again negative. The police didn't have the authority to issue process for apparent taxation offences. So, a missing person report was taken and circulated in Police Reports and the Police Gazette.

Mick Grant was less than forthcoming about his continental calls. The enquiry had been passed to Interpol.

I was given a travel warrant from Leeds City to Kings Cross. I had to be at the Old Bailey not later than 10.00hrs and Leeds not later than 16.30hrs on Sunday.

In Hambleton Nigel Ridley picked up the phone.

'... you're sure, Damian,' he said with a savage grin. 'That's where the bitch lives?'

'As I can be, Nigel. Good hunting.'

'I owe you big time. I'll be in touch.'

My application to marry came back approved by the Chief Constable.

Thirty-Six

Saturday a.m. The family piled into the personnel carrier heading for Boston Spa. Sandwiches eaten en route. I'm sure that the two Mums, Anne and Lucy didn't have one. But you can bet the others had a streak of morbidity driving their curiosity wanting to see the remains of the shed and where the murders took place.

Neil only too happy for a quiet one-to-one with Anne. They both had stories to share. I know the solace that Lucy and I took from our relationship following our shared experience. I needn't have worried about Anne.

Others sympathised. We could truly empathise.

I don't know exactly what the others were expecting to see, but unlike the ancient maps there were no signs indicating:

Here Be Dragons

Other than the fire-blackened earth where our coffin had been, the surrounding scorched grass and the patch of flattened grass where the shooting had taken place there was nothing.

We were all sitting in the top floor of the grandstand. Liz walked towards the Bar. The chatter ceased. She smiled thinly. 'For some time Bill and I had been discussing the future of the business. Whilst we hadn't broadcast anything, we had drawn up various options concerning the shops, track and the Spartans which we discussed with both our accountant and solicitor.'

She waited until the talk stopped. 'First the businesses. And Lucy is not privy to what is coming next.' She stopped and smiled at Lucy who returned the smile with a frown. 'I am giving The Spartans first refusal before we open it up to all comers as Bill and I agreed. This business was built on Bill's name, his reputation. I am going to franchise every retail outlet except Head Office. That means they are stand-alone businesses. You can use your link to the Spartans. You hire and fire your own staff. Pay their wages Pay your own tax and everything that goes with it. Any profit is yours. You can use the Vernon's name. You will get full support and advice and, we will supply your products. I've had some brochures printed. I'll put them out later. However, you do need legal advice before you make a decision.

'Brian and Lucy are getting married shortly,' she added to cheers from the Spartans.

Someone quipped. 'That's a bit quick, Lucy. I wonder why?' followed by laughter and applause.

'I am not pregnant,' said Lucy as she turned and laughed at the team of riders she had grown up with.

'Yet.'

'Yet,' she agreed and grinned.

'Congratulations to you both.'

We stood and bowed.

'Yes, congratulations, Love,' continued Liz. 'The volume of business is high and Lucy's workload is increasing. However, she will soon have other things to take care of. I'll still find something for her to do.

'If any of you are interested in a franchise it will not disqualify you from riding with the Spartans. Bill is no longer here and I'm sorry to have to say that I want to reduce the numbers. Nothing personal but that's the way it is. You could still ride as a Privateer. Also have free use of the track; that's another change.'

Vance will still be Race Captain and Neil, Engineering Captain.

Now the track. This Grandstand was to be the first in the development of the site after the track and the Go-Kart track was laid. Unfortunately Bill went astray. Very little has been done since.

The site will be re-named the Bill Vernon stadium. This grandstand the Vernon Stand. Every bike that Bill ever rode is in the garage at home. There will be a museum. The temporary stands round the site improved and extended as will the garages and the pits. And, there will be a business park. I'm waiting for the architect to come back with plans before I make an application to the council.

Now, immediately following your departure on Friday evening some pretty nasty things happened here. Had it not been for Brian it would have been our graves.'

'Had it not been for my presence here, Liz, it would never have happened.'

'Maybe. Maybe not. But it did and thanks to you we are here today. Exactly what I'm going to do I'm not sure. The site of the shed that was burned will be a garden with benches.'

'Will you call the bar in the grandstand The Spartans Bar?' said Vance.

'Yes,' she said and laughed. 'But it doesn't mean you can drink for free.'

'That's a shame,' was the reply.

'You will all remember Brian's mother, step-father Joe and his step-sisters, Neil more than most.'

'Thank you,' he said to cheers.

'I asked Joe to give me some ideas for catering. Both in here and fast food booths outside. I have them here,' she held up Joe's file. 'One thing I won't have are fly pitches. So everything is included in Joe's proposal. I'll digest these in due course.

There will be a major re-vamp of the Grandstand and of the site in general. We're going to push Go-carting and, next year if there is time we will be holding the Bill Vernon festival of racing. We will have to fit in with the racing calendar but hopefully an annual event. It's going to be busy.'

Thirty-Seven

Lucy and I headed for Bill's office. The others for the kitchen table. Lucy opened the safe and passed me Bill's diary. I checked these mysterious letters associated with the bets placed by Bill. A couple gave me the answer. The value of the winnings equated to the letter: A = £1000, Q = £17000.

Once the list of the dates when Bill made deposits was available it would indicate if they were linked.

Tea was out of the way. We sat there chatting. Not for the first time Frankie was a little reticent when Lucy joined in the conversation.

'You know, Lucy,' Joe said. 'I remember the day when I first met Brian and Dorothy. I was taking my usual Saturday morning class. There were about a dozen or so plus the girls, who as usual were doing their own thing. It gave us some time together and kept them out of mischief. Looking at them now you wouldn't believe they used to be six years old.'

The girls reacted. 'Cheek,' from Jennifer.

'Charming,' from Anne. 'Besides, we were only five.'

Strangely enough, nothing from Frankie. I could see that Mum had noticed it as well, but said nothing.

'Are you sure?' said Joe.

'Positive,' declared Anne. 'It was fourteen years ago when Brian was nine. There's four years between us. We were five.'

Joe laughed. 'I must be getting old,' he said. 'Anyway, the door opened and this cracking looking woman walked in with a little boy and sat down.' He put his hand on top of Mum's. 'She still is.'

There was a general chorus of 'Aaws' from around the table. 'I remember,' said Jennifer getting animated, 'You were teaching roundhouse kicks and Brian decided to join in and lost his balance. He fell over and bruised his bum.'

'You fell over?' Clive looked at me in disbelief. 'You never lose your balance.'

'I did then Clive,' I said. 'It was my first day. I thought it looked easy. It wasn't. Damaged my pride.'

'Poor little boy,' said Lucy, as she stroked my arm. 'He bruised his bottom.'

'It was a lot worse than that,' I whinged.

'You wimp,' retorted Anne.

'And these three,' I said pointing to the girls, 'rolled around the floor laughing like drains.'

'It was funny,' said Jennifer pulling what she classed as a sympathetic face.

'To continue,' said Joe. 'I didn't usually take children under ten, but I liked the look of Dorothy,' he winked at her. 'In her case I made an exception. I have to add I had no idea she was a widow. Brian picked it up quite quickly, and never gave in. Dorothy used to turn up every Saturday morning with Brian and bring a box of iced buns with cherries on top. One for each of the girls and one for Brian. She became an ex-officio baby sitter which I really appreciated. Every week they asked, 'Will Aunty Dorothy be there? Will she bring some buns?' Joe paused and took a drink of his tea.

'They were very nice,' said Anne licking her lips, 'They still are.'

Jennifer giggled. 'And then, Lucy, Mum began to bring two extra. I wonder who they were for,' she said steepling her hands and resting her chin.

'One for me and one for Dad,' Mum said, smiling.

'Yes, Lucy,' said Anne, 'Mum trapped Dad with her iced buns.'

'Did you, Mum?' asked Clive, as *all* the girls, laughed.

Liz's quizzical smile told me she understood.

Even now Mum could still turn heads and had no problems with wearing a swimsuit on holiday. I'm certain that the joke the girls were laughing at was not the same as Clive thought there were. I'd thought for a long time that had things been different, i.e. that there hadn't been the four of us to begin with, there would have been other little Mountains running around.

'Perhaps a little bit, love,' she replied. 'But for Lucy's benefit I'll just point out that your dad had found out that I was a widow. The girls had told me that their mother had died. Plus, we lived less than four hundred yards apart. Besides, I don't really think he needed much trapping.'

'I didn't need any trapping,' Joe said as he squeezed her hand again. 'I was a volunteer.'

'Are we playing gooseberry?' said Anne. Mum began to blush.

'Don't be silly, Anne,' said Mum and smiled at Lucy. 'We got married about a year after we first met. Joe and I had been down to the shops. Brian was playing rugby and the girls were playing by the gate. As we reached the house there was a bit of a rumpus. Some lad off the estate was teasing the girls.'

'Teasing?' said Jennifer. 'He was yanking our ponytails and pushing us around.'

'Then our hero arrived on the scene,' grinned Frankie.

'You?' Lucy looked at me.

'Of course,' I said. 'Who else?'

'Big head,' laughed Anne, as I wrinkled my nose at her.

'I was in a bit of a quandary,' I said. 'Joe always insisted that we do not fight outside of the club unless we were physically threatened.'

'Sorry,' queried Lucy. 'I don't understand, why not?'

'Karate is as much a discipline as it is a skill. There is no place for anger,' Joe explained. 'It's unarmed combat. A punch or a kick delivered incorrectly can hurt you, or, you could do some serious damage to someone else. I coach people wherever possible to walk away from trouble, not to provoke it. Brian was ten and quite a strong little boy. After twelve months beginning to develop some skill.'

'I understand, so what did you do?'

'I hadn't seen Joe's car coming up the street. This lad was a couple of years older than me and was really throwing his weight about. Although these three always used to gang up on me ...'

'Of course we did,' interjected Frankie, 'We're triplets.'

The girls looked at each other. 'All for one and one for all,' they chanted to Lucy and Liz's delight.

'And now there are four of us?' suggested Jennifer.

'Oh, I don't know about that,' said Lucy putting her hand on top of mine.

Anne grinned at her. 'Traitor,' she said as Lucy returned the favour.

'Back to the story. I told this lad to beggar off. He swore at me and pulled his fist back. That was my all clear. He threw the punch. I blocked it and hit him once in the stomach. He ran off saying that he was going to tell his dad. Joe jumped out of the car demanding to know what had happened. These three,' I indicated the girls, 'were jumping up and down and all talking at once, well, Anne was shouting ...'

'I was?'

'Yes you were. Eventually you all were. But Joe got the picture, patted me on the shoulder and said I'd done well. And for the first time I called him Dad.'

Nobody spoke for several seconds. 'I'll never forget that moment,' said Mum. 'I was so happy I thought I was going to cry.'

Joe squeezed her hand again. 'I did.'

'You cried?' queried Frankie. Everyone listened.

Joe nodded. 'Think about it. Your mother was diagnosed with leukaemia not long after you were born. She died two and a half years later. During that time when I couldn't be there, grandparents and neighbours all pitched in as baby sitters. You saw very little of her. Towards the end only when I could take you to the hospital. Yes, you missed her, but what direct memories do you have of her?'

'I see what you mean,' said Jennifer. 'We have photographs of when we were tiny. Fuzzy images, plus the things that you and Gran have told us.'

'That's right,' acknowledged Joe.

'But Brian was much older,' continued Jennifer. She turned to me. 'You were eight when your dad was killed?'

Lucy's grip tightened on my arm. This I hadn't anticipated. She knew nothing of this. Now it was in the open. 'Yes, it was two days after my eighth birthday.' I looked at Lucy and put my hand on hers. 'It was a long time ago.'

There was absolute silence until Lucy spoke again. 'But Jennifer made it sound as if he was murdered.'

There was an intake of breath from Liz.

'He was.' I squeezed her hand. 'Stabbed whilst making an arrest.'

'He was a policeman?'

I nodded. 'A detective sergeant.'

She took a deep breath. 'And now, you're getting too big to get a hug from your Mum, I'd better stick around.'

'Ha, ha. He'll never be too big for that,' said Mum. 'But you're welcome to share him.'

'For now,' she winked at Mum. 'I might lend him out from time-to-time.'

'Now then, where were we?' Mum smiled. 'How did you three know?'

Jennifer sounded quite nervous as she began to explain. 'It was only a couple of years ago when Brian was at university. We began to dig a little. We knew the approximate date when his dad died. That he had been a police officer. You would never talk about it when we were around. We went down to the Examiner office and had a look through their archive, found the article and decided we didn't need to know any more. I'm sorry.'

'There's nothing to be sorry about. We did it to protect you all,' Mum said smiling. 'I'm just surprised that you managed not to talk about it.' The smiles from the girls said, thank you.

'That was good thinking,' I said.

'We just wanted to know,' said Frankie.

'I think what Dad's trying to get across,' said Jennifer, 'is that at eight years old we've developed far more than at three. The impact of losing a parent hits far harder than it did with us.'

'That's exactly what I meant,' said Joe. 'Dorothy and Brian moved to Salendine Nook to be near her parents. Then we came on the scene. Joining the club was one thing. Dorothy and me getting married and us all living under one roof? Something else altogether.'

'Joe and Mum had explained about adoption and that would mean changing my surname from Blake to Mountain, but I didn't have to. My thoughts at the time were that it would be disloyal to completely cut myself off from my father.'

'Gotcha.' declared Anne. 'So, when you called our dad, Dad for the first time, it was your acceptance that he had taken your father's place in your life, but you still maintained the connection to your father through your surname.'

'Correct,' I said. 'Later on I often wondered if I had done the right thing ... '

'You did,' interrupted Joe. 'It would have been nice. To force you would have been wrong. But when you called me dad for the first time, it was voluntary, emotionally a bit of a shock.'

There was a silence for a few seconds when a young voice piped up. 'I'm confused.'

'What about, love,' Mum said. Everyone looking at Clive's puzzled expression.

'Well,' he began. 'If Brian's Dad hadn't been stabbed you wouldn't have come to live near Gran, and, if the girl's Mum hadn't died you and dad couldn't have got married anyway, and I wouldn't have been born,' he said with an air of finality.

Mum put a protective arm round his shoulders. 'That's true,' she smiled. 'But you are here, and we all love you very much.'

'I know,' he said. 'But isn't life cruel?'

Coming from the lips of an eleven year old that was quite perceptive, if simplistic.

'No son,' said Joe. 'It's not a question of life being either kind or cruel. Sometimes good things happen, for example, Brian meeting Lucy, unless you happen to think that's a bad thing.' He paused whilst most of us laughed and Lucy grinned and clung to my arm. Frankie's reaction was not so enthusiastic. 'Sometimes it's bad, nasty or cruel things happen to people and that's the way life is. In our case cruel things happened to two families, but your Mum and me found each other. That was a good thing. Between us we provided a stable home for Brian and your sisters, and then you came along. Without your Mum, none of you would have had the life that you have. We've got family photos of everybody. We remember those that aren't here. We celebrate the good times. The bad times fade and heal with time.' He paused and smiled. 'Just try to enjoy the good things and don't dwell on the things that you can't do anything about.'

Clive nodded. Whether that would work with him I don't know.

It was a quarter to nine when they left for Salendine Nook, Joe's voice ringing in my ears. 'I will collect you at 3.45pm tomorrow. You don't want to miss your train.'

Thirty-Eight

A whole minute early the train drew to a halt. My first time in London. Sauntering along the platform I gazed around King's Cross. It was huge.

The female voice yanked me out of my reverie. 'Excuse me. Brian Blake.'

It wasn't a question. I stopped and frowned. In front of me: Female. Late thirties. Five seven.

Brunette. Slim. Nice looking. No rings. 'You're the only one not making a dash for the barriers. First time in London?' she said and smiled.

I returned the smile. 'Yes and yes,' I produced my warrant card.

She nodded. 'Isabel Bond,' she said. 'No relation to James. Call me Isabel,' she produced her Id. 'Come with me, Brian, please.'

We hadn't gone twenty yards. 'Isabel, who's the man to the right with the camera?'

She stopped and looked. 'That's Sergei, my tail,' she smiled and waved. There was a reluctant response. 'Come on, I'll introduce you.'

The camera disappeared. 'Sergei,' she said with enthusiasm. 'How nice of you to watch my back.' She turned to me. 'Sergei is my body guard, always tagging along. Really he's registered as a military attaché at the Russian Embassy. That's a colloquialism for spy. Sergei, this is Mr Blake. Come all the way from Yorkshire just to meet you.'

I held my hand out and smiled, 'Pleased to meet you Sergei. I've heard a lot about you.' The handshake was tentative. 'I had expected someone much older,' Sergei said in a thick velvety Russian accent. 'Much more experienced.'

'You prefer older men, do you?' I said and gave the nerve point on the second metacarpal a tweak.

He winced.

I let go.

He scowled.

'Sorry Sergei, must fly. We must meet for a coffee sometime and exchange notes.'

We strode passed the ticket barriers away from Sergei. 'Won't he follow us?'

'He'll try.' She nodded to a couple waiting at the side of a news stand. The female dressed in a similar fashion to Isabel. They got into a waiting black saloon car and left the concourse via a goods entrance.

'There's a car outside which will follow them half way across London ... That was a nice touch about him liking older men. The Russians do set up honey-traps. Sergei is a homosexual and does prefer older men. It is a fact there is quite a percentage of all diplomatic corps and the British establishment who will drop their pants, full stop. And a surprising or perhaps not surprising number for the wrong gender.'

'In the circumstances it seemed appropriate.'

'Hmm,' she sounded dubious. 'What did you do to him when you shook hands?'

'It's a small nerve point. Quite tender.'

'You'll have to show me over dinner. Here we are.'

We exited via a side entrance and straight into the rear of a laundry van. Twenty minutes later I was taken via the service entrance into Tofts, an hotel in Giltspur Street.

Thirty-Nine

0900 The Old Bailey. Whether I had been followed or not I assumed that not all Soviet agents were as obvious as Sergei. I found one of the court officials and showed him my letter.

'Mr Blake. Ah yes. You're in court No.1. The Judge is Lord Justice Nevison. A bit of a stickler. Can be a crusty old devil when the mood takes him.'

'I'll bear that in mind, sir. I've only been out of training school for two months but I have been in a Magistrates Court. This is different,' he smiled and nodded. 'Do you think I could have a look in the court?'

No.1 Court was nothing if not imposing. It was huge. Designed to bring fear of being hanged to those convicted of capital offences. An Act currently going through Parliament would confirm abolition of the death penalty.

He took me to an anteroom. Knocked, opened the door and pointed to two barristers pouring over documents on a table. 'The gentleman on the right is Sir Henry Battle for the prosecution. On his left Sir Frere Jameson for the defence. Just introduce yourself,' he said and left.

I cleared my throat. 'Sir Henry?'

He spun round, 'Yes?'

'Pc Blake, Sir.'

'Good,' he looked me up and down. 'They said you were young. What service?'

'Two months out of Pannal Ash, Sir.'

He nodded. 'Ever been in court as a police officer?'

'Once, Sir. Hecton Magistrates Court.'

'That's something,' he paused and returned his attention to the table. 'Sir Frere and I were trying to make sense of these photos,' he indicated the scattering on the table. '

That was strange. 'There isn't a plan, Sir?'

His voice was terse. 'It's been lost.'

'Have you got a pad?'

'This do?' he said handing me a large writing pad.

'Fine, Sir.' I took the pad. 'You know York, Tadcaster?'

'Yes,' said Sir Henry. 'Traffic's a nightmare. They've been arguing about a bypass for years.'

'I live in Thirsk,' said Sir Frere. 'I travel a different route.'

A quick line-drawing showing where the stadium was in relation to Tadcaster, Boston Spa, the A1 and A64.

'Then Harewood House is across here?' Sir Henry pointed to the left side of the diagram.

'That's correct. The A659.'

On the next page I sketched the stadium and all the ancillary structures.

'Right,' Sir Henry picked up the photo of the burnt out shed. 'This photo is of that on the plan?' He pointed to the rectangle adjacent to the petrol pump.

'Yes, Sir. And the petrol tank is there.' I pointed it out.

'And the tank is higher because the land slopes slightly towards the River Wharfe.'

'That's correct, Sir.'

'And where did the shooting take place?'

'There, Sir.' I put an X on the map as close as I could. 'It's not exact.'

'It will do,' he perused the plan again and checked my statement. 'So, when you escaped you crossed diagonally to this building here.'

'Yes.'

'Then you went back here.' He pointed at the rectangle opposite. The one adjacent to our shed. Next in line for the flow of petrol. 'Where you had an uninterrupted view of the shooting. And you heard the conversation.'

'That's correct. It would be approximately twenty yards away.'

He turned to his colleague. 'You happy with that?'

'Better than nothing, officer. I appreciate the transport for the Spartans and their motor cycles had gone but will you mark where they were parked. Use dotted lines.'

That took ten seconds.

'Thank you. As near as you can, put an X inside a circle to where Kuznetsov was standing and where he initially produced his firearm.'

That done Sir Henry said, 'Put your head outside the door and collar the first usher you see. Tell them Sir Henry wants an urgent word.'

Within a minute the usher was on his way to secure the largest piece of paper or card he could lay his hands on. A straight ruler. Pencils. Sharpener and, an eraser. With instruction to return within a further sixty seconds.

'When he returns I want you to reproduce your plan on whatever he brings. As neat as you can. In the top left-hand corner mark it 'NOT TO SCALE', in capitals. Put your rank number and name in the bottom right hand corner.'

'Yes Sir.'

'That's out of the way.' He relaxed and smiled. 'Have you been told that the trial will be held *in camera*?'

'Yes Sir. Mr Syme told me.'

'Excellent. In this instance there will be neither members of the Press nor members of the public.'

'But there will still be a jury?'

'Damned right there will,' said Sir Henry. Sir Frere Jameson laughed. 'We're not a Banana Republic yet. If there is a guilty plea you may stay. If not then the usual rules apply. Wait outside and within hailing distance. Understood?'

'Yes, Sir Henry.'

'First things. The trial judge is Lord Justice Nevison. A stickler for protocol. Address him as My Lord. Answer the questions that I or he asks as succinctly as you can. Do not drift off into your opinion. Don't give this fella on my left any ammunition. Clear?'

'As crystal, Sir,' I said. Sir Frere chuckled.

'Good,' he smiled again. 'You may stay in court for any witnesses that are called after you. The procedure is that Sir Frere and I have agreed on the evidence contained in most of the statements provided. Therefore those witnesses will not be called and I will read their statements out to the court. There is no point in cross-examination where there is nothing contentious.

'Should His Lordship order that the court be cleared because of the nature of the evidence you as a police officer may stay. But beware, any evidence introduced should the jury be out is subject to the restrictions imposed by the Official Secrets Acts of 1911 and 1920.'

The usher returned bearing gifts. The paper was huge, 26x40 inches.

'Sir Henry, everything that happened on that evening happened on the right-hand side of the site. Do you want a drawing of the entire site or would an enlarged drawing of the right suffice?'

'Good point,' he turned to his colleague. 'Just the right?'

'I agree, the right would be better.'

I settled at the table and made room. I heard Sir Henry tell the usher to stay. Fifteen minutes later I finished.

'Very good,' Sir Henry said. Sir Frere agreed.

Sir Henry turned to the usher. 'Is the photocopier working?'

'As far as I know, Sir Henry.'

'Excellent. I want twenty copies, and this,' he indicated my original and looked over his glasses, 'Is for Lord Justice Nevison. I don't have to stress taking care, do I?'

Forty

The usher was only too pleased to surrender custody of the photocopies and original to me. All I had to do now was to find Sir Henry.

The two armed police officers on the door made it difficult, even with my warrant card.

'You're from the West Riding, what's your business in this court?'

'I'm the arresting officer.' The look he gave me was less than complimentary. I produced my letter. 'I should be on your list.'

'Problem, Mr Blake?'

Standing at my side was Mr Syme. 'Yes, sir,' I showed him the documents. 'I have this plan for Lord Justice Nevison and these photocopies for Sir Henry Battle.'

He turned and smiled at the two officers. 'For your information, Mr Blake is the arresting officer. I suggest that you either let him through or prepare to explain to his Lordship why you prevented him from entering the court.'

Without further comment they moved out of the way.

Plans delivered Mr Syme took me to one side.

'I hear you met Sergei yesterday?' he said, a smile playing on his lips.

'Yes sir. Didn't know what to make of him. Isabel treated him very lightly.'

'Don't be put off by this now you see me now you don't. He's very astute. But you've met your first Russian agent. They're not all as easy to spot.

'I assumed as much.'

Then he turned serious. 'The Russians found out the facts of what happened last month and have requested the return of Kuznetsov's body and Manville-Jones for trial. Kuznetsov is easy. However, Manville-Jones would be feted. We can't have that. By the time we have finished, if he is handed over, they will do what the law in the UK prohibits.'

'Execute him?'

'Precisely. But first we must have our pound of flesh. Of course, he may in the fullness of time decide to do the honourable thing. Save us the bother.'

'But …?'

'It will,' he interjected, 'somehow find its way to the Kremlin that the basis of those arrests you heard on the News were as a result of information supplied by Manville-Jones. That in itself will have the Russians jumping like fleas on a hotplate. There will be a purge. Many innocent Russians, both men and women, will pay the price.'

Further conversation was not possible. It was ten thirty. The door from the judge's retiring room opened. An usher entered.

'All rise.'

Everyone stood as Lord Justice Nevison, a short rotund man, non-smiling, characterful square jawed face, looking resplendent in his red robes and long wig entered, bowed to the court and sat.

Manville-Jones was brought into the dock and the jury sworn. There were no challenges.

Sir Henry Battle stood. 'My Lord, before we begin there is a small matter that I need to bring to your attention.'

'And that is, Sir Henry?'

'The official plans prepared by the police have been mislaid. However, Pc Blake, the arresting officer has, at very short notice, prepared one of the area in question but, not to scale. Although my learned friend and I agree that it is a reasonable representation.'

Lord Justice Nevison scowled, sat up and held his hand out. 'Let me see.'

I was standing too close to Sir Henry. He handed the plan to me, 'Hand it to the Judge's Clerk. He's sitting in front.'

It felt very lonely to walk that short distance. I handed it to the clerk. 'Wait there, officer,' he said. He turned and passed it to the Judge. After perusing the chart for several seconds he looked down at me. 'You are,' he looked down at the chart again. 'Pc 547 Blake?'

'Yes, My Lord.'

'What is not on here that was on the one that has been mislaid?'

'I don't know My Lord. I hadn't seen it.'

From the look he gave me I could see why he had been described as 'crusty'. 'Well, can you explain what might have been there?'

'If it was a plan of the full site, the Grandstand is approximately one hundred yards in length and there are stands around the motor cycle race track. Pits opposite the Grandstand and in the centre a Go-Cart track, my Lord.'

He nodded. 'And how accurate is your chart?'

'Everything is there that should be there, My Lord, it's just the exact dimensions that aren't correct. There are, or were, six sheds. The square building is for commentary and announcements. And the small rectangle adjacent to the garages, a petrol tank and delivery pump.'

He nodded then passed the chart back to the Clerk. 'Officer, There are several marks and symbols on the chart but nothing to differentiate between these sheds, as you refer to them. Please clarify and show any sightlines that you consider to be relevant.'

The Clerk handed me the chart. 'Yes, My Lord.'

I returned to Sir henry and exhaled. 'Phew.'

He smiled. 'You did all right,' he said and passed me the twenty copies.

'Can I use your anteroom, please?

'Yes you can. Come straight back when you've finished. If the plea is not guilty I'll send an usher to take them from you.'

I was about half way through when the door opened and the man I'd seen sitting on Sir Henry's left came in. 'I'm Sir Henry's second. Montague Blythe QC, can I have one of the copies, please.' I passed one across. 'A couple of things. This sightline.' He pointed to my sightline of the shootings. 'How far is it?'

'About twenty yards, sir.'

'And this one?' he pointed to where Lucy, Anne and Liz had been hiding. 'To where you saw the keys.'

'About thirty yards,'

'Thanks, that's all I want. And Manville-Jones pleaded not guilty to all charges: The murders of Lieutenant Phillips and Mikhail Kuznetsov. Your attempted murder. In addition there were seven counts of espionage.'

My gut started to churn. 'There will be an usher waiting at the courtroom door.'

It was eleven a.m. when the first witness was called. Where possible, statements were read to the court in chronological order. The Court recessed at four thirty. Perhaps I would be called tomorrow.

A couple of phone calls. Lucy at her mothers and then home to keep them up to date. Not that there was much I could say. Another great meal and an escorted walk. This time to the Tower of London. Must make the effort to bring Lucy to London and include the Tower in the itinerary.

I was called at two p.m. on Tuesday.

Forty-One

I was nervous the first time I had to give evidence at Hecton Magistrates Court. Being the focus of attention, even in a small court was novel and something I had to get used to. But this was the Circus Maximus. There were no possible distractions such as the Press and the public, just a Law Lord and two of the country's senior Queen's Council.

Take a deep breath. Be still my butterflies. Exhale. Time to go. At least the lions were on my side.

It was a lonely walk passed the man in the dock. The Captain in the Security Services who had betrayed his country. Had shot and killed two men in my view. In cold blood. And would have killed me, Lucy, her mother and Anne given half a chance; then blamed it on Kuznetsov.

'I'll affirm, please,; I said as the clerk approached.

He handed me a card. 'Read the words from the card with your name in the appropriate space.'

'I, Brian Blake, do solemnly, sincerely and truly declare and afform the evidence I shall give shall be the truth, the whole truth, and nothing but the truth.'

I handed the card back. The clerk departed.

Sir Henry stood. 'You are Police Constable 547 Brian Blake of the West Riding Police, presently attached to a unit of police detectives under the command of Detective Chief Inspector Graeme Valentine.'

'That is correct, My Lord.'

'How long have you been a police officer?'

'Approximately five months, My Lord.'

'Five months ago you left university and were sworn as a constable.'

'Yes, My Lord.'

'And amongst the documents you signed on that date was an extract from the Official Secrets Act?'

'Yes, My Lord.'

'Pc Blake, will you confirm this is the document you signed?'

He handed it to an usher who showed it to me.

It was the original. 'Yes, that is my signature.'

It was then showed to the judge and, the jury.

'Other than today have you seen that document since the day you joined the police?'

'Yes. My Lord, but it was a photocopy,' I paused and thought for a few seconds. 'Monday 15th July at approximately 1pm.'

'What were the circumstances?'

'I was at No. 3 District Police Training Centre, Harrogate. I had finished my midday meal and concluded a telephone call. I replaced the handset on the cradle when someone tapped me on the shoulder. It was Sergeant Faulkner our drill instructor. He whispered, "Commandant's office, now". So I knew it was serious.'

Sir Henry looked puzzled. 'How?'

'Sergeant Faulkner had been drill instructor at the Guard's depot at Pirbright, My Lord. He never did anything quietly.'

Several of the jury laughed. As did Sir Henry. 'I think My Lord we can all associate ourselves with Pc Blake's comment.'

'Indeed, Sir Henry.' He even smiled.

'What followed?'

'The commandant was seated at his desk, there were two men in civilian clothes seated between the desk and the bay window. The commandant told me the chief constable had consented to their request and they wished to ask me some questions. I did not have to agree to any subsequent request they made.'

'Are either of these two men in this court?'

'They are My Lord. Captain Manville-Jones. The prisoner in the dock. He was seated on the right. The other, a Lieutenant Phillips. The lieutenant showed me a photocopy of the document you have just shown me and asked me to confirm that the signature was mine. He then asked me if I was a Communist.'

'And you replied?'

'I laughed. I knew where the conversation was leading. At home there was, from my point of view, no real interest in politics. At university all things are available. Clubs, groups, associations. It was all new. I was away from the constraints of home. I chatted with other students and went to this talk which sounded interesting. It wasn't. I told the lieutenant I wasn't a Communist, neither did I read the Daily Worker.'

'Who or what is the Daily Worker, Sir Henry?' interjected the judge.

'A newspaper espousing extreme left-wing political sentiment, My Lord.'

He nodded. 'Carry on, officer.'

'He asked why I'd mentioned the Daily Worker. I said to save him the trouble of asking. And mentioned my passing involvement with communism'.

'I asked these two gentlemen who they were. They produced their identity cards showing they were members of the security services. They reiterated that they would not, under normal circumstances, contact anyone with as little service as I had. I could decline at any time. Although at that point they hadn't asked me anything contentious.'

'Pc Blake just what did they ask you to do?'

'I wasn't aware, but my girlfriend's father, William Vernon was the owner not only of a chain of retail motorcycle outlets but of the Spartans, a motorcycle racing team. I discovered later there were business interests in Italy.'

'I see,' said Sir Henry. 'The relevance being?'

'Documents were being stolen from top secret military establishments and smuggled abroad, My Lord. They didn't say which. It was always twenty four to thirty six hours prior to the Spartans leaving the country to race on the continent. The courier was known to be a man by the name of Peter Pederson and riding the same model of motorcycle that I rode.'

'That would be a Honda CB77, known as the Super Hawk.'

'That is correct, My Lord. The Spartans were scheduled to depart from the Spartans Training Track in Tadcaster for Holland on the 9th of August at 8.30 p.m.'

'And they wanted you to do what exactly?' said Sir Henry.

'If this Peter Pederson turned up, and they did warn me that he might not, I was to keep an eye on him, note whom he spoke with and pass any information to a teacher at my former school who would pass it on to the appropriate offices. But it does seem odd.'

'Odd? How so?'

'My Lord. If, as I was informed they, which I took to mean Captain Manville-Jones and Lieutenant Phillips, were going to keep an eye on me from a distance why the necessity of passing the information to a former school master. In the event they were at the stadium. To me it's bizarre.'

Lord Justice Nevison smiled inwardly. If this young police officer continued with this line of reasoning he would reveal some unpleasant truths. He made eye contact with Sir Henry and raised an eyebrow.

Sir Henry interjected. 'Officer, you are beginning to drift away from the question I asked. If there was anything else that the defendant or his colleague asked please inform the court.'

That stopped me. 'Sorry. No, there was nothing else.'

'And the reason they gave was because your girlfriend was Lucy, William Vernon's daughter?'

'It was, My Lord. They said it was too good an opportunity to miss. To have someone on the inside.'

'How long have you and Miss Vernon been in this relationship?'

'Technically, I suppose, since 7th July,' I said and took them briefly from the incident with the MG until the evening of 9th August when the police arrived and we were carted off to hospital; missing out anything that wasn't pertinent.

Sir Henry Battle nodded and looked towards Lord Justice Nevison. 'I have no further questions, Mi Lord,' he said and sat.

Lord Justice Nevison nodded.

Sir Frere Jameson stood. Checked his notes and faced me. 'Officer, your testimony I found to be very interesting. Although why you indulge in such flights of fancy I cannot imagine. You were, at the time, a police recruit with a matter of weeks service. Yet, you have told the court of this fabricated, harrowing experience that you, your fiancée, her mother and your step-sister endured. The injuries that you received and just how close to death you were. And yet, in spite of the pain of the burns. The heat of the fire. And, your worry about your compatriots, you still had the presence of mind to concentrate to such a degree you were able to remember, with defining detail, a conversation some twenty yards distant, with a raging fire between you and the defendant, Mikhail Kuznetsov and Lieutenant Phillips. And you claim that you can quote who said what verbatim. I put it to you that you included in your testimony a goodly measure of poetic licence. I am sure that your female compatriots were duly impressed.'

What the … 'My Lord I do not have to fabricate anything to impress anyone.'

'We shall see. Pc Blake, my client, when he gives evidence from that very witness box. A man who has served his country well for fifteen years will tell the court exactly what happened. How he and Lieutenant Phillips saw the fire and came to investigate. How Mikhail Kuznetsov shot and killed Lieutenant Phillips and was in turn shot by Captain Manville-Jones.'

Sir Frere Jameson paused too long. 'That My Lord is a fabrication,' I said, 'and doesn't answer the question as to why the defendant's fingerprints are the only ones on the trigger of Kuznetsov's pistol.'

Lord Justice Nevison sat bolt upright. My ego collapsed. 'Officer you are not a fingerprint expert.' He turned to Sir Henry. 'You have a fingerprint expert on the witness list?'

'Indeed, My Lord. The witness after next. He will confirm what Constable Blake has just said.'

He turned his attention to Sir Frere Jameson. 'Sir Frere. Thin ice.'

'My Lord. Thank you, officer. My Lord, witness statements provided by Lucy Vernon, Elizabeth Vernon and Anne Mountain have been read out. The testimony given by Pc Blake agrees in all regards. I have therefore no further questions.'

Lord Justice Nevison nodded. 'Officer you may step down.' He looked to his left. 'Sir Henry.'

He stood. 'Call Gilbert Syme.' The call was passed on.

There was a flurry behind me. The solicitor sitting behind Sir Frere Jameson detached himself from a conversation with Manville-Jones tapped Sir Frere on the shoulder and whispered. He turned to Manville-Jones who nodded.

Sir Frere Jameson stood and faced the judge. 'My Lord, My client wishes to change his plea from Not Guilty to Guilty. On all charges.'

The judge turned to face the Dock. 'Duncan Manville-Jones. You wish to change your plea to guilty?'

'I do My Lord.'

'Very well. Mr Clerk?'

The Clerk stood, turning to the Judge. 'Put the charges to him again.'

'Yes, My Lord,' he turned to face the prisoner. 'Duncan Manville-Jones, in relation to the charge of murder of Lieutenant Leslie Phillips, how plead you, guilty or not guilty?'

'Guilty.'

In relation to the charge of murder of Mikhail Kuznetsov how plead you, guilty or not guilty?'

'Guilty.'

In relation to the charge of attempted murder of Constable Brian Blake, how plead you, guilty or not guilty?'

'Guilty.'

So it continued. The trial was over. Lord Justice Nevison discharged the jury and adjourned the court for thirty minutes then left.

I was standing between Sir Henry and Mr Syme. 'What happens now, Sir?'

'The Press and the public will be allowed into court for sentencing,' said Sir Henry. 'Manville-Jones will be sentenced and we can leave early. But, a word of advice. If you intend to live so dangerously in future you had better buy some ice-skates.'

'Yes, Sir,' I said.

'Lord Nevison will,' said Mr Syme,' after sentencing will want to speak to you. But come with me. All right, Sir Henry?'

He checked his watch. 'That's fine but be back within twenty five minutes.'

The door was almost invisible. At the end of the corridor an anteroom with table, four chairs and a telephone. 'Brian,' he said.

'The room at Tofts is paid for until Friday breakfast. You can return to Yorkshire if you wish to arrange with DCI Valentine for a few days leave. You might also consider that your fiancée might not be averse to a couple of days in your company. There will be a train leaving Leeds at four thirty.' He pointed at the phone and smiled. 'It's your choice.'

DI Henderson answered. I explained about the change of plea but no sentencing as yet, Then my query about leave. 'Sorry Brian, we need you back here. Amongst other things Marjorie Simmonds has been seen again. Get the first train back in the morning.' That was that.

Mr Syme handed me a piece of paper. 'That's the telephone number of the Royale in Drury Lane. Please note, not the Theatre Royal. Gareth Jones is the Manager. He's a friend. Call him in the morning and tell him I gave you his details. He will understand. The show is Hello Dolly.'

We made it into court with five minutes to spare. It was packed. All come to see the hanging. Mr Syme and I sat behind Sir Henry.

The closing speeches made it was now the turn of Lord Justice Nevison.

Flanked by two officers Manville-Jones faced the judge. 'Prisoner in the Dock,' he said. 'Never in my service to this country have I come across such an abhorrent breach of trust as exhibited by you. As an officer in Her Majesty's armed forces you swore an oath of allegiance to The Crown which means nothing to you. Passing information to a possible enemy and committing murder to cover your tracks. Had it not been for the action of one young man you would still be free to continue your nefarious conduct. Were it not for the fact that in its wisdom Her Majesty's government has seen fit to abolish the death penalty, I would, without hesitation, sentence you to death by hanging. However ...

'For the murder of Lieutenant Leslie Phillips I sentence you to imprisonment for life.

'For the murder of Mikhail Kuznetsov I sentence you to imprisonment for life.

'For the attempted murder of Constable Brian Blake I sentence you to twenty five years imprisonment.

'In addition you have pleaded guilty to seven charges of espionage under Section one of the Official Secrets Act 1911. For each of these offences you will be sentenced to twenty five years imprisonment, to be served consecutively.' There was an audible gasp. 'Take him down.'

Manville-Jones disappeared down the steps. He would never be released. Lord Justice Nevison leaned forward. His Clerk stood, then all the strength seemed to go from my legs. 'Is constable Blake in court?'

'Your turn,' Mr Syme nudged me with his elbow. 'And keep your fingers crossed.'

I got to my feet. 'Yes, My Lord.'

'Come closer so that I can see you properly.'

I could feel the eyes burning into my back as I made that long and lonely walk. Or at least that's what it felt like. I stopped at the corner of the Clerk's desk.'

'Relax officer,' the Clerk said and smiled. 'He's not going to eat you.'

'Not today I'm not,' came the voice from on high. 'Do not do that again. It is not your job. In the future who knows? But today, you're safe.'

I looked up at the smiling face. 'Thank you, Sir. Sorry, My Lord. I apologise.'

He gave a curt nod and waved his hand. 'Don't worry about it ... This episode of the kidnapping etc. happened when you had been at Pannal Ash for eight weeks?'

'Yes, My Lord.'

His face broke into a broad smile. 'And the first thing you did after Kuznetsov locked the door of the shed was to propose marriage?'

'Yes, My Lord. There was nothing to lose. The promise of a future. Something to fight for.'

'It obviously worked. She hit Manville-Jones on the face?'

'Yes, My Lord. Lucy and the others approached from behind and she struck him here,' I put my hand down my right cheek. 'He wasn't impressed.'

'I'll bet he wasn't. Your father was, I understand, a serving detective sergeant murdered whilst on duty?'

'Yes, My Lord. Whilst securing the release of two hostages.'

'Like father like son. That level of courage is innate. Your action knowing the risks that you took was unbelievable. I agree with your summation. Had you succumbed to Manville-Jones he would have killed your fiancée, her mother and your step-sister and he would still be in the service of the Russians. Your country owes you a debt of gratitude. I shall be writing to the relevant authorities about you and your female compatriots. Good luck for your future career and your marriage.' Then his look changed. 'And remember.'

He stood. As did everyone in the courtroom.

The door to his retiring room closed. The Clerk said. 'He's normally very sparing with his time. He gave you a lot more. Should you come across him in future just try not to upset him.' He gave me a knowing look.

I called the DCI to give him the news and the sentences imposed. There was a loud whistle from the other end of the line. He promised to call the new Commandant at Pannal. I called home. Mr Syme smuggled me out of the building via a side door.

I called Mr Jones at the Royale. He was expecting the call. 'I know it's cheeky but I'm unable to attend at the moment, I have to return to Yorkshire. However I'm getting married on New Year's Eve. Would it be possible for my wife and I to attend?'

'Not a problem, Mr Blake, but it's pantomime season. It won't be Hello Dolly, but Mother Goose is a reasonable seasonal substitute, If you wish to avail yourself of the offer.'

I had to smile. 'That's very generous of you, Mr Jones,' I checked my diary. 'Would you have any seats for Monday January 4th?'

Two seats booked I put the phone down.

I called home. There was a train I could catch at 6pm.

Forty-Two

Mum collected me from Wakefield at nine. She and Liz had been talking and knew of our sleeping arrangements. 'I know it's only a few weeks to your wedding but please...'

'I know Mum, we'll be careful.'

I called Mr Valentine to let him know I was home early. 'Excellent, full uniform, best bib and tucker. Be at the office for nine.'

Now it was Lucy's turn. 'Why didn't you call me first?'

'Why do you think? There's only twenty four hours in the day.'

We talked for half an hour. Lucy said she was coming across to the flat tomorrow.

First task was to explain to the team the ins and outs of what had happened on that Friday.

'But why didn't you make a break for it once you'd escaped from the burning shed?' Said Jacko. 'You could have been killed.'

'They were nearly killed in the shed,' said DI Henderson. 'Besides, Brian had witnessed the captain swapping firearms in order to kill the lieutenant. If he knew there were four other witnesses he had nothing to lose by killing them. Brian's argument was, neither had he. Get the bastard before he could eliminate them.'

'That's the way I saw it, Jacko. He was a highly respected officer in the security service and I was what? A young copper with two minutes service. My word against his in an investigation and I was the only one who witnessed the assassinations.'

Next it was HQ and a meeting with the Chief, Chief Superintendent Sanderson the new Commandant at Pannal. And the DCI

They wanted from thread to needle.

'... and you believe, Pc Blake,' said the Chief Superintendent. 'That eliminating the Russian and the lieutenant was done to leave the way open for Manville-Jones.'

'Yes sir. It made sense from his point of view. I confirm that Bill Vernon and Lester Roberts are the principal suspects and are removed, which in my mind makes the two deaths in the road accident questionable. But who am I. That leaves the way open for him.

'Blake,' the Chief Constable added his two pence worth. 'Don't get tied up in trying to second guess what the security service are doing or thinking. It could drive you mad. Leave them to play their games and try not to get too involved.'

I didn't say anything but Manville-Jones did tell me they had me in their sights for the last five years.

'And Mr Syme told you the country owes you a debt of gratitude,' said the Chief Superintendent. 'You will get an official thank you but no suggestion what.'

I had to smile. 'That just about sums it up, sir.'

'Mr Wright, there are two police officers asking if you can spare a few minutes. A Detective Inspector Henderson and a Constable Blake.'

'Thank you, Kathleen. Show them in, please.' He put his Times back on his desk. The article concerning the trial at the Old Bailey foremost. The thought running through his brain - surely there can't be two constable Brian Blakes in the West Riding Police.

'This way, gentlemen,' The stern-faced redoubtable Kathleen stepped out of the way.

I followed the DI into the office. Jack Wright stood and walked towards us wagging his finger at me, a broad smile on his face. 'I knew it,' he said. 'There was something about you ...'

'You know what they say, sir,' I replied. 'Once a copper always a copper. Perhaps it's true.'

'Maybe you're correct,' he turned to the DI. 'Now Inspector, apart from parading Pc Blake, to what do I owe the pleasure. Oh, can you spare five minutes for a coffee?'

'We can, sir,' he replied. Mr Wright picked up the phone and waved his hand at two chairs.

'Can you arrange coffee for three, Kathleen, please,' he said, sat and turned to the DI.

'Now?'

'We've come to return some money, Blake?'

I passed an envelope containing the £120. 'It's all there, sir,' I said.

'And you want a receipt?' he said and smiled. 'Very big on receipts is Pc Blake, Inspector. And rightly so.'

We stayed for twenty minutes. First item the receipt. However, talk was more about the Old Bailey trial than Marjorie Simmonds. In the end Mr Wright was going to suggest to Mrs Brooks that the money be donated to the Police Widows and Orphan's fund.

I met Lucy with hot coffee and hotter kiss.

We were standing face-to-face. My hands clasped behind her waist. Lucy's round my neck.

'I've been thinking,' she said.

That raised a smile. 'Sounds ominous.'

Her frown said shut up and listen. 'I know we've never discussed children. But we both want them.'

'True, how many?'

'Not important at the moment.'

I wondered what was coming. 'Okay?'

'At first I was using our friendship to fight against my father. To be honest I would have gotten pregnant just to spite him. But after that Friday night everything changed. It dawned on me just how fragile we are and if it hadn't been for you we could all have died. I hate these snatched moments. I want to be with you always. I want to stop using contraceptives. It's only a few weeks and if I catch on, so what.'

That hadn't been foremost in my planning but contraceptives aren't guaranteed. 'You want to move in and start a family straight away.'

She smiled and nodded. 'Starting tonight. I've spoken to Mum and she doesn't object. Will it cause problems for you?

In certain quarters living together out of wedlock was frowned upon. 'Not if they don't find out and I won't tell anybody who could cause trouble.'

There was nothing further to say?

Forty-Three

Wednesday. With Neil there were nine round the table: piping hot pork pie, a tsunami of onion sauce and a mountain of cheesy mashed potato. Enough to drive away any autumn chill. Even Clive had enough to eat.

The main topic of conversation? The trial.

'What do you mean you weren't allowed in?'

'Frankie, it was a not guilty plea. All witnesses have to wait outside until they are called, if at all. In this case the trial was *in camera*. Not even the Press was allowed in'

'But you gave evidence.'

I'd been through court procedure plenty of times when I was at Pannal. They could be exasperating. 'Yes, Jen. And after I'd left the witness box and before the next witness could be sworn he changed his plea to guilty.'

'So those that hadn't been called wouldn't know anything.'

'Correct. However, once a guilty plea has been accepted it is open court and everybody can go in and listen to the closing speeches and the sentencing.'

'Can we get a transcript of the trial?'

I took a deep breath and exhaled. 'It was under the provisions of the Official ...' I looked at the three of them. 'Are you trying to wind me up?'

There were a series of grins around the table. 'Damn,' said Jen. 'It was just starting to get interesting.'

The look on Joe's face said I was getting slower.

When the laughter stopped it was Neil. 'You have to put up with this all the time?'

'All the time. Thank goodness for the flat.'

He and Anne were sitting next to each other. They made eye contact. Neil questioning. Anne all wide-eyed innocence. 'Help.' Was his only comment.

'Tell us about the sentencing,' said Joe.

This was easier. 'Life imprisonment for each of the two murders. Twenty five years for attempting to murder me. Twenty five years on each charge under the Official Secrets Act. To be served consecutively.'

'Just what were the details of these charges?'

I locked eyes with Frankie. 'Don't-start-that-again. Apart from anything else I don't know.'

'Ok, ok.' The grin broke through. 'Just testing.'

'Let me get this straight,' said Anne. 'This Manville-Jones character shoots the Russian with his service revolver. Then puts it back in his pocket. Takes the Russian's pistol and shoots the Lieutenant, wipes it down and replaces it in the Russian's hand. He believes we're all dead in the fire. When he sees you realises that there are four witnesses that he didn't expect. He can't use his own revolver because people will know who fired the shots. That's why he had to get the Russian's pistol and finish us all off?'

'Makes my blood run cold at the thought,' said Mum.

Neil slid his arm round Anne's waist. 'You ok?'

She nodded.

'You were all very brave,' said Joe.

Conversation began to tail off. 'Oh, by the way,' I said to Lucy, 'I've booked the hotel for our mini-honeymoon.' That put paid to the chatter.

She narrowed her eyes when I smiled. 'Oh, have you,' she said. 'And why haven't we discussed it?'

'You said you liked me when I was masterful.'

At least she blushed. 'You know very well I wasn't meaning that.'

'I know. Shall we talk about that instead?'

She hurled a wide-eyed *don't you dare* look in my direction. 'No.'

'I'm discussing it the same way we discussed where we're going to spend our honeymoon proper. And, I've got two seats for a show at the Royale for the Monday night.'

Lucy's 'Just you wait.' Drawing questioning looks. 'Ok where is this hotel?'

'Tofts, where I stayed. It's really nice.'

'Expensive?'

'It's where I stayed. The government doesn't throw money about. Besides, aren't you worth it?'

'Beside the point. And what's this show?

'Mother Goose, it's panto season.'

'That's for kids.'

'It's for everybody. Pity it's not this week they're doing Hello Dolly.'

'That's really good,' offered Neil. 'I'd love to see that.'

Anne leaned across and whispered in Lucy's ear. 'Would you mind if Neil and I came with you. In our own room?'

'You sure,' she replied in kind.

'Yup.'

'No problem.'

She leaned the other way and whispered. 'Neil, we're going to London with Lucy and Brian. Same hotel, double room.'

Saturday morning Mum dropped us off at the flat. I'd brought Lucy's leathers with me last Sunday. We travelled to Boston Spa on the bike.

One good piece of news was that Jeffrey Garden, Mr Cadogan's colleague had submitted a schedule of the bets made by Bill and the amounts won to the police. Amongst the data, statements from the bookies where Bill had placed his bets confirming the details. They didn't exactly say they were pleased he was no longer around but didn't sound sorry either.

They weren't an exact matches with the amount we found, in fact the amount won by Bill was a few thousand more.

We had a light lunch before making ourselves known at the track and salving a few curious minds.

Liz went through Joe's suggestions in detail, It looked good. She had taken the plans to her accountant. As yet nothing.

We spent most of the remainder of the daylight discussing the trial and our mini-honeymoon. And, would Anne let on, at least to Mum, about her plan to come with us and share a room with Neil.

Forty-Four

It was wall-to-wall sunshine. A great day to ride to Whitby. The A64, Leeds – Scarborough road could be very busy. Sundays it wasn't. Clear of York I opened the bike up. It's a beautiful part of the country. Few built-up areas. Winding tarmac. Trees. Fields. The occasional vehicle. Before long the sign for the A169. Malton to the right, Pickering and Whitby to the left.

Through Pickering climbing towards the North Yorkshire Moors. Fields giving way to heather. Unspoilt views stretching for miles from the top of Saltersgate Bank across the Hole of Horcum to the Pickering Forest and beyond. Saltersgate Bank with its very tight right-hand hairpin bend. Climbing to Fylingdales Moor, its newly commissioned guided missile tracking station, the three giant radomes nicknamed golf balls, prominent to the right. The long descent to Eller Beck. A wickedly tight left-hand bend over the old narrow stone bridge. A beautiful run over the tops and down the infamously steep Blue Bank with the view of Whitby Abbey, looking even more spectacular with storm clouds behind, into Sleights. From there it was five minutes to Whitby railway station where I parked the bike.

How far we walked that day I have no idea. I counted the one hundred and ninety-nine steps up to the Abbey. The view towards Sandsend was beautiful. Out to sea the approaching storm clouds threatened rain. When we reached the town the atmosphere was oppressive. The clouds appearing to sit on the Abbey ruins.

It was easy to see how the superstitious might believe in vampires and the Bram Stoker story.

Notwithstanding, the December sun had drawn the tourists towards this jewel of the Yorkshire coast. We took refuge in a fish restaurant for dinner. Fresh Whitby haddock must be one of the most delicious meals you can buy, supported by chips, mushy peas, bread butter and tea. Excellent.

The storm broke as our food arrived. The sound and light shows were impressive. Sitting in the restaurant window we could only sympathise with those caught unprepared, many of whom decided that now was the time to eat. Within ten minutes it was over, the sun broke through. Heading back towards the railway station we shop-dodged looking for Christmas presents. Climbed West Cliff to see the statue of Captain Cook.

It had been my intention to return home via the coast road and through Scarborough but it was half past three. The reverse route from this morning beckoned.

Forty-Five

My first job was to see the DCI. I needed two applications for annual leave for the New Year and Easter plus a request to carry five days over to the next leave year. All signed with the minimum of fuss.

Marjorie Simmonds was still missing. No doubt with *her* money. DCI Valentine wasn't interested in the affairs of the tax man. Security at The British Horseracing Federation and Weatherbys were happy that nothing illegal had occurred. There was no link between Marjorie Simmonds and any of the trainers or owners of the horses involved. The enquiry was now dead. I had less than six weeks service so I was tidying up loose ends, leaving the real detectives to get on with it.

Lucy broke the news. She wasn't pregnant. Disappointing.

Tuesday and Wednesday evenings we stayed at Boston Spa. I ran Lucy to work.

Liz had leafed through the book I'd taken her on exercise physiology. All she wanted to know was, could I help the Spartans and how.

Having worked until 3.0 a.m. on Saturday morning I spent a lonely night at the flat. Rose around 10.30 and left for Boston Spa. After a light lunch with Lucy behind me and Liz in the Bentley, Lucy's clothes on the rear seat. We set off in what passed for wintry sunshine.

It was Saturday and Huddersfield Town were playing at home. It began to rain when we reached Cooper Bridge. The match day traffic along Leeds Road was heavy. We arrived at two thirty. The wind was howling down from Bolster Moor. The rain of the town centre now wet driving snow, over two inches deep. Not good for two wheels. This was not in the weather forecast. Anne had been keeping a watch for us and opened the door as we made a dash for shelter. No sooner had we got the door closed than Gerald and the very pregnant Marianne arrived. Lucy had told me that if her father had still been alive Gerald and Marianne wouldn't have been there.

All eyes on the Christmas decorations. As a family we didn't hold back.

Including Neil and Tom, Jennifer's fiancé - they got engaged last month, there were twelve. With efficiency borne of practise the girls collected the coats and umbrellas. The question was: where was Clive?

Everyone was ushered into the lounge. And there he was. Stock still. Full Kendo armour and raised shinai in hand. I nudged Lucy and nodded towards our warrior. She nodded and grinned. How long before he made our visitors jump? We didn't have long to wait.

'Is that a model,' said Gerald stepping towards Clive. 'It's very good.'

'HAI!' Clive slammed his right foot forward and stopped the blow an inch from Gerald's head. Marianne screamed. Gerald and Tom jumped. Clive burst out laughing, put the shinai down and removed his helmet.

'Sorry if I scared you,' he said. 'Just a bit of fun.'

'You frightened me,' said Marianne, hand on her belly. 'I could have given birth.'

'No you wouldn't, Marianne,' chided Gerald. 'Relax and look at the workmanship.'

She wasn't impressed.

Tom gave Clive a dirty look and muttered something under his breath. Was there some history?

A five minute chat around Kendo with Clive and Joe, followed by introductions for the benefit of Gerald and Marianne. All went well until ...

Neil was standing next to Lucy. 'I thought I'd worked out how to pick Anne out from the others,' he said. 'But seeing them like this ...' then he whispered. 'Just as long as I take the right one to London.'

That drew a laugh from Lucy. 'I don't think Anne will let you make any mistakes.'

The girls were standing shoulder to shoulder. As usual, sporting identical hair styles dresses and shoes. The only identifying feature was Jennifer's engagement ring. An excited Lucy stepped forward. 'Let me, Brian,' she said in all innocence. She didn't know them well enough, yet. When I saw the girls smile, I knew I was right. 'The easy one to find is Jennifer,' she said. 'She's engaged to Tom and wears his engagement ring.' She put her hand on Jennifer's shoulder.

'Just a minute,' said Frankie. 'I'm Jennifer, this is Anne. I just lent her my ring to try it on.'

'No, you didn't,' said Anne. 'Hand it over. I'm Jennifer. The one wearing my ring is Frankie. Anne is at the other end.'

Everyone, including a puzzled Neil, stood there laughing. The girls smiled at Lucy. 'You rotters,' she said, returning their smiles. 'You've set me up.'

'Would we do that to you, our new sister?' said the real Jennifer with a glint in her eye.

Lucy scowled and then smiled. 'Yes, you would,' she said. 'Just give me a moment.' She took a pace backwards.

Standing next to Joe, Liz was trying her damnedest to work out who was who. 'Seeing them standing like that they really are like three peas out of the same pod.'

'They are,' he replied. 'They've caused no end of problems over the past eighteen years. Hours of endless fun for them, but they've never done this before.'

'All right you three,' said Lucy, her eyes narrowed. 'Since Brian put this ring on my finger at the stadium I only take it off to wash,' she turned to Jennifer. 'I'll bet the real Jennifer would do the same. You're Jennifer aren't you?'

'That was too easy,' said Clive.

'We didn't get that right, did we,' said the real Jennifer.

'Now,' she turned to Anne. 'After our incarceration I could never forget your voice, Anne, could I?' She turned to Frankie, 'Hi Frankie.'

Lucy curtsied at the ripple of applause which developed into an uproarious four-sister group hug.

'Come into the Library,' said Joe. 'We're into martial arts. You can try the armour on for yourselves. Being an engineer, Gerald, I think you would enjoy it.'

'I would love to,' said Gerald.

We all turned to follow. Mum stopped Anne. 'Will you take Lucy upstairs to get changed. Brian, can I borrow you for two minutes?'

'Ok, Mum,' said Anne. 'Come on Lucy.'

Mum sat at the kitchen table. 'Push the door to, Brian?'

I sat opposite. Sixty seconds later I was aghast. 'I had no idea. Are you sure?'

'Yes,' she replied. 'I think you noticed that she was a bit offhand when Lucy was here before, just as she had been when Pamela came.'

'I suppose she was but ... are you sure. Did she really think that I would fall in love with her?'

'She did. She thought that by playing the waiting game you would realise the way she felt and reciprocate.'

I stood and exhaled. 'She's ok now?'

'I hope so. But there's no guarantee,' she replied. 'I had a long chat with her after you left last time. I think she finally realises that it's never going to be. Please keep it to yourself. Whatever you do say nothing to Frankie unless she mentions it first.'

'Does Joe know?'

'He does, and he was as shocked as you.'

My mind in a whirl, I ran past the open library door and took the steps two at a time. *How on earth?*

We've always had a rule that if a bedroom door is closed you always knock first, just to make sure. But it was my bedroom, or had been. No-one was using it and I needed to get out of these leathers.

Lucy must have been to the bathroom for a freshen up when I barged in. She had asked Anne which my bedroom was. The curtains were pulled. The light on. Anne was sitting on the bed and Lucy? She had just taken off my bathrobe. Standing there, facing me, wearing only her bra and knickers, very lacy and sheer. What my Gran Westmoreland would have called *nearly knickers*. Lucy looked me straight in the eye and smiled. I walked across and put my arms round her. She reciprocated. 'You are so beautiful.' Anne sat there stunned as we kissed.

Lucy smiled at her as we untangled.

'But?' said Anne.

'The rules?' I said.

'But, yes.'

'You go and get washed, Brian. I'll explain.'

The door closed. Lucy sat alongside Anne. 'We're sleeping together. Sometimes we don't get much.'

Anne blushed to the roots of her hair. 'Does Mum know?'

'Your Mum? She does. We're getting married in less than five weeks. She just says be careful. My mum knows as well. In fact when Brian stays he shares my room.

'I don't know what to say, except I won't say anything to the others.'

'Thanks. I noticed that when you booked your room at Tofts you didn't book a twin-bedded room or two singles.'

'Oh, you heard,' Anne blushed again.

'Yup. You and Neil haven't yet?'

'No, but.'

'I know how you feel.'

She nodded. 'Mm.'

Lucy put her arm round Anne's shoulders. 'It's very busy downstairs. How about I send Neil up to your room?'

'Don't put ideas into my head. I'd thought of asking Brian if we could borrow his flat.'

'I don't think he would object. There are plenty of condoms. We won't say anything. But if you did get pregnant I don't think your Dad would kick you out.'

'Probably not.'

'And I don't think Neil would raise too many objections. I'll mention it to Brian. Just give me a ring. Now, help me with my dress, please.'

'No Marianne,' said Joe. 'This is nothing to do with religion. The fact that they practised Shinto or Buddhism is merely a coincidence. Pointed or bladed weapons have been invented across the globe numerous times and so has armour, it's cultural not religious. This armour and the *shinai* are training aids developed around two hundred years ago in Japan because swordsmen were getting killed or injured during practice.'

Marianne frowned. 'I understand,' she said, in a tone that suggested otherwise.

Forty-Six

Bathrobe hi-jacked and ablutions completed. Leathers in one hand, boots in the other I headed for *my* bedroom, arriving as Lucy and Anne emerged.

'Wow. You look stunning,' I was met by a radiant smile. She didn't have to do much with her hair, at least I thought so. It looked chic. Her dress was simple and figure hugging: midnight blue, half sleeves, knee length and high heels in the same shade. She looked perfect. Lucy put Pamela well and truly in the shade.

She made a little curtsy. 'Thank you kind sir,' she said. 'Just for that your intrusion is forgiven. You get a kiss.'

I dropped my leathers and boots. My attempt to put my arms round her firmly repulsed. 'No.' she said, 'You'll be wearing more than me. Now stand still.'

Anne smiled at us from the top of the stairs. 'Turn your back little sister,' I said. 'This is private.'

'Not on your life,' she exchanged smiles with Lucy. 'Lucy needs a chaperone.'

'Like Hell I do,' said Lucy, laughing as Anne disappeared down the stairs. 'Go on, shoo.'

'All right,' Anne replied. 'Shout if you need any assistance.'

'I will,' I called after her.

'Not you, you fool!'

There was no reply.

'Are you two having your own party upstairs or coming down?' Broke the moment. The humour in Mum's voice self-evident

'I wish,' whispered Lucy with a savage grin.

I gritted my teeth and rested my forehead on Lucy's. 'Lucy's on her way. I'm getting changed,' I called. 'You'd better go.'

'Just a sec'. Would you have any objections to Anne and Neil borrowing your flat?'

'Whose idea was that?'

'They're like we were. I suggested I send Neil to her room.'

'Now!?'

Lucy nodded. 'She said not to put ideas into her head and she'd thought of asking you about the flat. I said I'd mention it. There are plenty of condoms left.'

'If they want. No problems. As long as I'm not there. Let me know. But, was Anne thinking all night or just for a few hours?'

'I don't know. I'll check.'

One last kiss and she was gone.

'You look gorgeous, Lucy,' Mum said as Lucy appeared on the stairs. 'That colour really suits you.'

Lucy flashed her a smile. 'Thanks, Brian thinks so too.'

'He would. But he'd think you were gorgeous dressed in a sack,' Mum replied.

Lucy laughed. 'Yes, I think he would,' she said. 'But, whilst we're out here can we have a quiet word, please?'

The kitchen door closed; Mum motioned Lucy to sit down. 'Is there a problem, love?'

'It's a bit awkward and ... you can tell me to mind my own business but, has Frankie ever had a boyfriend?'

Mum told me later that alarm bells were ringing loud and clear. 'I'm not sure I understand why you're asking.'

'Well, Jennifer is engaged to Tom. Anne has Neil. I just wondered about Frankie.'

Lucy realised Mum was struggling. 'Believe me, Mum,' they exchanged smiles as Lucy called her, Mum. 'I'm not trying to cause any trouble but when I was here the last time Frankie acted as though she were jealous of my friendship with Brian. It was almost as if she was in love with him herself.'

Mum sighed. 'Has Brian said anything?'

'No,' she said. 'I've not spoken to him about it, and he's never volunteered anything.'

'You worked it out yourself?'

'If it's true, and you make it sound as though I am, then yes.' Lucy reached across the table and took hold of Mum's hand in hers. 'I want Brian and me to have a marriage like you and Joe's.'

'Me and Joe?' echoed Mum wondering what Lucy was going to say next.

'Yes,' she smiled. 'I understand the reference to trapping Joe with your iced buns.'

'You did?' she replied, hoping in vain that she wasn't blushing again.

Lucy nodded. 'Your blush and Joe's comment clinched it.'

'Between you and me subtlety didn't work, and that's as much as I intend to say on that matter, young lady,' said Mum. It didn't stop Lucy's broad grin. 'But as far as Frankie is concerned, she and Brian always hit it off more than he did with Jennifer or Anne. Probably because she was the dominant one of the three. Not so much now, but in the early days noticeably so. I don't think it was intentional, just a friendship that developed. With Brian, Frankie was one of his little sisters. He was the one who helped them with their homework. With Frankie that seems to have developed along a different route. I have to admit that I missed it until after your visit.'

'Brian knew?'

'That was what I wanted to speak to him about when you went up to get changed. His head must have been spinning when he went up a few minutes later. Frankie and I had a long chat and I think she's ok. It sounds as if it's been developing for around five years. I can only hope.'

Lucy gasped. 'Five years?' she iterated. 'Poor girl. And how did Brian react?'

'Totally shocked. He had no idea.'

They sat there in silence for several seconds before Lucy spoke. 'Thanks Mum, now I understand I can deal with it, and it stays private.'

'Thanks love, that's appreciated. I'll just check dinner then we can join the others before they send out a search party.'

Forty-Seven

We chatted in the library for the next hour until Mum called the girls to help her set the table. About the same time Gerald noticed the smell drifting from the kitchen.

He pushed his plate away. 'That was memorable,' he said patting his stomach.

Without exception there were general comments of appreciation from around the table. It was one of the best meals she had ever cooked. I suggested that *all* the ladies should move to the lounge. Before Mum could protest, Lucy and Frankie had linked arms with her to make sure she went.

With the six of us it didn't take long and we were in danger of falling asleep in the lounge, until Clive said. 'Can't we play games?'

Marianne pulled a face like a bulldog chewing a razorblade and was about to speak when the girls, as one, jumped up. 'Great idea, Clive,' said Anne. 'You get the chopsticks. We'll get the rest.'

There were ten dried peas, two saucers and one pair of chopsticks per couple. The object: using the chopsticks to transfer the peas from one saucer to the other and back, in turn, and in the fastest time.

'But I've never used chopsticks,' whined Marianne.

'Neither have I.' Gerald sounded exasperated. 'Come on Marianne, join in. It's Christmas time. Have some fun.'

'It's easy,' said Clive picking the chopsticks up. 'Look, I'll show you. You just hold them like this,' and demonstrated. 'Now you try.'

The first members of each team poised ready to start when Mum, the ultimate official, spoke. 'Clive, put that pea back in the saucer, please. The correct saucer.'

'Is he cheating again,' said Anne.

'No, I'm not,' he protested. 'It's only cheating if you get caught.' Which got everyone laughing.

'Well, you've just been caught, haven't you?' Anne retorted.

'No. We haven't started, so that doesn't count,' Clive's usual method of self-defence.

'You'll go far, Clive,' said Liz. Even Marianne smiled.

'Put-it-back,' said Mum trying to look threatening. 'In the correct saucer ... Thank you.'

The pea in its rightful place. Mum said. 'Ready? Go.'

It was a farce. It usually was. Peas and the occasional chopstick flew in all directions. Tom holding his chopsticks so tight that the pea hit the light fitting. Marianne's voice broke through the racket. 'We win. Can we play again?'

After that it was plain sailing, everybody joined in. When they got fed up with chopsticks we played Beetle, in pairs, and eventually charades.

In spite of their protestations that they couldn't eat another morsel, the cakes Mum produced were demolished. Clive making a valiant attempt to achieve that on his own until Mum banned him before he was sick. Liz invited us all to spend Christmas Day with them. Apart from Tom who was spending the day at home. We accepted. However, Tom did accept the invitation to our wedding.

We left around ten shortly after Gerald and Marianne.

Lucy and me? We snatched a minute or so whilst we got our leathers on before setting off for Mirfield. Liz, Neil and Tom following in the Bentley. She would drop Tom off at the bottom end of Greenhead Park. I took the scenic route to see the Christmas lights in the town centre.

It was raining hard in Mirfield. When I emerged from the bathroom Lucy was in bed.

Forty-Eight

The day of rest? Not today it wasn't. Breakfast by six and take Lucy to Salendine Nook. We would see Liz later.

Now I had to meet my new Inspector, Calvin Yates, at Westleigh, followed by Sunday dinner at Salendine Nook.

Jim Tyndall metaphorically picked himself up off the floor when I walked in. 'Bloody hell, Brian. We thought you'd resigned. Wotcha doing here?'

I met his shocked expression with a grin. 'I work here, Jim,' I replied. 'Have you forgotten? I've come to see Inspector Yates, is he in?'

'I wondered why he was here so early. He's in his office,' he laughed. 'I take it you remember the way.'

I grimaced. 'How could I forget?' I climbed the stairs and knocked twice.

Inspector Yates closed the folder on his desk. 'Come in,' he called.

He stood as I entered. I'm not sure how old he was. Not that much older than me. I put him between twenty-seven and thirty. Young to be an Inspector. Five feet eleven, around fourteen stones in weight, black hair receding at the temples, a winning smile, brown eyes and a firm no-nonsense handshake. 'Pc Blake, sit down, take the weight off your feet,' he said motioning to two armchairs either side of a small table complete with kettle etc. beneath the window. 'The kettle's just boiled. What can I get you, tea or coffee? I sat down and put my helmet on the floor beside me.

'Black coffee. No sugar, sir, please.'

'Great stuff,' he replied. Twenty seconds later he put two mugs of coffee on the table, retrieved his file and sat down.

'How long have you been a biker?' he asked.

'Almost two years, sir.'

'Enjoy it?' he asked with a quizzical smile.

'That depends who I'm sharing the bike with,' I said, drawing a laugh from him.

'Someone special?'

'Very,' I handed him the two approved annual leave forms, the approved request to carry the annual leave over to the next leave year. And my Application to Marry request authorised by the chief constable.

He looked at me, then the forms and smiled. 'You have been busy. Was this the girl from the RTA when you were at Pannal?'

'Yes sir, Lucy Vernon.'

He paused. 'I was called in to see Mr Williams on Friday. He told me about the incident at Tadcaster when you were on your initial course and the trial. Is there anything else you can tell me?'

'What do you want to know, sir? The only information that I was in possession of that might be seen as contentious was the fact that the security services were involved. Now that is public knowledge I didn't see a problem.'

He was more interested in the cumulative mental effects on me rather than what happened.

He handed me a minute sheet signed by the Chief Constable. 'Miss Vernon, her mother and your step-sister will be getting a letter to the same effect.'

We were invited or, in my case, instructed to attend HQ for a presentation on Friday 8th January. We could take guests. How many it didn't say. The main question in my mind: Were the Press going to be there?

'Anyway, many congratulation for the way you dealt with the situation. I'm pleased it wasn't me.'

I couldn't think of anyone who might have wanted to exchange places.

'After that it seems small beer but congratulations on your arrest of Sergeant Palmer at Pannal.

'You've created quite a few ripples in the short time since you joined the Force, which is why we're here. Before I forget you'd better read these.' He handed me a large card-backed envelope containing three sheets of paper. 'Acknowledge receipt on the minute sheet and keep the others in the envelope.

I signed the minute sheet and handed it back. The other sheets? A Magistrate's commendation re my arrest of Smedley. The second, a Chief Constable's commendation for the same incident.

I thanked him again.

He got down to the real reason I was there. The constant search for senior officers within the ranks of the police. The Chief Constable had decided that because I had a degree and my short history, I was one of those with the potential. I knew I had done well, but this?

Then he talked about the plans to re-organise the geopolitical boundaries of the country. For example, the West Riding, one hundred and fourteen miles in length and ninety-eight miles at its widest. Containing ten autonomous local authorities, each with its own police force, hierarchy, police authority and budget. A very inefficient system. With the intended changes to the political boundaries and amalgamation of police forces. The need for a more professional management a necessity.

'Any questions?'

'No, sir,' I said. But my heart rate had increased. I wondered what was coming next, and who did I have to kill to get it?'

'You've heard of the police college at Bramshill, in Hampshire?'

'Yes, sir.'

'Good. Now, have you heard of the Special Course?'

I didn't have to think. 'No, sir.'

'The Special Course is for Sergeants who are deemed to possess the qualities I mentioned a few minutes ago. Subject to completion of the programme I've set for you.' He removed a sheet of paper from his folder. There had been no option for me to decline. 'The report that I submit as your mentor, and reports from all the departmental heads where you will gain experience, together with an in-force interview you will progress to a regional extended interview. That will be the final arbiter as to whether you will be selected to attend the Special Course ... or not.'

I wore a wry smile. 'Sounds like a piece of cake sir.'

He smiled in return. 'It's not as bad as it sounds. One of the biggest things in favour is your degree. There's only a handful in the force at the moment and three of them aren't eligible. The biggest thing against you is the attitude of many officers of command rank. They think that the only way you should be able to progress is by walking the miles and fighting the battles, because that's the way they did it. So they would have you believe. The special course for these officers is anathema.'

'You mentioned that this is a course for Sergeants?'

'Next on the list,' he said.

For the next twenty minutes he talked about my promotion exam following my appointment being confirmed. Internal interviews. The Special Course itself and holding the temporary rank of sergeant. Assuming a successful outcome to the Special Course, what was possible afterwards.

I left his office my head spinning. The extended interview was a residential three day stay at a venue to be decided. I wouldn't have to sit the Inspector's exam and could achieve the rank with a little over four years in service. Nothing was guaranteed.

Forty-Nine

I remembered DCI Valentine's comment. Dad had done very well to reach the rank of detective sergeant in eight years. I had just been offered the opportunity to reach inspector in four. However, dad had achieved promotion on his merits as a police officer, not from passing an exam and a few interviews. At least that's the way I saw it.

En route to Huddersfield one aspect of that conversation kept springing to mind. They are looking for Officers of Command Rank - Superintendent and above. Officers who are prepared to listen. Make sound decisions. Take full responsibility for their actions. I would be working harder than I had ever done before. Amongst other things I needed to make contact with Inspector Meadowcroft. I was certain that Lucy would have an input into the conversation. She would be waiting for me at Salendine Nook. As important as she was, first I needed to speak to Joe.

It was one of those rare days that you get in late autumn. Yes it's cold, but the light when the sky was clear is so good that even the woods on the ridge overlooking Golcar stood out in sharp relief. It was a really beautiful morning as Joe and me took a stroll round the garden before lunch.

'Four years from now and you could be an Inspector?' The incredulity oozing from his pores. 'That's some going, Brian. What do you think?'

'Obviously it's tempting. I've always been determined to get to at least sergeant like Dad did. This, I had not anticipated. The money would be good as well. At the moment I think an Inspector earns somewhere in the region of fourteen hundred on promotion.'

'Bearing in mind what you're earning now the money's good, very good. But we're not talking about the money, are we?' Joe smiled and put his hand on my shoulder.

I didn't have to think about that. 'You're right, Joe, it's about me. As you've always said, it's about me.'

'Running a business is running a team. We all have our jobs. So is captaining a rugby team, and you did that bloody well. You've become a good instructor at the club. You managed three years coping with university. Got a 2:1. I read your dissertation. I couldn't understand most of it. What's the difference between that and running a team in police uniform? Eh? I'll bet over ninety percent is pure routine. It's the remainder that can cause trouble. From my experience during the war it's not just about waving a big stick, there is a place for that, but it's more about leadership and fairmindedness.'

'You're right again,' I said.

We stopped at the far end next to the fish pond, 'Look Brian,' he said. 'Forget this accelerated promotion lark for a moment. If you had, say,' he stood rocking his head gently from side-to-side. 'Five years in service and you knew what was what, promotion would be a change in approach because you'd become a supervisor. It wouldn't be the big step you're envisaging now because you'd have the experience. It's that, and what others will think ...' Joe paused, smiled and put his arm round my shoulders. 'Here's something for you to consider. I don't think you asked for my advice when you were sleeping with Pamela, and you didn't have any experience in that field either. Go give 'em hell, son.'

What else could I do but laugh?

Lucy wandered up to join us. 'All right, what's the big confab about.'

Joe as diplomatic as ever smiled at us both. 'I'll leave you two to chat.'

'Thanks Joe,' I said and faced Lucy, smiled and put both hands up in front. 'Now, don't get angry. Joe is a bit more dispassionate than you.'

The was an answering smile behind her eyes as she frowned. 'And?'

Her expression softened and eyes widened as I explained. 'That's wonderful,' she said and threw her arms round my neck. 'You deserve it.'

'Whoa. I've only been in the job a couple of months. This is about what could be and it's not going to be easy. I can't sit my promotion exams until I've been in the job for two years. A lot of water has to flow under a lot of bridges before that happens.'

'But you will pass. I know it.'

"Darling, I stand a chance. But nothing is carved in stone.'

Fifty

Sitting round the kitchen table during lunch I got the third degree about what Joe and I had been discussing. 'You're going to be an inspector in four years? That's brilliant.'

'No, Clive. It's not guaranteed. It's not even a probability. However, it is a possibility. Three years of working harder than I have ever done with no guarantees.'

The 'buts' came thick and fast. I had to agree that I stood the same chance as everyone else.

After lunch we all sat in the lounge before we made tracks for Boston Spa. I winked at Lucy and handed Mum that envelope. 'That's wonderful, love,' she said and gave me a bigger hug than she had the last time, passing the envelope to Joe, accompanied by calls of, 'What's it say?' from the girls and Clive.

Joe cleared his throat:

Chief Constable's Commendation

Police Constable 547 Blake is hereby commended for his dedication, courage and presence of mind in effecting the arrest of a violent criminal.

Signed
R. Barton
Chief Constable

'There's also one from the local magistrate's court for the same thing.'

The row they made you'd have thought that I'd rescued the Queen from a burning building. 'Yes,' I insisted. 'I told you four weeks ago.'

'You didn't say that you'd got commendations from the chief constable and the magistrates, did you?' from Jennifer; immediately echoed by Frankie, Anne and Clive.

This was ridiculous. 'I only received it this morning. Give me a chance.'

Within the next sixty seconds the girls had decided the certificates should hang in the hall alongside the other, where everyone could see them.

Lucy held her hand out. 'Excuse me,' she said. 'Could I see?'

'Oh,' said Jennifer. 'You're going to take them with you, aren't you.'

I nodded. 'All three.'

'For Liz to see?' asked Anne

I nodded again.

'Well, when Liz has seen them can we borrow them until you're married?' That was Jennifer.

Lucy nodded. 'I suppose so,' I said, which set them all off again.

As I was leaving I told Anne she was getting a letter from the Chief Constable about the incident at Tadcaster. They could sort that out between them

If anything, the greetings concerning news about the Special Course were even more effusive at Boston Spa than they had been at Salendine Nook.

Lucy and me hi-jacked the sofa. Chatting about the Special Course. Lucy, half-sitting half-lying to my right and resting her left elbow on the sofa backrest began to trace an outline of my right ear with the nail of her left forefinger. It was driving me to distraction.

'Lucy, please don't. I can't concentrate,' she knew exactly what she was doing and my brain was reacting as before.

'Good,' she said, and did it again.

'Please?'

'Just winding you up for tonight,' she whispered and did it again. An even more pleasant ripple ran down my spine. 'Get used to it,' she drawled.

I grabbed her hand. 'Stoppit.' I hissed through gritted teeth.

She looked mildly annoyed. 'Spoilsport,' she said and grinned. 'I was enjoying that.'

'Come on Lucy,' Liz smiled as she got out of her chair. 'Help me get the tea ready. He'll still be here afterwards.'

With a reluctant sigh Lucy followed her mother, as she reached the door she turned and winked.

Sunday tea was light: sandwiches and cakes which gave me the opportunity to hand *the* envelope to Liz. It was noisy.

As usual when we were at Lucy's we went to bed at ten. I put my arms round her. 'Now you've got me wound up are you going to behave?'

'No,' she began to unfasten my belt. 'This feels like a bad swelling. Do you want me to get rid of it?'

'Not yet,' I unfastened her bra, slid her pants down and pushed her back onto the bed. I leant over her kissed her gently and worked my way south paying attention to both breasts.

She grabbed my hair pushing me in the right direction.

We had a memorable night. I even got some sleep.

Fifty-One

The next morning I had to attend Hecton Magistrate's Court for the hearing against Alderman Cuthbert Wainwright. The pillar of society referred to by Inspector Jeavons. Pencils poised the gentlemen of the Press were there. We were first on the list. Mrs Brocklesby once again in charge.

The offence was leaving a vehicle in a dangerous position. He could be disqualified. A situation he brought on himself. The Clerk to the Court asked Wainwright to stand and confirm his identity and his guilty plea. This was the first time he had had to attend court. He looked embarrassed as he complied.

Inspector Felton read out the statement of facts. The Magistrates asked Wainwright if he had anything to say. His solicitor, Mr Reeve, made a few points: Busy businessman. Minor traffic offence etc. He had four previous traffic convictions, he was given a final warning and fined £10 on each offence and his licence endorsed.

The Alderman and Mr Reeve were leaving court. The latter saw me and raised his hand in acknowledgement. I returned the greeting. Wainwright followed suit and saw me sitting there in full uniform. He was under the false impression that I had resigned and looked as if his head was about to explode. Tough.

Back at the nick I was summoned to see Inspector Yates. He was quite amused at the Alderman's experience before the Bench. We discussed his mentoring programme. Not forgetting attachments to various departments including Force Control and the Forensic Science Laboratory at Harrogate.

An hour later the Chief Superintendent telephoned. First, he congratulated me and then asked to be put through to the Inspector. Thirty seconds later the inspector galloped downstairs. '0900 tomorrow, Chief Super's office.'

I called Liz and arranged to go over after work.

It was a fine evening so Lucy and I went for a walk followed by continuation of her plan to make me bandy-legged.

Fifty-Two

0900. I was ushered into Chief Superintendent Williams' office. What a difference from the last time. He was on the telephone and gestured for me to sit.

Call concluded he walked round the desk as I rose and shook my hand. 'Somewhat different from the last time you were here, Blake.'

'Yes sir, I was just thinking the same.'

It was a short meeting, but one he wanted to carry out face to face. We had a short discussion about the trial and about the effect on me. That smacked of Inspector Yates' concerns.

Then the main subject. I had been the subject of a case conference between the Chief Constable, himself and Inspector Yates. Apart from my degree, enquiries had been made with the Dean at East Midlands University. My exploits at Pannal and Westleigh. Last but by no means least my attitude towards authority. Meaning my volatile reaction towards Inspector Jeavons. I had been well and truly dissected,

The Chief Superintendent apologised for literally dropping this 'small matter' on my toes. He said that had they not been entirely sure that I was made of the right material we would not be having this conversation. I would have the full support of the Force. Any relevant expense including books, travelling, accommodation etc. would be met by them. That took a weight off my mind. One final point mentioned earlier by Inspector Yates. Stand up for what you believe in, but be selective.

He spent a few minutes discussing my pending marriage. That was it. I was on my bike and detoured to Hecton. I walked in through the front door as Inspector Meadowcroft was leaving his office. He was delighted. 'Brian Blake,' he declared. 'I've just had a call from the Chief Super. In a few years I'll be calling you, sir.' That let the cat well and truly out of the bag.

'Chuffin' 'ell, Brian, are you goin' on the bloody Special Course?'

The Inspector rounded on the unfortunate desk clerk, Pc Jack Briggs.

'First and last warning, Briggs, less of the language. As to your comment? That, is yet to be determined. First you have to put the work in and pass your promotion exam. If you're interested it's time you got started.'

'It came as a real bombshell, sir,' I said as we sat drinking tea in the canteen. 'I got this message to see Inspector Yates yesterday, that was it. I don't mind admitting it, I was staggered.'

'You'll be fine, Brian. Because of your father you've got that drive that very few have. In the few weeks you've been in the job you've proved you can do it. All that's lacking is experience. That and the knowledge will come together. I'll be honest, I know very little about the Special Course, but I'll lay a £1 to a pinch of snuff that you've nothing to fear from anybody. Yes, there'll be those who've been in the job a bit longer. Who know a bit more, but that's temporary. You mark my words.'

He was just as delighted when I told him about me and Lucy.

His expression changed. 'Er, before you go.'

I burst out laughing. 'Manville-Jones?'

He grimaced and nodded. 'Er, yes.'

I answered his questions.

'I suppose you were told never to mention it under pain of the Official Secrets Act.'

'True, sir. But the trial is over. The only thing that I knew that could fall under the Act was that the Security Service was involved.'

I got back to Westleigh just in time for my meal break.

I left the office armed with a complaint of criminal damage from the local rag, the Westleigh Guardian, just round the corner from the railway station. Guess what I found outside Wainwrights? He wasn't pleased. Not one iota. To be honest he was blazing mad. By the time he calmed down he had a small audience who found his angry little dance amusing. I have no doubt that he wouldn't remember anything I said. I reported him for the same offences anyway and put the ticket to produce his documents in his hand.

He was still wearing that bracelet, which caught the sun as he was remonstrating. 'What are you staring at?' he demanded.

I mentioned his bracelet.

He lifted his wrist up so that I could see. 'Take your covetous eyes away, constable,' he said, almost spitting the words in my face. 'This was part of my great-grandfather's Albert. He was the Mayor of Westleigh and my mother had this bracelet made for my 21st Birthday. I *never* take it off.'

I thought the bracelet ugly and effeminate and had no 'covetous' eyes for it. It was pointless to continue the discussion. I bid him good day and left him spitting feathers. I knew that if he turned up at the nick he'd get short change from Inspector Yates.

I took details of the damage from the office manageress of the Guardian; some clown had been daubing paint on the rear doors. A minor damage report and not a crime. One piece of paper instead of several.

Submitting the paperwork for the damage and Wainwright's offences took less than thirty minutes. Right on time I made my escape and set off to the jewellers in the Imperial Arcade to buy a watch. There was a complication. Not with the watch, that would be engraved within the next day or two. The problem was the brooch I bought earlier and gave to Lucy. She wore it all the time. It wasn't paste at all. It had been put into that display by mistake. He offered me £30 to buy it back. I'd paid 9/6d. When I told him I'd given it to my fiancé he offered me £35 plus a discount off the watch. I told him that I would ask her, however I doubted if she would want to sell it. He gave me the discount anyway, which was a good thing because I'd spent more than I could really afford and every little helps.

That evening I spent reading and re-reading the schedule that Inspector Yates had given me. I began to understand the magnitude of what was in store. Lucy rang at eight o'clock- I was neglecting her. I didn't mention the brooch, there was time for that later.

We chatted until nine before retiring to our celibate beds. Roll on New Year's Eve.

Fifty-Three

Wednesday. Two days before Christmas I had a trip to the Training School, Bishopgarth, Wakefield. From the outside it was a Victorian mansion that wouldn't have been out of place in a story by Edgar Alan Poe. Inside, the brooding atmosphere did nothing to lessen the effect.

My route was upstairs where I was introduced to Deputy Commandant, Detective Superintendent Hamlet LLB, who dressed and sounded like the Professor of Classics at East Midlands and nothing like a police officer.

He closed the file marked Pc 547 Blake on his desk and pointed to the two chairs across his desk. 'Interesting, Blake,' he said with a thin smile. 'DI Moore will be your tutor. Pay attention, learn and we might just be able to make something of you.' He nodded. That was it.

'You should take Mr Hamlet's comments as high praise, Blake,' he said as we left the office. 'For a probationer to get through his door?'

He showed me round the complex, which included the new and very modern 'A' block: three external classrooms and a fully equipped lecture theatre.

I left with a set of questions taken from the Junior Detective Course exam. My answers to be submitted by the third week in January. An extended period because of the Christmas holidays. I hope they didn't expect me to do clerical work on my honeymoon. A collection of legal reference books would be sent by divisional van to Westleigh.

Next, the Driving School at Crofton, three miles on the Doncaster side of Wakefield. My tutor, Sergeant Jerry Rolands, a Scot with a great sense of humour. An introduction to Chief Inspector Paulson, the Chief Instructor. The tour of the school completed in ten minutes. Once again, I was presented with a set of questions, this time from the final exam of the Road Traffic Law Course.

I was shown duty elsewhere for the whole day. By 1.15pm I was clear and retreated to the flat. I started on the questions from the Driving School. Ten minutes later Sergeant McGill called. The divisional van driver was enroute to the flat with a 'bloody heavy box' addressed to me. Thirty minutes later I had to agree, it was *bloody heavy*.

I invited myself to tea and sleepover at Lucy's taking the question papers with me.

Christmas Eve. Early turn. The usually level-headed citizens decided to buy everything edible on display just in case civilisation came to an end over the weekend.

0915 Meal. Out at 1000 My 1045 point was the bus station kiosk. No problems until traffic from Hecton began to back up blocking access and egress to the bus station. A young lad ran through the civic gardens and shouted. 'There's a lorry broken down blocking the road, Mister.' I waved an acknowledgement as the phone in the call box began to ring. It was Jim Tyndall. 'Report of a lorry snapping a half-shaft near the junction with St Peg Lane, Brian. Have a look-see.'

Pencils poised. 'Something's happening, Jim. Traffic from Hecton is backing-up and there's nothing coming through from Oakenshaw.'

' That's all we need. Sergeant McGill's on his way.'

It was worse. There's a small triangular one-way system in force. Vehicles travelling towards the main road keep to the left along Market Street. Vehicles travelling the other way along George Street. Simple.

A Speedy Fuel delivery tanker carrying 3000 gallons of petrol had snapped a half-shaft turning right from Market Street intending to turn left into St Peg Lane towards Gomersal.

The centre of Westleigh was now a car park. The late turn crew were fetched on early to deal with the operational side of the demands on our time. Pcs were borrowed from surrounding subdivisions to assist with traffic on what was one of the busiest days of the year. The roads in Westleigh were not designed to handle this volume of traffic. At least it wasn't me who dealt with Cuthbert Wainwright.

I got the simple job of controlling traffic in and out of the bottom end of the bus station; much to the chagrin of the bus company when they found out we were using their hallowed ground as an emergency two-way bypass. Any port in a storm.

An hour later another tanker arrived to tranship the load followed by a garage specialising in HGV recovery. Then it began to rain with a vengeance. At least I had my raincoat.

The main winner from this debacle was Gwynne. She owned Happy Days. The café next to the bus station. There was only so long I could resist the aroma of frying bacon.

Jim got away on time. I was second away at 3pm. What a day.

Scheduled to close at two for the holiday, Gwynne closed at 6pm when she ran out of milk.

I called Lucy from the flat, told her that we would see her around ten thirty in the morning. Showered changed and left for Salendine Nook at about five. Traffic was manic. It took me an hour.

It felt strange, all presents wrapped and packed. Not under the tree. We had decided to open them at Lucy's in the morning. The evening mainly watching the tv. Joe and me? We took root in the library. He wanted to know more about the Special Course. Just like old times.

Fifty-Four

Christmas morning. For once the traffic lights were in our favour we arrived twenty minutes early to be met by Lucy. The girls showed their pleasure at our reunion by gathering round, linking arms and squeezing us closer.

Lucy grinned. 'That was nice, do it again.'

I skipped indoors followed by calls of: wimp, misery and spoilsport.

One thing we all noticed was the large marquee and duckboards behind the house; something to do with the one hundred plus guests expected for our combined bash of wedding and Lucy's birthday, next week. The contractors got their dates wrong.

Half an hour later the party was complete as Gerald and Marianne arrived. Coffee, a little something of choice added, except Clive sitting there with a face like a wet weekend and a glass of dandelion and burdock. We put the smile back on his face - present time. To be honest I can't remember every present that was exchanged except there were a lot. Jet brooches for the girls. Joe and Liz received a bottle of Talisker single-malt each from the other family. I didn't realise Liz liked whisky. The Mums silk scarves each. I bought Lucy a watch engraved with her name and date of birth. Clive, inundated with books. For the most part Lucy and I received 'stuff': towels, bedding, kitchen utensils etc. Joe appeared carrying a large heavy looking box and put it on the floor. 'This is from the three of us,' said Mum.

'Come on Brian,' cajoled Anne. 'Open it up.'

Apart from the red ribbon tied round the box it wasn't sealed. When I saw what was inside I was gobsmacked. An Adler office typewriter. Ten reams of paper. Two hundred envelopes and stamps, and enough typewriter ribbons to reach the moon and back. I thanked them all profusely.

Then Lucy sprung her surprise. 'And this is from me,' she said and smiled. She was holding a smaller box. 'And don't say I shouldn't have done, or I'll hit you.'

I looked in the box then at Lucy. 'You shouldn't have done,' I said, she hit me in the chest. 'Thank you, it's perfect.' She'd bought me an Adler portable. If I remember rightly almost as expensive as its big brother.

'That's for you to take to Bramshill,' she said and smiled. 'Then you can type me a letter every day you're away.' What could I say?

'All right everybody,' said Liz. 'Have all the presents been handed out?'

There was a chorus of 'Yeses'.

For the first time in my life I'd had to borrow from Mum to be able to buy Lucy's watch; the look on her face was worth every penny. Thank goodness for overtime.

I told Lucy about my conversation with the jeweller and her brooch suggesting that she get it valued.

The two Mums turned and looked back as they entered the hallway. 'Just look at them, Dorothy,' said Liz as she smiled at Lucy and Brian. 'It takes you back, doesn't it?'

'It certainly does, Liz. Different world back then,' she laughed. 'Just fancy, cavorting round in front of strangers, even in private, whatever next?'

Liz nodded. 'How they would have tut-tutted and blamed the parents for permitting it ... Do you mind me asking, when did you meet your husband?'

'Douglas?' She cast her mind back and smiled. 'That would be, August 1936. I was eighteen, I worked for my aunt. She had a stall in Huddersfield market selling biscuits and cakes. Douglas was twenty-two. He'd been a policeman for three years before joining the RAF. He looked great in uniform, but didn't they all. He was taller than Brian is, black hair and blue eyes.

I'd see him looking at nearby stalls until I wasn't serving, then he'd bob over buy some biscuits and give them to the kids that used to hang around. There was real poverty round there in those days. Down the road from the market there were rows of small terrace houses, many not much better than hovels. Most of them occupied by the Irish navvies that came across to work on the railways or the canals. From the look of those kids they hadn't had a square meal in weeks. Buying the biscuits was his excuse to get chatting. It took a while before he asked me out on a date. Dad let us get married twelve months later.

At the start of the war he was shipped off to France and I moved down south and got a job in the NAAFI. He was one of the last to get away when the Germans invaded and insisted that I come back north because of the invasion scare. Brian was born in 1942.

But the night Douglas was murdered? I dealt with that pain a long time ago. The memory that I retain is the morning after and Brian calling the vicar a liar; well, to be honest he screamed at him.'

'Brian did?' was the incredulous reply.

Dorothy nodded. 'Yes, he asked the vicar if he'd been naughty. The vicar looked puzzled and told him that he'd been a good boy. Brian pointed out what the vicar preached to the children at Sunday School. If they were good and said their prayers, God would grant them. Of course Brian prayed that Douglas would come home. So, with all the logic of a distraught eight-year-old he pointed out that the vicar had said he was good, and God hadn't granted his prayers. Brian threw what he'd preached back in his face and called him a liar.

The vicar looked well and truly sick, didn't know how to answer that. Brian's been an atheist ever since. Never set foot in a church either; and, it made me think.

'No problem there Dorothy, we're not a religious family. I think that Lucy would marry him in a dustbin.'

'That's good. Brian carried a lot of anger. Joe's done a great job in helping him to get sorted out. The result is what you see, although meeting Lucy seems to have done something to his head.'

'That works both ways,' Liz laughed. 'She's never been like this before. Driving me scatty.'

'Sleeping together doesn't appear to have done them much harm either. Although finding out came as a bit of a shock.'

'Well, they're both sensible and getting married in a week. And Joe? you met him through introducing Brian to Karate?'

Dorothy nodded. 'I used to wait for Brian and kept an eye on the girls for Joe. They were a delight. He and I got on really well and I have to admit,' she smiled, 'that I fell in love with him after about six months when I saw how calm and patient he was. All the kids thought he was great. I was sure he felt the same about me but never took the next step. One day when the kids were occupied elsewhere, he called in for a cuppa. It was our first passionate kiss. I took him by the hand and led him upstairs. He didn't complain.

Liz laughed. 'Fantastic. Well done you.'

Dorothy grinned in return. 'I hadn't looked at anyone since Douglas. Almost two years. Three years for him since Geraldine. We had a lot of catching up to do.'

'And?'

Dorothy's smile said it all. 'But how did you and Bill get together?'

'He threw a half pint of beer over me,' replied Liz, poker-faced.

'He didn't?'

'Not quite. Dad owned a garage. Before the war we always took the Manx TT as holidays. As a result we got to know many of the riders. I'd seen Bill there with his family and I knew they sold motorbikes. He was a handsome devil, a good rider, young and slim. A bit of a jack-the-lad. My dad wasn't keen. I liked him, but dad... It was around what had been TT time, May 1942 we took a weekend at Scarborough. It was full of children evacuated from Hull and the north-east, poor kids. We were in the hotel bar and Bill was there with a few friends. We made eye contact. He was walking back to their table, tripped over the carpet and the beer slopped over my blouse. He was very cheeky and offered to sponge it down. I thought Dad was going to have a fit.'

'I'll bet. Was it deliberate?'

'The trip? No, purely accidental. He got the hotel manager to give him our home address and wrote to me. I answered and that was that. Nothing dramatic like yours, and in the circumstances I think you've done a wonderful job bringing up five children. But losing Bill the way we did was a real shock especially with the talk of espionage and drugs. It's still not settled.'

At one o'clock we sat down to a Christmas dinner as good as Mum's, the main difference being, instead of Christmas pudding Liz served an Italian dessert, *Tiramisu:* Cream, coffee and alcohol. Not long after we left the table Clive became giggly, he'd had a second helping of *Tiramisu*. Italy, it seems, was to play a large part in our lives.

The drizzle that had begun shortly after we arrived stopped about three. A setting watery sun showed its face. To get a bit of fresh air Liz suggested we take a turn around the garden. I'd thought before that it looked like a small park. It was almost seven acres and far too big for Bill and Liz to have managed on their own. I'll bet it was beautiful in spring and summer.

There were twenty-five tables stacked in the marquee along with well over a hundred chairs. No doubt the remainder of the equipment would be along later.

Fifty-Five

'Where are you going on your honeymoon, Lucy?' said Jennifer. 'Is it London and then Italy?'

'Yes, a few days in London in January then ten in Italy at Easter.'

A retreat to the house became the order of the day when it began to snow. The remainder of the afternoon was sedentary. It was the quietest Christmas Day afternoon I'd ever spent. Joe, me and Gerald talking shop in Bill's office. The five younger ladies talking and listening to Beatles music. Liz and Mum in the kitchen. Clive had his nose in a natural history book.

Tea was a smorgasbord of sandwiches, cake and something called *pannacotta* - cooked cream with a burnt caramel sauce, and some beautifully light lemon-flavoured sponge drops. Neapolitan in origin and made by Lucy. This looked promising.

The *pannacotta* was superb. I was replete. I'd just polished off the last spoonful. 'I'll get fat if you're making these all the time,' I protested, much to everyone's amusement.

'No, you won't,' chided Lucy. 'Don't be silly.' Then she leaned across and whispered in my ear. 'It's like sex, a little and very often.'

Lucy mentioning sex in the kitchen filled with family caught me completely by surprise. She sat back in her chair and howled with laughter as I felt myself starting to blush.

'Lucy, what on earth did you say to him? Look at his face. Brian, you're blushing,' said Jennifer, laughing at Lucy laughing at yours truly

'No, I am not,' I protested.

'Oh yes you are,' confirmed Anne. 'Lucy, what did you say?'

Lucy just about managed to stop laughing and motioned to Anne. 'I'll whisper it to you,' she said. Hopefully not the same as she whispered to me.

'That's not fair,' said Anne looking nonplussed as Lucy sat back laughing like a drain once again.

'What did she say, Anne?' demanded Frankie.

'Mind your own business,' said Anne giving the still laughing Lucy a sideways look.

'No, come on, Anne,' said Jennifer, echoed by Frankie. 'What did she say?'

'That's it. Lucy told me to mind my own business.'

'You're not going to tell us?' was the chorus as they rounded on Lucy.

'Nope,' Lucy confirmed with a grin.

'See what I mean, Dorothy? Seeing Brian blush like that, I'll bet Lucy was whispering something about sex.'

'Brian said she was direct. I think you're maybe right.'

'Oh she is. She's been like this since the day she woke up in hospital.'

No amount of scowls or cajoling would shift her. Eventually they gave up.

It wasn't long before everyone had had enough. Everything cleared away except the wine and Coca-Cola for Clive. Liz announced. 'We don't have any chopsticks yet, but we do have drinking straws dried peas and saucers, so, if you want to play a few games?' Off we went again.

It was Lucy who told me something that I should have realised long ago. She had just nipped upstairs to look for a game, when she came down Clive was sitting on the stairs. 'Is there room for a little one?' she asked. 'Budge up.'

Clive smiled and slid to one side as Lucy parked herself.

'What's the matter, Clive? It's not like you to look miserable, and it is Christmas. Cheer up.'

He looked up at Lucy. 'Everybody's leaving,' he said. 'Brian's gone already and you'll be getting married in a week.'

'Yes, we will, but we'll still be back. I'll be back more than ever on Saturday's when I begin to learn Karate.'

'I know that, you're ok.'

'Oh, thank you, you're not so bad yourself.'

Clive smiled. 'Anne's got Neil. Jennifer is marrying the Dork. Soon there'll be no-one except Mum and me. The house will be empty.'

Changing tack Lucy referred to Clive's comment about Tom. 'That sounds serious,' she said. 'Now, is Tom a Dork because he's simply a Dork, or is he a Dork because he's marrying Jennifer?'

Lucy smiled as a broad grin split Clive's face. 'No, he's always been a Dork, except Dad doesn't see it.'

'Why?'

'I don't trust him, he's snidey.'

'Have you said anything to your dad?'

He nodded. 'Dad just thinks it's because I don't like him.'

'How about I have a word with Brian, see what he says?'

'Ok,' he nodded.

'Come on then, let's go play Beetle.'

They left after ten. We went up at half past. Lucy discovered she wasn't pregnant.

'What's the matter with me?'

I put my arms round her and kissed her forehead. 'Probably nothing, love. Have a word with your Mum, see what she says and if it doesn't happen next time go and have a word with your Doctor.'

Liz had an answer to my problem. With stopping overnight I couldn't get any studying done. I could borrow what had been Bill's Bonneville, a 650cc Roadster, and fetch my books back here. Bill's leathers would fit. I had a volunteer navigator.

It was a monster. Max 120mph.

What a bike.

The ride via the scenic route. Tadcaster-Garforth-Oulton-Wakefield-Dewsbury-Mirfield. 34 miles. A few miles longer than via Leeds but a more pleasant trip and, fifteen minutes shorter. Lucy rode my bike on the return trip. The round trip took 90 minutes. This was the first time she had ridden anything over 250cc.

Lucy commandeered Bill's office to double as my study. Books at the back of the desk: Oakes Magisterial Formulist, Stones Justices Manual - both volumes, Kenny's outlines of Criminal Law, and one called The Blue Book – the manual of the Junior Detective Course. Apart from The Blue book they cost a small fortune

I got my large pad and writing implements. Lucy furnished me with a fresh pot of tea and some of her little lemony sponges. I wrote out the first question from the crime paper. Read it three times. Wrote down what I could call to mind and checked it against the Blue Book. It had taken over an hour but it looked all right.

Fifty-Six

Monday 29th December 1964. Three days to go. 1100. Liz would be giving Lucy away.

I had toyed with asking John Bradbury to be my best man, but in reality it had to be Joe.

All replies to the invitations had been received long ago. We were expecting in excess of 140 guests in the marquee. The contractors with their ex-army field kitchen plus the sound-people were already setting up.

Lucy and Liz had mentioned more than once that Cousin Raymond would be there. Who he was I hadn't a clue and neither of them were saying.

That week Inspector Yates had me on office duty where I shouldn't be able to get into too much trouble.

I spent Wednesday night at Salendine Nook and didn't sleep a wink, or so it felt.

It was very busy. There were more couples getting married today than I anticipated. And, a lot more guests heading my way than I supposed. I caught John, Christine and the boys and took them through. 11am approached, our guests settled.

One of the Spartans raised a laugh. 'Still time to do a runner, Brian.'

I grinned by return. 'No chance.'

Lucy was getting married in white. As she said. "I was a virgin before we had sex and It's sod all to do with anyone else."

Right on time she was there. She looked stunning. Her dress? Pure white, off-the-shoulder and knee-length. The girls in the palest of yellows.

Liz looked elegant. Don't ask me to describe what she was wearing. I didn't notice.

Lucy stopped alongside me and winked. 'Too late now,' she was exuding a confidence that had been increasing from the first time we had sex. Almost as if the death of her father and our relationship had unlocked her true personality.

It was a simple service concluded in no-time, or so it seemed. There was a buffet lunch at one of the town centre hotels.

Arm-in-arm we walked towards the door. I nearly fainted. Standing to our right, adjacent to the door was Mr Ray Barton QPM, my Chief Constable. 'Why's the Chief here,' I whispered. 'Did you invite him?'

There was a wicked grin. 'That's cousin Raymond.'

'What? You saw him at Pannal and didn't say anything?'

'I didn't think you'd want everyone to know.'

'Good point. Thanks.' We stopped. 'Good morning, sir. Mrs Barton. Lucy's just told me. Do you think it might be politic if we referred to you as a Vernon family friend?'

'I think that's a very good idea,' replied a smiling Mrs Barton. 'We can chat later.'

We took time for photographs on the Town Hall steps. There was some applause and even an unofficial camera or two. Plenty of calls of 'congratulations' and 'Good Luck', even one of 'Barmy bugger. Why buy a book when the library's full.'

It was a five minute walk to the hotel and the buffet. There were the briefest of speeches. And one from me – 'On behalf of my wife and myself.' And thanks to all those who had attended, with a reminder to come to Boston Spa for 2pm for refreshments and 7pm for food. Then it was time to eat and mingle. Lucy hadn't lost her appetite. John Bradbury's first question concerned the attendance of the Chief. 'You never told Brian he was a friend of your parents?' he said to Lucy.

'No. What would you have said if it had leaked out?'

John had a wry smile. 'Ok, fair enough.'

There were several envelopes passed by people who couldn't make our evening bash. They went into my jacket pocket.

Liz announced that the stadium would be open for visitors from 2.30pm.

Guests began making their excuses and leaving around 1pm. We did the same and travelled with Liz.

'Joe, She's nearly nineteen. Neil's a grand lad we don't have a problem with them getting married. And besides, I don't remember you protesting the first time we had sex. You didn't use anything.'

'True,' he blustered. 'But you caught me by surprise.'

'Oh did I?' she replied wide-eyed and tapped Joe on the chest. 'Pull the other one. If you weren't sure why didn't you say, no? Look, it came as a shock to me when Liz told me about Lucy and Brian. We've got to trust them. I'll have a word with Anne later.'

Joe sighed. 'All right, you win.'

There were no visitors, yet. The door was locked. I'd helped Lucy out of her dress and unfastened her bra.

The knocking on the door put paid to that. It was Anne. 'Come on you two. You have some visitors.'

I rested my forehead on hers and sighed. 'Ah well Mrs Blake. Plenty of time tonight.'

'All right Anne,' Lucy called. 'We're on our way.'

'Sorry,' was the plaintive response.

'It could have been worse,' I said.

'It could. A few seconds later.'

'How is it,' said Lucy knocking my hands away. 'You can always manage to unfasten my bra but you can never manage to fasten it?'

'I don't know. Perhaps men aren't built that way.'

'A likely tale,' she laughed. 'Well, can you manage to zip my dress?'

'I'll try,' I slid my arms round her waist and nuzzled her neck.

'Stoppit,' she hissed and grabbed my hands.

I did it again. 'Different now, isn't it?' I let go and finished zipping the dress.

She spun round trying not to laugh. 'You rat. Just you wait.'

I smiled and wagged my forefinger. 'Naughty. Love, honour and obey.'

She fixed me with a steely eye. 'I didn't say obey.'

I grinned. 'Oh no, you didn't did you?'

A wrinkled nose was the answer.

Fifty-Seven

The marquee looked superb. Drapes that looked as if they were redundant parachutes looped across the tent giving the appearance of the home of some desert sheikh. Heaters in the corners in full flow. A couple of chandeliers in the centre of the ridge and small lights strung around the walls giving the marquee a subdued and intimate atmosphere. Every table was laid. Small T-lights in holders the shape of hurricane lamps in the centre of each, in the process of being lit as the light faded.

There was a steady stream of neighbours and guests welcomed into the house and directed to the marquee for tea and coffee. Cards and presents placed on a table set aside for the purpose.

In front of the podium, where the band would be playing, a small square table with a lace cover that brushed the floor. In the centre was our wedding cake. A three storey confection in fancy icing.

Mum and Joe had discussed what they were going to give us. They suggested the flat we occupied if it was for sale. It was. The envelope marked Mum & Joe. Liz had given us an envelope the word CHEQUE written across the front. The amount? Not a clue.

Anne and Neil wandered across when the crush had eased. Anne gave us a nervous smile. 'When I knocked, Were you ...?'

Lucy giggled. 'About to. A few seconds later?'

Anne grimaced. 'Sorry.'

'It's ok. Brian will just have to work harder tonight.'

'Thanks.'

Lucy changed her attention to Anne and Neil. 'You two looking forward to London?'

They both nodded. Neil blushed.

'I was talking about The Tower of London and Mother Goose,' protested Lucy.

'No, you were not,' I said. 'You're embarrassing them.'

'Don't be,' said Lucy. 'It's how we all got here. Plus, Professor Lightman said it was part of our therapy. It works. It might help you. I remember from Pride and Prejudice Jane Austen used the word anoesis, although not about sex. I think that's perfect.

'Here, I've got something for you since you decided not to use the flat.' She passed Anne a parcel from the back of the table. 'You might as well have these. We don't need them anymore.'

'Are they what I think they are?'

'Probably.'

'I wouldn't unwrap them here if I were you, Anne. Mum's just walked in.'

Neil gave me a puzzled look. I nodded. He took the package.

'Dad found out about our plans.'

'We didn't say anything, Anne,'

'I'm sure you didn't, Lucy. But somehow Dad found out. He wasn't pleased.'

'Perhaps he overheard you on the phone when you made your reservation. Put two and two together but waited.'

'That's because you're his daughter,' I said. 'He knew about me and Pamela, and Lucy. And didn't bat an eyelid. He's all right now?'

'Mum had a word when she arrived. It was embarrassing.'

'Just use what we gave you. Brian has another box we won't use.'

'They should last us a couple of weeks.'

'As long as that?'

'You better have these,' said Anne handing Lucy an envelope and a gift wrapped box. 'From what you've said I think you'll like it. Neil thinks it's a bit soon.'

Lucy lifted the pink and blue checked woollen rectangle from the box and shook it open. 'No, it's perfect,' she said.

I was puzzled. 'It's a bit small, isn't it,' I said.

'I thought you were intelligent. It's a cot blanket, you idiot.'

'Oh. In that case it's perfect, thank you.'

Fifty-Eight

The earlier guests were gone. The invitees for the evening bash trickling in. Gerald and Marianne arrived and were directed to our table. To everyone's amusement Lucy had tied a sign to the marquee entrance:

PLEASE NOTE.
TO ALL POLICE OFFICERS
NO TALKING SHOP!

That would stifle conversation.

The caterers referred to it as a carvery. They carved the meats: beef, pork and turkey and then the guess helped themselves to the vegetables – if people hadn't had enough. They had excelled themselves. When the food was finished, Joe, as Master of Ceremonies, took over and introduced our family.

One problem was that Tom, Jennifer's fiancée had cried off. He had to go to a family do, which was understandable in the circumstances. Clive was pleased. He really did not like him.

Liz, as the mother of the Bride, created a bit of a stir when she told everybody our history. Made nice noises about me and how glad she was that I was taking responsibility for her one and only daughter etc.

I gave my second speech of the day which had to commence with, 'On behalf of my wife and myself.' It took a full minute for the applause and the cheers to die down. Mum told me later that even Frankie had joined in. I cracked a few jokes, clean of course. Thanked everybody especially Liz concluding by raising a toast to the bridesmaids, then presenting them with their gifts – small silver lockets on filigree chains. Joe responded on behalf of the Bridesmaids. It was a real family affair and told the story from the day that we met, getting in quite a few laughs at my expense on the way. Even mentioned the phone call after the accident when my boots were on fire. Mum thinking that my roast trotters might have been on the menu. It was a good speech with plenty of warmth and humour.

We cut the cake; well we stabbed the bottom of the three layers. The top layer by custom was taken and to be used to celebrate the birth of our first-born. Then we let the photographers and the band loose.

It was 7pm. Liz rapped the champagne glass in her hand. The chatter died. 'Good evening. If you are an adult and haven't got a glass containing alcohol raise your hands.' There were half a dozen. 'Ladies and gentlemen. A toast. The happy couple.'

'The happy couple,' Then someone added. 'And may all your troubles be little ones.' Which got a bigger cheer.

'Cheers to that,' said Lucy. 'The sooner the better.'

'You'll change your mind after the first one is born, Lucy.'

'We'll see,' she said.'

I don't know how many guests were there but there were more than I expected. Still we worked the room speaking to as many as we could.

'Brian?'

It was Bob Percival and his wife from Westleigh.

'The chief's over there,' he said and pointed. 'Are you related?'

'No, he's a friend of the Vernon's. Has been for years.'

'Ok. Seems a bit odd being at a do with him present.'

'Don't worry about it.'

It was good to see Jennifer dancing with one of the other guests. She was hacked off by Tom's absence. At least it took her mind off him.

Fifty-Nine

Lucy clung to my right arm. 'Can we get some fresh air?'
'You ok?'

She nodded. 'Just a bit peaky.'

'Not pregnant?' I said with a hopeful smile.

'No,' she shook her head and returned the smile. ' Just need some air.'

There was no-one about as we walked through the kitchen into the hallway. Seconds later Tom's strangled tones could be heard coming from the lounge.

'You little bastard. Wait 'til I get off this bloody floor.'

'What's Tom doing? He was supposed to be attending a family do.'

The lounge door opened and a frightened Clive appeared. 'BRIAN.' he shouted at the top of his voice. 'Oh.'

Clive didn't do frightened.

I pushed passed him into the lounge. Lucy put her arm round Clive's shoulders. If it hadn't been for the fact that Clive was scared it would have been funny. Tom was over six feet and a strong man, dressed in black tie, lying on the floor by the sofa cupping his balls with both hands.

'What happened?' I demanded.

'This little shit kicked me in the knackers,' he wailed.

'Watch your language, Tom. I wasn't talking to you. Clive?'

'I was going to the bathroom and I heard a noise. I thought it might be you two. I came in and Tom was putting something in his right-hand jacket pocket. When he saw me he put his finger to his lips.'

'That's bollocks. I've stolen nowt.'

'Be quiet,' I snapped. 'I won't tell you again. Go on, Clive.'

Clive stepped up beside me. 'He had something in his left hand as well, looked like a bunch of keys. He tried to barge passed me so I tried to stop him with a *kyobu geri,* but he was too quick and I was a bit low.'

I had to smile. 'So it seems,' I said.

Still in pain Tom lay there. He was about to say something but thought better of it.

'Anything missing, Lucy,' I said.

She had a quick glance round the room. 'There should be a small silver photo frame on that occasional table by the book case, it's a photo of my grandfather. At the moment I can't spot anything else.'

'Ok, go and find your Mum and Joe. Clive you stay here.' Before I could say anything else she was gone. 'Right, you, let's have a look.' I knelt on the floor by Tom's side and put my hand in his right-hand pocket. 'Well, what have we here,' I said as I pulled the photo frame into the light. 'Are you going to claim this is yours, or are you going to tell the truth?'

'Piss off.'

I demonstrated how painful things might get with a nerve hold if he didn't behave himself. I completed the search which produced the small brooch that I bought for Lucy. I held it up. 'And this?' I said. This time there was no comment neither a trace of any keys.

Before I could do or say anything else there was a kerfuffle outside as Lucy, followed by Liz, Joe, the girls, the Spartan males and about a dozen coppers crowded in. For the time being confusion reigned. Liz glared at the prostrate Tom. 'What the Hell is going on?' she said.

It was noisy. Clive told what had happened. I told what I had found, or not, in the case of the keys that Clive had seen.

Tom was lucky he wasn't strung up.

Jennifer was almost in tears.

Joe sacked him on the spot.

Lucy was furious. The brooch had been in the top drawer of her bedside table.

Neil and I moved the sofa where Tom was lying and there were the keys; he'd managed to slide them beneath the sofa in the confusion when Lucy and I arrived.

Lucy, and the girls went upstairs to check if anything else was missing. Liz now in possession of the office keys went to check. I asked Tom how long he had been here, in the house. 'About three minutes before this little angel barged in,' he said, nodding at Clive.

Jennifer was first back. 'How could you?' she said dabbing her eyes. 'You promised me that was all behind you.'

'I did it for us, babe,' he pleaded. 'Put some money together so we can get married.'

Jennifer's face was like thunder. 'Marry you?' She spat the words at him. 'After this? You've got a screw loose.'

'Don't worry. A piddlin' bit o'breakin', six months I'll be out.'

'Is he for real?' Inspector Meadowcroft was right behind me. 'Who goes thieving in a house where there are a couple of dozen police officers?'

'He does,' I said and laughed. 'And he's got his timing wrong. It's after 9pm. This is burglary in a dwelling house not housebreaking. Tom, you're going to the assize. But you don't drive so how did you get here?'

Tom sat there the blood draining from his face.

'I was wondering that,' said Jennifer. 'Oh, his brother's got a pick-up.'

'How many are you with?'

Tom said nothing.

I looked at him again. 'You haven't come all the way from Huddersfield in black tie on the off chance of a few things to stick in your pockets. What are you after?'

It was Vance who reacted first. 'Christ, I'll bet they're after the bloody bikes.'

En mass the Spartans followed by the coppers made a dash for the door, followed by Joe and me. I just heard Anne shout, 'You look after Tom, Jennifer. Come on Frankie they need some help.'

'Where do you think you're going,' Mum shouted at the girl's backs as they disappeared through the door.

'Out,' replied Anne.

'Not you, young man,' said Liz taking hold of Clive by the shoulders as he attempted to follow. 'You're going nowhere. You've done your bit. Without your intervention who knows what might have happened.'

Clive pulled a face, snorted and then relaxed as Mum took charge. 'Come on, Clive, let's go and have a drink, we'll come back when they've caught them.'

With the cheek of the Devil he said. 'Can I have a glass of champagne?'

'All right,' Mum agreed, laughing, 'but a small one and, I mean one.'

Cousin Raymond walked across to the telephone, dialled Force Control and spoke to the Duty Officer.

Jennifer ripped off her engagement ring, held Tom's nose and flicked the ring to the back of his throat and then rammed the heel of her hand under his chin. 'Swallow,' she ordered. 'If you want to breathe again, swallow.'

Sixty

We knew nothing of this. We knew nothing of the snow either. It was coming down thick and fast, big fluffy flakes that were beginning to build up on the lawns and as slush on the driveway. The Spartans might have been brilliant at racing motor bikes but they just weren't fit. Neither were the majority of the police officers. To make it worse they were wearing leather-soled shoes. Running on snow-covered grass was like running on a wet skating rink. There were five in the gang in total and thanks to Clive we had one, now for the rest. We poured through the door like something from a Buster Keaton film.

Tom's friends saw us and split into two groups. Half making for the pick-up, the other for the Tadcaster side of the house. I was faster than Joe.

'I'll go for the driver,' I called. Joe veered to his left to head off one of the others.

The driver reached the pick-up seconds before me but in his haste-cum-panic dropped the ignition keys in the footwell. I ripped the door open and grabbed hold of his collar. He swung to his right. I caught sight of a tyre-lever in his hand. Letting go of his collar I blocked his attempt to cave my head in, in the process slipped on the snow but managed to grab hold of his coat with my left hand and none too gently introduced his face to the door pillar. I handed him and the ignition key to Jim Tyndall and Sergeant McGill. Stan and Jack Kneeshaw took charge of Joe's prisoner.

'Brian,' Sergeant McGill was laughing. 'For God's sake this is your wedding day. Shouldn't you be playing footsy with Lucy?' That raised a cheer from my colleagues.

I grinned in return and nodded.

Liz was incandescent. She'd headed for the garage only to find the door forced. All the bikes were in the back of Tom's brother's pick-up. Six bikes that had been Bill's, two vintage bikes that he had been renovating. Plus Lucy's, Neil's, Liz's and Vance's. Another five minutes and we would have missed them altogether.

The penny dropped. 'You're Tom's brother,' I said to the one I arrested. I turned to Sergeant McGill who was standing over him. 'I saw him when he was fitting the alarm on this house. He denied ever having been to Huddersfield. How many more are there on his list?'

'Cheers, Brian. I'll let them know when they arrive.'

We sat them on the garage floor. Within the next minute all the Spartans, bar Vance and Neil, had returned empty handed. Several of the guests reporting that their cars had been broken into. Joe and I set off to look for the other two. If the missing thieves could get to the shrubbery they had a straight path to woodland which backed on to open pasture.

'They were heading over there,' I pointed to the trees on the far side of the lawn.

'Come on, let's go.'

Joe tapped me on the shoulder and pointed. Fifty yards away. A group of four. Neil and Vance floundering in the snow. Frankie and Anne running towards them illuminated by the light from the dining room.

'What do they think they're doing?' said Joe. Vance made a despairing dive for the one on the right, the thief caught sight of the girls and jinked to his right leaving Vance prostrate and wet. Neil had the same luck with the other, we were thirty yards away as the girls arrived. We heard Frankie call. 'You go high.'

'Okay.'

'Bloody tarts,' the one nearest gasped as both girls pirouetted. Anne's *mawashi geri,* taking him on the side of the head, Frankie's in the abdomen. High heels, party dresses, heavy snow and gravity are a strange mix and both ended up on their backsides in the snow. Joe and I collared the fugitive. He wasn't hurt much but whinged as we frogmarched him to join his friends. Neil and Vance helped the girls up out of the snow and donated their jackets. Except for a line of footprints in the snow heading for the shrubbery, of the fourth there was no trace.

Neil still hadn't mastered the ability to tell the girls apart. 'You *are* Anne, aren't you?'

Frankie grinned. 'Is she?'

'Stop it Frankie,' she said and kissed Neil on the cheek. 'Yes, I am.'

He breathed a sigh of relief. 'That was bloody good,' he said.

'Thanks,' Anne said. 'We've always wanted to try that in real life, just to see what it was like.'

'It was brilliant,' said Frankie. 'Mind you, slipping in the snow and getting a wet backside weren't in the plan. Will you excuse us both, we need a word with Lucy.'

Neil bent forwards and whispered in Anne's ear. 'I'll help you tomorrow night if you like.'

She reciprocated. 'Only if I can do the same for you.'

Some semblance of sanity restored; Mr Barton had taken charge. He announced to the guests that those responsible for spoiling the evening were either in custody or shortly would be. Other officers, including a senior detective would arrive shortly. He asked that the caterers do their best in the circumstances. If possible could he and his wife have a cup of tea and, would the band keep playing.

The first car to arrive was a road traffic car that had turned out from Tadcaster, followed two minutes later by a dog handler – I showed him where I'd lost sight of the thief. He let the dog off the leash. The dog tracked him for half a mile across farmland. He joined the others in the garage. I refreshed my acquaintance with Inspector Merton who arrived with a Sergeant Bruce and two uniformed constables. Thirty minutes later Detective Superintendent Horden arrived in a road traffic car.

Anne and Frankie had forsaken their party dresses and both were now wearing Lucy's jeans, T-shirts and underwear. I didn't ask but I wondered what they thought about Lucy's nearly knickers. Mum was consoling Jennifer over the loss of her ring. She really had made Tom swallow it.

The girls were giving their statements when Neil sidled up to me. 'Can I have a quiet word?'

'Sure,' I took him into the office.

'It's a bit embarrassing. I've never ... you know,' he dropped his eyes down to my groin. 'Pretended that I have, but ...'

'And you do love her? You're not just trying to get her into bed?' Not that he would have had to try too hard.

'No.' His look said - what do you think I am. 'I feel about Anne the same way you do about Lucy.'

'I know she feels the same about you. Or so Lucy tells me. I wouldn't be surprised if they swap notes. But I wouldn't worry too much. Look Neil, I can't claim to be an expert on women or sex but, for what it's worth ... '

Most were waiting either to give their statements or for the other cars to be moved out of the way. Liz stood at the front of the marquee with Clive and explained how he had interrupted Tom and tackled him. A very brave thing to do. And how that led to the arrests. 'I apologise for any damage to your cars but I think we ought to reward Clive in some way, don't you?'

He got a round of applause and almost £50 from a whip-round. He had the smile on his face for a month.

By the time they left for Huddersfield, Clive had been offered the position of the Spartan's mascot complete with his own personalised leathers. Plus a possible apprenticeship – if he wanted it. What a question.

Sixty-One

Liz's cheque was for £5,000! You could buy a good sized four bedroomed detached house in a nice area for £4,000. There were several generous cheques. Not of the same magnitude but we were not going to be short of money.

We didn't need to lock the door.

Lucy linked her fingers round my neck and smiled. 'Now then Mr Blake, do you think you can remember where we were?'

'I think it went like this,' I said, unzipped her dress and unfastened her bra. 'Is that right so far?'

'So far.'

I slipped the dress and her bra straps from her shoulders and slid everything down to her ankles stopping half way to bury my face.

She grabbed my hair pulling me closer and sighed. 'Perfect.'

'Perfect? Can I go to sleep now?'

'No, you bloody can't.'

'That was brave of him,' said Lucy as we lay in bed. 'Anne asked me the same question.'

'And?'

'I told her what we did. Or rather what you did my first time.'

I smiled. 'Giving my secrets away. But it does explain why they didn't ask for my keys.'

She rolled onto her left side. Slid her arm under my neck and her right leg over my thigh. 'Do it again.'

We caught the 1430 from Leeds arriving on time at Kings Cross. Outside, lights pushing back the darkness. The taxi dropped us off at Tofts. Christmas Trees either side of the door and the foyer reminiscent of a grotto.

'Mr Blake, welcome back,' said James, the duty manager. 'And Mrs Blake. Congratulations on your marriage. And,' he looked across at the register. 'Mr and Mrs Greeley, congratulations.'

Anne looked non-plussed. 'When you made the reservation, madam, you gave your name as Mountain,' he said and glanced at her left hand. 'Your husband has just signed the register. They're fine old rings. Family?'

'Yes, they are,' said Neil. 'My grandmother's.'

'Excellent. It's good to keep these traditions alive.'

'Sorry,' said Anne hoping she wasn't blushing. 'It's still so new.'

'Understandable, madam.' He was very discrete.

Lucy whispered something to Anne as we left them at their room door. Her parting shot - 'Don't forget, we dine at seven.'

They were late.

Liz said she felt as though she were playing gooseberry. Neil must have been doing something right, they could hardly keep their hands off each other. Nevertheless, everyone made time for a glass of complementary champagne courtesy of the management. The food excellent, as before.

It was a fine evening. I took them to look at the Old Bailey. They were suitably impressed. Followed by a walk along the Victoria Embankment. Plenty of festive lights strung between lamp posts.

Lucy and Anne had a girly huddle for a couple of minutes then linked up with Liz. Neil walked with me.

'Thanks,' he said. 'It worked.'

'We noticed, but no details. It's private and Anne is my sister.'

'I wouldn't. But I needed the walk. I was knackered.'

I laughed. 'Then you'll have to get fit. Don't want to disappoint *your wife*.'

'Ah. Yes. That nearly backfired.'

'If you come here again before you get married. If you get married. You're stuck.'

Lucy was lying on my chest resting her chin on her hands. 'Did you talk to Neil about oral sex?'

'Not specifically. I mentioned foreplay. Did he?'

'Hmm. She said he kissed her all over and then did this.' She pushed herself onto her knees and began to work her way down my chest and abdomen taking me in her mouth.

She lifted her head and gave me a playful squeeze. 'So easily led,' she giggled and rolled over. 'I've forgotten what comes next. Care to demonstrate?'

Sixty-Two

Sunday. We did the circumnavigation of St James' Park, the Houses of Parliament and Whitehall. In the afternoon Regents Park. The evening, tube to Leicester Square. Bought some cheap tickets from the ticket booth and watched Cleopatra at The Dominion.

'How do you think Joe will react if they want to get married?'

'Good question. I understand he wasn't too keen on them coming to London and sleeping together. But, Mum and Joe don't have a problem with Neil as a son-in-law. Why, has Anne said something?'

'No, but you've seen them. There's a genuine affection. It's not a simple infatuation. I think she feels the same as I did. She's reacting to what happened at the stadium and how different it might have been. It's the same for Neil. He was present when the accident occurred. Bill died and Anne could have. Plus he was sitting next to Lester. It wouldn't surprise me if they did.'

Monday, over breakfast. 'Do you think he would?' said Anne.

'Don't know. You've known each other over four months. A lot longer than Lucy and I had known each other before we decided to get married.'

'But you're not his daughter,' said Anne.

'Damn, you've noticed,' I said. To laughs and a wrinkled nose from Anne. 'I'll grant you it does make a difference. Why don't you give Mum a call and put it to her. They've no objection at all to Neil. You might get a pleasant surprise. Of course you might just want to live together and stuff convention.'

Anne grimaced. 'I think I'll give Mum a call.'

It was a fine, sunny but cold morning. Liz had paid for a group tour at The Tower of London. Yeoman Warder Eric Walker introduced himself. 'Is this your first time at the Tower.'

We agreed. 'I was down here a few weeks ago,' I said. 'I would have come but duty called and I had to return to Yorkshire.'

'Duty? You're in the forces?'

'He's a policeman,' interjected Lucy. 'He was giving evidence at the Old Bailey.'

Anne climbed on the bandwagon. 'He arrested that spy, Manville whatsit.'

I gave my grinning sister a quizzical glare.

Our guide looked at me. 'You're Brian Blake?'

'I am.'

'And these three ladies?'

'Were all with me. Only Neil wasn't there.'

'Let me shake you by the hand,' he said and shook everyone's, including Neil's. 'That changes matters. Follow me.'

Two minutes later he knocked on a door. 'Come,' said a voice from the inside.

'Just hang fire,' the Beefeater said and entered, returning seconds later accompanied by an elderly man with military bearing.

'Constable Blake?'

I hadn't a clue who he was but obviously in charge. 'Sir?'

'I'm a constable as well,' he said smiling. 'I'm the Constable of the Tower. Welcome. You have been the centre of many discussions over the past days. Perhaps after your tour you could spare us a few moments of your time.'

I didn't have to check. 'Of course, Sir.'

'Excellent,' he held his hand out to shake mine and shook hands with everyone. 'We will see you in approximately three hours.' He turned and entered his office.

'That was Field Marshal Earl Alexander of Tunis – Retired. Nice bloke.'

'Field Marshall and Earl?' said Lucy.

He grinned at Lucy. 'Retired. Shall we crack-on?'

To say that the tour covered everything was not an exaggeration. There was so many memorable subjects but the one that stuck in my mind was the execution of Lady Jane Grey, The Nine Days Queen, on the 12th February 1554 aged just 16.

After a short speech and reciting Psalm 52

Have mercy upon me, O God

The executioner asked her forgiveness, which she granted him, pleading "I pray you dispatch me quickly,' referring to her head. She asked "Will you take it off before I lay me down?" The axeman answered, 'No, madam.' She then blindfolded herself and had to be lead to the block probably by Sir Thomas Brydges, the Deputy Lieutenant of the Tower.

Jane placed her head on the block, and said her last words. "Lord, into Thy hands I commend my spirit."

The axe then fell, and one of the fairest and wisest heads that ever graced human form, fell likewise. *

There were about a dozen Beefeaters plus the Constable present in their club. We were allowed in only because it wasn't licensing hours. We got a round of applause and I introduced everyone and announced our wedding. Which received another round of applause.

They wanted an explanation from thread to needle. The few minutes suggested turning into three quarters of an hour,

'You know, Brian,' said Eric, our guide. 'Had you been under military orders you would have been in line for a VC. You'll get a gong of some description. You all will. Except Neil of course.'

'That's all right,' said Neil. 'I get Anne.'

Which brought the expected laugh.

They quietened as the Constable began to speak. 'He's quite correct Mr Blake. You will get an appropriate award. What, I do not know. You all will. But as far as you are concerned, you are earning, as a probationary constable, £800 per annum? £15 to £16 per week? The captain on the equivalent salary to a police chief inspector. You put your life on the line to make the arrest knowing that you could be shot. The captain, a member of the security services, is a traitor. It just goes to show that rank is not proof positive of a man's worth.

'There is not a man here in the Tower that, had we lived in a distant age, would not have gladly swung the axe. Blood-thirsty wretches that they are.' There was a pause for laughter and chorus of 'here heres'.

'Should you consider a change in your career and you wished to join the armed forces I think I can guarantee there would be regiments fighting to snatch you up.'

The last thing were the photographs. Lots of photographs.

Sixty-Three

There was another discussion in regard to a possible marriage. There would be no problem with Neil's family. They had already met Anne and thought she was a lovely girl. It was time that Neil was married.

After lunch Anne called home and asked the question.

'Leave it with me, love.'

We had an early meal and a taxi to the Royale. Liz had a surprise. We had paid for the seats but they weren't together. She had paid for an upgrade. We had a box and Isabel to look after us. 'Wow. Just look at this.'

'Lucy,' said Liz. 'You and Brian sit at the front. We'll sit behind.'

Lucy half-turned. 'Why is everybody staring at us?'

'I don't know,' said Liz and turned to Isabel.

Isabel took a couple of steps forwards. 'Like the Theatre Royal in Drury Lane we have two royal boxes. This is the one that the royal family rarely use.'

'Royal box?'

'Yes, it is used for other purposes and when your mother asked for an upgrade and knowing why you were here this was considered to be appropriate. But, please don't wave. They will lose interest once the orchestra begins to play. And, Mrs Vernon after the show I will take you to the managers' office. You will get a refund. It's been an honour to have you here.

Mother Goose was hilarious. The perfect end to our mini-honeymoon.

Joe, Mum and the others met us at Wakefield Westgate railway station. Anne's face dropped. I couldn't make out from Joe's expression what he was going to say. He looked stony-faced.

There was an uncomfortable silence. 'So, you want to get married?'

Anne nodded.

'Yes, sir,' said Neil.

His tone changed. I got worried. 'Have you any idea, Anne. Any idea at all ... just how many pies I've got to sell to pay for it.'

Anne was about to burst into tears when Joe's expression slipped. She flung her arms round his neck. 'Thanks Dad.'

'It's about time,' laughed Joe. 'I was beginning to think that none of you would leave home.'

Knowing how tight-knit the family was it must have been a wrench for everybody when Mum broached the subject of Anne's and Neil's marriage.

It would perhaps hit Jen and Frankie even more, as identical triplets there were times they had an almost psychic relationship.

Clive had already expressed his worries about people leaving home. First me. Frankie was moving into the flat in Leeds, rented by Joe. It was much more convenient for the university. Now Anne. The only one left was Jennifer.

Mum wouldn't think like that. To her it would be of marriage joining two families, in the same way that Lucy had brought the Vernons. She would be thinking grandchildren. Lucy and I were trying our best.

It was a great night.

My bike was at Boston Spa.

Sixty-Four

I've begun to learn Italian. Lucy thought it would be a good idea if, when we went on our honeymoon proper, I could at least buy a couple of coffees without having to resort to English. No pressure then.

My next meeting with Inspector Yates.

Sitting comfortably coffee at the ready.

'Right Brian, how are you settling into married life?'

'Fine sir. It's good.'

'Excellent. Any residual effects following Tadcaster?'

'None intrusive, although I've been advised there may be something nasty lurking in the undergrowth.'

'Understandable. Now, mindset. I want you to write these four words down. When you've a spare few minutes give every letter of each word the same value as its position in the alphabet: Altitude. Attitude. Aptitude. Bullshit. See which get you closest to 100% without going over. Take a lesson from that.'

'You told me earlier that your aim when you joined the police was to reach the rank of detective sergeant in eight years, as your father had done. Having had some time to think, where do you see yourself in ten years?'

Being a sergeant was a given.

It was a lively discussion. Lively in that he thought I was selling myself short.

It was centred around the rank of inspector.

The first rank where you were given the chance to take full responsibility for a shift, or a full Section, without looking over your shoulder. A means of proving you were capable of greater things.

It boiled down to a series of bullet points:

- Never be afraid to express your point of view. – If a senior officer doesn't want you to speak he will tell you.
- Never ask permission. Always say, 'This is what I propose.' With supporting evidence. Leave it to others to express an opposing position.
- If you think you are right stick to your guns until a senior officer pulls rank.
- You will be the superintendent's eyes and ears on the ground. If you think remedial action is called for, begin action, then put pen to paper with all the details. That way they don't have to think. That is the way you get noticed,
- You won't get it right all the time but never be afraid to make a decision and take action.
- Finally: Keep a copy of all your reports and keep them safe.

Sixty-Five

Nigel Ridley took a step back and scanned the front of Simmonds' house. 'Hide all you want you sick bitch. One of these days ...'

He climbed back into his Jaguar spinning the wheels as he left.

Lucy and I were at the Doctor's. Once again her period had started and she was upset. 'What's the matter with me, Doctor. Why aren't I pregnant?'

He gave her an examination and sat back behind his desk. Completed a pink form and handed it to me together with a clear glass screw-capped receptacle.

'Mr Blake, provide a fresh specimen of semen. Complete the form and take it to the address at the top.' He sat back and smiled. 'Mrs Blake as far as I can ascertain there is nothing wrong with you. The semen provided by your husband will confirm whether he has sperm in sufficient number and motility to impregnate you. Now, one of the reasons why healthy young women do not conceive is stress. Is there anything in your recent past that could have had such a deleterious effect?'

We looked at each other and laughed, then told him. His face was a picture.

'I see,' he said. It looked as if he were having a problem trying to process the information. 'That would no doubt have the effect.

And, if that is the case then try not to worry. And providing your husband's sample is up to the mark it's just a question of time.'

Lucy took the call from the Doctor. 'Your husband could impregnate half the women on the planet, Mrs Blake. Try to relax.'

Sixty-Six

Sightings of Marjorie Simmonds were rare and she was still adrift. There had been no communication with any of her business interests.

A letter had been received from her mother's solicitor regarding the enquiry. A search of all her business addresses provided the break we needed. We would be in Italy thinking about them.

A screwed up telex was discovered beneath the files in the bottom drawer of the filing cabinet of her Horsforth office naming St Paddy for the 1960 Epsom Derby. It was endorsed in red ink: Won. SP 7/1.

The telex was sent to Simmonds from a Feed Merchant with regional offices who supplied all the stables involved in Simmonds' gambling syndicate.

Sixty-Seven

1100 Easter Saturday. Anne and Neil were married at Huddersfield Registry Office. Lucy as Matron of Honour. Jen and Frankie as bridesmaids.

The reception in a marquee in the back garden. The Pc on the gate preventing any would be problems.

They left at 1930 on Neil's bike.

Gemma, one of her friends from school commented. 'You haven't got many clothes, Anne.'

'I shan't need them,' was the reply.

I hoped Neil had taken my advice about exercise.

Easter Monday we took the bus to Knaresborough spending the day doing very little: Mother Shipton's Cave. A rowing boat on the Nidd. A light lunch in a small riverside café. Returned to the hotel and caught up, followed by an excellent meal in the restaurant.

0700 Easter Tuesday. Leeds-Bradford airport courtesy of Liz. Lucy looked great in her cream-coloured slacks and blouse with a navy-blue jacket and matching shoes.

We had a good send off. both families plus the Spartans minus Anne and Neil. Handshakes and hugs all round with an extra hug from the Mums. A quick wave. We booked in, joined the throng and disappeared through the barrier.

Lucy tapped the back of my hand. 'I forgot to ask, Mr Blake, have you ever flown before?' She said stroking my whitening knuckles.

It was noisy. The propellers a blur. Fifty feet in the air and climbing fast – unlike my stomach. All thoughts of looking for the family long gone. 'No, Mrs Blake, I haven't,' I replied through gritted teeth whilst trying to squeeze the life out of the armrest. So many people were flying these days I hadn't thought it would be a big deal. Wrong again.

Lucy squeezed my hand. 'You'll be ok in a few minutes,' she said. 'When the seatbelt light goes off you can unfasten yours.'

'I'm not so sure that's a good idea,' I said as the stewardess sitting across the aisle looked at me and smiled.'

'Are you all right?'

'He's a flying virgin,' Lucy held her left hand up and grinned.

The stewardess smiled in return. 'Honeymooners?'

Lucy grinned and nodded. 'Si,' she replied.

Two minutes later the plane levelled off. Noise abated the seatbelt light extinguished. The stewardess disappeared into the galley reappearing with two small bottles of champagne and two glasses. 'Congratulations,' she said and smiled. 'With the compliments of Yorkshire Airlines.'

The flight didn't seem too bad after that, although the turbulence was unnerving.

A short flight to Croydon, perhaps a larger aeroplane would be better.

The first few thousand feet were stomach churning. This time I was more prepared. From twenty-five thousand feet we crawled across France. The ground laid out below us like some gigantic Ordnance Survey map. It leant an air of reality to those small squares of paper I had seen so often. Town after town slipped by, woodland, rivers, farmland, you could even make out what appeared to be orchards, even vineyards. It didn't seem long before the

Mediterranean appeared. We had been up since five thirty, combining that with the drone of the engines we took forty winks. I'm not sure which was worst, take-off or landing. I didn't care. It was just good to be back on terra firma – the more firma, the less terror.

Sixty-Eight

At last, we reached the immigration officer. I'm pleased Lucy spoke fluent Italian, apart from one or two words that reminded me of Latin I didn't understand a thing. Lucy first and then my turn. She'd told him that I didn't speak much Italian. He held his hand out, '*Le tue passaporto, signore,*' he said slowly.

That I did understand and handed it over. As he took it he noticed the badge I was wearing in my lapel; I'd joined the International Police Association only six weeks before. He frowned, checked my passport and looked at me. '*Sei un Poliziotto?*'

Out of the corner of my eye I could see Lucy smiling. *Poliziotto*, I knew was a police officer. Here goes nothing. '*Si, sono un poliziotto, signore,*' I replied, metaphorically crossing my fingers.

He inclined his head and smiled.

'*Mio marito,*' Lucy said placing her right hand on my forearm.

'Ah,' he replied and smiled. He stamped my passport without further delay and handed it back. 'Have a nice holiday, signore è signora,' he said in heavily accented English.

'*Grazie mille,*' responded Lucy and we were through. 'That's handy, it can take forever sometimes. Is that the IPA badge you talked about?'

'Yeah,' I said, 'I remember what you told me. Interesting response.'

I followed Lucy through the crowded halls into the public area. Everything, sights, sounds, smells, different. Most of the people Italian speakers, just a few French. 'Over there,' she said, pointing to her right where a man was holding a hand-written card - BLAKE. Lucy waved. He responded.

Lucy beamed a smile as we neared, 'Buonasera Luca,' she called. 'Thanks for meeting us.'

'Buonasera, Lucy. Welcome back,' he replied kissing her on both cheeks. 'It was terrible news about your father. Your mother wrote to us about the other matter but I sensed there was a lot she didn't say. We would have come over, but with the new baby?'

'I understand. It would have been nice but it was for the best. But we're here now.'

Luca nodded. 'Signora now, is it?' he glanced at me and winked. Luca was about five feet five tall, broad shoulders and stocky with a chin that looked as though it could look after itself, swarthy complexion, black hair, dark hooded eyes with in-built sparkle and hands like shovels.

Lucy didn't manage to prevent the blush. 'Si,' she said, smiled and gestured towards me. 'This is Brian, mio marito.'

'Buonasera, signore,' said Luca as we shook hands.

'Brian, please,' I replied. 'Buonasera. Congratulations on the new baby. Boy or girl?'

Luca nodded, tapped his chest and smiled, 'Luca,' he said. 'Another son, Pietro. Two of each. And Brian it is. I hear you are a British bobby?'

'*Si, sono un poliziotto, Inglese.*' I replied and grinned in return.

'*Eccellente.*' he declared with a beaming smile. 'The locals will treat you with great respect and speak to you in Italian.' That brought a grimace. 'We appreciate people making an effort,' he said, his face wreathed in smiles. 'We are very forgiving. Everyone will correct you.'

'*Grazie,*' I said. 'I'll bear that in mind.'

'That is good. The British police are respected, even in Napoli,' he said, making a joke that I didn't understand at the time.

'We should go,' he picked up Lucy's case. 'They are waiting and I will be in trouble. Plus, the crew will want to be away.'

Without further explanation we followed Luca's shoulders as he clove a path through the crowd and into the sun. It was hot. He made a bee-line for the taxi parked at the front of the line. The driver acknowledged his wave and opened the boot. Luca in the front, Lucy and me in the back. It felt like I imagined the beginning of a grand prix would feel when the flag dropped. Even with Lucy's commentary it was confusing. The nearer we got to the centre of Naples the more the traffic resembled a Gordian Knot. Nevertheless, we made it through without too much trouble. It was a very large, very busy city, people and traffic everywhere. Horns blaring, drivers gesticulating, it looked a fun place to spend our honeymoon.

Sixty-Nine

Over his shoulder and noise of the traffic Luca explained that had we arrived between Good Friday and Easter Monday Italy stops. Nothing interferes with religious devotion. On Little Easter - Easter Tuesday, nobody works. They all push off into the countryside and have a holiday, even the hotel staff. I'll bet the police and customs officials didn't. However it did explain why we travelled on Easter Tuesday.

Thirty minutes later, the Mediterranean. Sunshine. Seagulls. Beautiful blue water. Boats. Hundreds of boats. We drove past a solid line of hotels on the right. So, what was Lucy's secret that she just happened to mention when I threatened to withdraw my services, getting a thump for my troubles. Had it anything to do with the fact that on my annual leave application I had no address other than the *Villa San Pietro, Naples,* Italy, and a referral to Inspector Yates if I had to be contacted in an emergency. He had Liz's telephone number. The taxi driver pulled up at the quayside. Two boats moored close-by. Of our destination I had no idea. We and our cases disembarked. Luca paid the fare. 'You know who to call if you need a taxi, Lucy,' he said.

'Of course,' she said smiling at the taxi driver, 'Giancarlo.' The driver returned the smile, climbed into his taxi and re-joined the throng.

'Just where are we going?'

'Over there,' Lucy smiled and pointed south-west into the afternoon haze. I still couldn't see anything.

Luca collected Lucy's case and headed for an immaculate fifty-foot motor cruiser moored twenty yards away. 'Come on, they're waiting.'

'We going on a tour round the bay?' I asked as we followed. In view of the lack of information it seemed like a reasonable question to ask. Lucy's scowl said otherwise.

Was this luxury water-taxi part of Liz's treat? It mattered not; the boat could have been conjured up from a manufacturer's brochure. It was as immaculate inside as out and had a crew of two. I followed Lucy on board. The helmsman in the wheelhouse. Luca and the other crewman cast off, coiled the ropes, within seconds we were under way.

Luca set Lucy's case on the cabin floor.

'What did Mum tell you?'

'Very little, Lucy.'

Lucy looked at me. 'I can't tell you everything, Luca, because some of it falls within the provisions of the British Official Secrets Act. This is what happened ...'

Luca looked worried. 'You were sent to spy on Bill?'

I shook my head. 'No. Just to note who this courier spoke to. There were several but in the main it was Bill and Lester. I had to report back with the details. But it never came to that.'

'I'm pleased you told me here. I wouldn't want the children to hear the story.'

I shook my head. 'I wouldn't have told that in front of any children.'

He nodded and turned to leave. 'I'll leave you two to freshen up,' he said in a tone that sounded diplomatic. 'There are some refreshments in the galley. When you're ready come up to the wheelhouse.' He left, closing the door behind him.

Lucy locked the cabin door. Turned and threw her arms round my neck. 'Whose boat is this?' I said when we came up for air.

She broke into a broad grin. 'I keep wanting to say it's Dad's but it isn't, It's Mum's,' she said. 'Luca is her business partner in Italy.'

'Ok, that makes sense,' I said and paused. 'Will there be anything else, signora?' I trailed my fingers across her breast.

Her eyes widened. 'Now?'

I leaned forward and whispered. 'Luca said to take our time. The blinds are drawn. *You* locked the door. It's not going to take an hour.'

Less than thirty seconds later there was a jumbled pile of clothes on the cabin floor. I nodded as she pointed to the table.

The earth might not have been moving yet but the boat certainly was as the helmsman navigated some choppy water. Lucy bent forwards supporting herself against the table. I closed up behind letting her take some of my weight, her hips moving as she felt my erection at the base of her spine. I slid my right hand up the inside of her thigh tugging her bush. My left hand stroking her left breast. I kissed the nape of her neck and blew gently into her left ear. A deeper massage brought muted squeals of pleasure and took her gently from behind. It was exquisite. The frisson of Luca and the crew being only the thickness of a pane of glass away adding to the pleasure. It didn't take long. The boat pitched and rolled across the wash from a speedboat throwing us to the floor. That was some blast. We lay on the cabin floor in a tight embrace, kissing more to stop the laughter than anything else. It was a full two minutes before we managed to get our legs to coordinate. Now we couldn't stop giggling. A quick wash and change, we were almost back to normal.

The food was excellent. Wonderful bread. Butter at the side - for the *Inglese*. Italian meats and a bottle of red. The vineyard owned by Liz and Luca. Now, there's a surprise. I recognised the label from our wedding feast. I'd drunk plenty as a student, mostly beer. Compared to this red the rest was plonk. Lucy explained the sausage was cooked but the *prosciutto*, the thinly sliced ham wasn't. I was apprehensive. It was on the chewy side but tasted good. The wine was in a different league altogether. Quaffable.

We pulled ourselves on deck. For now it was fine and sunny but the onshore wind was stacking the clouds. The seabirds low over the water held a promise of rain. Lucy pointed out the Yacht Club *Canottieri Savoia* and the *Castel dell'Ovo*, the Castle of the Egg, so called because it was supposed to have an egg buried in the foundations, although she couldn't remember why. The traffic flowing along *La Via Francesca Caracciolo* looked like Dinky Toys. Pedestrians like ants.

Half a mile from land and on the same heading, the number of small boats appeared to have multiplied threefold. Naples was a large city, nevertheless I hadn't expected so many. Lucy drew my attention to Vesuvius. So close to Naples. The mountain of fire that had laid waste to Pompeii and Herculaneum almost two thousand years ago. Even asleep it was threatening.

We shambled forwards to where Luca was chatting to the helmsman. Lucy pointed at another mountain appearing out of the sea. Turning to me she kissed my chin. 'That's Monte Solaro, the highest point of Capri.' She glanced at her watch. 'We should be there in less than an hour.'

'What? Capri, as in Gracie Fields?'

'That's the one,' she replied in a wistful tone, as if she were recalling some pleasant memory. 'I'll show you her villa later. But it's pronounced Cap-ri, with the emphasis on the first syllable.'

We were thrown about as the boat danced across the wake of a ferry en route to Naples. I had a firm grip of the rail with my right hand and my left arm around Lucy's waist. It seemed unbelievable what had happened in the last nine months. And now we were traversing the Bay of Naples heading for Capri.

Luca turned as he heard Lucy's voice and motioned that we join him in the wheelhouse. Giuseppe, our helmsman handed over the wheel to Lucy. No stranger to the task. Then it was my turn. The instructions from Luca were: Watch the compass heading. Do not do anything stupid with the wheel. Simple enough. Ten minutes later. Even I could see that there was a fairly large boat having left some harbour that I couldn't make out sailing from port to starboard. On its present heading guaranteed to cross our bows sooner rather than later. I handed back control to Giuseppe.

With every minute Capri's grandeur became more imposing. The massive lump of Monte Solaro, nineteen hundred feet, its spectacular cliffs dwarfing everything. The Marina Grande at its northern foot our immediate destination. Capri, the capital, Lucy said wasn't any larger than a decent sized English village. It sat on what looked like a saddle, several hundred feet up, resting between the mass of Monte Solaro and Monte Tiberio, a mere shrimp at nine hundred feet in the east. There was too much to take in. However, Lucy did manage to point out *la funicolare*, the little cable railway that ran between *La Marina Grande* and *La Piazzetta*, our preferred manner of transportation. The address was still a surprise.

In the lee of Monte Solaro the wind dropped. The sun reappeared. Everything clean and bright. It was a very pleasant afternoon. People waiting for the ferry. Motor scooters, one of the main methods of transport on the island plus a few small cars and taxis which seemed to have their own fair share of bumps and scrapes. The roads were, it seems, narrow.

Seventy

We disembarked leaving our thanks with Giuseppe and Marco. Luca would see us later. Lucy's case in hand I followed as she made her unerring way past the tourist shops, cafés etc, through the crowd to where we could catch the funicular. We arrived as it drew to a halt. The jointed-car more similar to a small train in appearance than those at Scarborough and held many more passengers. It was almost full. Lucy smiled at the two men pressing against the rear window. 'Posso?' she said and indicated we would like access. Perhaps it only worked for beautiful women but they replied in kind. 'Signorina,' and moved.

'Grazie mille,' I said and smiled. I'm pleased they didn't try to engage in conversation.

The views spectacular. As we climbed the horizon extended. The cliffs even more massive. We became enveloped in the Island with its citrus groves. La *Marina Grande* below, Vesuvius to the right and Naples, a smudge on the horizon. It took less than five minutes to reach *La* Piazzetta, having passed its twin on the descent, the upper station platform so steep it was stepped.

We spent a silent few minutes taking in our surroundings and the views. Lucy's head on my shoulder, my arm round her waist until she looked up, kissed me on the cheek and uttered those fateful words, 'Come on, time to go.' There were roads on Capri that carried cars and buses but not up here. They were referred to as Via i.e. road, but they were alleyways, pedestrians only, lined with shops, boutiques, cafés, restaurants, ice-cream parlours, some had eye-watering prices until I realised the prices were shown in Lire, there were 1800 to £1, still a lot. It was a rabbit warren. Within seconds of turning this way and that I was hopelessly lost. We left the shops behind. High walls on either side. Waterfalls of Bougainvillaea. Every so often a gate or doorway. Was one of these mysterious entrances our destination?

Through the large ornate gate we could see a pergola smothered in Bougainvillaea, dripping colour and trapping the scent as it threaded its way to a large white-painted villa. It was incredible. I recognised palm trees and yuccas from the Hot House in Greenhead Park. There were others I didn't know but just as beautiful. A scattering of statues. I don't know how much Liz was paying to rent the villa but it must have been a bomb. Lucy pressed the buzzer on the right-hand post, answered by a young female voice. 'Prego?'

Lucy winked at me and replied, 'Signore e signora Blake.'

There was delight and excitement in the reply, 'Lucy!'

'Ciao Carla, come stai?'

'Ciao Lucy. Mama Lucy ...'

I got the gist.

There was a sharp click. The gate began to swing open. The door to the villa opened and a torrent of children appeared racing towards us. Well, three of them, two big ones and a little one, all as excited to greet Lucy as she was to see them. Following the children a smiling very attractive raven-haired woman, aged I would think in her late thirties, carrying a very small baby.

After a great deal of hugging, hand-shaking and kissing of cheeks, Lucy did the introductions: Claudia, carrying the latest member of the family, Pietro, just two months old and the reason why none of the family had been at our wedding. A tall dark-haired good looking seventeen year old Cristoforo, who preferred to be called Chris. An even darker haired fifteen year old Carla, the spitting image of her mother. Last but by no means least, seven year old Maria.

I remembered that 'pleased to meet you' in Italian was *piacere*, which was met by a torrent of Italian. Thankfully, Chris and Carla asked if we could speak in English to help with their studies. Claudia spoke excellent English with a strong Italian accent and Maria was, well, Maria. All the others did any translation required. Maria was delighted that she could call me *zio*, 'uncle', Brian; *zia* Lucy and *zio* Brian. In Maria's eyes it was if Lucy were now complete, I knew I was.

En masse we ambled through this delight and into the villa, the marble floor with its panels of Roman style mosaic cool against the heat outside. It was beautifully furnished, again with its statues and potted palms. At the rear, a much larger walled garden with a raised terrace at the far end. Mature palms casting their welcome shade. A full width pergola immediately outside the door. On the right a table with unhealthy but delicious looking cakes, and, if I was not mistaken, a tiramisu. On the left, twin tables and innumerable cane chairs, attendant Bougainvillaea at one end and a climbing vine covered in brilliant red flowers with white edging at the other, identical to one in the Greenhead Park hothouse, I'm sure it was called Gloriosa. Between the terrace and the pergola, apart from the fountain with its tight triangle of dolphins spouting water over the back of the one in front, a myriad of plants including: palms, roses and rosemary. I had no idea what most of the plants were. The garden was a blend of palms, succulents and shrubs with a curved path winding between them. It was fantastic.

Chairs unstacked; a happy Lucy given charge of an uncomplaining Pietro. 'This feels good,' she said and smiled at everyone.

'It looks good,' I confirmed and got a kiss on the cheek for my trouble. Claudia and the children busied themselves making fresh coffee, re-appearing a few minutes later accompanied by Luca. Lucy offered Pietro to Claudia who declined, saying that she needed a rest and it would help Lucy to get used to the feeling. There were no objections.

The food was beautiful. My waistline had better watch out. All those dishes that Lucy had made in England plus several others. The most spectacular of which was a cake they called *Baba alla crema con Macedonia,* pronounced Machedonia. It looked obscene, smelled fantastic and tasted out of this world. A confection of sponge, rum, syrup, fresh cream and fresh fruit. Superb.

Lucy presented Claudia with an album of the photographs from the combined celebration of our wedding and her 21st. A quick flick through and the album set aside, we sat talking. In the main Lucy talked with Claudia and Luca, with me being brought in as required. I talked with Chris and Carla, for the most part about being a policeman in England and not carrying a firearm. Something they found very strange and dangerous. I must be very brave.

It was five when Claudia announced they were leaving. She put what was left of the food back in the larder and relieved Lucy of her charge. 'Children, time to go and leave these two time for themselves. And,' she said laughing to quieten the howls of protest from Maria, 'They're here for the next nine days. I'm sure we'll see them again.'

Lucy crouched in front of Maria. 'We'll see you tomorrow at six, before you go to bed, Maria. All right?'

Maria pulled a face and nodded. 'Mi prometti?'

Lucy tapped her on her nose. 'Prometto.'

As Luca scooped Maria up my confusion got the better of me. 'But I thought Claudia and Luca lived here?'

'No, we live in Anacapri,' said Luca, pointing, 'the other end of the island.' Lucy broke into a broad grin.

'Don't tell me this villa belongs to your mother as well?'

'Of course,' she laughed. 'This is the Villa San Pietro. I'm surprised you asked. We rent it out from May 1st until the end of

September each year, unless the family want it. Now, that includes your family. Claudia manages it for a pittance.'

'I get paid very well,' protested Claudia to a grinning Lucy.

'Aren't you pleased we met?'

'Seeing that we're married I suppose I'll have to say, yes,' I grabbed Lucy round the waist. It's very difficult to punch someone if you hold them close to you. There's method in the madness.

After much shaking of hands, hugging and waving, Maria was carried away from the gate by Luca. Lucy locked the door. 'First things first,' she said with a beaming smile. 'Then I'll show you around.'

Seventy-One

Three minutes later there was a sun lounger erected in the garden where we had a full view of the sky. 'Take your clothes off and lie on your back,' she said and began to get undressed.

'What do you want me to do?' I asked as I lay down.

'Anything you like that doesn't involve talking, singing or getting up,' she said and pushed me back onto the sunbed. Then straddled me. 'This, is *my* welcome to Capri.'

The light was fading when I opened my eyes. How long I'd been asleep I had no idea. Lucy was fast asleep, spread-eagled on top of me her head resting on the right side of my chest, her right hand on my left shoulder, breathing slow and rhythmic. I wondered if she had settled for the night. In the meantime, I took stock of my surroundings. It was a new moon and in the gathering darkness the sky was already ablaze with stars. I had never seen so many. No artificial light anywhere. The villas either side were either unoccupied or were showing none. However, the starlight reflecting from the walls was sufficient to bathe everything in a suffused almost surreal light. The trees over the terrace silhouetted against the Milky Way. In the confines of the garden, with its high walls, the scent was fabulous. The silence almost total, just the water in the fountain and the occasional sound of a motor scooter or music in the distance.

Lucy's head moved followed by a yawn. 'This is nice,' she said as she stirred and slipped to one side. I put my hand round her behind to stop her from falling.

'Your bottom's cold.'

'Your hand isn't,' she kissed my chest. 'That was special,' she whispered. 'We'll have to do that again.' We had been lovers since forever. If she found that the way we made love was special who was I to argue.

'Yat chime eyit?' she yawned.

'Yown yo,' I followed suit. 'Yi?'

Lucy pushed herself up into a kneeling position astride me. 'We've a table booked for eight. I want to show you something.'

She was naked, kneeling astride my thighs her body illuminated by starlight and she's wanting to show me something? 'You already are.'

'She looked puzzled until she realised where I was looking, and smiled. 'You like what you see?'

'Stupid question,' I said as she leaned forward and kissed me gently on the lips. This time we both stayed awake.

A gentle but cool breeze intruded, I put my arm round her. 'You were saying something about a table?'

She nodded and grinned. 'Yup. For a meal.'

'I'd worked that bit out,' I replied. 'But who? ... Oh, Claudia.'

She yawned and nodded. 'Let's go shower.' She slid onto the floor and took me by the hand. That's when I discovered that the demand on the water supply during the holiday season meant there are no leisurely showers on Capri.

Bearing in mind we had only fetched a single case each, I wondered where she had hidden her clothes. I soon found out. She hadn't bought them, yet. Plenty of underwear. A couple of blouses. One sweater. One dress. One skirt. One pair of slacks, and, a mysterious pair of well-worn jeans, plus shoes. I'd wondered why the case was so light.

Seventy-Two

Lucy insisted that I put on a light sweater. We left the villa at six thirty. Following the *Viale Amedeo Maturi*, a comfortable uphill stroll to the cliff top above the *Villa Jovis*, built two thousand years ago for the Emperor Tiberius. Six hundred feet straight down into the Mediterranean. The emperor used to have troublesome staff and unwelcome guests removed from his presence via this unofficial but scenic back door. A Roman version of high-board diving.

'We can come back in the daytime to see the villa,' she said.

What she wanted to show me, apart from the stars, was the view. The view north across the Bay of Naples from *Ischia*, its' most easterly point, the darkening skies and brightening glow of the city lights, sweeping round to the east, *Ercolano*, or *Herculaneum*. The darkness of Vesuvius. *Pompeii*. The lights of Sorrento. Further to the south the faint glow from the Amalfi Coast. From our height of almost nine hundred feet the three-mile strait between Capri and the Sorrentine Peninsula looked narrow. As Lucy had predicted, there was a cool wind blowing off the sea carrying the fragrances of the mainland. This was the view she had first seen when she was just five years old. A memory she made sure she refreshed every time she came to the island. A view that she found enchanting and magical. Who was I to disagree?

Coached by Lucy on what to say, *in Italiano,* when we reached Da Manico's, her restaurant of choice I was sort of looking forwards to the event. It never happened. Da Manico's was secluded, somewhere in this rabbit warren. It was warm and dry. We were to eat outside, although I couldn't see any free tables. Taking my cue from Lucy we stood and waited for the waitress to notice us and show us to our table. She noticed Lucy, her eyes lit up and Lucy was enveloped by the waitress. Not much older than I but of more ample proportions. The only word I managed to grasp was, Lucy. The conversation continued at about half the speed of sound for a couple of minutes. An examination of Lucy's wedding and engagement rings. Me getting the once over with the description: *Lui è molto bello.* To which Lucy smiled and simply replied, *si.* This was Elena, wife of Frederico, the restauranteur. This short cabaret concluded when we were escorted between the diners to the only unoccupied table in the square. The other customers returned to their eating.

Lucy told me that all meals served on Capri were either local or Italian recipes. She was certain there were one or two things that I'd never eaten before. Would I like to sample them? That seemed fair enough. She and Elena exchanged a few words. Elena disappeared into the kitchen, re-appearing a few minutes later with a small plate with what appeared to be rings of hardboiled egg, and something else that reminded me of Twenty Thousand Leagues Under the Sea, but much smaller and with only eight tentacles. It was good, much better than I thought it would. My first taste of *calamari*, and *polpo*.

The highlight of the evening? I ordered dessert. The coffee was no problem – *due caffè nero, per favore,* simple: two black coffees, please. The ice-cream, g*elato?* We both decided to have an *affogato,* that's ice-cream drenched in hot espresso with a shot of Amaretto. I tried to be clever and order them with peaches. Now, in Italian the word for peaches is *pesche*, which has a hard 'k' sound. The word for fish is *pesce*, which is soft. Yes, I ordered *due affogato con pesce,* two ice-creams with espresso, Amaretto and fish. Elena stopped writing, smiled, and said in very good English, 'Almost, but not quite, signore.' Lucy smiled and raised an eyebrow. As I looked from one to the other hoping for inspiration the penny dropped; and so, we were each served with *un affogato senza pesche,* no peaches, and not a taste of fish anywhere. I wouldn't do that again.

Surprise. Lucy intended to take me on a guided tour of the shops, until it rained. Heavy rain was as good at clearing the street on Capri as it was back home, only warmer.

Seventy-Three

It was wall to wall sunshine. Light that you only tend to get in the UK when there isn't an 'R' in the month. Breakfast out of the way it was a brisk walk up to the *Villa Jovis*. It didn't fully open until June, nevertheless we were allowed to wander, which we did for about an hour. Two thousand years ago it must have been fabulous. Now, just a few remnants still standing: The bell tower and signal station. However the views hadn't changed. According to Lucy's guide book this was just one of the fourteen villas that Tiberius had built on the island.

Leaving the *Villa Jovis*, we took a wander clockwise along the *Via Tiberio* away from the mainland. Superb views across the island and south towards Stromboli and Lipari. After a while we sat at the edge of the road and drank in the panorama.

The funicular to the Marina Grande. Colourful and busy. A light lunch. We rented a scooter for the afternoon. Booked our day trip round the island by boat and tour of the Blue Grotto, the *Azzura Grotta*, for tomorrow. Riding pillion to Lucy I confirmed that the only level piece of road on the island is *Via Cristoforo Colombo*, the quayside of *La Marina Grande*; everything else is up or down in varying degrees, combined with sharp or even hairpin bends, not the place to be reckless. Nevertheless, someone once said that second class riding beats first class walking. Not something that I held to be a universal truth. However, the thought was to be entertained when considering whose hips I had my hands on.

It was a fun afternoon. *Via Castiglione* twisted and turned like a skein of Mum's knitting wool. We spent an hour in the *Giardini*

Di Augusto. It was cheap. An hour. Too short. However, it gave me a taste of some wonderful gardens, certainly one to re-visit. Looking down on *La Marina Piccola* and *Via Krupp* – a spectacular vertiginous zigzagging footpath down the cliffs. The peaks of *Monte Solaro* and *Monte Tiberio*. The sea stacks – *Faraglioni,* and everything else on the south east of the island. All framed by this wonderful azure sea.

All too soon we had to travel back along the skein, turning left and left again heading downhill along *Via Marina Piccola*. It was fine on two wheels, plenty of room. On four? Care was certainly required; but it was a beautiful ride. Lucy negotiating the hairpin bends with aplomb, past innumerable hotels and villas. We reached the bottom and parked the scooter a few yards from the water's edge. Plenty of vehicles and people coming and going. It was hot. The *Marina Piccola* a perfect sun-trap.

Looking back along the route the island towered over us, but for the most part all we could see were the trees. Wending our way through the holiday makers brought us to *La Canzone Del Mare*, the significance of which completely defeated me until Lucy informed me that this was where Gracie Fields lived. 'Here?'

'She owns it.'

As she spoke a taxi exited *La Canzone Del Mare,* in the rear seat Gracie Fields, or Gracie Alperovici to use her married name, and her husband Boris. She waved and smiled. That was it. We spent the next hour mooching about but found time for a long cool drink in one of the waterside bars.

It was almost three when we left, Lucy deciding on a tour of spectacular views of which there must have been thousands. We had to make do with three; I was running out of film. Returning the scooter we took the funiculare. Lucy's first port of call was the bank. She had an authority signed by Liz for her to draw from the company account. Senore Sentore, the manager satisfied, Lucy drew her cash and we went shopping. No, the money she drew from the bank was for our forthcoming tour of inspection. I stood guard outside a shop that sold expensive lingerie. Several parcels, carrier bags and boxes to the good we were back at the villa. Yes, I was given a private viewing where it was suggested that I might like to see just how easy they were to remove. Successfully achieved. Lucy had also bought presents for the girls, and the two Mums. The mind boggled. Something that would spark Joe's interest.

Seventy-Four

The taxi dropped us off outside Luca's villa, somewhere off *Via Li Campi*, in Anacapri. The church clock struck six. It was beautiful. As large as Liz's but definitely a family home. Lucy and I got the private tour of the rear garden from Maria whilst Chris and Carla helped Claudia with the meal. Luca arrived ten minutes later. To call it simply a rear garden was somewhat misleading. It was a garden at the rear of the villa, and it had a patio where we were going to eat. However, the sight and smell of over one hundred lemon trees bearing both flowers and fruit were amazing. A scattering of fig trees put it into a different class altogether. Anacapri was twice the height above sea-level as Capri itself. The views to the west spectacular. Maria was allowed to stay up and participate beyond her normal bedtime as we all watched the sun sinking into the Mediterranean. You could almost hear the sizzle as the sun hit the water. The dying rays striking the flanks of Vesuvius fading until dusk claimed dominion. The glow from Naples breaking the darkness. To the east the mass of Monte Solaro blocking everything except millions of stars.

Luca tapped me on the arm and motioned with his head to follow. Out of earshot. He looked uncertain. 'Was Bill ...?' he hesitated.

'A spy?'

'Si.'

'Not according to the man I met. Bill was being used as a postman, a diversion. The courier, I'd been told, was Lester's cousin who likewise delivered various items. I had to report back so that the security services would concentrate on those two.'

'There was another?'

'Yes.'

'So Bill was a dupe?' He was happy with that. If I were being honest I don't know and nobody would tell.

At 9pm the taxi arrived to transport us to the other side of the island, dropping us off in the *Piazza Angelo Ferraro*. It was a beautiful evening for a stroll by the waterside.

The scream split the air with all the finesse of an axe. A young voice. Female. Fifteen yards away a young woman was struggling with three young men who were dragging her to a nearby motor cruiser, bearing a fourth. All were shouting. After being repulsed by the scream, sightseers were beginning to press and joined in the chorus. Lucy translated. 'The tall one is shouting, "You are mine. You were promised to me"'

'I take it the girl disagrees?'

'That's about right. The crowd are on her side.'

'We can't do nothing.'

'Could be a family feud.'

'Ah well. We must do something. You get the girl. I'll deal with the others.'

'Be careful, I was just getting used to being married.'

The crowd were noisy but no-one intervened. I did. A couple more strides and I was at the front. 'Leave-the-girl-alone,' I said. "She-doesn't-want-to-go-with-you.'

The tug of war stopped. The tall one said. 'English? Not your business. Leave or you might get hurt. Angelina is mine.'

'She doesn't seem to think so.'

'She was promised to me at birth.'

A few of the crowd understood and translated for the others. There was general disagreement. 'At birth?' I iterated. 'She's what now, sixteen or seventeen. She's not property. She doesn't agree. Let her go.'

'Keep out of this or you *will* get hurt,' he turned to the man on his left and said something I couldn't hear. But Lucy did.

'Brian, be careful. He's carrying a knife.'

He let go of Angelina's wrist and took a step towards me. Put his hand behind his back and pulled a knife, drawing a few protests and screams from the crowd. He took one pace forwards as my *yoko geri* struck him full in the chest knocking him off the edge of the quay. He missed the cruiser. There was a spontaneous eruption of laughter and applause which seemed to upset the other two. They let go of Angelina, who clung to Lucy. Both stepped towards me. They hadn't been paying attention. A *mawashi geri* cannoned the tall one into his friend who joined number one in the harbour, much to the amusement of the crowd. I pointed at the last remaining assailant. 'Don't, unless you want to join your friends.' He stopped and thought about it.

Two things happened in quick succession. A man in his fifties wearing a smart business suit pushed his way through the crowd from the left. 'Angelina.'

The girl turned, 'Papa,' she let go of Lucy and threw herself at her father.

I heard someone say, 'Carabinieri', as two uniformed officers appeared from the other direction.

They split, one addressing me in a torrent of Italian. The other to Angelina's admirer. I held my hands up. 'Signore, non parlo molto bene l'italiano,' I indicated Lucy. 'Mia moglie lo fa.'

'English?'

I smiled and nodded. 'Si.'

He nodded and turned to Lucy, 'Signora?'

She told me afterwards what she's said. The scream. What we had seen, indicating Angelina. What I'd said and the threat with the knife and what I'd done. He found that amusing. Then asked Angelina and her father if what Lucy had said was correct. Why did Antonio Bruni think that Angelina had been promised to him from birth.

The answer was simple. Angelina's parents, the D'Agostinis, had always wanted a daughter. They had four sons. When Angelina was born it was an occasion for much celebrating. Lorenzo D'Agostini got drunk with his friend Tommaso Bruni. He had three daughters and one son. Someone, no-one remembered who, suggested it might be a good idea if Antonio and Angelina got married in years to come. Five year old Antonio heard this and it stuck. Tonight, he decided that he had waited long enough.

The police station was full, for the most part with dry people. We were interviewed first. Sergeant Giuseppe Massimiliano's English was excellent. He frowned and pointed at my IPA badge. 'You are a police officer?'

'Yes,' I said and produced my warrant card. 'In the West Riding, in the north of England.'

'Yes, I know it,' he said handing my warrant card back.

'You know the West Riding?'

He had a wistful look in his eyes. 'Yes. I suppose you could call him a hero of mine from long ago. Bill was his name, Bill Vernon. I saw him win the Senior TT race on the Isle of Mann. He was a brilliant rider. He lives there and gave me an invitation to visit him.' He had a sad smile. 'Life got in the way. Look.' He removed his wallet and passed Lucy a photograph.'.

She smiled and passed it to me. 'How long have you worked on the island, Sergeant?' she said. I had to smile. It was Bill, Liz, Gerald and Lucy with the sergeant in his leathers.

'Whenever necessary. I'm not stationed here. Why do you ask, signora?'

'Because the man on the left is Bill Vernon, my father. Unfortunately he died in a road accident last year. We have a villa here. It's where Brian and I are spending our honeymoon. I remember this photograph being taken. It's my mother, father, me and Gerald, my brother.'

You would have thought he had just discovered some long lost relative. Lucy gave him a business card with our contact details. Luca's address and phone number. I typed my statement out, in duplicate. Then Lucy's, also in English. Then she translated both into Italian. Someone else could copy-type those. Did we want to press charges? Not if they were apologetic. They were more of a danger to themselves than they had been to me. It would all depend. As we were leaving the police station Lorenzo D'Agostini assailed us in Italian, thanking us for our intervention and an open invitation to dine at his restaurant as often as we liked, there would be no charge.

Finally, an instruction from the sergeant to produce our passports at the police station the following morning.

We missed the last *funiculare* and caught the bus.

Seventy-Five

How do you describe something that is simply indescribable? Sometimes words like the page they are written on are too two-dimensional. Under a cloudless sky, looking from the cliff tops north into the Mediterranean, the water wasn't just blue or azure or cyan even cerulean, that was relatively easy. It held the promise of a very warm day.

0930 We left the Marina Grande for the circumnavigation of the island. Brilliant in its own right. Clear of the harbour sailing clockwise through the *Villa Jovis* 'drop-zone' where the cliffs towered six hundred feet and beyond. The geology was impressive. According to Lucy's guide book the island was formed between 65 and 190 million years ago. Geological forces had pushed this block of limestone vertically. The seabed was now *Monte Solaro*, nineteen hundred feet above sea-level. Rocks had been tilted and pushed about as if they were plasticine. Corals, grottos and rock formations fantastic.

Dependent upon tide and weather the entrance to the Azura Grotta was reputed to be three feet high and seven feet wide. It wasn't. You had to get your head down low or literally *face* the consequences. And although I hadn't thought to bring a tape measure I doubted whether it was anywhere near seven feet wide. The weather was living up to its promise. Between bursts of O Solo Mio, Giovani our gondolier explained. There are two entrances. The one we had entered by. The second six feet below, but ten times larger, both allowing the sunlight access to the cave. From where we were sitting it was almost as if we were surrounded by an unreal glow rather than just light. The sunlight outside the grotto was reflected upwards from the white sandy bottom four hundred and fifty feet below giving this amazing effect. I'd heard about the Grotto before but you had to experience it to understand. We were the only ones there so Lucy asked if we could swim. Within seconds we were both in the water. Lucy wearing her brand new brief bikini. She did that on purpose. Drops of water turned to silver, our skin appeared to glow. Weird? No not weird just wonderful. The cave was about one hundred and eighty feet from entrance to rear, We spent five or ten minutes exploring the recesses. In the absence of artificial light we gave up and climbed back on board over the stern. Me first. Lucy's body glistened as I hoisted her out of the water and into the boat, cascading water appeared to be blue. Just surreal.

If possible, the remainder of the day was even more relaxed. One of the things that Capri was not short of were places to eat. You could probably eat at a different one every day and still not visit any one of them twice throughout the year. Even when you took into account that most of them closed throughout the winter months. Once again Lucy introduced me to someone that she was familiar with: Alanso and Paulo Vaccaro owners of *Il Vinyard*, even I could translate that without too much trouble. The food was excellent. I managed to order from the menu without any problems, at least she understood what I said. Afterwards we repaired to their very busy club next door: discreet tables, bar and entertainment. It was interesting to see how the Italians plus their visitors had taken to the music of the Beatles, Stones and a myriad of other groups; it was a pleasant way to spend a few hours.

Seventy-Six

0955. Temperature 70⁰. Wall-to-wall sunshine. A gentle off-shore breeze wafting the scents of the Sorrentine Peninsula across the water. It took thirty minutes to travel from *La Marina Grande* in Capri to *La Marina Piccola*, Sorrento's only port.

Ferry secured we disembarked and mingled with those waiting to take the reverse journey. There was no rush. We walked up to the *Piazza Tasso*. Managing to find a vacant table outside an attractive looking hotel where they were serving coffee.

'*Due caffè e cornetti, per favore, signore. Caffè latte per mia moglie e caffè nero per me*,' I said as the waiter appeared at my elbow. A stream of Italian flowed in the opposite direction. All that I could make out was, '*Grazie signore ...*' I looked helplessly at Lucy as she laughed. She explained that I was learning to speak Italian and would he repeat what he said more slowly.

He smiled and nodded at Lucy, then replied in English, 'Thank you, sir. Are you here on holiday?'

I looked across the table at Lucy. She smiled.

I grimaced in return, took a deep breath and faced my inquisitor. '*Siamo in luna di miele*,' I replied with great care. '*Siamo venuti da Capri per la gionata*.'

His face lit up. '*Molto bene. La* m*ia congratulazione, signore e signora*,' he replied with a broad smile, then shook his head sadly and lapsed back into English. 'But a day is not long enough. You must come back to Sorrento for longer.'

'*L'anno prossimo, forse*,' said Lucy, and smiled.

'*Si signora*,' he smiled and left to get the coffees.

'Next year.' I confirmed. Lucy nodded. 'But ...*forse?*' that was a new one.

'Perhaps,' she smiled and winked. Tonight was a certainty.

Cornetti are delicious bite-sized Italian breakfast pastries, flavoured with lemon and vanilla or chocolate almond cream. They went down well with the coffee. What did we do the rest of our stay? We walked. Explored the Old Town, Corsa Italia and the Cloister of San Francisco. Enjoyed the sunshine. The ambience. Admired the architecture and the views. Window shopped. Made a few purchases. Had lunch with a glass of Pinot. Spoke with a few English holidaymakers, a couple of whom had difficulty in understanding why Italians could neither understand what they said nor speak English. Neither did they appreciate our suggestion that they learn a few words in Italian. Of course, it's not what you do but who you do it with that counts. We had a beautiful meal at Giancarlo's parent's hotel, where we had our morning coffee. Caught the ferry back to Capri at 8.00pm. Relaxed on the terrace and counted the stars.

Seventy-Seven

Saturday dawned. The mystery tour loomed. I found out why Lucy had insisted that we each bring a pair of old jeans and decent footwear. Today was the day we climbed Monte Solaro - the hard way – *Il Sentiero del Passatiello,* the footpath of Passatiello. Information regarding the route conspicuous by its absence, other than Lucy flashing that wonderful smile and the light-hearted comment: 'It's uphill.'

She produced a small back-pack for me to carry the water, snacks and first aid kit. Ten minutes later we reached the spot known as *Due Golfi*, the point where you could see both *La Marina Grande* and *La Marina Piccola*. Headed towards *La Marina Piccola,* past the hospital taking the path to the right, *La Via Torino* and then left along *La Via Milano*, the old mule track, until recently the only way to get between Capri and Anacapri. *Monte Solaro* rearing in front. Soon, we would be climbing.

All signs of habitation behind. There was just us, the sun, trees, shrubs, spring flowers and the gentle breeze; plus numerous birds, various rodents and a small snake, which Lucy advised me was a non-venomous whip-snake. Just us communing with nature.

It was a steady climb. Even without the sunshine it was warm work. Eventually the path levelled off. The views stupendous. From *La Marina Grande* to *La Marina Piccola,* we were even looking down on the *Villa Jovis* and Sorrento. Lucy took my arm, 'We turn up here,' she said, pointing into the trees on the left.

'You sure?' I said.

'Sure I'm sure.' Grinning, she took my hand. 'Come on you don't want to get lost.'

This was a different beast altogether. Narrow. Well-trodden but faint. A severe slope. Massive blocks and pinnacles of limestone littered the ground. The path zigzagged. Trees. Thousands of oak trees, and what looked like holly; known as the *Anginola foresta*. Well-polished lumps of limestone protruding through the thin soil helped; had the ground or the rocks been wet it was a long way to roll for the unwary. Lucy's small packet of sticking plaster would not have been adequate. We were climbing through dappled sunshine. I did the sweating. Lucy just glowed.

I didn't know how long we'd been walking when Lucy called a halt. 'In a few yards we'll be getting to the fun bit,' she inclined her head and smiled.

I looked around for clues. My view obscured by trees. A few yards behind her a rock wall. 'Hmm, is that fun as in ha, ha? Or interesting?'

She grinned, 'Interesting.'

It was. Very. It wasn't a path, more a cleft and the way we had to go. From where we were standing short stretches looked almost sheer. A huge jumble of rocks looking like some ancient rock-fall. The interesting bit? Fastened securely into the rocks on the right-hand side were strong chains, not taut, but there for a reason. It was not as bad as it appeared provided you were careful. It didn't take long before we completed this rock scramble. Followed by a steady if steep uphill walk through the woods and back into the sunshine. High above, the peak of Monte Solaro. There was no-one else in sight. Lucy draped herself round my neck and we shared a long lingering kiss. 'What do you think of the view now?'

I kissed her on the nose. 'I think that you're just as beautiful as ever.'

She scowled, 'Thank you,' she said. 'Now turn around.'

It was a WOW moment. I stood behind, my arms round her waist. Laid out before us was the entire eastern half of the island. The Villa Jovis outlined against the Sorrentine Peninsula, Vesuvius, and the Bay of Naples with the city shrouded in haze. We stood silently until we heard a hullabaloo behind us with a smaller voice shouting, 'Zia Lucy, zio Brian.'

Lucy looked up and kissed me on the chin. 'That will be lunch.'

We spent the next few hours eating, drinking, talking, playing and taking lots of photographs. After we'd exhausted talking about our climb, the conversation switched to where we'd left it the other day. It was after three when we left to walk down the mountain to the *Villa San Michele* where we said our good byes - for now. I was to experience *La Scala Fenicia*, the Phoenician Steps, all 921 of them. I have to admit that it was easier going down though not as much fun as following Lucy up the rockfall. The climb to Whitby Abbey was 199 steps. Enough to raise your pulse. But 921? And the locals used to do this all the time.

Seventy-Eight

Sunday. I'd slept like a log. I didn't take a photograph all day.

1000 Monday. We were an hour's drive east of Sorrento on the Amalfi Coast. This was the first of Liz and Luca's business enterprises we had visited on the mainland. It was a beautiful country, hot and sunny. The people friendly.

The legend on the sign read:

La Frutta della Terra
Azienda Vinicola
(The Fruit of the Earth
Winery)

Lucy's first tour of inspection. Luca leading. She pitched in where she wanted clarification and translated for me. Over the next two hours we had a thorough grounding into viniculture. A tour of the Vinyard: the number of vines per hectare. The weight of grapes they could harvest. How much wine they could extract? It was a lot. However, had they been producing white wine and not red it would have been a lot more. Apart from this vineyard there were a dozen they had bought when the elderly owners had no family to take over. This was Luca's territory. We had a tasting; I could get to enjoy this country even more. We even had to fly to Turin for a night; it was terrible. We saw several similar enterprises and the one that brought Bill and Luca together in the first place. Luca was an engineer and used to do work for Bill when he was racing in Italy. One day whilst Bill was visiting Luca, unwelcome visitors arrived who were determined to burn Luca out of business, and put him permanently out of action. They lost. Luca and Bill between them saw them off and managed to save most of Luca's business. Bill loaned him the money to get back on his feet. That was that.

Wednesday, one more day before we returned to reality. We ate. We shopped. We ate. We shopped. The last evening meal of our honeymoon courtesy of Senore D'Agostini.

Sooner or later all good things come to an end. A slow dawn stroll around the garden. A kiss under the palms followed by our last ride in the *funiculare* to meet Luca, Claudia and the children at the quayside. They delivered us safely to the airport and after many hugs and handshakes they returned to that beautiful island that we would see again.

Seventy-Nine

We were met by Liz and taken to Salendine Nook for a reunion including Anne and Neil.

Lucy and I were given the flat that Mum and Joe had been renting for us. We knew that all five of us would be treated equally. As soon as Lucy and I married my rent allowance had increased. It covered the expenses of running the flat. Well within our finances and with enough cutlery, towels, sheets and 'stuff' to stock an hotel.

Anne told us that their wedding present had been a three bedroomed house on the outskirts of Tadcaster for the same money as the flat. It needed a lot of work, much of which could be done by them. It was a good start. And as soon as it could be arranged volunteer working parties would meet up with Neil's family to start the work.

Frankie arrived in time for tea. Clive got stuck into his homework. Joe, I and Neil went for a walk up the road towards Outlane. It might have been a warm Spring evening by our standards but I still put a jumper on. Lucy was grilled by, guess who? Whilst I was guarding the lingerie shop, Lucy had bought Mum and the girls identical presents; apparently Mum turned slightly pink when she opened her package, the girls as one declared, Wow! I don't think Joe and Neil would object.

We walked and talked. Liz had told them about the use of the villa on Capri. They were delighted. Liz had filled them in to some extent but Joe asked my opinion. I told them everything that I knew about the island, including *La Sentiero*. The date would be about this time next year. They were looking forward to seeing our photos.

Lucy came up with a couple of photographs from the Isle of Mann. They showed the meeting between the family and Sergeant Massimiliano. That was a whole new conversation. Liz said she would write and invite them over.

Eighty

Returning our lives to the tick of various clocks was a wrench. However, the old routine was waiting and it had to be done. Mum had re-stocked the flat. There was plenty to do. Contact Dermot Reeve about the flat. Take the photos to be developed - that would cost a bomb. I called the Training School and left a message for DI Moore and one for Sergeant Round at the Driving School. Then I called work for a chat. It sounded like work.

'I'm glad you're back,' Sergeant McGill said. 'I want you to work 2-10 today. I know you're still on Annual but we can put that back on your card. We've a young girl missing and we need all the extra hands we can get.'

I called out to Lucy and told her. Her reply. 'What do you want in your sandwiches?'

The sergeant heard Lucy's reply and told me to go straight to Gomersal and liaise directly with Sergeant Sedgewick. Then he asked how the honeymoon had been. By now Lucy was standing at my shoulder. 'It was fantastic, Sergeant,' she laughed. 'I'm glad I was there.'

'Well, Mrs Blake,' he replied. You could hear the humour in his voice. 'You can have him back later.'

1330 Gomersal. Wall-to-wall cloud. About twenty volunteers milling round waiting to find out what was required. The area we had to search was behind the police station. Perched at the top of a long and steep wooded bank. Sergeant Sedgewick, a twenty year veteran and definitely built for comfort, carried out the briefing. He introduced me and Pc Carl Haig to the volunteers. 'The area we're searching runs from the back of the nick across to Marsh Lane. That's about a mile. It's also a mile to where Angela Scarfe's grandmother lives. It's not a race. Take your position from these two. Pc Blake will be at the bottom of the hill. Pc Haig at the top. Make sure you keep in line. If the line stops, so do you. If you find anything. Stop. Raise your hand and shout. Then wait until we've had a look. Any questions?'

Angela Scarfe was seven years old. Described as four feet tall, slight build with brown eyes and hair tied in a ponytail. Wearing a green gingham dress with belt, brown shoes and dark green gabardine raincoat. She was carrying a small amount of cash in her pocket when she left home at half past eight that morning to catch the bus to school in Oakenshaw. She never arrived.

It was a pig. It took twenty minutes to get everyone in line. I gave a single blast on my whistle. Answered from the top. It took almost five hours to travel that single mile. We must have stopped over a hundred times to check things out. Apart from my ripped trousers when I slipped and a selection of dead dogs and associated skeletons there was nothing. Which I suppose was good news, but as the Sergeant said later, you always hope against hope that you will find them safe and well, or, that you don't find anything.

With mixed emotions we returned to Gomersal. Sergeant Sedgewick was thanking everyone for their assistance when a Road Traffic car pulled up. Angela had been found safe and well in York. A patrolling police officer found her near to Clifford's Tower, tired, hungry and in tears. She just wanted to go home. There was a cheer when we found out that she was safe. It was almost as if we had found her. It didn't matter who had. I had my somewhat curly sandwiches and a cup of tea. Put a report in about my torn uniform trousers, I needed a new pair. As dusk was falling, they sent me home. I still got a full day put back on my card. At the same time I arrived a young Miss Scarfe was given a warm welcome by her mother.

Eighty-One

There's one thing about routine, it's easy to drop back into, only mine was different from that of the normal probationary police officer. Yes, I still worked a beat most days dealing with whatever was thrown in my direction. I still had to attend court. I also had the additional massive workload from the Academy and the Driving School. That workload was constant. One treat though was that I was to meet the Forensic Science Liaison Officer, Detective Chief Inspector Tim Gough, a six feet four inch Irishman. I spent a day in his company at the Forensic Science Lab at Harrogate. Most of what they showed me was way outside my area of expertise. Nevertheless, they took the trouble. Just as important, I met the scientists who did the work.

Having been lovers eleven months or so and not used contraceptives since the beginning of March I was used to these regular breaks in our sex life. One night in July I realised that there hadn't been one for a while. I asked the question. 'Is there something that I should know?'

From the knowing smile she knew exactly what I meant. 'What do you mean?' She enjoyed playing the game.

I slid my arms round her waist, smiled and kissed her on the nose. 'You know exactly what I mean, Lucy Blake.'

She smiled that smile. It still worked. 'Give me an idea.'

'Oh, I've got ideas,' I bent forwards and rubbed noses. 'Are you pregnant?' I whispered.

She pulled a face. 'Not sure,' she said. 'I can't say that I feel different, but if I'm not I'm very late.'

'Have you spoken to your mother, yet?'

She shook her head. 'I want to make sure first, besides,' she replied adopting a hurt expression as she stroked my cheek, 'I want to tell you first ...' then that grin appeared. 'Make love to me, again.'

The things I have to do to achieve perfection.

It was a tragedy bordering on a disaster – Lucy went off wine all together. Not that she drank a lot, but became less keen on alcohol. Hopefully that would be temporary.

A week later the Doctor confirmed that Lucy was three months pregnant.

I know that Gerald and Marianne had produced Bill and Liz's first grandchild, but the relationship between Lucy and Liz had always seemed so much stronger. Liz was over the moon and got out the whisky. Orange juice for Lucy. Gerald and Marianne gushed as much as Liz. Marianne told Lucy what to expect in terms of pain; she was such a sharing person.

We invited ourselves across to Salendine Nook. Lucy gave Mum her usual hug and whispered, 'Hello Grandma.'

You can imagine the response.

I don't know who stayed on the ceiling longest, Mum or Joe. Jen and Frankie weren't far behind. Even Clive became caught up in the excitement. It was a good night.

We got home to the sound of the telephone. Liz had told a delighted Anne.

The following morning I received notification that I was required to attend York Assize in relation to the trial of Donald Palmer. A charge of murder.

At the weekend with Lucy on the pillion we went to introduce my biological father to his first grandchild.

Eighty-Two

It was the happiest of times. We knew it wouldn't be easy with all the extra work that we had to contend with. The Special Course and Lucy still working. But somewhere around the middle of January there would be three of us. We had long chats with both Mum, Joe and Liz about several things including investments; and ourselves. 'Where would we live?' The flat was fine at the moment, but there was no garden. There was the cobbled area at the side for the dustbins and a small fenced off area where we parked the bikes with little room for a washing line. We had to consider the options. We could apply for a police house: no rent, rates or repairs to pay. On the down side, no independence, no rent allowance and we would have to live where the Force dictated. And, because I hadn't been in the job for the required twenty-two years I didn't have the automatic right to buy. If the Force wanted to be bloody minded they could transfer me anywhere they wanted at any time and insist that I lived in accommodation of their choosing. The second option, not one we wanted, would be to make do with the flat. Okay for now, but only one bedroom, no garden etc. My next day at work I took that problem to Inspector Yates.

Two days later he paid us a visit at the flat and presented us with an option which seemed perfect. A non-standard police house that would become vacant in two weeks. Non-standard because it had been purchased and not constructed to the police pattern. The officer who lived there was due to retire. He took us to meet the occupants, a DC Kevin Starkey and his wife Eva; they were moving to Chester to be closer to their daughter. It was small. Stone-built and according to the date carved in the lintel in 1921. Situated on the main Huddersfield – Leeds Road, the A62, about one and a half miles from where we lived at the moment, and a half mile from the White Gate pub. It had a small front garden but a huge one at the rear; an eighth of an acre; half of it an allotment with a greenhouse. A timber and asbestos garage to the side with a shed behind. Two bedrooms, bathroom, lounge, living room, a small kitchen and laundry. Much smaller than any police house I had seen but big enough for the next few years. There were a few issues: Pointing. Damp on the first floor. And a gas cooker that Kevin described as having been first used by Noah on the Ark. One black mark I didn't mention was that the cottage was about a mile from the spot where Christine Jones was murdered by Magnus Yarney, who, twelve months later murdered my father. That was ancient history.

I received an answer to my application within ten days, offering me the opportunity to occupy Hartshead View Cottage. A schedule of works was drawn up for the repairs. It was to be gutted: new kitchen and bathroom suite, gas central heating installed, new bathroom suite – both to be re-tiled, complete re-wiring. At least the address would still be the same.

Eighty-Three

I was on loan to DCI Valentine, again. There had been several sightings of Marjorie Simmonds in the area of a supermarket and a filling station about half a mile from her home in Park View Grange, Leeds 16. I was the only member of the team who had met her. And now we had a reason to interview. Neither her mother nor her solicitor claimed to have had any contact.

Park View Grange. Detached houses. Expensive. High hedges. Gated. Plenty of adequate private parking. Nevertheless there were vehicles left on-street. A motor cycle was more manoeuvrable. Enquiries had been made at her home. No answer. The Farrell family, her next-door neighbours, were asked to let us know should she reappear.

One improvement over last time. I had one of the new multi-channel radios at my disposal. It was a simple but often boring task, you just had to keep your wits about you and not drift into reverie. Not always easy.

The second day. Fine with no threat of rain. I was working the evening shift. At 22.30 a call came through from the Farrells reporting a blazing row at Simmond's house. DC Mark Wilby was the nearest. I wasn't far away and didn't hang about. I was lucky to survive the left turn into Park View Grange. A dark red Jaguar being driven at speed cut the corner forcing me onto the footpath and a couple of pedestrians to leap out of my way. The street lights were dim. Nevertheless, the driver looked straight at me. I could have sworn it was Nigel Ridley, Simmonds' ex. Why the hurry? Had he just paid Marjorie a visit? I apologised to the pedestrians and told them to contact the police who would be behind me.

Simmonds lived in the last house on the right. Twin entrances to the drive. Mark Wilby's car was stationary opposite the door. Headlights on. Driver's door wide open. Mark was hanging onto the door and leaning against the windscreen. Radio by his feet. Blood dripping from his left wrist and his jacket sleeve. Blood stains right chest and left shoulder. 'Mark. What happened?'

He shook his head. His breathing was laboured. 'Guy ran out ... large ... hold-all ... got out ... bastard ... revolver ...shot me twice.'

'OK.' I pressed the talk switch. '547 urgent.'

Sergeant Nicholson answered. 'Go ahead, Brian.'

'Mark Wilby's been shot, twice.' Penny, seated on the next console, flinched, grabbed the handset and dialled. 'Right chest and left shoulder He's conscious and able to talk. Haven't been in the house yet.'

'Ok. Penny's ringing the ambulance. Mr Valentine?' he called.

The DCI dashed out of his office. 'Yes, I heard. Let me talk ... Brian, DCI. How is he?'

'Conscious and talking, sir,' before I could say anything else there was the sound of running feet behind me.

'Are you police officers?'

'Just a sec, sir.' I turned. The speaker a man in his late forties. A woman of the same age and a younger man. 'We are,'

'We called your chief inspector regarding the row. My wife and I are doctors. Farrell. My son is a medical student. We heard gunshots.'

'My colleague's been shot. His name is Mark.'

'Let's have a look at you young man,' the lady said easing me out of the way.

'Did you get that, sir?'

'Yes. Fortuitous. Can you shed any light on what happened?'

'Mark said that as he arrived a man carrying a large holdall ran out of the house. He exited and was shot twice. He said it was a revolver.'

'Do you know how bad the injuries are?'

'Looks like right chest and left shoulder, sir. He's upright and talking if that's anything to go by. Oh, they've just sat him down. One more thing sir. As I turned into the Grange I was nearly taken out by a dark red Jag. Forced me onto the footpath. The light wasn't good but I could have sworn that the driver was Nigel Ridley. He might be heading for the A1.'

'Ridley?'

'Couldn't swear to it sir, but I think so. From memory the No. is 129 C something. Definitely the same model and colour as Ridley drives. If there's nothing else, I'll check the house for signs of Simmonds.'

Sergeant Nicholson's voice. 'Ok Brian. Well done. Assistance is en route. We'll get the obs out. Keep the channel open and give me a commentary. One room at a time. And, take care. With your history ...' There was a hint of humour.

'Noted,' I replied with a grin.

I took one last look at Mark Wilby in the safe hands of the Doctors Farrell and turned to the house. 'Could I come with you?' The voice of the youngest Farrell.

'Sorry,' I smiled 'This is a crime scene. I'll have to do this on my own.'

Leaving the disgruntled medical student behind I took my elevated heart rate with me. 'Sarge, from where I'm standing all downstairs lights to the front of the house are on. The front door is wide open.'

'Noted.'

This was going to be a very deliberate process. 'I'm entering the hallway. No sign of a disturbance.'

I held my breath. Other than my heart pounding in my throat it was silent. Slowly does it. Five paces to the first doorway. 'Reception room to the left. Again, no sign of a disturbance.'

'Crossing the hallway.' Three paces. 'Reception room cum library to the right. There are a few books strewn around. Going to the rear of the house next.'

Eight paces. 'The dining room is a mess.' Then I saw the body. I took a deep breath and exhaled. 'Fully clothed female lying on the kitchen floor behind the table. Prone position. Not moving. Blood on her head. Hang on a sec.' The blinds hadn't been drawn. I could see from the reflection there was no-one else present. I knelt at the side of the body and spoke. 'Sarge, it's Marjorie Simmonds. There's a small hole in her left temple with what looks like residue around it. The shot taken at close range. He was taking no chances that his ex-wife would talk.'

'Ok, Brian. Well done. That's enough. Leave it for C.I.D. They should be with you very shortly. Wait at the door. DI Forrester will be taking charge. Keep *everyone* out until he arrives. Ok?'

I took a deep breath and sighed. 'Will do.'

I didn't have long to wait. First the ambulance arrived and left with Mark in the back accompanied by the female Dr. Farrell. The other Doctor Farrell and his son hanging around, waiting.

Seconds later three cars arrived and disgorged their occupants. They stood to one side allowing an officer to walk through. Five eleven. Greying hair, dark suit and shoes. 'Pc Blake?'

'Yes, sir.'

'DI Forrester. Who's been in?'

'Only me, sir.'

'Moment.' He turned to one of the officers. 'Forbes, detail some of these,' he indicated the spare officers. 'Get all these vehicles off the road and into their drives. I want full details of the occupants of every house on this estate and where they've been over the past two hours. Details of all comings and goings. Then speak with Doctor Farrell, ascertain the details of the injuries to DC Wilby and arrange to take their statements, asap. Two at the end of the Grange. Details of anyone leaving including their address. Intended destination and reason for the journey. Likewise everyone trying to enter. Where they are going and why. And, if I find any members of the Press within fifty yards, I'll have your balls for breakfast.' He turned to me. 'Who went with your colleague?'

'A lady doctor, Doctor Farrell.'

'Ok, she's a surgeon. Oh, sergeant, one on the gate. There'll be a County DCI name of Valentine. Allow him and his party access. Other than that, only studio and forensic.' He turned his back on the others. 'Blake, something about a red Jaguar?'

'Yes sir. As I was turning into the Grange he was leaving at speed and cut the corner, forced me onto the footpath.'

'See the number or the driver?'

'Not the full number but I half-recognised the car and the driver. If I'm right it's Nigel Ridley, the deceased's ex. Lives in Hambleton in Rutland.'

I was on the receiving end of a questioning look. 'And how, pray, do you know that?'

'When I worked for DCI Valentine before, sir. I was under-cover acting as a courier for Marjorie Simmonds. My first call was to her ex, Nigel Ridley. A nasty piece of work. He drives a dark red Jag, same colour and model.'

'You've passed these details on to your team?'

'Yes, sir.'

'Fair enough. Talk me through.'

Sixty seconds later we were in the dining room. 'Shall I wait at the door, sir,' I said.

'No, come and confirm this is who you say it is.'

I crouched at his side. 'Yes, this is the woman I know as Marjorie Simmonds.'

'How often had you seen her?'

I did a quick count. Eleven times over six days. The first time I was in her company for almost twenty minutes. The last was when the operation blew up. She's not been seen since until a few weeks ago.

He nodded. 'Did you check the rest of the house?'

'No, sir. Once I'd reported finding the body I had instructions to leave it for you.'

'Fair enough.'

I left Inspector Forrester and his team to get on with it and chatted with Bob Robshaw, the local beat bobby on the door. I didn't have long to wait. DCI Valentine, DS Cartwright and DC Myers arrived.

'Brian, are you ok?'

'Fine, sir.'

'Good,' he laughed. 'You'll get a reputation if you're not careful. Getting yourself so close to firearms and bodies.'

I grinned in return. 'Just as long as I'm not one of the bodies.'

'Agreed. You think it was Ridley?'

'It was a dark red Jag, same model and colour that I saw at Hambleton. I only got a glimpse of the driver when I swerved. That's the impression that I got. When I first spoke to him there was definitely some animosity between him and Simmonds. She laughed it off, but ...'

'He seems to have had a history of running out of cash, sir,' offered Derek Myers.

'True. Brian, you get off. Get the paperwork done and then off home.'

'Yes, sir. Er, do we know how Mark is?'

'No. He'll be at LGI. Max and Penny have gone to collect his wife.' I nodded and put my helmet on. My heart rate was still elevated.

'Try to stay out of trouble,' was the DCI's pained parting shot. I waved over my shoulder and turned left out of the drive.

Eighty-Four

The closer I got to Leeds City Centre the slower the traffic. Was this the norm or were there ongoing road checks? I was all right paddling down the centre of the road checking the cars in front. The Jag would stand out like a sore thumb. It did. Three cars in front. My heart rate took off, again. How many rounds he had left I didn't know. It was not good. One occupant. Gender unknown. I kicked my bike into neutral and tapped on the offside window of the car on my left. The driver wound the window down. 'I don't know this area of Leeds well,' I said. 'What road is this please?'

'Roseville Road,' he said and looked at the bike. 'Nice bike. Can I have a look?'

He made as if to open the driver's door. The last thing I wanted were innocent pedestrians milling round. 'Stay in the car, please,' I said.

'Just a look.'

'I'm a police officer. Please stay in your car.'

'It's only a look. I'm not breaking the law.'

'Later,' I said. 'And what's that side street on your left?'

He wasn't happy. 'Gledhow Place,' he muttered.

My radio was clipped onto my jacket lapel. '547 urgent.' Now the driver was listening.

'Go ahead, Brian.'

'Roseville Road, Leeds junction with Gledhow Place. Traffic stationary. The Jag is three cars in front. One occupant, over.'

'Jesus! Try and keep people out of the way and keep your channel open.'

'Will do.'

Someone tapped on my helmet. 'You're a copper? Problem with that Jag?'

I glanced over my shoulder. 'Get back in your car, please. Keep out of the way.'

'Why, what's up?'

I was getting ratty. 'Get out of the blood...' I froze as the driver's door opened. 'Move, now,' I snapped and almost spat into the mike. '547 he's exiting.' I kicked the bike into first and slipped the clutch as Ridley, now clear of the car, revolver in right hand. holdall in left, turned in my direction. Now I was feet away. He fired two shots in the air creating the effect that I wanted. Everyone disappeared.

Ridley pointed the revolver at my face. My heart rate took off again. *Oh shit!* Not exactly what I wanted but I noticed the hammer was down. However, he had fired five shots and unless he had reloaded there was one left. The odds were better but still in his favour. Holdall in his left hand he climbed onto the pillion and stuck the revolver in my back. 'One wrong move and I will fire. Understand?'

'I understand,' I said into the mike. 'With a gun in my back you're the boss. Where do you want to go?'

'Just ride.'

'He said he had a gun in his back?'

'Yes.'

'Ok. Ridley is likely to be heading south. You get onto Force Control. Jenny, call Leeds. Pass details of Brian's bike. Stress obs. only. Advise re armed pillion passenger. No attempt to intervene. We don't want any bloody heroes or dead probationers.'

'Ok. Keep me posted. I'll be with you in a few minutes.'

Ridley pushed the revolver hard into my back. 'Why have you stopped?'

'I can't hear you for the traffic noise. Just tell me then I'll know what I'm doing.'

'Pont ...'

Our conversation was interrupted. 'Just a minute.' A fresh-faced constable, pocket book in hand, appeared at our side. 'What are you carrying in that holdall. I was watching you from the traffic lights. You're all over the shop. It's dangerous. I want to see what's inside.'

'It really is nothing to do with you, officer,' Ridley was getting very twitchy.

Good grief. What next? 'Officer, you don't want to do this,' I glanced over my shoulder and pressed the talk key. 'You were going to say, Pontefract?'

'Yes. Now get out of here.'

I kicked the bike into first and left the open-mouthed probationer on the footpath. 'What! ...' he pressed the talk key. 'Pc 1034, I've ...'

The road to Pontefract was straight ahead. Through Hunslet and keep left along the A639 at Thwaite Gate. A journey impeded by Ridley's holdall. Whatever it contained was heavy. I pressed the button on the radio and shouted over my shoulder. 'We keep left here towards Pontefract.' I hoped Sergeant Nicholson did not reply. Ridley replied by pressing the revolver into my back, hard.

Traffic was backing up fast and nothing was coming towards us. 'Take this right,' my passenger said almost too late. I braked hard and managed to slow enough to make the turn and stopped.

I realised that I had forgotten that I could lock the channel open. They would hear everything and wouldn't be able to speak. I stopped.

'I told you not to stop. Now get going.;
'Look, you've proved your point ...'

DCI Valentine, DS Cartwright and DC Myers dashed into the squad office.

DS Nicholson put his finger to his lips. 'Recording's on, sir. Brian's locked the channel open.'

'... *You've got a revolver and it's loaded. All I want to do is get home to my wife. We've just got back from our honeymoon. I'm not going to do anything stupid. Now where do you want to go? And please take that fucking gun out of my back. I don't want to hit a pothole and you fire it accidentally.*'

Several seconds later. '*You know the area?*'

'*Yes, where do you want to go?*'

'*There's a truck stop on the A1.*'

'*Charlie Fortes?*'

'*You know it?*'

'*I'm a biker. Of course I know it.*'

'*Side roads. No towns. Now move.*'

''*Side roads probably. Towns? If you want to get across the river I've got to go through Castleford. I'll stay out of the town centre. Then past Fairburn Ings. It's a nature reserve in the middle of nowhere*'

'*How long?*'

'*Twenty five to thirty minutes ... The revolver?*'

'*All right but no funny business.*'

DCI Valentine stepped back. 'Peter, ring Mr Handerson, he lives at Whitwood, next door to Castleford. Get him down to Castleford nick pronto. Stress the delicacy of the situation. Keep Pandas out of the way. Obs. only.'

'Sir.'

'Jenny, speak to the Duty Officer in Force Control. Bring him up to speed. Stress to keep traffic cars out of the way unless specifically detailed and, all obs to be passed here ... Derek, the Leeds Control Room. Tell them it's in our area and to liaise with Castleford. Then put the kettle on.'

'Sir.'

'John, you keep the log. No doubt Force Control will have their own. I'll call Mr Creighton.'

'Shop!' Detective Superintendent Creighton slapped his hand on the public counter. 'DS Creighton,' he waved his warrant card as the office PC appeared.

The atmosphere in the office was oppressive.

'John,' he said shaking hands with Superintendent John Stilwell, Pontefract divisional officer.

'Vincent, welcome. What's the story so far?'

He held his hand up. 'Moment. Mark do you know where they are at the moment?'

Detective Inspector Mark Henderson moved to the large wall map. 'He's sticking to the back roads where possible, sir. He was here,' he pointed to a road junction 'Methley Junction about a minute ago. Providing he sticks to what we've heard this is the route we expect him to take. Follow the main road and turn left here towards Castleford town centre. Across the river bridge heading north along Barnsdale Road. At this crossroads turn right along Newton Lane passed Fairburn Ings, the nature reserve, to Fairburn. Ridley's intention was to travel south from Fairburn to Charlie Fortes. After that we don't know.'

'Thanks. Sorry John. The pillion passenger is Nigel Ridley, a former army officer. Wanted for murdering his ex-wife in her kitchen with a shot to the head and putting two bullets into the chest of one of my DCs. He's still in surgery. Plus the kidnapping of PC Blake whose wife is expecting their first. All less than an hour ago. We know Ridley fired two shots in the air when he kidnapped Blake. We don't know if he reloaded or how many bullets he may have in reserve.'

'Christ. This Blake, he seems to have a cool head.'

'He has ... Has everybody been warned to keep out of the way?'.

'They have. And, that Ridley is believed armed. There's a traffic car parked well back out of sight in Park Lane. He will let us know when and if Blake takes the right turn into Newton Lane. Then follow at distance. There are two Pandas out. One is tied up dealing with a domestic and Maltravers, in the second, has been told to keep clear for now. He's to follow up and stop any traffic from entering Newton Lane. There's a phone box about thirty yards from the river bridge with a PC close by. He'll ring in when the bike takes the Barnsdale Road. If he takes the right-turn into Newton Lane we have a surprise for him at Caudle Hill. Inspector Rodgers, DS Gray and PC Smith, the Fairburn beat officer, all ex-military, two of them armed, have arranged with a local farmer to drop several hundredweight of pig slurry on the road. That will stop anything.'

DS Creighton laughed. 'I think the smell would do that on its own.'

'Probably. But what's the significance of this holdall Ridley is carrying?'

'His ex-wife ran a successful gambling syndicate. We suspect it's cash.'

The desk phone began to ring. DI Henderson snatched it from the cradle. 'DI Henderson ... Thanks.' He redialled. 'Duty Officer ... DI Henderson, Castleford. Inform your car the bike is heading north on the Barnsdale Road.'

So far so good. Ridley had his left hand full of holdall. His right hand on my shoulder. The revolver tucked somewhere out of sight. Let's hope the two didn't get together again. I glanced in my offside mirror. There was a Panda about one hundred yards adrift. POLICE sign off it still stood out like a sore thumb. I hope he had the sense not to get too close.

'John Needham and Greg Marsden sitting patiently in their Austin Westminster flinched when the message came through about the bike.

'Whisky 89 all received.'

'Who wants to live forever, John,' said Greg.'

'Just don't get too close then they won't spot the lights.'

'You know I hadn't thought of that.'

'Smart arse. Here he comes,' said Greg as Blake with his passenger slowed and turned into Newton Lane. 'I wonder what's in the holdall. He's carried it from Leeds. Must be valuable.'

'Don't give a shit. Make the call.'

John Needham grinned at his friend and pressed the talk clip. 'Whisky 89 to control, urgent.'

'Go ahead.'

'The bike has now turned right into Newton Lane. Will follow shortly.'

'All received.'

Seconds later. 'Christ, what the fuck does Maltravers think he's playing at?'

'Whisky 89 urgent. The panda is following the bike. He was supposed to stop traffic.'

'Noted, stand by ... Whisky 89 follow at safe distance.'

'Noted.'

'He's what? Thanks, leave it with me.' DI Henderson replaced the handset. 'The Panda has followed the bike in front of the traffic car.'

'The stupid bastard,' Superintendent Stilwell spat the words out. 'What does Maltravers think this is, a glory hunt.' He leaned forwards and pressed the switch on the radio. 'Pc Maltravers, this is Superintendent Stilwell. Your instructions were to prevent traffic entering Newton Lane. You will comply. Acknowledge.'

Pat Maltravers turned his radio off. *Bollocks,* he thought. *'traffic getting the glory again. They can stuff that.*

'Inspector Rodgers, did you get that, over?'

'All received, sir. It will take then a good five minutes before they reach us. The slurry has been poured. We are ready.'

'Thank you.'

I just had time to see the Westminster tag on behind the Panda before the bends blocked my view. Besides this was a narrow and twisty road and a good chance that some of the water fowl from the flooded mine workings might be taking an evening stroll. The last thing I needed.

My passenger was getting twitchy. 'Can't you go any faster?'

I slowed. 'Look through the shrubs on your right you'll see the moon shining on Fairburn Ings. Flooded mine workings. I don't want to go round a bend at speed and find a couple of dozen geese or swans in the way. In five minutes we'll reach Fairburn village then it's the A1. Fifteen minutes to Charlie Fortes.'

There was a grunt from the rear.

All was going well until a figure emerged out of the gloom. Waving his arms and shouting something about slurry. Was this what I was hoping for? 'What the hell was that?'

'Don't know,' he said.

'He shouted something about slurry.'

'Whatever it was keep going, or else.'

'Slurry is liquid animal shit.' Too late! I saw the farm trailer across the road and the slurry spreading towards me. I hit the brakes. My rear wheel locked and slid violently to the nearside. We hit the deck with a thump and slid. Ridley parted company from the bike. The smell indescribable. All Hell broke loose.

The scene suddenly floodlighted as the Panda pulled up ten yards short, headlights blazing and blue light working overtime. The sound of running feet. The unmistakable sight of a police uniform. Another set of headlights behind. Slamming doors and more running feet.

My heart missed a beat as Ridley, still hanging onto the holdall, plunged his right hand inside his coat. The running feet stopped. The road surface was slick but I managed to get my foot against the bike's fuel tank as a pair of hands grasped Ridley's coat. 'Kidnap a copper you bastard. Your arse is mine. You're nicked.'

When a revolver is cocked the cylinder revolves. If the cylinder can't move the weapon can't be cocked. The bike slid backwards as I launched myself reaching for the revolver. Too late.

The first shot smashed the officer's breastbone. The second keyholed to the right. He collapsed in a heap across Ridley. I managed to get a hold of Ridley's coat with my right hand pulled and scrabbled as he swung the revolver towards me and pulled the hammer back. I managed to get a grip on the cylinder and push it away as he fired.; the bullet striking my bike. Ridley fighting to re-cock the weapon.

'Let go, Ridley. It's over.'

The two traffic officers grabbed hold of their fallen colleague. 'Pat,' one shouted. 'Are you all right?'

What the fuck? 'Get the fucking gun!' I shouted.

Ridley screamed as a police truncheon landed across his radius.

'You heard what the officer said. Let go.'

I took the revolver from Ridley's nerveless fingers. The two traffic officers removed the holdall from his left hand and cuffed him where he lay, accompanied by screams as the cuff bit into his wrist.

I manged to relax a little. 'Your colleague took two in the chest. From the way he fell he's dead.'

'Oh fuck. Greg take Pat's other arm. Let's get him out of the way.'

Between them they manoeuvred their colleague to the grass verge. 'He's no carotid pulse,' said the second.

'Shit.'

'It's over,' I said to Ridley.

'He said you were a copper. I should have shot you whilst I had a chance.'

That would go down well in court.

Illuminated by the headlights I could see Ridley's right wrist swelling. 'My wrist. These cuffs.'

'Sorry, is it hurting?' said Greg. 'If you can't take it, sunshine, don't dish it out.' He looked down at me and smiled. 'You ok, kid?'

'Better now, thanks. Give me a hand up will you?'

Three more officers arrived. 'Where's Maltravers?'

'Over here, sir. He's dead. Two bullets in the chest and no carotid pulse.'

'Christ. The stupid bastard.' He turned to me. 'You're PC Blake?'

'Yes, sir.'

'Are you injured at all?'

'Apart from the eau de cologne and being a bit shaken, sir, I'm ok. At least I think so.'

'Whatever, bloody well done. Sergeant Gray? Come and take possession of this firearm.'

Inspector Rodgers took the few steps to the Panda picked up the radio. 'Inspector. Is the Super there?'

'No sir. He's en route with a Detective Superintendent Creighton and DI Henderson. Should be with you in five minutes.'

'Yes, OK. I don't care who but find someone to close off Newton Lane. Try Force Control. The van out at Caudle Hill for the prisoner and the police surgeon and photographer, yesterday?'

'Will do, sir.'

'Before you finish, sir,' I interjected. 'Could someone get a message to DCI Valentine to let my wife know I'm going to be late. And can someone check Ridley's pockets for spare ammo. He fired five shots before I came across him and three just now, so he must have reloaded.'

'We'll do that, sir,' the traffic officer called Greg said. He and his colleague, none too gently, set about the search.

'Inspector Rodgers. Inform DCI Valentine that we have the prisoner and PC Blake reports being uninjured.'

'Yes, sir. I'm on with them now.'

DS Gray smiled at Blake. 'I'll take that revolver if you can bear to part with it.'

'Sorry, here,' I handed it over. 'How can I get this shit off my leathers?'

The DS grimaced. 'We've a fire engine up the road to wash the road down. I'm sure they can spare a drop or two. Are you sure you're ok. You look a bit rough.'

'I've felt better. I want to check my bike. It went down with a hell of a thump. And the last shot that Ridley fired hit it somewhere.'

'There's time for that later, Blake,' said DS Gray. 'I want photographs of the bike in situ.'

'Here you are Sarge,' said Greg. 'Five spare rounds in his pocket. A one man war.'

'So what happened at the house?'

'Shot his ex-wife in the head and hit DC Wilby twice in the chest. The last I heard Mark was still in surgery. Fired two in the air to get rid of bystanders before pointing the gun at my face.'.

DS Gray nodded. 'Needham.'

'Sarge?'

'Accompany Ridley back to the nick and stress to the duty sergeant to put a POL1 on the detention sheet. Tick the appropriate boxes'

'Will do.'

He picked the holdall up and turned to me. 'Now then Blake, just what is in this holdall?'

'Don't know exactly, Sarge but I suspect a lot of cash.'

'Let's have a look.'

Bag unzipped DS Gray looked inside. 'Good God!' he gasped. 'Where did this lot come from?'

'Ridley's ex-wife ran a very successful gambling syndicate. She was paid two grand commission per member per race.'

'What!'

I smiled to myself. 'Somewhere there's just shy of £1,000,000 floating round.'

'I'm in the wrong bloody job,' he gave me a strange look. 'What service have you got in?'

'I came out of Pannal in September last year.'

'September?'

'Yes, Sarge.'

He shook his head. 'OK, let's get you and the holdall cleaned off.'

'If you have no objections, sir,' said DI Henderson, 'You've got Blake's statement I'll be in touch in the morning.'

Superintendent Creighton looked at his watch and smiled. 'That's today.'

DI Henderson glanced at the office clock. 'So it is.'

The office clerk picked up the phone. 'Castleford,' he held the phone out.

'It's DCI Valentine for DI Henderson.'

'Sir?'

'... That's great, I'll tell him. His bike has a ruptured fuel tank so that's staying here for now. Perhaps the Spartans can fix it for him,' he laughed. 'Yes, I agree. He's at the Assize in a couple of days and he does need a couple of days off, at least. He's very tired. He's going to call Lucy then I'll take him home ... I'll see you later this morning.' He handed the phone back to the clerk and turned to the others. 'Mark Wilby's out of surgery and off the danger list.'

'Did you say, Spartans, Mr Henderson?' said Superintendent Stilwell.

'I did, sir. Blake's wife, Lucy's father was Bill Vernon.

'I see. Then you were at Tadcaster, Blake?'

'Yes, sir. That was an interesting night.'

'Hello love,' I'll be home soon, Mr Handerson's bringing me ... No I had a bit of a spill the bike's got a ruptured fuel tank. (It wouldn't do any good to tell Lucy it also had a bullet hole) ... no, I'm Ok, just a bit stiff and tired. See you soon.'

The next morning the cash was taken to a local bank and counted. The total £260,000. Where was the remainder?

Where had Marjorie Simmonds been for the past weeks?

Mick Grant's house.

Grant might have been in prison but his wife and children were still living close-by. How she came to be in contact with Ridley was, as yet, unknown.

Over the next days, with the exception of the Vernon's and The Grange all members of the syndicate were visited once more to see what information could be elicited in regard to Marjorie Brooks.

The members were informed that in all probability their investment was ended. There was nothing new.

Eighty-Five

Being tied to the house was a novel and unwelcome experience. The DCI paid me a visit and told Lucy to call him should I attempt to leave the house prior to my attendance at the Assize. 'You're in danger of burn-out if you don't rest. Once the trial is over take the medication. You're no good to anyone if you can't function properly.' At least he didn't mention the bullet hole in the tank.

0915 Two days after the event. York Assize. Courtesy of the DI, complete with butterflies, I arrived ten seconds after John Bradbury. Together we found the Court Calendar. Palmer was the first case in No.1 court. We arranged to meet later in the foyer. John and I went to find where we should report.

The Usher brought us to where a man in a periwig and gown was leafing through a very large file. He cleared his throat. 'Sir Garson?'

He looked up and nodded. The usher left. 'Sir Garson Grayling QC, Prosecution,' he said. 'Which of you is Pc Blake?'

'I am, sir,' I said.

He looked at John. 'And you're Pc Bradbury?'

'Yes, sir.

Another periwig-sporting lawyer sauntered up. 'Ah, Garson,' he said. 'Your probationary constables, if I'm not mistaken.' He smiled and ran his tongue across his lips. 'Yummy.'

Sir Garson laughed. 'This is Sir Alistair Black QC, for the defence. Ignore him.'

I looked from side-to-side. 'Sorry, Sir, but, ignore who?'

Sir Garson laughed again. The man who wasn't there narrowed his eyes and sauntered off. 'He does like his thin ice,' he said to his opponent's retreating back. 'Right, have you both been to court?' We had. John only Magistrate's Court.

'I've been to the Old Bailey, Sir.'

He peered at me over his glasses. 'Why?'

'Manville-Jones, Sir. I was his arresting officer.'

His face became wreathed in smiles. 'Were you indeed? So you've met Lord Justice Nevison.'

My smile matched his as I nodded. 'Yes, Sir.'

'For the benefit of your colleague, Lord Justice Nevison, very proper and a stickler for etiquette. Address him at all times as, My Lord. I will lead you through the evidence. Just answer the questions I put to you. Do not run off at a tangent.' He smiled. 'Trust me. I've done this before.' Had he heard about my faux pas? He ran through several other points and then asked if either of us had any questions. John hadn't.

'What are the chances that Palmer will plead guilty, Sir?'

'If he's any sense he will. There's too much evidence. He has no wriggle room. But you never know until it happens. However, if he has been given the appropriate advice he will know that pleading guilty now will count in his favour when he comes round to a parole hearing.'

We were in the Well of the court when Lord Justice Nevison took his place. Palmer was produced from the cells and jury sworn. The Clerk read out the charge. 'Donald Palmer, you are charged with the murder of Julie Slater, contrary to Common Law. How do you plead?'

There was a lengthy silence. 'Mr Palmer?'

There was a gasp as Palmer replied. 'Guilty.' At least Valerie Johnson would not have to give evidence. Perhaps he did have feelings for her after all, even if not for Julie Slater.

I felt a pat on the back. 'Well done.' Behind me was DI Vellander.

Lord Justice Nevison laid his pre-sentencing comments on with a trowel. His betrayal of his position in society. The fact that he was married and Julie was only nineteen years of age. He was sentenced to life imprisonment. The only sentence available for convicted murderers. As Palmer was being taken away the Judge leaned forwards and said something to the Clerk who came across and spoke with Sir Garson. Five minutes later John and I were in the presence of Lord Justice Nevison, minus his wig. He was scratching his head. 'Damned nuisance,' he said and smiled.

He looked at John. 'Pc Bradbury.'

'My Lord?'

'I understand you had to wake Pc Blake up when he was late for duty?'

'Yes, My Lord. It happens.'

'Indeed it does. I served in the army as well. I hope Pc Blake remembers that.'

'I'm sure he will, Sir.'

He turned his attention to me and smiled. 'We meet again.'

'Indeed, My Lord.'

'How is your wife. You are now married I take it?'

'Yes My Lord. Since the New year.'

'Good. Serving in the police is akin to serving in the army. Neither, in the long run are the best option for the single man. But having a husband in either isn't the best option for the wife. Always worrying about the unexpected knock on the door.'

'I concur, My Lord. From personal experience.'

He thought for a moment. 'Oh yes, your father.'

'Yes, My Lord.'

'Well done both of you. And Pc Blake, try not to make a habit of having to rely on your friends too often. Now, if you will excuse me.

John's parting shot was – Can't you o anything without somebody trying to put a bullet in you pr burn you to death. How many lives have to got left? You'd be safer if the army.'

I couldn't think of anything sensible to say

I began the medication that evening and slept for almost five days, apart from visits to the bathroom and finding time to eat.. I have to admit I did feel better.

Liz had my bike literally brought up to speed by Neil. New tank with the flying **S** on the tank. And a few modifications you don't get on standard production bikes.

Eighty-Six

The day we moved in Lucy was looking even more beautiful, just three months to go. We had numerous visitors from Salendine Nook and Boston Spa. Our new neighbours were pleased to have another policeman as a neighbour – I wasn't too sure about that. I worked at Westleigh and the house was in Mirfield. Some education would be called for.

Inspector Yates, or Calvin as he now insisted we call him when we were not on duty, his wife Caroline and Michael, their fifteen month old son, became regular visitors. They lived a few miles away at Clifton. That was good for Lucy, she didn't have many friends in the area as yet. We'd decided to keep the flat and rent it out. To get round any problems accruing from the additional income stream, our solicitor, Dermot Reeve, recommended setting up a separate company in Lucy's name to manage the affairs; the force agreed. They couldn't make us sell the flat but we had to submit an annual set of accounts, a bit of a bind. Joe's accountant sorted that out.

We settled in well, travelling to work was easier, we were a mile and a half nearer. Lucy loved the house. It was perfect. The female neighbours soon made themselves at home. They were impressed with the photographs of us in Capri. They didn't travel abroad. The second bedroom, decorated as a nursery, was accumulating baby paraphernalia, most of it grandparent derived. Lucy was ensuring that I kept up with my studies. And the girls? Just try and keep them away. Anne, as always, riding pillion to Neil when they could make the time. It was a fifty mile round trip and, because she had transferred her course to York we saw even less of her. Frankie, of course, Vance's pillion. Jennifer? Still suffering from the after effects of Tom's arrest was on her own. She bought her own bike.

On the advice of the County Prosecuting Solicitor, the charges in relation to Tom and Co. were reduced from burglary to theft. They could be dealt with at Quarter Sessions instead of the Assize. Not such a hit on the public purse. Nevertheless, because of the breach of trust, Tom and his brother had been sentenced to four years imprisonment. The others to thirty months.

Eighty-Seven

The flow of shoplifters from Buy Smart had eased considerably since opening. That didn't stop the dedicated from trying it on. Anyone convicted of theft on the premises was permanently barred. There were, however, always those who liked a challenge. That explained why, the following Saturday, I was having a coffee with assistant manager, Mike Preston, whilst I took his statement for an arrest the day before. His desk in the glass-fronted office, eight feet above the shop floor, providing great views. Access was via a short flight of steps on the left. Immediately below Mike Preston's desk was the access door to the basement storeroom, on the right of which was the hoist for moving products. Between the two doors the light switch for the stairs and the basement.

Unbeknown to anyone in Buy Smart, at 3pm yesterday, a driver delivering to Tomkins's shoe shop was turning his van round in the same yard where I'd made my first arrest. He misjudged the distance and reversed into the wall at the side of Buy Smart's delivery doors with a hefty thump.

Buy Smart might have been a new build from the ground upwards, but the gas supply and meter were not. The impact cracked the union between the pipe and the meter. The meter was in the basement storeroom directly beneath the safe in Mike Preston's office. The driver examined the rear of the vehicle but all he could see was a dent and a few scratches. He was late and didn't take the trouble to tell anyone.

I thanked Mike for the coffee, shook hands, pocketed the statement and left the office. At the bottom of the stairs was Saturday boy, Norman Jones. Always smiling. 'Morning Norman,' I said. 'Are they keeping you busy?'

He grinned and nodded, 'Morning Pc Blake, just going to the cellar to play with the spiders.'

'Have fun,' I said and headed for the door.

'Thanks,' he replied. 'I will.'

My next call was to serve a summons on my old friend Cuthbert Wainwright. Not for parking offences this time, but for failing to stop at a red traffic light in Huddersfield. Would he never learn? Normally this would be served by post but he was likely to be disqualified, therefore the summons had been marked for personal service and his attendance in court was mandatory; no guilty plea by post this time. It was good to renew old acquaintances.

Mike Preston poked his head out of his office door. 'Just a sec Norman, before you go downstairs.'

The drizzle had stopped and the sun trying to make its presence known as I mingled with the shoppers in Bradford Road. There were still several weeks to Christmas, nevertheless, everywhere was busy. A few seconds later I was assailed by a shrill, 'Yoo hoo. Mr Blake.' I smiled and waved. Coming towards me was a local celebrity. She must have been over eighty if she was a day, no-one knew for certain. President of the local WI since the year dot. Mind as sharp as a tack and dressed more smartly than anyone else on the street. Mrs Violet Carson, the same as the actress who played Ena Sharples in Coronation Street, but I'll wager that she had never worn a hairnet in her life. A widow; her husband had been a local haulier and left her financially secure. What she didn't know wasn't worth knowing. But where she got her information from nobody knew. If she liked you she was a gold mine of information.

'Good morning, Mrs Carson,' I said and smiled.' You're looking well this morning.' She looked well every morning.

'I'm fine Mr Blake, thank you for enquiring,' she replied. 'And how is that lovely wife of yours? When is the baby due?'

'She's fine thank you, and the baby's due in mid-January.' I replied.

Norman, having had his instructions from Mike Preston switched on the light as he opened the cellar door. The gas had been leaking for almost twenty hours. There was a spark from the light fitting at the bottom of the steps. The explosion blew the front of Buy Smart into the middle of the road.

Eighty-Eight

I'd never heard a noise like it. It felt as though the air had exploded. The pressure wave hit. For several seconds I was disorientated, as if a giant invisible hand had grabbed hold of me and given me a good shaking. It was lucky we were a few yards passed the Buy Smart window otherwise I might have been wearing it. My greatcoat gave me some protection but my ears were ringing and my back felt odd. No pain. Just odd.

The sounds of broken glass. Cans of food flying round like unexploded hand grenades. The explosion reverberating around the surrounding buildings, car horns, fire and other alarms mixed with the screams and crying of the injured.

I'd instinctively wrapped my arms around Mrs Carson who was shaken but otherwise appeared all right. I guided her to a small café two doors away and sat her down inside as everyone else rushed out. 'Stay there, Mrs Carson. I'll be back as soon as I can.'

It was overwhelming chaos! The pavement and the road were littered with glass, debris, foodstuffs and the injured.

What the Hell do I do now?

Where do I start?

Why couldn't I think straight?

Somebody must have heard that. The injured. A woman in a blue coat lay on the floor not moving. I knelt at her side. Two young women knelt opposite me and were covering the woman's face with a pocket handkerchief. Why?

Then a demanding female voice. 'Brian,' she sounded worried. 'Are you ok, Brian?'

I raised my head and looked at the two young attractive and very worried young women. Did I know them? I wasn't sure. 'A bit shaken but I'm fine, thanks,' I said. 'Do I know you?'

The one who had been speaking shook her head. 'Brian, I'm Rachael, Rachael Reeve, Dermot's daughter. Are you sure you're ok?'

'Yes, of course. Sorry. I'm fine,' I lied. Now I was feeling like crap. This was not the time to be a casualty.

She put her hand on my arm. 'Christine and I are both staff nurses,' said Rachael. 'We'll look after these with the ambulance crew. Apart from this one. She's dead.'

I looked down. Of course she was dead. She had a large piece of plate glass embedded in her throat and wasn't bleeding. I recognised the royal blue coat she was wearing. She had been a foot to my right when the explosion occurred. Come on, Blake pull yourself together. I left Rachael and her friend to look after the casualties. How could I not know it was Rachael?

'Brian,' a voice yelled. I looked to my left as a Road Traffic car pulled up. Andy Evans jumped out. That was strange. Andy never did anything fast.

'Hi Andy, welcome to the fun house.'

'The circus is on its way. They've told me to act as comms.'

'Great,' I replied. 'I'm just going to take a look inside.'

As I turned he shouted after me. 'Brian. The back of your greatcoat is ripped to shreds.' I raised my right hand in acknowledgement and headed for what had been Buy Smart.

I wasn't sure how many customers there were when I left, about a dozen I thought, plus several staff. There was so much dust in the air, everything was covered. Most people coughing. Struggling to get out or just to stand.

'Margery? Are you all right?' Margery was the shift supervisor working on the tills. Kneeling on the floor beneath her till, covered in debris and bleeding from a head wound.

She looked up. Tears in her eyes. 'Mr Blake,' she said. 'I just bent down for a new till-roll. What happened?'

'Not sure,' I said helping her up. 'There should be an ambulance arriving shortly,' at least I hoped so. 'Let's get you sorted.' She didn't answer as I guided her to the door to be met by a couple of ambulancemen. 'This is Margery. Was on the floor behind her till. She's got a cut scalp.'

Next an elderly man who had propped himself against one of the shelves. 'Can you walk?' I said.

He looked at me. 'I think so, officer,' he said.

I put my arm round his waist. 'Lean on me. It's not far to the door.' Safely dispatched I returned. There were several walking wounded. I hadn't seen any bodies, yet, but there was time.

'Can you stand?' I asked the lady lolled against the freezer. 'I don't know. Help me up, love.' I crouched alongside her. I was feeling bloody awful and still had the noise in my ears. With a bit of trial and error she managed to stand.

'I only slipped out from work for a packet of cigs.'

I had to smile. 'Dangerous habit smoking.' I said.

'Too bloody true.'

I walked her slowly to the door into the arms of two more ambulancemen then I was ambushed, at least that's what it felt like. Confronted by half a dozen firemen accompanied by Dr O'Keefe from the Health Centre.

'Now Pc Blake,' For the first time since I met him Dr O'Keefe wasn't smiling. 'You've been in the wars.' I nodded in agreement and wished I hadn't.

'Officer.' One of the firemen grabbed my attention. I knew his face but couldn't put a name to it. 'Apart from the people we can see in here is there anyone else in the building that you know of?'

I had to think hard. My brain felt disconnected. 'Erm, just before the explosion the manager was in his office. Oh, and Norman, one of the Saturday boys was heading for the cellar.'

'Was there any strange smell, gas for example?'

I shook my head and winced. 'I didn't notice any. Sorry.'

There was a rapid exchange of looks between the firemen as they hurried off. I looked towards the rear of the store. There was no office. Just a huge hole. No trace of Mike or anyone else.

Dr O'Keefe took me firmly by my right sleeve. 'And you young man are coming with me.'

'No, Doc,' I protested. Dr O'Keefe tightened his grip on my sleeve. 'I'm fine really.'

'Pc Blake,' the tone was demanding.

I looked up as Inspector Yates appeared from the direction of the nick. 'Sir, I'm fine, really.'

'Listen carefully Brian. This is an order. You will go with Dr O'Keefe, now. Do you understand?'

I was confused and I must have looked it. There was so much to do.

'Sergeant McGill?'

'I'll make sure he does as he's told.' The Inspector turned away to speak to the senior fire officer as Sergeant McGill continued. 'Brian, come on. You need a check-up. If they say you're all right to return I'll fetch you back. Is that all right?'

I nodded.

'You were going to get a statement; did you get it?'

'Yes, Sarge,' I retrieved the statement and the summons from my pocket handing them to him, the movement sending a streak of pain across my back. I bit my lip. 'And there's this summons to serve on Wainwright.'

'Fine. I'll see to that. Right let's go. Ok Doc he's all yours.'

'Pc Blake, do you think you can make that ambulance in front?'

I looked up. All I could see were blue lights. Four fire engines, a lot of ambulances and uniforms. Who they belonged to I had no idea. A sizeable crowd was gathering including a couple of reporters I sort of recognised. It was fuzzy. 'I think so.' It became difficult to walk. I thought that my knees were going to buckle. Sergeant McGill took a hold of my left arm.

'Arrgh.' I yelped. 'That bloody hurts.'

'Where?' the Dr demanded.

'The side of my upper arm.'

Dr O'Keefe took a quick look at my sleeve. There was a piece of glass protruding from my greatcoat. 'Don't touch his back Sergeant, and support his left arm under his armpit.'

'Ok doc,' he acknowledged and turned to go.

'Just a moment, Sergeant,' said Dr O'Keefe as we approached the ambulance. 'Pc Blake, before we get you on board exactly where are you feeling pain?'

I had to think hard. 'The back of my head,' I said. 'My back and my left arm and thigh.'

'Have you any pain in your ears?'

'Ears? No.'

'What about your chest?'

'No.'

'In the area of your stomach?'

'No.'

'Your intestines?'

'No, should there be?'

'Hopefully not,' he smiled, 'but let me finish asking my questions first. Your testicles?'

I grimaced. 'Not so I've noticed.'

'Good. Now, this pain in your back, does it feel deep or superficial?'

I looked at him gone out.

He repeated the question. 'Does it feel deep or superficial. In the muscles or deep inside the chest cavity?'

'On the surface, I think.'

'Anywhere near your kidneys?'

'I don't think so.'

'That will do for now, let's get him on board.'

'Just a second, Doc. Brian, is there anything else before you go?'

I had to stand a few seconds to collect my thoughts. 'I think so,' I said. 'Oh, I was with Mrs Carson when it happened. I sat her in the Corner Café and told her to wait.'

'Old Mrs Carson, Violet Carson,' Dr O'Keefe demanded.

'Yes Doc,' I managed a smile.

'Was she exposed to the blast?'

'I was between her and the blast if that helps.'

'I still want her to go for a check-up in hospital. Many problems with blast aren't immediately visible.'

My head was a bit muzzy. 'She seemed all right,' I said.

'You thought you were,' Dr O'Keefe smiled.

I agreed ...

Another ambulance pulled up, two doctors and five nurses exited. Dr O'Keefe collared one of the doctors, directing him and one of the nurses to the Corner Café with instructions to get Mrs Carson to an ambulance. If she were in any way awkward to say that Pc Blake had personally asked to let them check her out. Not to take no for an answer. I wondered if they had ever met anyone like Mrs Carson before. To be honest everything after that became very hazy. I have brief recollections of the shocked reaction when they cut my greatcoat and the rest of my uniform off in Casualty. The piece of glass that killed the woman in the blue coat made a mess of my uniform and back on its way through, accompanied on its journey by several dozen shards of glass still in situ. Three of them lodged in the back of my head, sort of glass hatpins. That was the last I remembered.

Eighty-Nine

I was trussed like an oven-ready turkey. Someone, I assumed Lucy, was holding my right hand. I'd felt better. How long I'd been out I hadn't a clue. But my head felt clearer. I remembered being told they were taking me to Leeds General Infirmary.

I opened my eyes. Lucy was sitting at the bedside. She'd been crying. She cried again. Mum and Liz were sitting at the foot of the bed. They'd been crying as well. Everyone else outside in the corridor. They walked round the bed and gave me a kiss on my bandages. 'We'll give you some time to yourselves,' Mum said as she closed the door behind them. The sudden flurry of chatter greeted Liz as she announced that I was back in the land of the living.

Lucy leaned forwards and gave me a kiss on the lips. I kissed the tears from her eyes. 'I suppose that's it for now,' she said with that wicked smile of hers. That particular thought wasn't uppermost on my mind, but I wasn't about to say so. 'If that door locked from the inside ... but it doesn't, so that's that.'

The mental picture tickled my funny bone. Me being trussed like a turkey and Lucy weeks away from giving birth. Us having sex in a hospital bed? That would have been a good subject for one of Bamforth's postcards.

'You've thought about it, have you?'

It was a great distraction for us both. She was at her mischievous best. 'Of course,' she said, as if it was the most natural thing in the world, 'Haven't you?'

'I like the idea, but I've not been conscious of anything ... Like the first day on Capri?'

'When I get you home, I promise.'

'I like the sound of that,' I smiled.

There was a pause of several seconds. 'How do you feel? We came yesterday after Calvin told us you were injured. But you were in the operating theatre. When we got here last night you looked so pale ... they'd given you something to make you sleep.' She stopped talking. I thought she was going to cry again. She squeezed my hand. I responded. That's when I realised I wasn't in pain and why I'd slept for so long. I was still confused and for some reason I didn't understand, feeling guilty. Was it because I had survived when the woman in the blue coat hadn't? I certainly didn't intend to raise this as a point of discussion with Lucy.

Don't cry,' I said,' and kissed her hand. 'I'm all right, well, I am now you're here.'

She smiled and wiped the tears from her eyes with the back of her other hand.

'Do they know what happened?'

She sighed. 'Nothing official. Calvin says the fire brigade and the gas board think it was a gas leak. The explosion triggered when someone went into the cellar and switched the lights on.'

I thought for a moment. 'That makes sense. That would be Norman, one of the Saturday boys. He was on his way, as he put it, to play with the spiders. I spoke to him as I was leaving Buy Smart. How is he?'

Lucy looked troubled. 'We've been asked not to mention casualties,' she sniffed and changed tack. 'You're famous,' she perked up and smiled again. 'Mentioned on last night's news bulletin on the telly. You're a hero.'

'Why?'

'In spite of your injuries you rescued three people from Buy Smart. We're all proud of you.'

'At the moment it's still fuzzy. The cashier, but after that not a lot. But hero? All I did was help her up off the floor and walk her to the door.'

She was happy. 'Well, you are,' she kissed me again. 'So get used to it. They had a TV crew in Westleigh showing the main road and Buy Smart. It's a real mess. They interviewed someone from the local council. They're going to have to demolish what's left of the building; maybe even the shops either side.'

I nodded. Any collateral damage I hadn't even considered. 'Is there any water, darling. I feel as dry as a bone.'

She almost leapt from the chair, 'Sorry, I'll get you some. I've baked some of those lemon drops. It gave me something to do.'

I managed a couple of lemon drops and a glass of water whilst Lucy was explaining. My suggestion of ringing cousin Raymond when Calvin couldn't find the Vernon's telephone number worked a treat. I couldn't remember a thing after that.

'The Chief was aware of the explosion but not that you were involved. He sends his love.'

'No. He didn't,' I chuckled.

'Well, that's what he meant,' she giggled. 'He sent his best wishes for a speedy recovery.'

I smiled and nodded. 'That's better,' I said as Lucy grinned. The thought of the Chief sending me his love was unlikely. 'Oh, there's some flowers,' I'd just noticed the smell. There were three vases of flowers on the bedside table along with a bowl of fruit and several cards.

'From Mums one and two?'

She grinned and nodded. 'Everybody. And there's been loads of calls, and, there's some more cards to open. Do you want to open them or shall I?'

'You do it, please.' For the next few minutes Lucy was happy to rip the envelopes open, read the dedications aloud and put them on a desk unit against the wall opposite my bed; the bedside table was full.

Those lemon drops had made me feel hungry. Before I could say anything the door opened, a nurse walked in followed by a doctor. Nurse Briggs had come to find out if I wanted anything to eat for tea.

'Tea? What time is it?'

The nurse smiled as she watched my face. '3.30pm on Sunday.' She handed me a menu of sorts. 'It's a long time since you had anything to eat.'

It was nearly thirty hours. No wonder. 'The soup, chicken sandwiches and trifle, please.'

The nurse left the room. The doctor sat on the bed and smiled. 'Nigel Farmer, Senior Surgical Registrar. You're looking better, Mr Blake. How do you feel?'

'Better than the last time I was conscious, Doctor,' I replied. '

'That's a good start,' he said. 'Your wife tells me that you have a degree in physiology.' He smiled at Lucy.

'It's exercise physiology,' I said.

Lucy glanced at us both. 'Is there much difference?'

'There is, Mrs Blake,' Dr Farmer replied. 'But that's not important. Your husband will understand what I'm about to tell him. No disrespect to you but I'll keep it simple. If you have any questions, please ask … Mr Blake, what do you know about blast injuries?'

I grimaced. 'Apart from the fact that they hurt?' I attempted a smile. 'Next to nothing. But I've never given them any real thought.'

He smiled and relaxed. 'Okay. Two things as far as you are concerned. The blast wave can affect both air and fluid filled organs and cavities by compressing the contents. It chucks around anything loose. You're ok with that?'

I was. Lucy told me later that my expression was a cross between shock and fear. I have no doubt that Doctor Farmer noticed it as well. 'Yes, I understand,' I replied. I really understood. You can compress a gas which in itself under these circumstances can radically increase the pressure within the lungs, gut etc. However, you cannot compress a liquid which is why the cardiovascular system works. The potential for serious damage to the fluid filled organs e.g. the heart and brain etc didn't bear thinking about.

'In your case, Mr Blake, you were incredibly lucky. I understand that you were not in the direct line of the explosion?'

'No,' I said. 'Outside in the street and standing several yards to one side.'

'Good. We know that the eardrums are vulnerable. When we found that yours were intact and there was no bleeding, we knew that it was *less* likely to be too serious.' I noticed his emphasis on the word *less*. 'But even so there was an effect. For want of a better word you had a concussion. Why you felt disorientated and why we need to keep you in hospital for a few days for observations. The bed rest will also help. Just to be on the safe side.'

'Do you know for how long, Doctor.'

'Frankly, Mrs Blake, no. These things don't manifest themselves as we would like. A few days observations will help us to spot anything nasty that may surface.'

'I see,' she looked disappointed.

'We know you want him back as soon as possible,' Doctor Farmer smiled. They were a good-looking couple and she was about seven months pregnant. 'When's your due date?'

She smiled, 'Mid-January.'

'I understand. These things take their own time. It's better to keep him in a day or so longer than not.'

'I suppose so,' Lucy sighed. 'You mentioned there were other types of injury.'

He nodded. 'The second type of injury is caused by objects which are basically chucked about by the explosion causing blunt trauma or penetrative injuries, such as in your husband's case. We removed more than thirty fragments of glass from his upper back, most of them small and none of them penetrative, in that they did not penetrate his skull, chest or abdominal cavities. And by the way, if you hadn't already guessed, we had to shave your husband's hair off. All of it.'

'I'd thought my head felt different. I'd put that down to the injury.' I patted my head gently. 'Yes, now I can feel it.'

At least Lucy found it funny and giggled. 'Aw, that's a shame. You're a baldy.'

'It's not that funny,' I protested.

'Yes, it is,' she said.

'No, it's not.'

'We've had this conversation before,' she said. 'Yes, it is.'

I sighed and smiled. 'Ok, you win.'

Doctor Farmer was smiling at the exchange. 'The first conversation that Brian and I had,' Lucy explained, 'He and his sister Anne laughed when I got Jimmy Cagney and Jimmy Durante mixed up. They laughed like donkeys. Now it's my turn.' Lucy looked worried. 'It will grow back, won't it?'

He had a sympathetic smile. 'It will Mrs Blake and won't take long, and remember,' he turned to me, 'you have a large laceration to the right-hand side of your back. Healing will take some time. You need rest and keep as still as possible. But you're young and have excellent musculature. Unless something nasty rears its ugly head, in time there should be no or very few residual effects. However, you will have some interesting scar tissue. Now, have either of you any questions?'

Lucy didn't have any. I had one that was nagging. 'Yes Doctor. Can you explain why, when I had the injuries that I did, I had no initial pain and still managed to operate?'

'Good question. Sorry I can't give you a definitive answer, it's not my speciality. I can tell you it's not fully understood although well documented on the battle field; which is basically where you were when the explosion occurred. We call it stress induced analgesia. If you really want to know, I will find out?'

'No, I'm happy with that, thanks.'

The doctor gone the hoards were about to enter en masse when Sister Sheldon appeared and pointed out the *Only two visitors at a time* notice.

'He requires as much rest as possible. Would you please restrict the visit to no more than thirty minutes in total.'

There were gentle kisses from the ladies and waves from the men. Two minutes passing the time with everybody asking the same questions.

I must have fallen asleep because when I opened my eyes there was only Lucy in the room. I was greeted with a kiss and, 'Hello sleepy. Your sandwiches have arrived but no soup.'

I managed to shuffle into a more upright position and wondered what they had given me for the pain. Vague memories that it hadn't been so pleasant. Lucy adjusted the pillows and pressed the call button twice. A pre-arranged signal for fresh tea.

I'd fallen asleep after fifteen minutes. So, having made sure that I was all right, all except Lucy left. We chatted for about an hour. Liz popped her head round the door to take Lucy back to Boston Spa until I was discharged. Tomorrow she promised me some proper food: homemade Bolognese sauce, and spaghetti cooked in the ward kitchen. Already arranged with Sister Sheldon. It was certain to be good.

Ninety

Monday morning. Awoke feeling fully refreshed. The blinds already opened. The sun shining. Rosebay Willowherb sprouting from the concrete rendering opposite. What a pity it wasn't in flower. I tried to sit up and get a better look. My back and left arm screamed in protest as I collapsed against the pillow. Sweat running down my brow. Trying to get my breathing under control. Tracing the bell-push by the simple expedient of following the wire through the bedclothes I gave it a couple of hefty presses. Seconds later the door opened and a couple of nurses waltzed in. One of them I knew. Carol Kingsman from Dewsbury General. She was working in casualty when Smedley was taken there following his arrest. She looked at me and frowned. 'Brian Blake, what have you been doing? Trying to sit up?'

I nodded, 'Big mistake.'

'Ok, lie still,' she motioned to her younger colleague. 'Teri, you take his right side.' Between them and my right leg, the backrest and pillows were adjusted. I felt more or less human.

'Thanks Carol.'

'You were caught in the explosion,' Carol said as the covers were straightened and she handed me the bell push. 'You were lucky.'

'So I realise,' I replied. No doubt that would be brought up ad nauseum. 'I'd only left Buy Smart a minute earlier. I was talking with a Mrs Carson in the street.'

'Yers,' Carol replied and frowned. 'She's in Women's Medical creating havoc. Never shuts up about her Pc Blake, his wife and baby. That's what threw me, I didn't know you were wed.'

'I am, seven months ago, her name's Lucy.'

'Seven months,' she gasped in mock horror. 'I wouldn't have believed it of you, how old's the baby?'

I grinned in return. 'Young people these days. Due in January.'

'Tch. That's spoiled a good bit of gossip,' she shook her head and smiled. 'Before anything else, Teri, let's get the chart done.' With a thermometer in my mouth. Teri taking my blood pressure. Carol my pulse. I kept still until they completed the chart.

I was hungry and could have eaten the proverbial scabby donkey. Did they have any in the fridge? Scabby donkey or reasonable substitute ordered. I requested something for the pain.

'I'll see what I can do for the pain,' said Carol. 'Is there anything before we go?'

'Yeah, when did you move from Dewsbury?'

'I'm a Staff Nurse now,' she replied with a smile. 'It's a bit further to travel but it's more money and a step nearer sister.'

I congratulated her on her promotion and asked her if I could get a paper.

'After breakfast. Your money's in the top drawer,' she pointed at the cabinet.

'Thanks. Have a word with Mrs Carson. Tell her you've spoken to me and she can visit providing she doesn't cause the ward staff any trouble.'

She laughed. 'Worth a try,' she said as they left.

I got my shot of morphine five minutes later. 'Don't get the idea that this is on demand, Brian,' said Carol, 'because it's not.' That was fair enough. But I hadn't realised how much pain I had been in, until I wasn't in any.

Breakfast tasted very good. They'd run out of scabby donkey. I had to settle for bacon, scrambled egg, tomatoes, beans, bread and tea.

The consultant, Mr Carthew and entourage came round at ten. 'How are you feeling this morning Mr Blake?'

'Better than I was yesterday, Doctor.'

He had a pleasant smile. 'Early days, Mr Blake,' he checked my charts. 'Nothing untoward. I'll arrange for the physios to pay you a visit. There's no reason why we can't let you out of bed providing that you don't try and do too much.'

'I'd like that. But how will I know?'

'If you're doing too much?' I nodded. He laughed. 'Believe me that will become self-evident.' That confirmed that I was nowhere as bad as I might have been.

The physios arrived forty-five minutes later. I quickly found out just how little too much was. Still, I was vertical and mobile, just unable to get to the bathroom. After my miniscule perambulation they sat me in my armchair supported by a marshmallow of pillows. Blanket over my knees. Bell-push in my lap.

It became a parade with plenty of comments about the time I spent in bed. DI Henderson and Liz Farthing. DCI Valentine with some grapes for me and flowers for Lucy. Calvin Yates, with best wishes from himself, Caroline and the staff at Westleigh. That was a sombre meeting. I pressed him about the casualties. Norman, just sixteen, was killed outright. He caught the full force of the blast as he opened the cellar door.

The blast destroyed the Manager's Office. The safe fell into the cellar taking Mike with it. Apart from blast injuries he had numerous wooden splinters embedded in his legs, back, neck and skull. He was placed on the critical list. His chances of survival were slim. He was in LGI. I could visit him later. The wounded taken to one hospital or another, a couple even to Pinderfields at Wakefield. All were hospitalised. So far five people had been killed in the blast, including the lady in the blue coat. The cause of the gas leak was still being investigated.

We finished on a happier note when I queried the use of the word, hero. He laughed. 'Just how much do you remember?'

'My memories are vague. I remember the cashier. Everything else is fuzzy."

'Well, before the Fire Brigade arrived and not knowing if it was safe, in spite of your injuries, you went back into Buy Smart three times to guide people to safety.'

'That's what Lucy told me.'

He nodded. 'The press are pestering for an interview. They've been told, no. You need rest.'

I thanked him. Reporters and cameramen were not something that I wanted to think about for now.

There was some quite edible stew for lunch, except the cabbage was wearing water-wings, the jam roll and custard were rib-sticking. Roll-on Lucy's Bolognese.

Half an hour later Mike Preston died. He was married with three children under ten. The total was now six.

Shortly afterwards Francis Grogan, the store manager, arrived for a two minute visit. He had taken the day off on Saturday to visit his mother who had suffered a stroke. He apologised and asked how I was feeling. I told him and asked that he pass on my condolences to Mike Preston's wife and family. There wasn't much else either of us could say.

Ninety-One

1345. The door opened. Frankie's head appeared. 'Hello bro, room for a little one? You were asleep the last time I was here.'

'Free time?' I said as she sat on the bed.

'Yup,' she said. 'No lectures this afternoon.'

I nodded. 'You and Vance ok?'

'Yeah, we're fine. Everything's fairly smooth.' Whatever that meant. I didn't pursue it.

Before we could continue the door burst open. Two men in raincoats bustled in; like refugees from a Raymond Chandler novel. One taking photographs as he moved round my room. The other scribbling. Frankie didn't need to look at me for confirmation. She stood up and spun round. 'Out!' she almost screamed at the two men. 'He needs rest and quiet not a couple of idiots pratting about.'

'Nice one Frankie,' I said to myself assaulting the bell-push. With the racket Frankie made I thought that the seventh cavalry might already be on its way.

The cameraman kept moving. The reporter stopped writing. 'Calm down girlie,' he said. 'Why don't you make us a cuppa or fetch a bedpan or whatever you do. We just want a word with your boyfriend.'

Her eyes narrowed. A danger sign to anyone with a whiff of intelligence. 'He's my brother,' she growled. 'Now, get out before I throw you out,' she said, with as much menace as I'd ever heard.

He looked Frankie up and down. 'Whatever.' He took a step forward. 'Now Pc Blake, what ...'

That was his second and last mistake. Frankie's *Yoko geri* landing squarely on his chest propelling him into the door slamming it shut. He collapsed on the floor. Frankie picked up his notebook and tossed it onto the bed. 'Now,' she said to a startled cameraman. 'If you don't want to join your friend, I'll have your camera.' She held her hand out.

'You're bleedin' jokin',' he protested. 'I can get these syndicated. They're worth a bomb.'

Her voice was calm. 'The camera?'

He must have thought that because he was half as big again as Frankie she had just been lucky. He tried to push past her. I pressed the buzzer four times.

Frankie seized his outstretched hand twisted his wrist viciously anti-clockwise and swept his legs away. He crashed face first into the floor. She picked up the camera and removed the film. Massaging his elbow the erstwhile cameraman got to his feet and kept his distance looking on in horror as Frankie fully exposed the film against the light. 'Nope,' she said. 'Sorry, you've no exclusive.' Then tossed it back to him as the Chief Constable opened the door stepping aside to allow Sister Thewlis access.

'Mr Blake?' she demanded as she entered the room. 'What the ...What are you two doing in here?' she demanded of the intruders. 'You've been told more than once you're not allowed ... Well?' Without waiting for a reply, she turned to me. 'Are you all right?'

'I am now Sister, thank you. I could do without the hassle.'

Frankie handed the book to the Chief. After a quick glance he pocketed it. 'I shall report this intrusion to your employer. With immediate effect your Press accreditation for all future Press Conferences is withdrawn.' He turned to the door, 'Sykes.'

Bill Sykes, the Chief's driver appeared and nodded. 'Sir,'

'Escort these two gentlemen of the Press to the hospital doors and advise them about the Justice Of The Peace Act, 1361. Should they appear again they will suffer the consequences.'

They wouldn't be back. If they were lucky that would mean a night in the cells.. Otherwise a binding over at Magistrate's Court.

The Chief was smiling. 'We meet again, Miss Mountain,' he said as the two dejected reporters moped out. 'Thank you for looking after your brother.'

'But I always have done, Mr Barton. He's always in trouble.'

I refused to be drawn.

The Chief found that funny. 'And Lucy is well?' he said to me.

'Yes, thank you, sir. Only nine weeks to go.'

'Congratulations Blake. What you did was exceptional. In the highest traditions of the service. As was you activity at Castleford. You and everyone else should be proud. Not least this incident at Leeds and Castleford. I have read the file and will be in touch later.'

He stepped forward to shake my hand as Chief Superintendent Williams entered followed by Sister Thewlis bearing a tray of cups of tea.

Mr Williams enquired as to how I was and shook hands. When he and the Chief had drunk their tea they left with *instructions* to get well. Frankie followed, promising to return when things were quieter.

It was becoming a carousel. I wondered who would be next. Hopefully Lucy. It was Mavis, the tea-lady with the tea-trolley-with-the-wonkey-wheel, she deposited a second cup of tea. Lucy arrived with John Bradbury in tow. John's wife Christine had seen a piece on the News and told John. Today was his rest day. He had come by bus from Brighouse, nevertheless gave Lucy and me a few minutes.

After John it did quieten. My mind stopped buzzing. Mrs Carson arrived in a wheelchair. I introduced her to Lucy. I'm pleased she was there. I fell asleep and woke up after she had been returned to Women's Medical. She came back the following day but only for thirty minutes. She was a very nice old lady, but you can have too much of a good thing.

I was allowed an evening visit by Anne and Neil. It was good to see them both.

'Attention seeking again?' said Anne to Lucy's amusement. 'Haven't you learned your lessons at all?'

The Bolognese sauce was wonderful. With the home-made pasta, herbs, black olives and red wine it was so full of sunshine we could have been back on Capri. She'd even sought permission from Sister Thewlis for me to have the glass of red with the meal. Bribing her with a spoonful of Bolognese sauce, and, a promise of the recipe. No shame some people.

Three days later I could walk unaided. A further two days and Mr Carthew had my dressings removed. The feeling on my skin was fantastic although it itched like hell. The stitches removed from my scalp and smaller wounds on my back. I still had to take it easy. Should I re-open the wounds I would be ordered back to bed. However, I could now have my hair washed. Pity I didn't have any. Still, the first sightings of fuzz were on the horizon. I had to suffer the ignominy of having Teri wash my scalp. The things you have to do.

Ninety-Two

Ten days after the explosion the last stitches were removed. My head more like a billiard table than a billiard ball. I got the all-clear to leave at three pm. Destination, Salendine Nook. I wasn't allowed to drive so Mum would take Lucy to her doctor's appointments.

Joe carrying my case we left after hugs all round at the nursing station. An excited Lucy between me and Mum. A quick check of the house. Followed by an even quicker check with the neighbours. An hour after we left the hospital Joe pulled up at home. Mum and Lucy made for the kitchen. Joe carried my case upstairs and motioned me to follow. He sat on the bed and pointed to the stool in front of the dressing table. I sat down. 'Has Lucy seen your back?'

I said not.

'Some of my friends were badly injured during the war. Injuries caused by shell splinters, flying masonry etc. Do you think it might be an idea for her to see yours now whilst your Mum and me are here and the others aren't, rather than just give her a nasty shock?'

That seemed like a good idea. I stood and stripped to the waist with great care, turning so that Joe could see. The sharp intake of breath said it all. He passed me a dressing gown to put round my shoulders whilst he went to fetch the wall mirror from the bathroom. He adjusted the wings on the dressing table, sat me down and held the mirror so that for the first time I could see. Even I was shocked. I still had a bit of colour although most of my Mediterranean tan had faded. The injuries didn't *all* stand out in sharp relief. It was very neat but to be brutally honest my back was a mess. The scars might well fade with time, nevertheless, it looked on the raw side; some of the puncture wounds looked worse.

Lucy took one look at my back and burst into tears. One look had brought it all back. I stood with my arms around her whilst she cried and motioned for Mum and Joe to leave us. Once she realised that when she touched my back I wasn't leaping in the air, she accepted that I wasn't going to be consigned to a wheelchair. Nevertheless, it was ten minutes before she felt composed enough to go downstairs.

Clive came home from school and without thinking gave me a hug. I fought the temptation to pick him up and his request to see my back. Bloodthirsty wretch. Once I'd pointed out how upset Lucy was, his level of inquisitiveness dropped and he took himself off to talk to her.

Jennifer arrived home at quarter past five and immediately put me in my place by giving Lucy a hug, ignoring me for a couple of minutes until she *realised* I was there. I got my hug accompanied by hands being rubbed up and down my back trying to work out just how bad it was. It was obvious it was pre-planned. She didn't ask.

Braising steak with carrots, onion and mushrooms, frozen peas and mashed potatoes followed by spotted dick and custard. That was my sort of comfort food. Lucy's cooking was excellent, but no-one cooks like your Mum.

The conversation was a little strained after dinner. No-one wanting to be the first to talk about what happened. Lucy took the initiative and my shirt came off. A minute later everyone had had enough and my shirt went back on. After that we had a normal family evening arguing over some quiz show on Granada.

We went up around ten. Lucy fulfilled her promise. It was as good as Capri except that it was indoors and colder; but we didn't care. Lucy got some support for Junior who gave his football boots an airing against my uninjured side.

The next morning, just as he was leaving for work, Joe called me into the library. 'Have you given any thought that you might be too badly injured to carry on?' he asked.

'I'd be lying if I said I hadn't,' I replied. 'However, it's early days.'

'That's true, but it won't hurt to bear it in mind. In any case, you're entitled to a payment for industrial injuries. It's the sort of thing I have to deal with on a regular basis. If you've no objections I'll get you some information.'

I wasn't au fait with this but there was nothing to lose. 'Ok Joe, I'll see you tonight.'

It wasn't a bad day providing you wrapped up against the wind. After the local children had gone to school I borrowed one of Joe's flat caps. We caught the bus into Huddersfield getting off outside Ralph Cuthberts, the chemists. Now we had the time to admire the Christmas decorations. Nothing dramatic, just strings of coloured light bulbs back and forth across Westgate, above the trolleybus wires. There were small set pieces on the lampposts and trolley bus poles. Cowlings, the Florists, looked like a Christmas tree. St George's square, between the railway station and the George Hotel hosted a twenty-foot Christmas tree. A slightly smaller one in the old Market Place adjacent to the Police box. Even though it was mid-week there were enough excited children about to add to the colour.

Walking along Buxton Road we reached our favourite coffee shop, this time we took a table away from the window. With her elbows on the table Lucy took a slow sip of coffee holding the cup between her hands. She looked across at me. 'I've been thinking,' she said and smiled.

I reached across and stroked the back of her hand, returning her smile. 'That sounds ominous, what about?'

'Ha, ha,' she replied, smiled and took another sip of coffee. 'You know Huddersfield far better than I do.'

I nodded.

'You know that Joe and Mum are planning this joint venture with upgrading the motor cycle track, corporate facilities, restaurant etc.'

I nodded again.

'Well, one of the things they've decided on is to employ an Italian chef so that the meals they provide are as authentic as possible. I was wondering what you thought about a shop, here in Huddersfield town centre, one selling genuine Italian produce. You know: meats, cheese, pasta, pastries, wines etc. We could work with the local travel agents. Spread the word.'

I thought about it for several seconds. 'I don't know to be honest,' I said. 'I've never thought about it. Have you discussed it with anyone?'

'No, I haven't said anything, but I thought about it when you were first injured.'

I looked her in the eye and smiled again. 'In case I was retired on medical grounds?'

She returned the smile and nodded. 'What do you think?'

'Irrespective of what happens to me, and you know far more about business than I do, it's different and I think it's worth considering. We can talk about it later, with Joe if you like.'

She nodded; it was her turn to squeeze my hand. She perked up. 'Let's do some Christmas shopping,' she said, then paused. 'I want to go home whilst I can still move. I want our first Christmas together to be at the cottage. Junior won't be far behind.' I had no problems with that at all. We did our shopping at the Co-op on Buxton Road. It was a real lift. With our 5'6" Christmas tree, lametta, tinsel, baubles for the tree and not a few decorations. How we got on the bus never mind off it without poking someone in the eye I don't know. I did manage to thwack someone quite hard with the end of the Christmas tree box. If Mum was disappointed when she saw our treasure trove she hid it well. 'You're going home,' she said and smiled. More of a statement than a question.

Lucy gave her a hug. 'Brian's much better than either of us expected,' she said. 'I'll be honest, I miss the cottage. Besides, before much longer Junior will get too big for me to do anything.'

'Oh, get on with you,' Mum replied and wiped her eyes, 'There's plenty of time, but we'll run you home after breakfast tomorrow.'

I think that Jennifer and Clive were expecting us to stay longer, resulting in a few long faces over dinner, but we weren't that far away. Lucy called Liz to pass on the news. She would let Anne and Neil know.

We had a chat with Joe about Lucy's idea for a shop. He thought it might have legs. Best to wait until the baby was born and long enough to see how I recovered. There was no rush.

Ninety-Three

Within five minutes of Joe and Mum leaving, Lilian Frith from two doors up the hill arrived to welcome us back. It had long been recognised that she had the twitchiest curtains in the area. Less than thirty minutes later Lucy was hosting a tea-party. Seven of them in total. All knitting little things. We would have the best dressed baby in the area.

My first sick note was for a month. We had a plan. Weather permitting, in the mornings we would go for a gentle walk together. In the afternoons I would go for a longer walk or, perhaps Lucy was right, a hike. I'd discussed it with the physios before they kicked me out: no running, no weights or other heavy lifting, but walking, stretching and swimming were not a problem. They even said that I could do *kata*, that made me feel more like my old self.

Slowly our rhythm established itself. Through trial and error I found out what was possible. According to Doctor McFarlane, Lucy's pregnancy was progressing normally.

I had to visit Force Headquarters to see the Force Medical Officer. He was quite positive and gave me a thorough check-up, including a series of stretches and exercises. He told me that although it was early days things were far better than they might have been, much of this because no spinal ligaments had been damaged. I had already been made aware that the FMO's assessment would be about my health with regard to my ability to carry out my duties as a constable. A much higher level than had I been an ordinary member of society. There was still a long way to go. My future was far from certain.

We put the Christmas trimmings and the tree up the first weekend in December. I needed a rasp and a pair of pliers to assemble it. It was a mammoth job which I managed without any undue problems. Two hours later it was complete. It looked so real those who saw it for the first time were fooled.

One thing we almost missed was the social highlight of the Police year, the annual Christmas dance. Normally I would have pitched in with the rest of them. This year it wasn't possible but we did manage an appearance, if only for a couple of hours. I'd paid for the tickets only the week before the explosion. It was held in the Merryweather Hall in Hecton. Transport courtesy of Jim and Sally Turnbull who lived at Hartshead Moor and had to drive past the cottage en route. The food was good, although neither of us participated much in the seasonal beverages and certainly not the dancing. But there was the chatter, with the ladies coming across to speak with Lucy. Next year perhaps we would be able to participate fully. The last thing in the evening was the raffle. Lucy won a nice set of crystal sherry glasses and I won the booby prize, a giant baby's dummy made of Blackpool rock. Ah well, you can't win 'em all. Towards the end of the evening one small fly in the ointment became apparent. A handful who had decided that because I had been proposed for the Special Course with less than two minutes service, and, being retained in the Service after the explosion I must have been brown-nosing the Chief Super. Inspector Meadowcroft had overheard the comments suggesting that they either put up or shut up.

Once or twice, Glenys Foster, the midwife had queried Lucy's dates believing she was further on. The date was much closer to Christmas. However, there were no problems, slightly raised blood pressure but nothing to give cause for concern.

Everyone came to us early on Christmas Day morning. Gave our kitchen and new cooker a real test. We ended up with a houseful. It was noisy, fun and wonderful. Lucy's waters broke that evening. She gave birth to our healthy, noisy, beautiful, 6lbs 14oz daughter: Claire Elizabeth Dorothy, at noon on Boxing Day.

As you would expect it was chaotic. Lucy had decided weeks ago that she was going to feed Claire herself. Access to the bedroom was restricted. When the family arrived our new arrival was sleeping soundly, for how long we didn't know. The latest package in our new game of pass-the-parcel had done the rounds of the Vernons, now it was the turn of the Mountains, beginning with Clive. That was Lucy's idea. Apart from being nervous he was very proud. The only problem being that no matter who was holding Claire no-one wanted to let her go, even Joe, he was as proud as anyone, and rightly so.

That night we stood in complete silence, arms round each other just looking at our new and helpless member of humanity, lying flat on her back, arms in surrender mode.

Listening to her breathing was magic, simply magic.

Epilogue

There had been no more snow. I'd opted for a cross-country walk towards Hartshead and Brighouse. I was ready for a hot drink as I opened the front door. An excited Lucy was on the phone. 'Hang on, Anne, he's here now.' She lowered the phone and handed me a letter. 'This arrived whilst you were out. We've all got one.'

'I thought I might put the kettle on,' I said. 'It's cold out there.'

I could hear Anne's laughter when Lucy replied. 'You'll be wearing the kettle if you don't open it.'

I grinned. 'Ok. You win.' I rang my thumb under the flap and extracted the missive. 'Good grief.' It was unbelievable. I looked at Lucy as I lowered the document.

'Well,' demanded Lucy. 'We've all been awarded the British Empire Medal, what have you got?'

I almost couldn't say it. 'The ... the George Cross?'

'Did you hear, Anne. The George Cross.'

'Whereabouts does that sit in the awards?'

'I'll ask him?'

'I heard,' I said. 'If I remember correctly, it's the highest award for bravery you can receive as a civilian. The equivalent of the VC.'

A couple of raps at the door. A beaming Calvin Yates was on the doorstep.

'You'd better come in, Calvin.'

He looked at the pair of us as he stepped over the threshold. 'I see you've heard.'

I handed him the letter. 'From the Palace.'

'Brian,' said Lucy holding out the phone. 'Mum wants a word.

'Hello, Liz, congratulations ... Yes, thanks. I'm still in shock. I never expected anything of this magnitude ... Yes, my boss has just arrived ... I suppose I'd better call Joe and Salendine Nook. See you later.'

I handed the phone back to an excited Lucy. 'Can I ring Salendine Nook?' she said.

I nodded as Calvin seized my hand. 'Fantastic, well done.'

'But how is it decided who gets it?'

'I'm positive it's a committee of the Cabinet Office. So it's pretty high level and the investiture will be at Buckingham Palace unless I'm sadly mistaken.'

The phone rang again. 'Lucy Blake ... yes, I'll put him on. Brian,' she held the phone out. 'Cousin Raymond wants a word,' she said and grinned.

'Good morning, sir.'

'Lucy likes her little games.'

'Indeed sir. She is annoying at times.' Lucy grinned and wrinkled her nose.

'Many congratulations. From what I have been told the award is richly deserved.'

'I'm still shocked.'

'That is understandable. The reason for my call is to explain about the finance ...'

Call to the chief ended, Lucy picked the phone up. 'Who are you calling?' I said.

'Salendine Nook then Joe.'

'Ok. Then call your Mum and tell her that she and Anne will have their fares paid and one night's accommodation. If Neil wants to go with Anne, they will have to fund it. Ok?'

Lucy waved her hand and dialled. I motioned to Calvin. 'Come on, the kettle calls,' I said.

Four weeks later. We met Luca, Carla and Chris at Kings Cross and took them to Tofts. Liz had booked their accommodation. After our evening meal we walked along the Strand returning to the hotel along the Victoria Embankment.

At ten the next morning the four of us plus our guests showed our letter to the police officers on the gates and joined the group walking across the courtyard and into Buckingham Palace.

This mysterious building that everyone knew yet almost nobody did.

The newsreels and photographs could not do it justice. Magnificent wasn't the word.

The stream of visitors was split. Recipients going one way and visitors another.

'One moment madam.' A man in a frock coat stopped us. 'I'm sorry but you cannot take your baby with you. It's not that Her Majesty doesn't like them, but she insists there are no distractions during the ceremony. Is there no-one who could take care of her. I take it the pink ribbon indicates that.'

'Yes, it does. And, sorry, no there isn't.'

He turned to me. 'You are Police Constable Blake?'

I agreed.

'Just a moment, please.'

'... Police Constable Blake is here to be invested with the George Cross. It's his infant daughter. His wife and two others with the British Empire Medal. I thought perhaps Lillian might be free for an hour or so.'

'No, she's busy at the moment. Leave it with me. I'll think of something.'

'I'm sorry for the delay but someone will be here shortly.'

We hadn't long to wait when a smartly dressed young woman hurried up. She looked vaguely familiar. 'I understand you need a babysitter for a while.'

'That's very kind of you,' said Lucy.

'It's not a problem. Can't have you missing the investiture. She's lovely, what's her name?'

'Claire.'

'She's tiny. When was she born.'

'On Boxing Day.'

'Congratulations. Quite a Christmas present.'

'Thank you, it was,' I said

Our babysitter took possession of the most valuable thing in our lives. 'Hello Claire, haven't you got beautiful eyes? Let's go for a walk and I will show you a picture of my grandfather.' She turned to us, 'Don't worry, she will be fine.' She turned and strolled the way she had come although I'm sure she winked at our friend in the frockcoat.

I think everyone had the same alarm bells ringing when Lucy said. 'Grandfather?'

He smiled. 'King George VI.'

Shocked looks were exchanged. 'Then that was Princess Anne?'

'It was,' he smiled and gestured with his left hand. 'Now, if you care to continue.'

We were gathered in what I suppose was an ante room. A man in uniform with masses of gold braid from the Lord Chamberlain's office was spelling out what followed.

He smiled at everyone. 'Ladies and gentlemen, today's investiture will be carried out by Her Majesty in the Grand Ballroom which is somewhere about half a mile behind me. We have you all on our list so there is no need to worry that you will be missed. When Her Majesty arrives the room will stand and the National Anthem will be played. No singing. Constable Blake,' he paused and looked at me. 'Yours is the highest award so you will be first. We will tell you what to do. One thing for you in particular,' That made me feel a lot better. 'This is not a parade ground. Relax,' easier said than done. 'No headgear so no saluting and no drill movements. Your name will be read out and why you are there. When you feel the tug on your arm just walk until you are opposite Her Majesty. Turn and bow, head only. Ladies a slight curtsy. Please do not try to go so low you can't get up or that you fall over. Take three short paces. Her Majesty will affix your award to the pin on your left side. She may ask you questions. When you first speak address her as Your Majesty. After that call her Ma'am as in ham - short A. Do not initiate conversation yourself. When she offers her hand that is a signal the conversation is over. Take the hand gently. Release. Take three steps backwards, head bow again, or curtsy. Turn and walk away.'

Apart from the route march around the palace it was a doddle. Good luck and quick kiss from Lucy and it was time. With my heart bouncing round inside my chest I was placed in the doorway. Then the next step. Facing me the man began to read out the dedication.

'Your Majesty. Constable Brian Blake for the award of the George Cross.' The tug on the sleeve. I began my walk. 'For displaying the most conspicuous courage in the circumstances of extreme danger.'

I turned towards the Queen. Bowed. Took the three steps.

An official held a velvet pad with the George Cross in the centre. She took the medal, smiled and fixed it to the pin.

Within sixty seconds it was all over. The conversation was ended. I shook the hand. Took the three paces to the rear. Bowed. Turned to the right and walked.

I don't know what Lucy said to the Queen but she laughed louder than she did when I spoke to her. She joined me with her medal followed by Anne, and last but by no means least, Liz.

We were standing near to the top of the Grand Staircase, everyone clustering round to look at the medals when a lady aged about forty and dressed in a business suit approached. 'Mr and Mrs Blake would you and your party come with me please.'

The pace was brisk so it was impossible to appreciate the artwork. After passing through several doorways our guide stepped to one side. 'Her Royal Highness,' she indicated. 'I will wait here for you.'

'Here you are Mrs Blake, safe and sound. And I have to say that your daughter is a fine judge of works of art.' Claire was now safely in Lucy's arms.

Lucy offered a nervous smile. Thank you your Royal Highness. It was very good of you.'

'Not a problem.' She smiled and looked round the group making eye contact with each of us in turn. 'Now, you're Pc Blake. You're Lucy and Anne Greeley and Mrs Vernon. I take it this is Neil your husband and who are the others?'

'This is my mother, Dorothy' I said. 'And Joe my step-father. Jennifer and Frankie my other step-sisters. And the little one is Clive, my half-brother.'

'Hello Clive,' she said. 'What's it like having identical triplets for sisters?'

Clive answered in his usual tactful manner. 'They're a pain,' he said scowling.

Princess Anne laughed. There was a frowning objection from the girls. 'Clive,' Mum scolded. 'Mind your manners.'

'Sorry,' he said and grinned. 'They're all right, I suppose. '

'I've got three brothers so I understand. But it's nice to hear people being honest instead of saying what they think one wants to hear. And who are the last three?'

'We live in Capri, your Majesty,' said Luca. 'My name is Luca Paffetti. I am Mrs Vernon's business partner in Italy. These are my two eldest children Cristoforo and Carla.'

'Please, not Majesty, that's my mother. Address me as Ma'am. And your wife?'

'She is at home with Maria and the baby, Pietro.'

'And how do you like England?'

'I have been several times but coming here, in Buckingham Palace, is beyond my wildest dreams and it is good for my children. My daughter was whispering a few minutes ago that she would like to have her photograph taken with you.'

There was a gasp. Carla looked horrified.

Princess Anne narrowed her eyes then smiled. 'A group photograph. Yes, why not. But not for the Press. Do you have a camera?'

Lillian, our guide was summoned, and took two photos of the group with Lucy's camera. Princess Anne in the centre, Lucy and me on one side, Anne and Liz on the other. Clive at the front with Cris and Carla in the middle. The others either side.

We were in the quadrangle mingling with other recipients and waiting for a slot to have our photos taken with the Beefeaters.

'Are they real?'

'Yes Carla,' Lucy laughed. 'They're all retired soldiers. They're very real. And they're nice as well. The one on the left, Brian and I met some time ago. His name is Eric. Their history takes them back to the reign of Henry VIII in the 16th century; his personal bodyguard. Those pikes they carry are very sharp. I'll introduce you.'

After the investiture this was the most popular part of the day.

At last. 'Hello Eric.'

'Lucy. You got your gong. Well deserved. Congratulations.'

'Thank you. This is Carla, her brother Cristoforo or Chris is behind us.'

'You're Italian?'

'Yes, we live in Anacapri.'

'Naples?' He pointed at Luca. 'That man is your father?'

'Yes, is problem?'

'Luca Paffetti. We met many years before you were born.'

Carla turned round. 'Papa, this Beefeater says he knows you.'

'Yes,' he replied. 'His name is Eric Walker. We meet during the war. I do not talk about the war. It was a very bad time.'

'He's right,' said Eric. 'It was. But your father is a very brave man. He fought with the partisans. But if you don't want to talk about it, Luca, I won't press you. Now young lady, would you like a photograph?'

Everything wrapped up we left the palace and returned to Tofts Hotel to get changed.

I took everyone to the Old Bailey and by chance No1 court was free. Clive slipped out of the way and found his way into the Dock. Not for long. Someone below heard him and open the cell doors.

After a quick bite we took them to Regents Park. The evening meal, for eleven, was paid for by Joe and Liz splitting the bill.

I don't know whether the meeting with Eric had stirred up unwanted emotions in Luca but he was out of sorts and said very little all evening. Tomorrow morning we had booked a visit to The Tower. What Luca would do was anyone's guess.

Right on time we arrived at The Tower. I don't know who was the more excited Carla and Chris or Clive – all looking forwards to the torture chamber and the executions. What else?

We entered via the main entrance. Luca paused. 'You go on. Carla, Chris stay with Liz and Lucy. There is something I must do.' He approached a nearby Yeoman Warder. 'Excuse me. Yesterday I met Yeoman Warder Eric Walker at Buckingham Palace. We fought together during the war. He told me that if I want to talk to ask for him.'

The last we saw of Luca was him accompanying the Yeoman Warder. When and if he was ever ready to tell us about his meeting it would have to wait.

When we finished our tour he still hadn't shown up. Lucy and I had a train to catch. We said our goodbyes promising to see the Paffetti's in the springtime.

* The Tower of London 1840 W. H. Ainsworth

THE END

Acknowledgements

Grateful thanks to Eve Seymour, my editor. Deborah Paffetti who for three years tried to teach me to speak Italian and who ensured that I hadn't insulted the language with its appearance in the book. The team at More Visual for their stunning covers. To Damian of Sabretooth-Designs for his brilliant website and last but by no means least my Beta Readers

Don't miss out!

Visit the website below and you can sign up to receive emails whenever Jon Mason publishes a new book. There's no charge and no obligation.

https://books2read.com/r/B-A-ZRTW-FFVKC

BOOKS 2 READ

Connecting independent readers to independent writers.

Did you love *Nemesis*? Then you should read *Counting The Dead*[1] by Jon Mason!

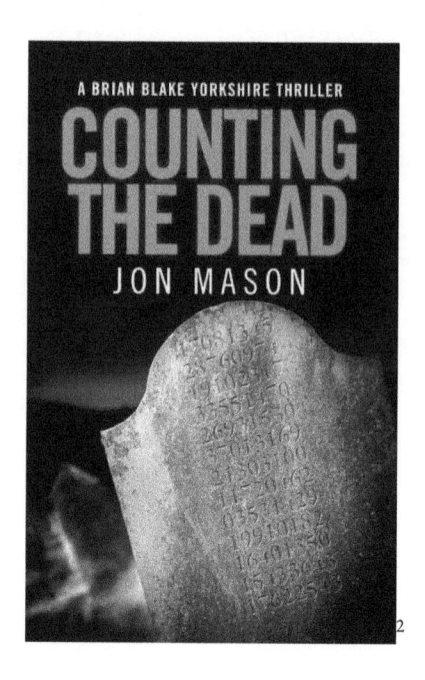

Enquiries following the arrest of a local dignitary for attacking two young boys out birdwatching lead to a further association with DCI Valentine and his team. The start of a chain of events that unleash Blake's childhood demons and an enquiry stretching back decades. Those evil forces now working directly against him putting his entire future at risk.

No stone left unturned. Enemies, both old and new, play their part, even unwittingly. As the story races towards its climax Blake is tested to the limit.

Read more at www.jonmasonbooks.com.

---

1. https://books2read.com/u/m0o5wA

2. https://books2read.com/u/m0o5wA

Also by Jon Mason

Blake Detective Series
The Blooding of Brian Blake
Nemesis
Counting The Dead

Watch for more at www.jonmasonbooks.com.

About the Author

JON was born into post WW2 Yorkshire in England. His brother Stuart was born in 1938. His father, demobbed from the RAF where he had been a Dispatch Rider, returned to the tailoring industry. His mother had spent the war years x-raying wheels for battle tanks.

They lived in a small, inner two-bedroomed terrace house. There was no damp-proof course, double glazing, central heating or hot water on tap. The tin bath hung from a nail under the stairs and the lavatory was across the back yard..

Leaving school in 1962 he joined the West Riding Constabulary as a Cadet and as a Constable in 1965. His initial training carried out at No3 District Police Training Centre, Pannal Ash, Harrogate, in the then North Riding of Yorkshire.

Over the next three decades he gained experience across much of what the police service has to offer. 1965-70 on uniform beat patrol. From 1970-75 in the Road Traffic Division as an advanced driver and also where he was firearms trained. From 1975-77 Force Control where he learned his radio and computer skills before being promoted to the Western Area Control Room in January of 1977, Twelve months later he was seconded to the fledgling Computer

Development Unit working with Ferranti International in the development of Stage 4 of a resource handling and incident recording system known as Command and Control (Not big Brother) and the setting up of the Communications Training Wing at the West Yorkshire Police training school. December 1983 saw him transferred to an inner city sub-division where he spent the last 10 years of his service as uniform patrol sergeant where he also worked closely with the Air Support Unit, Custody Officer and the last four years as the Station Sergeant.

In May of 1967 Jon and his fiancee married. A marriage which so far has lasted for over 56 years. They had two children, tragically Andrew, the elder, died of a heart attack in January 2018 - he was 48. Their daughter is still going strong.

Prior to retirement Jon qualified as a fitness instructor and subsequently head-hunted to work in a new community based cardiac rehab programme where he had the opportunity to study cardiology at Leeds University Medical School and exercise physiology at Carnegie. He also studied bio-mechanics.

All that knowledge and experience Jon brings to his books.

Read more at www.jonmasonbooks.com.